TITLES BY D.N. SIMMONS

THE
KNIGHTS OF THE DARKNESS
CHRONICLES

# THE
# LION'S DEN

### KNIGHTS OF THE DARKNESS CHRONICLES
### CHRONICLES
### BOOK FIVE

# D.N. SIMMONS

RUSHMORE PUBLISHING
CHICAGO

FIRST EDITION

Copyright © 2012 by D.N. Simmons
Edited by H.I. Gantt
Rushmore Publishing
ISBN-13:978-0615689098
ISBN-10: 0615689094

# <u>Dedication and Acknowledgments</u>

As always, I dedicate this novel to my absolutely wonderful, loyal, understanding and *truly* patient readership. I thank you all for the opportunity you've given me to entertain you. It has been my greatest pleasure. I want you know that your unwavering support inspires me and I am honored to have you all as readers.

I'd like to thank my mother for being the wonderful, supportive and loving person you are. Thank you for pushing me to meet my potential. I'd like to thank my father for your support, love and guidance. Last, but not least, I'd like to send a special "thank you" to all of you who have supported me in life and in my career.

Love Always
D.N.

# Author's Note

I want to apologize to all of my readers for not being able to publish this novel according to the scheduled date I had promised. As you all know, I hate to disappoint you, however, I have an obligation to all of you to give you the very best I have to give. It's an obligation that I take very seriously, therefore, I may take longer publishing a novel than I had intended. I do this to make sure I have edited the novels to the very best of my ability so that all of you will be able to have a delightful reading experience.

Once again, I thank you for your patience and understanding.

Love
D.N.

# CHAPTER ONE

Natasha entered the bedroom she shared with her two lovers. Both men, lounging on the bed watching television looked up at her.

Xavier chuckled. "You have that, 'I have a favor to ask of you', face," he said, noting Natasha's expression.

"Do I?" Natasha asked.

"Yes," Xavier answered.

"Wow, you can read me really well. Do you mind?" she asked.

He shook his head. "No, of course not, what's the favor?"

Natasha smiled. "These cravings are driving me crazy. I actually think they're stronger than before. Anyway, I would really, really, really–"

"Oh-oh, she said 'really' three times, this must be a big favor you're getting ready to ask of us," Xavier teased.

"Well, that depends," Natasha began. She climbed on the bed, sliding closer to her two men. "I really want a big, juicy burger loaded with all kinds of trimmings like the one I saw on TV yesterday. That thing looked like it was the bomb, don't ya'll agree?"

"Are you talking about the one that's a pound of ground beef, three different cheeses, six slices of thick-cut bacon, honey-glazed-deep fried onion rings, a potato pancake and a layer of marinated beef brisket sautéed with mushroom in au jus sauce?" Xavier asked.

Natasha nodded. "Oh yeah! That's the one. Although, when you put it like that, it does sound like a ridiculous burger, doesn't it? But it looked soooo good and the dude eating it on TV was chowing down and made me want it even more."

"That burger looked like it would give someone instant diabetes and a stroke at the same time to me," Xavier commented. "You sure you want to eat that while you're pregnant?"

Natasha pouted; her lover was making perfect sense. "I know it's not the healthiest thing a person can eat. That's why I only want one. I've been eating enough fruits and veggies to balance it out."

Darian laughed. "So you've been preparing yourself for this, have you?"

"Maybe," Natasha said, smiling.

"Wasn't that restaurant in New York?" Xavier asked.

"Was it? I don't know," Natasha said.

"I believe it was," Darian confirmed.

"Well see, that's why I said 'really' three times," Natasha said. "Because I knew it was a huge favor to ask."

"I guess I'll get it. We both know Darian won't," Xavier said.

"I resent that, I would go," Darian said.

"Oh really? All right, do you want to go instead?" Xavier challenged him; one eyebrow cocked.

"Well, you've already offered, far be it from me to cast a shadow on your chivalry and outshine you. By all means, my young one… you may go in my stead," Darian retorted.

Xavier laughed. "Full. Of. Shit."

Darian only laughed. "You know; you're just spoiling her, doing irreparable damage."

"Excuse, how are you going to talk about me like I'm not sitting here?" Natasha asked, poking Darian in the arm. "And by the way, I'm not spoiled."

"Yes you are," Darian laughed.

Natasha smirked. "Shut up, whatever," she said, laughing at Darian. "Anyway, I do appreciate it. Thank you for going for me." She kissed Xavier twice on the mouth. "I love you so much." She stroked the strong line of his jaw with her finger, causing him to moan.

"So gullible," Darian jested.

"No, I'm not. You're just mad she didn't kiss you," Xavier teased.

"Oh, I'll have her all to myself when you go on your little errand," Darian retorted, laughing to himself.

"Oh boys, there's enough of me to go around, especially with this big-ass belly," Natasha said, pointing to her expanded stomach, which was quite large as she was nearly seven months pregnant. Both men decided to play it smart by not commenting on her joke, they just smiled. They had learned in the past just how sensitive a pregnant woman could be.

"You're beautiful to me," Xavier said, playing it safe. "I'll be back shortly." He exited through the balcony's double doors making sure to close them behind him before disappearing into the nighttime sky, flying toward New York.

Inside the bedroom, Darian leaned forward, kissing Natasha's cheek. He remembered the last time she made a joke about her weight while pregnant with their son. Both men laughed innocently and she got offended thinking they thought her to be fat. After the emotional onslaught of her tears and rants, she apologized to them, blaming her hormones. Since that time, both men had made a mental note to not fall for *that* one again.

Natasha lay next to Darian, snuggling closer resting her head on his muscular chest. He wrapped his arm around her while his other hand rested on her swollen belly. Even though it was the second time around experiencing her pregnancy, it was still a complete marvel to him. Laying there beside her, he began to reminisce about their first experience. How happy and excited Natasha was the day she discovered she was pregnant. He also remembered his own excitement and Xavier's; the moment they knew they were going to be fathers.

Throughout her term, they pampered her endlessly. Whatever she wanted, they got it for her. Darian had joked that they were ruining her--to which--Natasha would just laugh and nod. He had thought her all day sickness was interesting as well as unpleasant. He couldn't quite understand why everything seemed to nauseate her, even scents she had once loved. Xavier was more in tuned to her needs and he helped him to understand. Both men had delighted in hearing the tiny heartbeat and feeling their son move underneath her soft skin as their child began to grow larger and healthier inside her. Night after night, he and Xavier would lie beside her listening and feeling the baby while Natasha twirled her fingers through their long silky hair.

The day Natasha went into labor was another new experience in and of itself. Never had either man heard her curse so much. Never had they seen her in so much pain. Apparently, asking her questions about the birthing process during the moment it was happening was a terrible idea. Natasha didn't seem to have any tolerance for Darian's inquiries, which was pointed out when she yelled at him to "shut the fuck up, or leave". Xavier had laughed and learning from Darian's experience, he kept his own questions to himself until she was more receptive to them. Darian was extremely curious and stood behind the doctor and nurse as their son began to enter the world. It had been centuries since Darian had witnessed the miracle of life and this was the first time that life was going to be a child of his… that was human. Once it was all over, after twelve hours, the three rejoiced in the little baby that was bundled in Natasha's arms.

Xavier managed to capture the birth on video and they enjoyed watching it once they came home from the hospital. Even all of the cursing seemed funny after the experience was over. Natasha had to apologize to her two lovers once she saw and heard all of the awful things she said and done to them in her haze of unimaginable pain which the drugs given to her didn't seem to lessen fast enough, that much she remembered. They had been all too forgiving, as they understood.

Taking care of the baby proved somewhat difficult for Darian in the beginning. The tiny infant seemed so delicate, so completely dependent on them. He loved his son instantly. His vulnerability and innocence were just so precious. It gave Darian a different perspective on the value of human life. How it begins, how truly fragile it was. It was a gift much like his immortality. That was how he saw it, now.

Xavier, on the other hand, had taken to fatherhood naturally, impressing both Natasha and Darian immensely. They figured

Xavier's human experience with his siblings gave him the knowledge he needed to care for their own child, that and the fact that he really wanted to be a dad and had read many books on the subject of parenting. It was Xavier along with Natasha, who helped Darian understand their child's needs and desires. He smiled to himself over the memory as he felt his second child move slowly inside Natasha's abdomen.

She looked up at him. "What are you smiling about?"

"I was thinking about our first born, how easily Xavier took to fatherhood, how eager he was."

"Oh yeah, I kind of knew the moment he put those headphones on my stomach to play classical music for the baby, he was going to be a great father."

Darian looked down at her. "What did you think about me?" he asked.

"You? ... You were adorable, really. You cracked me up."

"How so?"

"Darian, baby, the first time Matthew puked on you, you held him out at arm's length." She began to laugh, remembering his appalled expression as creamy infantile vomit slid down the front of his Egyptian cotton, hunter-green, shirt. "For a second there, I thought you were going to toss him to Xavier."

"I wouldn't go that far. I remember that, he did it without warning and it was projectile vomit. One minute, he was giggling and having fun and the next he was spewing all over me. I've never had anyone vomit on me before ... Well, not since becoming a vampire, that is. It was hot and thick and sticky. As you know, the only human fluid I don't mind with that combination-"

"Okay, I'm going to stop you right now, because you're starting to go to that place you like to go to." Natasha poked him in the chest.

"What place?" he asked with a mischievous grin.

"Darian."

He snorted. "You're no fun. By the way, I suspected it wasn't an accident when Matthew regurgitated on me, because he laughed afterward."

Natasha burst into a fit of laughter. After a few seconds, she regained her composure. "Think that was his master plan?"

"I'm not putting it past him. He's tried to catch me off guard dozens of times since then with his carefully planned projectile vomit and urine attacks," Darian joked.

"That first time was because you didn't burp him properly before playing bouncy-bounce with him. Imagine how he felt! Besides, his stomach was still developing, babies spit-up all the time. It's got nothing to do with master plans."

Darian arched an eyebrow. "Explain the urine, then," he said somewhat suspiciously, still believing his son may have planned some of those "attacks".

Natasha chuckled.

"Well?"

"He never pissed on you."

"That's because I was too quick for him. It was funny when he got Xavier ... and John. I'm simply saying; I think he knew what he was doing. How can I not suspect him?" Darian smiled, flashing his pearly whites.

"Maybe that was his way of toning down your arrogance. Children do humble you, ya know." She giggled once more.

"If you say so."

"Well, maybe not you, but other people have been humbled by the experience of having babies. That new born life is so precious, so beautiful."

"He is that and I'm humble enough."

"I remember one time you changed Matthew's diaper. You laid him on the changing table and your nose was all wrinkled up, eyebrows all furrowed." She continued to laugh.

"I could smell what was inside his diaper a mile away. You forget, my senses are a thousand times more acute than yours. Besides, I remember you complaining about his bowel movement just the other day after he had broccoli."

"Hey, that was some serious shit. You didn't see what I saw. I had nightmares after that!" she joked, chuckling.

"Nightmares, eh?" he smiled. "I got used to fatherhood all in good time, if I may say so."

Natasha struggled to catch her breath, she looked up at him. "Yes you did, darling. You caught on very fast. I knew you'd be a perfect father, too." She leaned upwards, kissing him passionately.

They laid quietly together for several minutes before Darian heard the little chatter coming from the nursery. "He's finally awake!" He swiftly unraveled himself from Natasha, letting her fall face-first back onto the bed.

She looked up at him with a snort at having been tossed to the side, so to speak, then she chuckled to herself as he climbed out of the bed, leaving the room. He returned two minutes later carrying their year old son in his arms. Little Matthew, as some called him, knowing he was named after his biological father, was dressed in a light blue t-shirt and white and blue elephant-spotted pajama bottoms over his pull-ups. His green eyes stared at his father as he carried him towards the bed. Darian leaned forward, kissing his son's soft, curly, dark brown hair. He inhaled deeply, taking in his sweet baby scent.

"Is he wet?" Natasha asked, reaching over testing his pamper. Darian shook his head. "I'd be able to smell if he was. He's just hungry, lonely and he wants to play."

"I bet he is. He had a very long nap. I'm going to make him a little something to eat." Natasha began to roll off the bed.

"No, you should be relaxing. I can take care of his dinner." Darian walked out of the room, taking their son with him and leaving her alone, smiling.

Natasha was both overjoyed and relieved that not only did her two lovers love their son, and were anxiously awaiting the arrival of their second child, but the entire coven grew closer because of the infant. John, Tony, Gary and Christopher took to their "uncle" roles immediately. Even before Matthew was born, they had purchased clothes and toys in preparation of his arrival. Annabelle adored the little infant and enjoyed nuzzling, playing and holding Matthew whenever she could pry him from the hands of his uncles and fathers. The biggest surprises were Miko and April, who were oftentimes reserved; even they couldn't help making cooing sounds and "baby talk" in the infant's presence. Matthew, Warren's lover, S.U.I.T. partner and the biological donor of Natasha's two children loved him very much. He visited often, playing with his son for hours on end. Natasha's parents, and Matthew's mother were constantly spoiling her son, so much so, Natasha found herself having to put her foot down.

She didn't want a spoiled brat for a child. Darian's fawning over him was bad enough. Xavier and Matthew understood where she was coming from, and toned down their blatant adoration enough not to spoil their son rotten. Darian, on the other hand, needed more restraint. He finally submitted and resisted the urge to carry his son constantly. He also refrained from making exuberant purchases, like the several pairs of thousand dollars infant loafers he had bought several months ago. Even Xavier chastised his lover for that decision. Darian's reason for having done so at the time was, "only the best for my son." All in all, everything was wonderful as far as Natasha was concerned. She'd never been happier. She only wished her best friend, Annette were alive to share the experience, too.

Darian came back into the room ten minutes later, carrying his son and a jar of food. He sat on the bed and began feeding Matthew puréed vegetables. Natasha lay next to them watching; secretly hoping Darian couldn't hear her own stomach growling.

"Xavier should be here shortly. You sound ravenous," he said, smiling slyly.

Natasha smirked. "Oh, I see you've got jokes."

"Ah, was that your stab at being sarcastic?" Darian smiled.

Natasha giggled. "Maybe, I can't help it if I'm hungrier than a hostage."

"You know, some hostages are well fed," Darian remarked.

"See, there you go again, talking shit," Natasha joked.

Darian laughed and she kissed him before taking hold of her son. She lifted Matthew's tiny shirt, inhaling deeply, she blew a loud gust of air over the surface of his belly, causing the toddler to burst into a fit of laughter.

"He's ticklish, just like his mother," Darian commented.

"I know," she said, giggling. Her slender delicate fingers moved erratically over her son's soft skin, ticking him. He cackled loudly as he thrashed on the bed, smiling beautifully at his mother. Several minutes later, Xavier entered the bedroom through the door, and not the window like the last time when he scared Natasha out of her wits causing her to spill her nachos all over Darian's three-thousand dollar sheets.

"Hey baby, tell me you've got something good for me," Natasha begged, arms outstretched before her, fingers wiggling.

Xavier smiled wickedly as he approached her. He began to unbutton his pants.

"Oh, now you're just being lewd." Natasha laughed, slapping Xavier's thigh.

"Hey, you're the one who asked for 'something good'," Xavier teased.

"There's nothing I can say that I don't think you're going to make sexual, so just hand me my food," Natasha said, chuckling.

Xavier laughed as he dangled the still hot bag of food just out of her reach. "How badly do you want it?" he teased seductively.

With one eyebrow arched, and in her most threatening tone, she said, "you should know by now not to come between a pregnant woman and her cravings." Natasha lunged for the bag, which Xavier raised, keeping her at bay.

Darian chuckled. "I believe she's serious, Xavier. It might be best for you to just lay the bag down gently and take several very slow steps backwards … *easy* now."

Natasha turned toward him. "I see the two of you are going to gang up on me now, is that it?"

"Maybe," Xavier leaned forward, lips pursed, waiting for his kiss.

"I don't even know if I should give you one for all of the trouble you've caused me," Natasha said, pouting playfully.

"Awwww, don't be that way, Tasha." Xavier handed her the bag.

"That's better." She gave him his kiss.

Xavier went into the bathroom, washing his hands. When he came back out, he immediately scooped up his son tossing him in the air as if he weighed nothing. Little Matthew laughed and babbled as his father played with him.

"You returned faster than I expected," Darian said, mentally calculating Xavier's traveling time and distance.

"Yes I did. Turns out, they have a location in Indiana. I didn't have to fly to New York after all," Xavier replied.

"That's good to know," Natasha said as she began eating the

burger that was so huge, she had difficulty opening her mouth wide enough to bite it.

"That's just ridiculous," Darian commented at the sight of the burger.

Natasha giggled as she continued to stuff her face.

"Oh, but look at how happy we've made her," Xavier said, pointing at Natasha.

Darian regarded her gleefulness, he nodded. "Indeed, she is quite jolly."

Natasha swallowed her food. "Stop talking about me like I'm some sort of lab animal."

Both men laughed heartily, tickled by their own jokes. Xavier lay on the bed and released his son. Matthew climbed over both men towards his mother, opening his mouth wide once he reached her.

"Oooo! You little greedy baby! I didn't beg for not one bite of your food. I swear, if Matthew wasn't human when he first donated his sperm, I would have sworn you got that trait from him." Natasha leaned forward, kissing her son on his nose. Relenting, she gave him the tiniest bite of her hamburger. His little mouth couldn't open wide enough to take in the entire sandwich, but he was able to bite off a tiny portion of meat and cheese. "I bet you drooled on my sandwich, too. You drool over everything."

"That is so very true. Even his little kisses are full of spittle," Xavier teased. He leaned forward, burying his face against the crook of his son's neck, inhaling deeply. "Ahhh, I love that smell."

"Everyone loves the way babies smell." Natasha finished her meal. Resting her back against the headboard of the bed, she watched her two lovers play with their son until the toddler was exhausted enough to curl up beside her and fall asleep. Both men laid bedside her and the baby, watching their son sleep.

"You two can do that forever, can't you? Just sit and watch him sleep?" she asked.

Xavier nodded. Darian smiled.

"He's amazing. We witnessed him growing inside of you, living off your body and what you had to give him. We heard his tiny heartbeat before he was born. And then we saw him come into this world. I don't remember them being that small when they're first born," Xavier said. He leaned over and kissed his son's forehead. "And now, we're going to have another child. I can't find the words to describe how happy and anxious I am. I don't know if the baby is a boy or girl!"

"Do you have a preference?" Natasha asked.

Xavier shook his head. "No. What about you, Darian?"

"I don't have a preference," Darian said. He looked at Natasha. "Would you want any more children after these two?"

Natasha shook her head. "N.O.-- no. I've always wanted two kids. I'm getting exactly what I want, even more so with the two of you in my life," she caressed their cheeks.

The three of them talked about various topics as Xavier rested his head on her belly, hearing and feeling his second child inside. He smiled. Darian watched him in silence. He was happy that Xavier was able to experience fatherhood. He knew it was something his young lover had always wanted and thought he'd never have. They stayed inside the bedroom, enjoying each other's company for the remainder of the night until Natasha fell asleep, and the sun forced the two men to rest. Before she drifted off, she told them she couldn't wait until the next evening when they'd all be together again.

# CHAPTER TWO
## THE NEXT EVENING

Christopher dashed through the red velvet curtains exiting the stage after he finished his routine. He pulled the crumpled bills from what remained of his costume and began counting the money. He opened the door to the dressing room and was greeted by Gary.

"How much did you make?" Gary asked as he zipped up his black leather pants.

"Enough to buy my little brother that toy he wants for his birthday, about two hundred," Christopher said.

"I bring in more than that in an hour," Gary bragged.

"Hey! Don't cheapen this, two-hundred dollars is more than what most people make in a day. My parents don't even bring home two-hundred dollars in one day. This is fucking great to me."

"You know, if you switched to what I do, you'd double that... a pretty boy like you, yeah. See, I make no less than a thousand on nights like this, the weekend is a goldmine." Gary zipped up his black leather, sleeveless shirt.

"A thousand bucks?"

"No. Less. Than."

"Damn. Okay, you've got me there, a thousand is better than two-hundred. I still think it's good."

"See, it not that the women don't tip well, because Ignacio makes damn near fifteen hundred stripping and giving private dances on nights like this."

"I see where you're going with this."

"Oh, do you?"

"Yeah, you're going to tell me what my problem is," Christopher said, one eyebrow cocked, waiting for Gary's enlightening response.

Gary nodded. "I am. It's because you look too young. See, we provide a sexual fantasy for them. Many of them want a strapping man with muscles rippling and bulging everywhere, not a skinny boy with slender, but well-toned, supple limbs, prancing around in his undies."

Christopher looked down as his semi-nude figure. "I'm not that skinny. I'm the perfect weight for my age and height."

"That may be, but your pubescent body just doesn't do it for many of them. Have you seen who graces the covers of those romance novels? Not one of those men looks like you."

"Dude, that was low."

"I'm just being honest."

"Okay, so for men … My body would appeal to them?" Christopher asked.

Gary nodded. He pulled out a wad of cash from his side pocket, wiggling it in his face. "I bet you thought I was just happy to see you, didn't you? No, my friend, it really *was* a lot of money in my pocket." He smiled.

"You know, nobody likes a smart-ass." Christopher playfully tried to snatch the money from Gary's hand, but missed.

"Oh no you don't! See, that's how you get beat up in the dressing room at the strip joint." Gary laughed, stuffing the dollar bills back into his pocket.

"Awww, that's so sweet. You know you can't take me," Christopher teased.

"Oh, see, now that was low, low, loooow. I still say it sucks that you're stronger than I am, and I'm older than you are. I've been a vampire longer than you, too!"

"Don't beat yourself up over it. It's fate," Christopher said, patting Gary on his shoulder, feigning sympathy.

"Don't touch me," Gary joked, playfully knocking his hand away. Both men laughed.

After the laughter faded, Christopher began to speak. "So, you think I'd do better with the men?"

Gary nodded. "Gay men, that is. See, the way you look is more appealing to many of them. The crowd is filled with stallions and they like to look at pretty boys they can imagine themselves mounting, so to speak. It also works the other way around for the more robust strippers here and the pretty boys in the audience. All I'm saying is; think about it."

"I know that's your thing. I also know what Darian told me-"

"Darian gave you the talk?" Tony asked as he entered the dressing room.

"Yeah, he passed on his knowledge which was extremely insightful, but that's to be expected. I'm just not ready to go there yet. Having sex with men is just not something I'm ready to embrace, vampire or not. I still like the ladies," Christopher said.

"Who said anything about fucking them? I'm just saying dance for them." Gary sat down at his mirror and began combing the kinks and tangles from his silky blonde hair.

"I know, it's just ... they'll be looking at me, wanting me, wanting to touch me and then doing so."

Gary laughed. He turned, looking at the younger man. "I bet you're scared you'll get turned on by that and start questioning your sexuality, right?"

Christopher shrugged one shoulder, looking away, he nodded once.

"Newsflash! We're vampires; we don't have a sexual preference. We don't live under the human moral code of ethics either, hell even they don't want to live under that. That is why we're desired by everyone and everything." Gary finished combing his hair.

Christopher thought about what he was saying. He had been experiencing feelings of arousal whenever he fed. It was increasingly difficult to resist the temptation. Because of that, he found himself feeding on more women, even though the blood of a human male gave him more pleasure. When he'd asked Darian about that, it was explained to him that men have more minerals in their blood because they don't have menstrual cycles as females do. During his nearly two year stint as a vampire, he had noticed that men were the preferred choice for vampires, both male and female. All conflicts aside, he really was just curious.

Tony watched him standing there in his string bikini. He laughed. "I think I know what's got you so conflicted."
Christopher looked at him. "What's that?"

"You're still thinking like a human man but you're feeling a freedom inside you that you never knew was possible. When you feed from a man, you want to take him in every way imaginable. You want to take his life, his blood and his body. You believe that just because you don't kill your victims, you can resist all the other temptations as well."

Christopher's mouth dropped open, shocked that Tony knew his innermost thoughts better than he did. Hearing his own subconscious feelings spoken openly helped him better understand his dilemma. "So what are you saying... that I should just give in?"

Tony shook his head. "Not necessarily. You don't want to kill, that's understandable. That's going to be something you're going to have to continue to fight against. Your natural instinct is to hunt and kill. But I think you should enjoy what your life has to offer. There's no harm in enjoying the pleasures of the flesh. Remember that. There's a whole new world out there that you're denying yourself."

Christopher didn't say anything, only reflected on Tony's words. Truth be told, it wasn't the first time one of the vampires in Darian's coven had told him that. Still, he had his reservations.

Tony looked past him to his lover. "Are you ready to go?" he asked Gary.

"Yeah." Gary walked toward him.

"Hey, where are you two going?" Christopher asked, feeling a little left out. He didn't want to be alone. His other partner-in-crime, John was with Devin. Everyone seemed to have plans except him.

"You're not ready to go where we're going," Gary teased.

"And where's that?" Christopher asked.

"We're going to a party. Another little vampire shin-dig," Gary continued teasing.

"A lot of vampire sex?"

"Oh yeah! Everywhere you look, somebody will be getting busy," Gary said.

Tony looked at Gary, smiling. "No we're not."

Gary slapped him on his arm. "I really had him going. You

ruined my fun. Did you see the look on his face?"

"Very funny, jerk," Christopher said to Gary, who only smiled coyly.

"We're going to this new club that just opened, *Eclipse*. Personally, I think it's a blatant rip-off of *Desires Unleashed*, with the whole dance and strip club combo. But we're going to see what the buzz is all about." Tony looked at his watch. "Come on, we need to leave now if we plan on having any fun in before the sun rises."

Both vampires turned to leave, Christopher called out to them. They turned around.

"Can I go with you?" he asked.

"Get dressed-quickly," Gary said.

Without another word, Christopher dashed into the shower, washing away sweat, glitter and other needless things. He dressed quickly in a pair of blue jeans, a snug-fitting white t-shirt and white sneakers. When he joined the other two vampires, and looked at their matching black leather outfits, he felt a bit out of place.

"Well, well, well, don't you look wholesome," Tony jested.

"I do feel a bit underdressed for the outing."

"Doesn't matter, come on." Gary beckoned for him to join them.

The three vampires left *Desires Unleashed*, heading toward the newest club on the supernatural strip called Eclipse. As they rounded the corner, they noticed several police and S.U.I.T. squad cars parked in front of the building. Red and white "S.U.I.T." tape blocked off the building from the several dozen onlookers peeking over each other's shoulders trying to get a look at what was going on.

"What the fuck happened here?" Gary asked to no one in particular. "I smell blood and ... ."

"Death," Tony finished his sentence. "We need to get a closer look."

The three inquisitive vampires mentally forced the crowd to part, allowing them to walk past the spectators toward the front where they could get a better view of the situation. Once there, they saw something they had never seen before.

"Oh my God!" Christopher exclaimed, backing away several steps.

"Why would anyone do that?" Gary asked, not fully grasping

what he was seeing.

"I don't know. But Darian and the other leaders need to know about this shit right now," Tony said. Leaning forward, he looked closer at the mutilated corpse of a shape-shifter. The body was lying in a pale, crumpled heap on the ground right in front of the club. He had been flayed from head to toe, so perfectly that not an inch of skin was left on the victim. The blood vessels had collapsed and looked like dark blue roads over the mass of pale flesh. It was apparent that the body had been completely drained of blood. Every bone in the corpse appeared to had been shattered to bits inside it's flesh casing. It was hard to tell if it was because of the very powerful impact of flesh hitting concrete or something else entirely.

"We need to find out who or what did this," Christopher said. "God, I think I'm going to be sick."

"Come on, let's get you some air." Gary took Christopher by his shoulder and led him away from the crowd.

Christopher leaned against the brick wall of the adjacent building, a restaurant that catered to both humans and supernaturals. "I still feel sick."

"That's definitely the humanity inside of you at work. I'll admit, I haven't seen anything like that in my life. Because I'm so young, I've been pretty protected from the more gruesome sights. Like that battle we had, I wasn't allowed to go, I stayed with you. Seeing that corpse like that is kind of bothering me, too, so don't feel bad about feeling si-" Gary managed to dodge the stream of bloody vomit that spewed from Christopher's mouth.

A second later, Christopher spat the last of his meal on the concrete. "Holy shit! I didn't even know I could still get sick like that."

"It's a mental thing. You must have kept thinking about it and you made yourself worse." He patted the younger vampire on his back. "Are you going to be okay?"

Christopher nodded. "Yeah, I think so. I just don't want to see that body anymore."

"You know, we've got to be two of the most pampered vampires in the city," Gary joked. He couldn't believe that he was feeling a bit queasy as well. He thought he'd be feeling bloodlust instead.

Nonetheless, he managed to keep from getting sick. In that moment, he realized just how much he had been kept from danger. His lover, Tony seemed to have no problem looking at the corpse and he figured it was only because he'd seen far worse atrocities. He was grateful to Darian for keeping him out of harm's way. Both he and Christopher decided to wait where they were for Tony to rejoin them.

As Tony examined the body from the distance that separated them, he saw Warren and Matthew walking up, each man flashing their S.U.I.T. badges.

"Why the hell are all of these people standing around? Can you do something about this shit? This isn't a damn Broadway show," Warren complained to the uniformed officer who had inspected their identification.

The officer nodded. "Yes sir." He went to work dispersing the crowd. Several squad cars turned on their sirens, causing the onlookers to become alert of the oncoming patrol cars. They backed away from the red and white tape allowing the squad cars to park in front of the tape, blocking them from the scene. Unable to get a better view, the disappointed spectators grumbled but continued observing in hopes of catching a glimpse of the body again. Tony was part of the crowd that was pushed away. He called out to Warren who turned around immediately, zeroing in on his voice.

"Officer, let him through!" Warren called to the uniformed cop. He pointed toward Tony. The cop nodded and lifted the tape as Tony slid underneath.

"Thanks, do you know what's going on?" Tony asked once he reached Warren. He looked at Warren's partner. "Hey Matthew."

"Hi, Tony," Matthew greeted. He kept a few paces back because the sight of the exposed flesh was beginning to entice him.

Warren looked over at his partner and lover. He walked towards him. "Look, Matthew, why don't you go inside and talk to the witnesses. I can handle this out here," he suggested, seeing that his lover was having a hard time controlling his hunger. Without saying another word, Matthew walked inside the club to where witnesses were being held for questioning.

Tony watched him disappear into the club. "He's still having trouble at the crime scenes, I see."

Warren nodded. "Yeah, it's been pretty peaceful around here for the past several months. And when it wasn't, we didn't really have a lot of gruesome murders. So he hasn't seen anything that can really set him off, mostly just petty crimes. Darian must have the vamps in this town scared shitless to cross him."

"Hey, we vamps aren't the only ones committing crimes, Warren, damn," Tony complained.

"I know that. Xander, Richard and Elise are keeping the shifters in check, so I just assumed Darian was handling his business as well, that's all. No need to get testy."

"I'm not getting testy. Besides, that's not even important, this is." Tony pointed to the mass of broken bones and flesh that used to be a living being.

"I've never seen anything like this before, that's for damn sure." Warren walked to the body, squatting beside it for a closer inspection. "It's definitely a lion."

"Yeah, and the fact that it's apparently bloodless does suggest vampires. Well, that and the scent I'm getting," Tony said. "Not that something else couldn't have drained him, though."

Warren nodded. "This reminds me of a case Matt and I had a few years back. A vampire and shape-shifter were leaving bodies in remote locations public enough to get noticed eventually, but not enough to be a target audience spot. The bodies were found mutilated, drained of blood and all of them were headless."

"Well, whatever did this wants notoriety," Tony said.

Warren nodded. "I agree. Witnesses said it fell from the sky and it's no coincidence it happened smack in the middle of one of the most popular strips in the city." He rose to his full height and began circling the corpse, trying to find any evidence that could help him piece together what had happened and why?

"I'm going to tell Darian about this. If we have another rogue vampire on the loose, he's going to want to put an end to this asshole before more bodies start dropping in," Tony said.

"You got that right," Matthew said as he came up from behind. He stood several paces away from the body and beckoned for the two men to join him. They did. The three men took their conversation away from prying eyes and ears towards the alley where Christopher and Gary waited.

"Tell me more," Tony said.

"Every witness I spoke to inside the club all said the same thing. They were standing in line waiting to get in, when all of a sudden a body dropped out of the sky landing right in front of them."

"Did anybody s-"

"No, not one person could tell me any more than that," Matthew said, interrupting Warren's question. "No one saw where the body came from. The building itself is only two stories and I don't think falling from that height would do that kind of damage to the corpse."

"I agree, we can probably rule that out, it's highly unlikely," Warren said.

"Shape-shifters are pretty strong, right?" Christopher asked, drawing everyone's attention.

"Yeah," Warren confirmed.

"Well, wouldn't that mean that someone stronger than that shifter had to kill him? I mean, he was really fucked up, he looked gross." Christopher swallowed hard.

"You're not going to puke again, are you?" Gary asked him. Embarrassed, he shook his head. "No!"

"Vampires get sick?" Warren asked; his eyebrows cocked in amazement. He looked to Tony for an explanation.

"We can. Not like humans. We don't catch colds or anything like that. But my specialty drinks have been known to put a few vamps on their asses or their heads in the toilet," Tony answered.

"He just got nauseous at the sight of the body. His virgin eyes never seen anything like it before outside of a movie screen," Gary explained.

"Oh, I didn't know that, I learned something new." Warren looked at Matthew. "We need to get back to the scene."

Matthew nodded. "Look guys, we'll keep you in touch when we find out what's going on."

"I'm thinking about what you said, too, Chris. Because the shifter is dead, I can't get a read on his aura, so I don't know how powerful he was. But based on what we know about vampires, they have to be as strong as Xavier if they're flying," Warren speculated.

The other men nodded in agreement.

"We'll keep you posted," Warren said. He and Matthew walked back to the crime scene.

Tony turned toward the other two. "Okay, so our night of fun is officially ruined. Let's get back to the mansion."

"Before we go back home, can I get something to eat?" Christopher asked.

"Feeling hungry?" Gary asked.

"Yeah, I am."

"Fine, let's make it quick," Tony said.

The three vampires walked with Christopher until he found his victim, feeding quickly. Afterward, they headed back to the mansion to tell their Master what they knew.

Tony knocked on Darian's bedroom door. He waited for permission to enter. Once he heard his Master call to him, he opened the door. "Master, I think we have a problem."

Xavier turned towards Tony. "What's the matter?"

Darian sat up in the bed, swinging his legs over the edge. "Tell me."

"A body was found right outside of that new nightclub, *Eclipse*. We were on our way there when we saw all of the S.U.I.T. surrounding the building."

"Human?" Darian asked.

Tony shook his head. "No, shifter. Warren and Matt were there on the case. They said they would keep us posted. It looks bad, Master. The body was completely drained of blood; I'm talking gone, bone-dry. It was also flayed from head to toe, not a piece of skin to be seen. All of the witnesses said the body just dropped out of the sky, no one saw by what or whom."

"Were you able to catch any scents off the body?" Xavier asked.

"A vampire's scent, but no one I recognized. I know another shifter didn't have anything to do with it, at least I don't think so. The shifter scents I smelled on the body were too faint to be recent." Tony looked back at Darian. "Master?"

Darian was thinking about his next move. He didn't have an answer for Tony yet. "Thank you, Tony for getting this information to me. You may go."

Catching the hint, Tony left, leaving the two vampires alone.

Xavier looked at Darian. "What do you think is going on? Think it's a challenge?"

"I don't know. I'd be lying if I said this didn't alarm me. We could be dealing with one very strong vampire or even two. I can't determine that now because I don't know how powerful the shifter was. I have to go on the fact that this vampire may have the ability of fight or an airplane," Darian smirked.

"Do you need my help?" Xavier asked.

Darian shook his head. "No. I don't think I'll have any trouble tracking down this menace on my own. If this vampire is killing in so bold a manner, they should have an aura I can detect easily."

Xavier nodded slowly. "So, first thing tomorrow night … "

"I'll hunt." Darian finished his sentence for him.

Xavier laid down beside his son, but not taking the toddler into his arms. The sun was rising and he was feeling the effects. He kissed his son, Natasha and Darian before his body relaxed to rest. Darian laid beside him, snuggling next to his cooling form. He closed his eyes, letting his body rest.

# CHAPTER THREE

The loud ringing on the telephone woke both Xander and Tatiana up immediately. He reached over her, snatching the cordless off its base.

"Hello?" he asked in a groggy, annoyed tone.

"Xander, I'm sorry if I woke you, but this is important." Warren began to tell his Alpha about the death he was investigating. "What do you think is going on?"

"This is disturbing. I can't tell you anything yet, I've never heard of a shifter being murdered and disposed of in such a brutal fashion before, believe it or not. At this point, there's not much to go on. Please keep me updated with whatever you discover. I'll contact Richard and Elise, let them know what has happened," Xander said before ending the conversation with Warren.

"I heard everything. You'll need to get in contact with Darian as soon as the sun sets. Since this appears to be a vampire crime, he'll be the one to deal with it," Tatiana said.

"True, but I still want to contact the others; they need to know that a shape-shifter was the target of this attack." Xander dialed Elise's number, and waited for her to answer.

"Hello?" answered Sergio, his voice gruff as he forced himself out of his slumber.

Xander greeted him before requesting to speak with Elise.

"She's still asleep, Xander, what's going on?" Sergio asked.

"I assure you, it's important, I'd rather you both hear what I have to say."

Taken aback by the urgency in his tone, Sergio woke Elise up, handing her the telephone. He propped himself up on his forearms, listening as Xander told her everything that he knew about the murder.

"My goodness!" Elise gasped softly, appalled by the viciousness of the crime. She thanked Xander for telling her before ending the call.

Xander called Richard next. When the other Pack Alpha answered, he greeted him and told him the situation.

"We need to find out how old the shifter was. That will help us determine just how strong the killer is. Tell Warren to focus on that. I'll talk to Matthew," Richard said.

"My guess is, Darian may be taking care of this later on tonight when he wakes up. I just wanted the three of us to be on guard until then," Xander said before saying his goodbyes. He climbed out of bed, stretching his long form, working the powerful muscles underneath his skin.

"Why don't you come back to bed, staying up worrying about this is not good," Tatiana suggested.

Xander turned towards his wife. "Perhaps, dear, but I can't help it." He smiled sadly.

"Very well." She sat up, brushing her long dark brown bangs from her eyes. "I'll start breakfast." She climbed out of bed, gave her husband a sweet kiss before entering the bathroom to freshen up. When she was done, she headed toward the kitchen. Xander stepped out onto the balcony of their bedroom, relishing the crisp, fresh morning air. The delicately cool summer breeze helped relax him as he thought about the complexities of Warren's new case.

*** 

"So there's another dumb-ass rogue vampire on the loose," Sergio stated as he watched Elise combed the tangles out of her long, wavy, brown hair.

"It looks that way, but we're not sure. Xander, as always, never rules humans out of the equation," Elise said.

"Shit, I don't blame him. Humans have been responsible for the deaths of a lot of supernaturals. Our history with the bastards proves this to be more than a notion," Sergio said, pulling the cool silk sheets up over his chest getting more comfortable.

"I agree. Warren and Matthew are investigating the crime. I want you to go to the scene. Take someone with you, see what you can find out," Elise ordered.

Sergio looked at her from his relaxed position. "Now?" he asked slightly disappointed.

She nodded. "Unless, of course, you'd rather go back to sleep."

"Is there any way to answer that question truthfully and still get some tender lovin' later on today?" he asked, grinning wolfishly.

"Not if your answer is 'yes', there isn't." Elise's eyes met his and she smiled slyly.

"Ahhh, shit," Sergio groaned as he tossed the covers aside, climbing out of the bed. "Of course not, darling. I would rather investigate this silly-ass crime than get much needed rest. As a matter of fact, I'm betting Danny would agree. I'm taking him with me."

"Sarcasm will get you nowhere," Elise commented.

"Who's being sarcastic?" Sergio tossed her a mischievous grin as he walked into the bathroom. Showering quickly, he then dressed in a pair of black jeans, boots and black t-shirt. He walked towards Elise, standing behind her chair. Leaning over, he began to kiss her neck, tickling her with his perfectly groomed goatee.

"Stop tickling me with your whiskers!" Elise said, giggling.

"Okay," Sergio said, he began licking down the length of her neck, hoping to get her in the mood.

"Sergio, sweetheart?"

"Yeah, baby?" he answered as he trailed his kisses over the creamy smoothness of her bared shoulder.

"First business, then pleasure."

Getting the hint, he ceased his seduction. "You're no fun," he whined before leaving the room, heading towards Daniel's and Miranda's shared bedroom. He knocked hard, purposely, hoping to jar the couple out of their peaceful sleep. A second later, Daniel swung the door opened, a look of pure outrage plastered on his face.

"What the hell?!" Daniel exclaimed.

"Congratulations! You are the unlucky winner of an early morning, one hour commute to a downtown club to investigate the murder of a shifter. Hurry now, get dressed and come with me!" Sergio said, feigning enthusiasm.

"You're an asshole sometimes, you know that?" Daniel said, rolling his eyes.

Sergio laughed. "I've been called that by other people with much more conviction behind that word than you. But seriously, I'll fill you in on the way there, get dressed. I'll be waiting downstairs." He walked away, leaving Daniel to get prepared.

Ten minutes later, Daniel joined Sergio in the foyer. "Let's go."

The two men climbed into Sergio's Sidewinder SUV, traveling down the winding scenic route towards the interstate.

"Okay, what the fuck's going on?" Daniel asked.

"Some other asshole killed a shifter. Elise wants us to search the crime scene and see what we can find. Warren and Matthew are on the case, but she wants to do her own investigation. They're young, we may pick up on something they didn't," Sergio informed.

"Oh." Daniel looked out the window at the beautiful flowers and trees as they passed by. "Did this happen last night?"

Sergio nodded. "Yeah, from what we were told, well, actually, it happened around three or four this morning."

Daniel didn't speak any more about the murder; he and Sergio discussed other matters until they arrived at their destination. S.U.I.T. tape blocked off the entire *Eclipse* nightclub, which meant the new establishment was not going to do any business until the matter was settled and the club and its' employees were cleared of any involvement. There was a police squad car parked in front of the building. A uniformed officer exited the car and began walking towards the two men as they approached the scene.

"I'm sorry gentlemen, but no one is allowed near this crime scene."

"I left my wallet here last night, they told me to come in today to pick it up," Sergio lied, hoping it would get him some kind of access.

"I'm sorry, sir. But there's no one inside to retrieve your wallet for you. Why don't you write down your name and I'll forward the information to the club owner. That's about all I can do for you at the moment, I can't allow you inside." The officer handed Sergio a pen and paper and told him to describe his wallet.

Sergio scribbled a brief description with a fake name on the paper and handed it back to the officer. "Thanks."

"No problem," the officer said, taking the paper and pen back.

"Hey what happened here anyway?" Daniel asked.

"I'm not at liberty to say, sir." The officer stood his ground, silently letting the two men know that he wasn't going to let them pass. The expression on his face told them he wouldn't answer any more of their questions either.

"I'll call and check back later," Sergio said, tapping Daniel on his arm, leading him away. The two shifters climbed back into the Sidewinder SUV. "Fuck! That was a waste of time."

"I guess having a vampire now would help. John or Xavier could have hypnotized his ass and got him out of the way," Daniel said, slightly disappointed that they couldn't do their own investigation.

"Yeah, I agree. Hey, did you manage to catch the scent of the shifter or anything else?"

Daniel nodded. "I did, confirming what Xander told Elise, It's definitely a lion."

"You know that's an interesting aspect. Lions are extremely territorial. I wonder where he came from."

"They are also the strongest of the feline species," Sergio said.

"Depends on his age. I wonder if he had a Pride with him?" Daniel speculated.

"I was wondering about that, too. If he did, where are they?" Sergio asked.

"If they aren't dead, they should be looking for another alpha male to protect them."

"True. We should see if there's been any movement among lion Prides as of late." Sergio pulled out his cell phone, calling Elise. Once she answered, he told her that they were unable to investigate the scene. Also, he told her about his and Daniel's opinion on the situation.

"I was thinking the same thing, I'll call Xander, he may already be on the same page," Elise said.

"Okay, I'll be home soon." Sergio hung up. He and Daniel ate at a restaurant before returning home. He searched for Elise and found her with their two children, playing a board game specifically designed to help kids learn the basics. He sat down beside her, kissing her softly on her temple.

"Hi Daddy!" his twins exclaimed at the same time, excited to see their dad for the first time that day.

"Hey you little munchkins!" He scooped up both kids tickling them and nuzzling them as they cackled and squirmed, loving every moment of their father's attention.

"I love watching you with them. So precious," Elisa said, watching her lover and children.

Sergio smiled. "I love my family, I love being a part of your lives." He continued to play with his family, including himself into their board game. "Did you speak with Xander?"

"I did, he's going to look into it."

"That's good." He bounced his son on his lap. "So, did you learn any colors today?" he asked his son, Caesar.

The toddler nodded his head enthusiastically. "Yes! I did! I know blue, red, pink ..." his son listed the colors he'd learned. He had a little trouble pronouncing "purple" and Sergio assisted him. Caesar was pleased with his accomplishments, as was Annette-Naté when her father asked her the same question. The four of them spent quality time together, teaching their children more colors, numbers and shapes. It was a great way to spend the early part of the day, especially when sundown seemed so far away.

# CHAPTER FOUR

Warren closed his cell phone, disconnecting his call from his Alpha. He looked at Matthew sitting in the passenger seat. "That was Xander, the heads of our groups are looking into lion Prides to see who's missing a King or male member."

"That should be easy information to find out, right?" Matthew asked.

"That depends if they're willing to talk. Lions are the most secretive and territorial of all the shifter species," Warren paused.

Matthew looked at him. "Are you going to tell me more, or are you just going to leave it at that and hope I figure out the rest on my own?"

Warren blinked, as if bringing himself out of a trance. "Sorry, just thinking about something. I've never met a Lion Pride, but I do know that the King of the Pride is both protector and provider. The women are the nurturers and homemakers. Without a King, they are extremely vulnerable. So, if one happens to be missing a King, they might not want to broadcast it. They'll lose their territory, possibly. Other Lion Prides will seek to kill them or the Kings of other Prides might take the women for their own, expanding their Prides."

"But if they need a King to survive, wouldn't it be in their best interest to broadcast it?"

Warren shrugged one shoulder. "That depends. If handled diplomatically, so to speak, one could choose their King, instead of being forced under the ruling of a less desirable one."

"Do you think this shifter was a King?"

"I don't know. Unfortunately, my superior sense of smell, which far surpasses yours, is unable to tell."

"You think you're better than me just because you're some mangy wolf?" Matthew asked, playfully.

Warren tossed a sly glance his way, shrugging one shoulder. "Well, one isn't going to dispute such glaring and irrefutable facts."

"Fuck you and your entire mutt breed," Matthew retorted with a wicked grin.

Warren laughed outright. "Can I help it if we're the shit?"

"Full of shit, is more like it." Matthew looked away, smiling to himself.

"Don't think I didn't catch that sly-ass comment."

"Oh, I'm sure your super heightened *wolf* ears can pick up everything," Matthew said sarcastically.

"I see, I've talked myself into a hole. I'm going to stop now. Besides, we're at the precinct." Warren pulled their car into a parking spot closest to the door. The two men climbed out and entered the precinct. They walked to their desk, turning on their computers simultaneously.

Matthew sat down and began sifting through the notes he took of the crime scene. "We caught the scent of a vampire on the victim; do you think it's working alone?"

Warren ran his fingers through his luxurious black hair. "Most likely it is, although I'm not willing to omit human involvement. For all we know, the vampire scent we smelled could have been another victim waiting to be disposed of. I mean after the way Annette died, puncture wounds and drained blood, I'd be foolish to not add humans to the list of suspects."

Matthew nodded. "Not to mention those rich assholes a few years back had no problem drugging shifters and a vampire, kidnapping them in the process. It's easy to see why we can't rule humans out, if one is involved, how are we going to begin tracking them down?"

"Matt, right now, I have no idea. I haven't slept in twenty-four hours. We've been up all morning at that fucking crime scene and all we have to show for it is that the body wasn't thrown from the rooftop, that's been ruled out. It's frustrating."

"If we're not going to cancel out humans, we need to check the air traffic control reports to see if any planes were flying over Chicago at that time, in that location." Matthew began looking up the telephone number so he could call and get the report.

"Good idea, no planes, no humans."

"Well, I wouldn't go that far. It just means that no humans were flying over at that time. Doesn't mean they aren't involved. Let's not get too ahead of ourselves," Matthew said. He found the number and looked at Warren. "Do vampires register on the radar when they fly?"

"I don't think so. If they see anything at all, they'd probably mistake it for a glitch in the system or a bird. The government doesn't even know vamps can fly. The Council kept a lot of our secrets ... secret." Warren began reading over his partner's notes.

Matthew called the Air Traffic Control Center, using his federal S.U.I.T. status to get the report. He kept his fingers crossed, hoping to get some kind of lead. After requesting the information and getting the results, he was slightly disappointed. He stood by his fax machine looking at the total amount of aircrafts that were in the air for that day and their point of travel and destination.

Warren came up from behind, peeking over his shoulder. "So what do we have?"

"Jack shit. There weren't any planes flying over the area at that time, let along, over the *Eclipse* nightclub."

"Well, it's what we suspected. A vampire is definitely involved." Warren walked back to his desk, sitting down. He began to brainstorm. "Xavier was strong enough to fly, even though he's young by vampire standards. We also know that it was Darian's blood that increased his strength. There's really no way of telling just how powerful this vampire is or why he or she did what they did. I've got to tell ya, Matt I'm not thrilled about working on this case."

"We should check in with Marshall, see if he's found out anything more," Matthew suggested.

"Yeah, he should have something by now."

"Let's hope so."

The two detectives walked past a few dozen S.U.I.T. officers. With their superhuman hearing, they could hear many of the conversations as they walked by. A few of the officers were buzzing, spreading gossip and speculation about the current crime. Some were jealous that Warren and Matthew were chosen for the case. Many felt their captain gave a lot of high-profile cases to them because they were her favorites. Some of the other officers didn't envy them; they were glad that they were chosen instead of themselves. High-profile meant longer hours, more media exposure and harder work. Ignoring all of the comments, the two men made their way to the morgue to speak with Marshall. They entered without knocking, which was one of the few pet peeves the quirky medical examiner had.

"Sure, come on in officers. You're not disturbing me," Marshall said, jokingly.

"I'm sorry. Did you want us to knock?" Warren asked, pointing back toward the door.

"You two, and Marks and Julliano are the only S.U.I.T.s who don't knock. It just wouldn't feel right if you started now. I've grown far too accustomed to your 'barge-in' style entrance." Marshall gave the two men a sly smile.

"Everybody's a fucking comedian today," Warren mumbled as he walked closer to Marshall, who was still examining the body of the shifter, giving the corpse a full autopsy. "So what did you find out, please give me some good news."

Matthew came up beside Warren, standing slightly behind him. "Marshall did a vampire do it?" he asked, his breath increasing slightly.

"Oh, I have no doubt that a vampire did this, but not just one vampire, you're dealing with at least four different vampires. I found what I think may be two male vampire bites and two female," Marshall informed.

"What the fuck?" Warren asked, hating the case even more than before.

"The news gets better, so please try to contain your excitement, this is a morgue." Marshall gave the two officers a crooked smile as he leaned over the ice cold body. "Look here." He pointed to a set of puncture wounds. He placed a ruler beside the wounds. "The centimeters spacing between the punctures indicates, male."

Matthew leaned over, getting closer to the corpse. Without realizing he had begun to salivate, a low growl bubbled up from his throat and grew fiercer as he lunged forward towards the body. Instantly, Warren caught him, dragging him backwards away from the corpse as he snarled. Marshall had taken several steps backward, pressing himself against the stainless steel drawers. Warren used his strength to suppress his lover as he whispered for him to calm down. Several seconds passed before Matthew was able to regain control of his composure. A minute later, he nodded, letting Warren know that he was calm. His face reddened by embarrassment at the loss of control. Warren continued to monitor to him, making sure he wouldn't try to feed again.

"So ... did you do that to him?" Marshall asked, looking at Warren.

Warren turned sharply, looking at Marshall. "No! I didn't turn him-Wait a minute? ... You know about me?" he asked, shocked by the revelation.

Marshall nodded. "I've known for some years. Perhaps he should wait outside then."

Warren turned to Matthew. "I think that's a good idea, get some fresh air."

Without arguing with the two men, Matthew left, knowing he needed to get away from the scent of raw flesh. Breathing fresh air into his lungs was the best thing to do at that point.

Warren watched him leave, before returning his attention to Marshall. "You've known about me being a shifter for years? How? I was being so careful."

"Don't get upset. I'm a pathologist. It's my job to pay attention to every detail. It's also my duty to know everything I can about supernaturals. Their habits, instincts, et cetera. I've noticed you at crime scenes and I've seen your hunger growing. Human men usually don't get that glazed-over look in their eyes at the sight of blood, gore and body bits, that you do. Then I noticed it when Matthew did, about a year and a half ago."

"How come you've never said anything?"

Marshall shrugged. "Figured you didn't want anyone to know what you were. By the way, which breed of shape-shifter are you?"

Warren looked at him sideways, still in disbelief. "I'm a wolf."

"Ah, and Matthew?"

"He's a coyote, long story."

Warren took a few steps closer. Marshall did the same and the two stood face to face with the corpse between them on the cold metal slab.

"So, how come you didn't expose us?" Warren asked. "The S.U.I.T. is against supernaturals joining."

"Because you're damn good cops; the best on this force, regardless of your species whether everyone would agree or not. As far as I'm concern, that's just an added bonus. It's why you get the high-profile cases, because you get the job done better than most. And if the entire S.U.I.T. Organization would get its head out of its bureaucratic ass, they'd realize that by hiring supernaturals and pairing them with their human officers would save more lives, and stop more crimes."

Warren was amazed. Here was a human who had kept his secret for years, and now he was keeping Matthew's. Marshall had no inclination to turn him in, he respected them, acknowledge their contribution to the S.U.I.T. and the people they've protected and saved.

"I'm still in shock here. You've never let on that you knew, you never treated me differently." Warren smiled at him. "You're a cool-ass dude, you know that?"

"You're just now realizing that?" Marshall adjusted the collar of his white lab coat, flicking it. "I'm cool as hell."

Warren laughed, feeling a bit more relieved to know that he had a human ally within the division. "I'm glad it was you who found us out."

Marshall nodded. "What you need to do is make sure Matthew doesn't flip out at the wrong time. If he does what he did here somewhere in public, you two can expect a *public* execution."

"I know. We're still working on his control. He hasn't seen anything this … I guess the right term would be, 'appetizing' since being turned. I'll take care of it."

Both men nodded in agreement.

"Okay, let's get back to this here, what else can you tell me?" Warren gestured towards the body.

"Right, I've sent a sample of his organs to toxicology to check for any foreign substances. If there is any sign of drugs in his system, we'll know soon enough. I've also pulled a tooth and scraped a flesh sample and sent that to the DNA lab. Because this poor guy didn't have any skin on his body, that killed any chance of us getting identification off his finger prints."

"The fingerprints probably wouldn't have been on file anyway."

"Why do you say that?"

"He's a Natural Born."

"I'm still unclear."

"If he was turned by another shifter, then he may have had a record. I know that in the States, they take your foot prints when you're born."

"Yeah, our little antiquated tracking system," Marshall smirked.

Warren chuckled. "Yeah, well, shifters who are pregnant don't go to hospitals to give birth. The birth of a Natural Born is very private and sacred to Packs and Prides, a special occasion and not for human scrutiny. The Matron in each community assist in the birthing procedure and most shifter communities have people they can contact to get the proper paperwork they'll need to cover the newborn. That's how it goes."

Marshall reflected on the new information he'd just heard. "That's very interesting, very organized."

"Yeah, and if my Pack Alpha knew I told you even that much, he'd kill me, figuratively speaking … maybe." Warren had to think about the last thing he said.

"So why did you?"

"Because you've proven that you can keep a secret. I trust you with that information."

Marshall nodded. "Thank you for trusting me." He looked back at the corpse. "Every bone in his body has been shattered; I believe the fall from the sky did that. It must have been from a very high distance, at least ten-thousand feet, but probably higher. I'm just giving you a ball park figure."

"What did the killer use to skin him?" Warren asked.

"See, that's what's so interesting about this body. I couldn't find one shred of evidence to prove that an actual weapon was used at all. There were no serrated engravings in the flesh to prove that a knife of some sort was used."

"What about a filet knife? I mean, the guy was flayed, that would be the weapon of choice and if done well, might not have left any signs?"

Marshall shook his head. "I'm afraid not, Warren. Even a filet knife, as sharp as can be, still would leave some kind of engraving. That's not the really, really fascinating part of this tale. Look here?" He pointed to a tiny puncture in the meaty mass towards the victim's thigh. A sharp jagged piece of white bone jutted through the flesh, causing that part of the body to look deformed and the muscles were twisted around the bone underneath the flesh.

"What the fuck am I looking at?" Warren asked as he gazed down at the horrendous sight before him.

"Well, the 'fuck' you're looking at is this here." He made a circular motion with his silver pointing pen around a partial moon-shaped puncture. "This wasn't made by a set of fangs. It's far too shallow. If I had to give a professional calculated guess, I'd say it was a nail mark. The curve of the wound isn't comparable to the nail of a human, it's sharper, pointier, but considering the supernaturals responsible for this murder, it's not outlandish to assume they flayed the skin of this shifter with their bare hands."

"Jesus Christ!" Warren gasped.

"I know. I've never seen anything like it before since the *Exposure*. You've got some really sick vamps on your hands this time."

Warren looked over the mangled mass of flesh stretched out on the slab. "God, this is a real fucking mess, and I don't even want to think about what they did with his skin." He thought about everything Marshall told him, he had to tell Xander, right away. "Thanks for everything, Galen. I'll get back with you if anything else comes up."

"Don't you want to know how he died?" Marshall asked.

Warren mentally cursed himself for forgetting such an important detail. He was so preoccupied with telling Xander the news, he'd gotten sidetracked. "Yeah, of course, I had assumed being drained of all blood killed him? What do you medical types call it, exsanguination?"

"Yeah, but I haven't come across a shape-shifter who's died that way. Has a shape-shifter ever been killed from massive blood loss?"

Warren nodded. "It's rare, but if we don't regenerate fast enough, it could happen."

"His neck was broken by the fall that much I know. The lack of blood and the condition of his veins indicates that he was alive when he was drained once again before being dropped from the sky. Although, I'm sure he would have died anyway from the blood loss."

"It also means he was alive when he was being flayed," Warren added.

Marshall nodded. "The rest is up to you."

Warren nodded once as he turned around, heading towards the door. "This case just hit ten on the 'Holy shit!' meter," he said, once he rejoined Matthew at their conjoined desks.

Matthew looked at him. "I really fucked up in there, didn't I?"

Warren nodded. "Yeah, you did. You have to fight harder to control yourself, Matt. Had you did that at the crime scene ... I don't even want to think about what would have happened. You have to watch yourself," he whispered low enough for only his lover to hear.

"What did you and Marshall talk about?" Matthew asked.

"First off, he supports us," Warren told him everything that he and Marshall discussed, ending it with the details of the corpse.

"Holy shit," Matthew said, after getting all of the particulars. He slouched back into his chair, running both hands through his brown, silky, hair with the loose curls Warren adored so much. He locked his fingers behind his head as he leaned back.

"I'm waiting for the results from the DNA lab and from toxicology. Meanwhile, I'm going to call Xander, let him know what's going on. You need to call Richard, tell him everything and by that, I mean you losing control as well."

Remembering the embarrassment he felt then and was now feeling, his face reddened once more. "All right."

Neither man wanted to take the risk of calling their respective Alphas inside the S.U.I.T. precinct due to the busy atmosphere, someone may overhear them. They rose from their seats, each man heading in separate direction to make their very personal phone calls.

Matthew went outside, walking to a restaurant where he was going to get lunch for himself and Warren. He entered the one-occupancy bathroom to make his call, dialing Richard's cell phone. His Alpha picked up after four rings.

"Hello Matthew," Richard greeted.

"Hi, Richard. I've got some new information." He began telling him everything he knew.

"At least four vampires, you say? I take it that Xander and Elise are being notified as well?"

"Yeah, Warren's calling Xander and he'll most likely call Elise."

"Looks like this is something Darian will have to deal with. If there was more to go on, I'd be willing to hunt out their resting place and burn them to ash, but they were cleaver enough to not leave a trace, which is just mind boggling to me. I don't know how they could mutilate a body and not leave all their scents."

"That's what's got Warren and me so confused, too. What are you going to do now?"

"Same thing I was doing before you called me, contacting other lion Prides I know of. Keep me posted as you discover more."

"All right … Umm, Richard, there's something else I need to tell you," Matthew said apprehensively, regretting having to tell his Alpha about his blunder. "I lost it today at the job."

"How? What happened?"

"Warren and I were in the morgue speaking with the M.E., when I lost control-"

"In front of the medical examiner?! What happened?"

"Don't worry, everything went fine. Surprisingly enough, he already knew about us." Matthew began to tell Richard what Warren told him about Marshall.

Richard listened carefully. "Listen, I want you to remain cautious around him, still. It's good that he's kept your secret this long, but never trust him completely, tell Warren to do the same."

"I don't understand?"

"Keeping your secret now doesn't affect him one way or another. If push comes to shove, he may use the knowledge he has over you to make you do things you may not want to do. Be careful."

"I will. I've tried very hard not to react the way I did. One look at that body, the way it smelled … ," his voice trailed off.

Richard was silent for a few seconds. He understood what his young shifter was going through. "I know Matthew. We're going to have to help you focus on your control with different, more challenging techniques. Until then, keep a full stomach. The more hunger you feel at the moment you see something like that, the more likely you are to have an episode."

"I'm getting something to eat right now. I'll keep that in mind, I'll make sure to not have an empty stomach next time."

"Make sure that Warren tends to your needs. Don't let so many hours pass by between meals."

"All right, I have to go now, need to get my lunch. I'll call back if I find out more."

"Good."

Both men ended their conversation and Matthew left the bathroom and walked up to the counter to order and pay for their lunch. When his order was ready, he left the restaurant, food in hand.

He entered the precinct, walking back to his area where he handed Warren his lunch. "Did you contact Xander?"

Warren opened the brown bag, releasing another wave of succulent aroma from the food inside. "Yeah, he's going to call Elise. He's still trying to figure out which lion Pride is missing a member."

Matthew chuckled. "That's exactly what Richard is doing ... well, the calling Prides part. That really proves how much they have in common."

"All three are great leaders, well ... all four, let's not forget Darian."

"I'll be glad when he wakes up, he should be able to track these vampires a hell of a lot easier than we can," Matthew said, digging into his lunch. Each man wanted to see what Darian's next move would be.

# CHAPTER FIVE

As the sun disappeared behind the red and golden horizon, Darian opened his eyes to see his son looking down at him. Little Matthew smiled widely, giggling as his father smiled back at him.

"Hello, little one," Darian said as he sat up, scooping his son into his arms.

"Evening baby," Natasha greeted, leaning over kissing him softly on his lips.

"How was your day?" Darian asked.

"It was nice. I finished that book I was reading, kind of disappointing, anticlimactic, ya know." Natasha ate one of the strawberries she was snacking on. "Elise called today, she had a little more information about the murder that happened last night. How come you didn't tell me about that? I saw some of it on the news today. It was horrible!"

"Because there was no need to wake you up and tell you about the dead shifter at five o'clock in the morning." Darian kissed his son's forehead.

"Spare me your signature sarcasm, babe."

Darian smirked. "So what did Elise say?"

"I told her you'll give her a call once you woke up. The information was pretty detailed and I thought you two needed to touch base. Here." Natasha handed him the cordless telephone.

Taking the telephone, he called Elise and waited for her to answer. She did.

"Hello, Elise. This is Darian."

"Good evening Darian, this is what we know so far." She wasted no time telling him everything they knew about the dead shape-shifter.

"Are you certain of this?" Darian asked, visibly disturbed by the news.

"Very. It's what we've manage to gather while you were resting. I know it's not much, but at least you know you're dealing with four vampires. Do you need our help?" Elise asked.

"Let me look into this first and I'll get back to you tonight. I need to visit the crime scene," Darian said. He'd been getting all of his information second-hand, and he wanted to see things for himself. They all claimed there was only one scent on the body, but he needed to be sure. Not only that, he may be able to detect remnants of the vampires' auras they couldn't.

"Of course. I think that would be wise. Call me immediately if you discover anything, or if you need our help," Elise requested.

"I will." They ended their conversation.

Natasha was watching him, noting his furrowed brow. "It's worse than you thought?"

Darian looked at her. "I hadn't really had a chance to put much speculation to this crime until now." He handed her their son. "I have to go out tonight. Based on Elise's information, I'm looking for a vampire coven with at least one member strong enough to have the ability to fly."

"Xavier can fly and he's only one hundred years old," Natasha pointed out.

Darian slipped on a pair of black pants, buttoning them. "Actually, he's been a vampire less than that. More importantly, he has my powerful blood flowing through his veins. He can fly, but not over great distances and not very high. It takes a lot of energy and power to levitate one's body in order to take flight."

"So you think one of them is really old?"

"Old or strong enough to fly at least ten thousand feet high."

"How high can Xavier fly?" Natasha asked genuinely curious. She was also trying to figure out for herself how old and powerful this new vampire coven was.

"He can take flight at six-thousand feet above ground at the most and travel as fast as three-hundred and fifteen miles per hour. But he needs to take frequent breaks if traveling over great distances. And what I mean by that is, every hundred or so miles he needs to have a break."

"So basically, it wouldn't be wise for him to cross the pond?"

"Not if he didn't want to fall out of the sky into the ocean, no."

"Can you?"

"Yes. But as with all attributes for our kind, certain abilities come with age, no matter how much another's powerful blood moves you along."

Natasha nodded, gaining an even better understanding. She now knew why it took Xavier so much longer to return home than Darian even when they had traveled to the same locations. "Do you think this coven is old like the last one?" she asked getting back on topic.

Darian pulled a black v-neck t-shirt over his head, slipping his arms though the sleeves. "I really have no way of telling at this point. I need to conduct my own investigation. When Xavier and the others awaken, tell them I'm looking into the situation. I'll elaborate more once I return." He approached the bed, kissing both Natasha and his son before turning to leave.

She watched him walk out onto the balcony and disappear into the late-evening sky. Only once he was gone, did she remember what she had wanted to ask him. He'd said that Xavier could only levitate six-thousand feet high. She wanted to know how old does one have to be in order to fly ten-thousand feet high or higher, with or without powerful blood from another. "I suppose I'll ask him that once he returns," she muttered, then frowned. "Gee, now I'm starting to talk like him, too." She shook her head, chuckling softly as she continued to play with her son.

***

Darian flew fast through the sky, faster than human eyes could see. He wondered if the marvel of human technology had come up with a device that could track vampires' speed and direction through some sort of high-tech radar? He'd have to look into that one day real soon to see if the government had any hidden secrets. One can never be too cautious and he wouldn't be thrilled about the realization of humans knowing vampires could take flight at all, if that was the case.

Landing silently on the edge of a downtown skyscraper near the *Eclipse* night club, he peered down at the city below with its sparkling golden lights illuminating each building. He could feel the vibrations of the city, the millions of lives thriving filled his body with energy … and lust. Taking a deep breathe, he could smell the blood pulsing through millions of veins. He loved breathing in the city and did it often. It was one of his guilty pleasures. His hunger rolled inside of him, beckoning to him to feed.

"Soon," Darian whispered to himself. His eyes scanned over the skyline as he mentally searched the minds of the surrounding mortals going about their day for any information they may have. He wondered if anybody had seen any strange figure flying by at the time the shifter was dropped from the sky. After several minutes, he received a mental answer. Someone had seen something they couldn't explain. Darian opened his eyes, looking in the direction of his target. In front of him stood a skyscraper condominium, one of the few dozen or so buildings that had been constructed with amazing speed over the past two years. Towering forty stories in the air, on the top floor was the single condo where a man was sitting on his sofa, drinking bourbon. With lightening quick speed, Darian flew towards his balcony which sported a state-of-the-art high-powered telescope with night vision lenses.

"Interesting," Darian muttered to himself as he admired the telescope. Telepathically he unlocked the sliding glass doors, silently sliding them open. He entered the man's condo, coming up behind him with the stealth of the world's greatest predator. The unsuspecting man had no idea he was no longer alone, let alone being approached. Quickly, Darian covered the man's mouth with his left hand while he held him in place with his other. He could smell the intoxicating aroma of fear dripping of the man in a steady flow. It called to him to drink, begged him to devour its essences as he devoured blood. *I will,* he thought.

"I'm not going to kill you. Just relax," Darian whispered as he bent forward, sinking his fangs deeply into the man's throat, piercing the vein. He closed his lips over the wounds, sealing his bite as the delicious blood flowed into his mouth and the man's memories flowed into his mind. He preferred to gather information this way. Reading minds was a great way to get information, but it wasn't nearly as satisfying. Not to mention, if the target was strong of will, they could block off such a mental intrusion. Natasha had that skill because of the increase in her telepathic ability, so did many others, including other vampires and shape-shifters. It would take more focus to break down those barriers and Darian would rather not bother. Very few could hide their deepest thoughts when the blood flowed.

The man had seen what Darian assumed was the vampire responsible for dropping the shifter *fifteen-thousand* feet to the ground causing practically every bone in his body to snap like matchsticks. To the man who had been looking behind his telescope, the vampire looked to be a shadow surrounded by the mist of clouds, and then it was gone in a blink of an eye. That was it. No face, no other identifying features, just a shadow. Darian released the vein, pulling back from the blood, his tongue running along his bottom lip. The man himself rested against the cushions of the sofa. His muscles were relaxed and the dark stain on the front of his pants was already starting to stick.

Darian chuckled as he leaned towards the man's ear. "You will not remember me, you will not remember what you saw last night. There was no shadow, only the brightness of the stars."

He knew his subliminal persuasion would take care of any unanswered questions the man might have, all except why his groin was in the shape it was in. Darian decided to leave that a mystery. Once he was done with him, he left. Finding a secluded area in a dark alley to land, he placed his feet on the ground and walked towards the *Eclipse* nightclub which was still closed due to the ongoing S.U.I.T. investigation. Immediately, he could smell the blood scent left behind by the corpse. He walked toward the area where the body landed and eyed the blood splatters. He was not surprised that there were very few. There wouldn't be a lot of blood if the shifter was drained nearly bone dry. He looked upwards, judging the distance the shifter had fallen. He wanted to see the corpse and knew Warren would be his best ticket into the heart of the S.U.I.T. facilities. Reaching into his pocket, he pulled out his ultra-thin, internet-equipped; high-tech cell phone with the touch screen he'd recently purchased only two months into his contract, replacing the one before it that wasn't "ultra-thin". At that point, Natasha had teased him, calling him a "techno-addict". He had replied, telling her, "that's how he *rolled*." using her own slang term.

He dialed Xander's number.

"Hello Darian?" Xander greeted, recognizing Darian's cell number.

"Good evening, Xander. As you may know, I'm performing an investigation of my own, but I really do need to see the body. I was wondering if Warren would be able to assist me with this?"

"Ah, he should be able to. He's not here right now, but here are his numbers." Xander gave Darian, Warren's home and cell numbers.

"Thank you." They disconnected and Darian called Warren's cell.

On the third ring, Warren answered. "Warren." It was a greeting and a prompt for the other person to introduce themselves.

Darian smiled at the crude greeting, but answered. "Hello Warren, this is Darian. I need a favor from you tonight."

"Sure, what's up?"

"I'm looking into this murder, but I really do need to see the body. Is there any way you could get me into the S.U.I.T.'s morgue tonight?"

"Yeah, I'm actually glad you called me, I was going to suggest that you do just that. I can meet you-"

"I can be there in three minutes, literally."

"Yeah, I bet you can. Unfortunately, I can't. I'm at a restaurant right now getting dinner, so I'll be able to meet you in about fifteen minutes," Warren said.

"Very well, I'll wait for you in the parking lot."

"Why wait? Can't you just hypnotize your way through?"

"And mentally exhaust myself when I have so much to do tonight? Do you realize how much concentration it takes to perform such a skill and on so many people. Trust me, it's easier for you to escort me in," Darian replied.

"Okay, I was just asking. I'll be there shortly. "

With the call ended, Warren finished getting his and Matthew's order, then he climbed into his car, heading for the precinct. He pulled into a parking spot closest to the back door. Leaving his dinner in the car he walked towards Darian who was standing where he said he'd be, beside the back entrance.

"Hey, I take it you don't want to sign for a visitor's pass?" Warren asked, knowing full well that Darian wanted nothing to do with the S.U.I.T., especially after the last encounter he had with them.

"No." Darian smiled and watched as Warren slid his ID into the electronic key card slot.

Warren punched in several numbers and the red light turned green, indicating the door was now opened. Stepping inside, he motioned for Darian to stay by his side.

"I figured as much," Darian replied dryly to Warren's silent command.

"Do you want my help or not?" Warren looked over his shoulder.

Darian's mouth opened to respond with a condescending comment of his own, then he reconsidered. Their routine banter could wait for lighter circumstances. "No need to get testy, I need your help."

"Okay, we're still going to do this the legal way, whether you want to or not. Reason being, there are cameras all around the building, and I don't want to have to explain why I let you walk around with me without signing in."

Darian sighed, but decided not to argue. "I guess it's a good thing I didn't hypnotize my way through here as you suggested earlier."

"I guess, but at that point, I wouldn't have been with you. You were on your own." Warren smiled wickedly.

Darian rolled his eyes, but he understood. The last thing he wanted to do was get Warren into trouble. They walked towards the front desk and Warren signed him in.

"You need to sign right here, too." Warren pointed to the blank line beside the line where he'd signed his name.

Darian obeyed, scoffing at the entire situation. "This is annoying."

"Yeah, I bet. I'm sure you're used to getting exactly what you want without all the messy paperwork or explanations," Warren commented.

"As a matter of fact, yes." Darian refrained from telling him about how he obtained information earlier that evening.

Warren smiled. "Then you're really going to hate this part." His smile widened as he handed Darian a white sticker with his name on it under the word "visitor".

Darian looked at the sticker. "I think you're enjoying this far too much. I'm not wearing that."

"Do you want to see the body or not?" Warren asked, sticker still extended.

Darian huffed, but snatched the sticker from Warren. Peeling off the protective paper, he pressed the sticker on his shirt. "Can we go now?"

"Do you always make simple things hard?" Warren asked as he led the way to the morgue. Darian decided to not answer the question. The two men entered the morgue and saw the medical examiner bent over a body. "Hey Galen, need a favor from you."

Marshall looked up from yet another corpse, a victim of a vampire attack. "I'm going to have to start charging you for favors really soon, I see." He looked at Darian. "Traded up on Matthew already?"

Warren gestured to Darian. "He's an expert in this field, so to speak. I wanted him to take a look at that body from the club. He may be able to tell me a bit more." He knew that Marshall was fully aware of who and what Darian was. The incident three years ago sort of let the cat completely out of the bag, not that Darian himself seemed to mind.

Marshall pushed his glasses up on the bridge of his nose. "If you think you can find out more about this murder than I did, please be my guest." He walked towards the many stainless steel drawers and pulled one out. Laying there on the cold stainless steel slab was the corpse in question. Even before Marshall unzipped the thick plastic bag, Darian could smell the blood. He could also smell that it was a shifter from the feline lion breed.

Darian stepped up to the corpse, studying it. He didn't need Marshall to tell him how the victim had died or how the victim had been flayed. Even if he hadn't already been told, he could see the handiwork of the vampire coven responsible for killing on his territory. They'd pay for their offense, of that, he was sure.

"So, see anything we didn't catch?" Marshall asked.

Darian's forest-green eyes locked onto the slender, unkempt man. "You did a very good job with your autopsy. Thank you for letting me view the body."

"Not a problem." Marshall zipped the body bag up and slid the corpse back into its slot.

Warren took a look at the body lying on the table under the bright halogen light. "What's this here?" He pointed.

Darian turned towards the corpse as did Marshall.

"Ah, he just came in about twenty minutes ago," Marshall said, walking towards the corpse.

"What's the COD?" Warren asked, approaching the table as well.

Darian followed the men, secretly impressed with both the human and the shifter in their abilities to do their jobs well.

"Another vampire attack, only this time, one is responsible. See here," he pointed to a set of puncture wounds on the shaft of the penis. "He pierced the vein. I was able to match this set of bite marks to a pair I found on the other corpse. So it looks like at least one of our guys fed again."

The muscles in Darian's jaw tightened. How *dare* some unknown coven enter his territory uninvited! How *dare* they *kill* in his city and with such callousness!

"Shit, why the fuck weren't Matt and I called in for this?" Warren asked, pissed that he wasn't notified about the body until now.

"Because the M.O. didn't match, that is, not until now. Your DB was a shifter, between the ages of twenty and thirty based on the size of his bones. This guy is a human, and looks to be fifteen, no more than seventeen. Your DB had multiple bite wounds; this one only had a single wound. Your DB was flayed alive, this one-"

"Galen, I get it. I'm not dense," Warren huffed.

"Okay, all I'm saying is, easy to miss. It wasn't until I had a closer inspection did I recognize the space and size between the two punctures and was able to match them to your DB." Marshall nodded in the direction of the steel drawer. He was quite pleased with himself for being able to make the comparison.

"Fuck me," Warren hissed as he ran fingers through his dark locks. "Who's on this case, now?"

"Currently, Johnson and Weinstein, but that'll change once I pass my findings over to the captain." Marshall and Captain Michelle Lawrence were in a pretty serious relationship outside of the precinct. Inside, however, it was strictly business, so no one had anything to say about it.

"Yeah, that ought to please them greatly, having their case yanked out of their hands and given over to us," Warren stated sarcastically.

"I'd be happy if it were me. Your case isn't looking any prettier now than it did last night." Marshall looked at Darian. "Are you able to catch a scent off this body?"

Darian looked up from the corpse to Galen with a start. He was surprised to find the man so blunt. "You know who I am?"

Marshall nodded. "Who and what. I remember you from a few years back. The remains of a crime you were accused of did come across my path. To tell you the truth, I'm glad you were cleared of all charges. Looking at you now, something tells me I wouldn't have wanted to see the outcome of a guilty verdict."

In spite of himself, Darian had to smiled the comment. He liked the human. "No one was more please than I was with the outcome of that particular case."

"And the lawsuit that followed, no doubt." Marshall nodded, remembering the high profile case and the multimillion dollar suit that followed, which set a new precedent for standard procedures on proper investigating of crimes involving murders by a supernatural.

"To answer your question," Darian began, getting back to the matter at hand. "I did catch a scent." He decided against elaborating on how useless a scent on the body was now if he couldn't track it later.

"Well, it's a start," Marshall said. Darian nodded.

"Is there anything else, skin particles, hair follicles, anything?" Warren asked, hoping that since the newest victim still had his skin and nails, maybe he took something from his killer that would be able to put them on the right trail.

"I scrapped under the nails, sent what little I found there to the DNA lab. Like the body found last night, he was also naked."

"Where did they pick this one up at?" Warren asked.

"Hyde Park, he was laying between two parked cars in that huge lot over there off 53st street." Marshall's cell began ringing. He looked down at the little device, noting the number. "Well, looks like we may have another DB."

"What the fuck?" Warren tossed a glance at Darian then back at Marshall who was returning the call. Both Darian and Warren could hear the conversation. Apparently, another victim was found, this time a female adolescent, the bite marks were very visible as the body was also naked. Once Marshall hung up, Warren's cell phone rung.

Marshall chuckled at the accuracy of the S.U.I.T.'s hotline. "I take it you already know what that phone call is going to be about," he said, letting Warren know that he knew he heard his conversation due to his superhuman hearing.

Darian caught the subtle hint and wondered if Xander was aware that a human knew about Warren and quite possibly Matthew's nature.

"Yeah, but I have to keep up appearances anyway," Warren replied as he called the number back. It was the same conversation Marshall had, only he was instructed to get there ASAP.

"My team is already on their way to the scene. I'll be here still going over this one. Seems like the two patterns that's tying all of these corpses together are their lack of clothing and loss of blood," Marshall pointed out.

Both Darian and Warren nodded.

"Okay, I'm going now, I'll be back later." Warren tapped Darian on his arm, gesturing for him to follow.

Once outside of the precinct, Darian looked at Warren. "He knows about you?"

"You caught that, eh? Yeah, he does. I just found out earlier today that he knew."

Darian arched one jet-black eyebrow. "Is Xander aware that this human knows your secret?"

Warren froze.

"I'll go on ahead and assume that your sudden silence means that he doesn't know." Darian shook his head with a sigh.

"I'm going to tell him."

"When?"

"Tonight."

"*Now.*"

"No, not now. I want to be face-to-face with my Alpha before I drop a bombshell like that," Warren said, convinced it was the best thing to do.

"Do you think this human is trustworthy?" Darian studied the young shifter closely.

Warren nodded. "I don't have any reason to think otherwise. He said he's known for some years now. I was none the wiser. Besides, he saw Matt in the throes of bloodlust and he hasn't rat us out yet."

"Matthew lost control?"

"Yeah, the first corpse you saw brought it out of him. Supernatural crime has been down since we took out those three bitches and their clans. Matthew hasn't really had to deal with a bunch of blood and guts, until now. Richard knows all about that."

"Ah, so Richard knows about this human knowing your secret, but your own Alpha does not. For your sake, I hope he doesn't get the information second hand." Darian gave Warren a wicked smile and took off into the air, heading towards the location of the second crime scene where the young boy was found.

"Damn vampires," Warren muttered. He understood where Darian was coming from, especially since the soon to be sixteen-hundred and fifty-three year old bloodsucker was one of the fiercest leaders he had ever met. Darian was right; he should have told Xander right away about Marshall knowing what he was. He wasn't sure why he hadn't. There were many reasons he'd thought of. Xander would want to kill the pathologist, or Xander would have Darian erase his memory ... but he knew the truth. Xander would be disappointed that Warren had lost enough control to get discovered. He hadn't been as careful as he thought he was and it was the main concern his Alpha had when he agreed to allow him to join the S.U.I.T..

*Be careful, don't get discovered or it'll all be over for your career.* Xander's words echoed inside his head as he drove to the new crime scene. Perhaps Darian was right. He should call Xander right away. Any delay would only increase his Alpha's irritation, especially if he found out that Richard knew hours before he did. Even more so if he found out from Richard instead of him. Reaching into his pocket, he retrieved his cellular and dialed Xander's.

"Hello Warren?" Xander greeted.

"Hey Xander. I've got a couple of updates for you, some good news, some bad, or it could all be bad depending on how you want to look at it."

"I'm listening?"

Warren took a deep breath, releasing it in a sudden rush. "Okay. I'm just going to come out and say it. Marshall Galen, our resident M.E., knows our secret, and by 'our' I mean, Matt and me."

"Go on," Xander's tone was reserved. Warren didn't know if that was a good sign or not. He figured he'd gain a better understanding once he told him the rest.

"Earlier today, Matt had an episode. The bloodlust got to him really bad and he lunged for the remains of last night's corpse. Marshall was there, saw him, saw me contain and calm him."

"*Earlier* today?" Xander's tone was a little less reserved.

*Oh boy, here it comes*, Warren thought, but he decided he'd take his medicine. "Yeah … um … I was going to tell you face-to-face. I was on my way out there to see you when Darian called me."

"Warren, I must say that I am disappointed by the fact that you've waited hours to tell me something so very important. What if he wanted to expose you, you would have needed my protection. Why did you wait so long to tell me?"

Xander didn't raise his voice, but that didn't mean the anger wasn't palpable, even over the phone.

Warren winced. A scolding from his Alpha always affected him, making him feel as if he were a small child being chided by a parent. He wanted to say; *because I was scared you'd be mad at me*. But what came out was; "I don't know."

"To quote my wife, 'I wasn't born yesterday'." Xander knew that his young Pack member was fully aware of his reasons. He wanted the truth. He felt he deserved that much.

Warren sighed. "Because I was afraid that you'd be disappointed at me for failing to cloak my nature."

Xander thought about chastising the young wolf even more, then decided against it. Admitting his faults was punishment enough. "Tell me about this human who knows?"

Surprised that his Alpha changed the subject, Warren answered him, hoping he would also agree with him that Marshall wasn't a threat. "He's known about me for years and he's known about Matthew since his change. He's trustworthy."

"That may be, Warren. I know that you have a lot of respect for this human. I've heard you speak of him favorably, so allow me to give you advice in this matter. Do not trust him as you would trust your own."

"He hasn't betrayed us, Xander."

"Not yet and he may never, but that's no reason to let your guard down." Xander couldn't resist. "Once was more than enough."

Warren winced again at Xander's clever jibe at his failure to keep his guard up enough to fool the inquisitive M.E., he agreed. "I understand. I'm sorry."

"Very well. What are the other updates?"

Warren told Xander about the second corpse. "... And right now, I'm on my way to the scene of another. I'll be able to tell you more about this later."

"Three bodies in less than twenty-four hours and one was a shifter. I'm wondering if this is the morbid idea of a vampire coven's hi-jinks or something much more sinister."

"A flayed shifter points to sinister for me. I just want to catch these bloodsucking sons-of-bitches and roast their asses!"

"Agreed. Keep me informed."

The two men ended their conversation just as Warren pulled into the parking lot where the third victim lay. He killed the engine and climbed out. Walking towards the S.U.I.T.'s red and white tape, he was approached by a member from Marshall's coroner's team.

"Did you get a chance to talk to Marshall?" Janet asked, her dark hair bounced with each step she took struggling to keep up with Warren's long strides.

"Yeah, the second victim is linked to the first."

"I'm glad I'm not you and Matt, I'd hate to be you two when Johnson and Weinstein get the news."

*Shit Matt! I forgot to call him!* Warren remembered he'd been so busy with his Pack Alpha, he hadn't told Matthew about the third murder. He was reaching for his cell phone when he caught a familiar scent.

"About time you made it. I've been here a full minute before you," Matthew said, walking up to him.

"Had something to take care of first, that's my excuse and I'm sticking to it. So … ," he looked at Janet. "… What do we have here?"

"Some very sick shit, a female DB about twelve years old with multiple puncture wounds on her wrists, breast, throat over the jugular and over the artery near her groin. That's what we have for the preliminary report. Once we get her to Galen, we'll know more. Cause of death looks to be massive loss of blood which lead to a cardiac arrest." Janet swiped at her bang with the back of her gloved hand, freeing her vision.

"Twelve years old. Jesus!" Matthew whispered.

They stood looking down at the little girl lying naked, cold and dead on the crude pavement. She appeared as though she'd been posed. One hand was positioned by her head, the other rested on her stomach.  One leg was propped up, slightly bent, the other lay flat. Her breast; barely developed were marred by two sets of puncture wounds on each small mound. Her pale blue eyes, which were once bright and full of life lay opened, blank and staring off into nothingness.

"I think I actually feel sick to my stomach right now," Warren spoke his innermost thoughts vocally without meaning to.

"I'm right there with you. I have a daughter around her age. We've got to catch these sick fucks and make them pay for stealing the lives of three people." Janet hated this part of her job the most, viewing the discarded victims where they lay. She, however, loved discovering the clues that led the trail to their killers.

Warren and Matthew slipped on a pair of latex gloves.

"Are you done with her?" Matthew asked.

Janet nodded. "I've gotten everything I can get at this point. CSI will be here soon to do the rest. When you're all done, Roberts and Marks will remove the body."

"All right," Warren said. "Take care."

"See you back at the precinct." She walked away towards her SUV.

"We don't have any witnesses, no one who may have seen who put her here. That was my first question when I got here," Matthew said, walking around the body, memorizing every detail.

The two detectives performed their investigation, speaking to the confused and horrified person who had the unfortunate luck of discovering the body beside his car. Both men eliminated him from being a suspect because he wasn't a vampire, and his scent wasn't on the body. Of course, that wasn't the reasons they listed for eliminating him. After a few hours of investigating, they drove back to the precinct, expecting the body to have beaten them by at least an hour. They entered the morgue, wondering if Marshall would have anything new to tell them.

"Hey Marshall, what can you tell us?" Warren asked.

Marshall lifted his head from the desk. "I know I've complained in the past about being overworked, but today, I really mean it. I don't think I've been this busy since a horde of bodies were discovered in that building almost two years ago. Not to mention the two dead bodies that were found in that apartment," he said, expressing his exhaustion.

"Yeah, I remember that, a real fucking mess that was." Warren was a part of that 'real fucking mess' when his Pack, Elise's Pride and Darian's coven had been attacked by three different supernatural factions using humans to do their dirty work in efforts to gain their territory. It started in Illinois and they had ended it in Florida.

"Did you guys ever catch the killers in that case?" Marshall asked with one eyebrow cocked.

"You know we didn't, but we will." Warren wondered if Marshall suspected he had anything to do with it.

The expression on the coroner's face proved that he did. It also said that he wasn't going to press the issue. "That's the past, this here is the very present, therefore, priority." He rose from the stool he'd been sitting on and walked towards the newest corpse on his table. "I haven't had much time to go over this one thoroughly, but I can tell you what I do know now then finish my report later."

"Whatever you have will help," Warren said as he and Matthew joined Marshall. The three men looked down at the body.

Marshall eyed Matthew's expression. "Are you going to be able to handle this?"

Surprised, Matthew looked up. "Yeah, I'm going to be just fine."
"Why so surprised?" Marshall asked.
"I'm still trying to get used to the fact that you know about us."
"Fair enough."
"You don't have to worry about me right now," Matthew began. "I was able to control myself at the other scene, so I think I can handle this. Besides, I ate dinner on the way here.

Marshall nodded. "Good." He gestured to the body. "Okay, gentlemen, this body has multiple bite wounds ..." He went on to point out the areas Janet had listed before, plus a new one. "... And one more right here." He pried apart the little girl's legs, exposing her hairless pelvis.

"No! Hell no! Please don't fucking tell me these motherfuckers did that," Warren placed his hand over his mouth, visibly horrified.

"My God," Matthew lowered his head, aghast.

"My sentiments exactly." Marshall pointed over the adolescent's labia where the two puncture wounds were, one on each side. "I don't think I need to tell you what happened here."

Warren shook his head, both hands now at his sides. "No, you don't. Same coven?"

Marshall nodded. "Same coven. The first thing I did was measure the distance between each puncture wound and they were identical to those on the first victim and one was identical to the bite wound I found on the second victim."

"Anything else?" Matthew asked.

"That's all for now," Marshall answered.

"Okay, thanks Galen," Warren gave the slimmer man a pat on his back. He left the morgue with Matthew behind him. They went to their desks and sat down. "We need to find out if there have been any murders similar to ours in other cities."

"I was doing that earlier with the first victim." Matthew rose and left, returning minutes later. "I had this in the car, here." He handed Warren a file-size manila envelope.

Warren pulled out its contents and began scanning the documents.

"From what I could gather, there's been a series of skinless or naked, bloodless corpses discovered in various cities around the world and several in the States." Matthew picked up their coffee mugs and walked way, returning once again with both cups filled to the brim with the bitter hot liquid. "Here." He handed Warren his mug.

"So," Warren began, pausing to take a sip, grimacing slightly. "Tastes like shit." He looked into the mug. "Why is it black?"

"Because we need all of the caffeine we can get," Matthew said.

"A little sugar and cream wouldn't hurt." Warren placed the mug on his desk. "It says here there's been at least fourteen dead bodies of shifters that have been found flayed like ours over the past four years. Why are we just finding out about this shit now?" He looked up at Matthew.

"Other countries don't have our resources, knowledge--hell--other countries, with the exception of England and Japan; don't even have a S.U.I.T. organization. You and I both know that local cops aren't equipped to handle what we do. Shit, we're barely equipped our damn selves."

"You've got a point there." Warren ran his hands over his face. "What time is it?"

Matthew looked at his watch. "Two A.M.."

"Fuck, when was the last time we slept?"

"At least thirty hours ago."

"I can't fucking think straight right now and I don't even know where to begin." He looked up just in time to see detectives Johnson and Weinstein approaching them.

Detective Gabriel Johnson slapped a folder on Warren's desk. "I just want you to know that it's really shitty that you two get all of the high-profile cases, and I'm not above declaring it favoritism either."

"That's what we had on the second victim. Do with it what you can," Barry Weinstein said. He was upset as well, having their case yanked away from them and given to the famous "Golden Boys", but he was a bit more contained and professional than his partner.

"Look, Johnson, neither Matt nor I asked for this case," Warren said, biting down on his own rising temper.

"Just like you two didn't ask for the last one, right?" Johnson shot back.

"Right. We're just here trying to do the best we can, and we don't have time for your fucking petty-ass jealousies."

"Then explain to me why our fucking case just got snatched away?" Johnson waited for a response.

Matthew remained silent as he reached over his desk, picking up the envelope Gabriel had slammed on Warren's desk. He began searching through it, reading the information.

"Trust me; we didn't ask for your case either, but unfortunately, it's a part of ours. And if I remember correctly, one of the biggest high-profile cases that the S.U.I.T. had didn't go to us. It ended in a million-dollar lawsuit and a bunch of new bullshit-ass procedures. I also remember it wasn't Matt and I that fucked that one up." Warren watched the other two men's facial expressions. He remembered how most of the officers were pretty high on themselves for having arrested Darian Alexander and how lacks the investigation had been to the point where the entire S.U.I.T. had to be held responsible when a group of civilians solved the case the S.U.I.T. was supposed to.

"That wasn't us, had it been, it would have turned out differently!" Johnson was getting more agitated. His partner grabbed his arm, attempting to calm him down.

"Enough! Shit, what are you guys, twelve?" Weinstein whispered, "at least keep your fucking voices down."

Warren tossed him a glance before returning his attention back to Johnson. "Listen, Johnson … Weinstein, Matt and I respect you two. We don't doubt your ability to do your jobs; you're two of the best on the team. But the truth is, whether you like it or not, we've solved more cases than you that may be why the captain picked us for his case."

"That's only because you're assigned more cases." Johnson crossed his arms over his muscular chest.

"I'm not going to argue with your ass anymore, you've got a problem with us taking your case, take that shit up with the captain. Go and blow smoke up her ass!" Warren rose from his chair and stalked off.

Weinstein patted his partner on this arm. "Let's go." He walked away. Johnson gave Matthew one last look of pure rage, before he followed his partner back toward his desk.

Matthew watched the two detectives retreat to their side of the room. He understood why they were so pissed, although, he didn't approve of the exchange of schoolyard insults between his partner and Johnson. Warren returned fifteen minutes later. He was more composed.

"Are you okay?" Matthew asked.

Warren nodded. "Yeah, I'm fine. Can you believe that asshole? Like I asked to be up for thirty straight hours!"

"Warren … drop it."

Warren opened his mouth to protest and then closed it, knowing that his partner was right. It was over and done with. "What does the file say?" He pointed to the papers Matthew was holding.

"That this case just took yet another turn for the worse. The second victim was killed hours ago. Galen has the TOD clocked in at 3:00 P.M.."

"What the fuck?" Warren reached over, snatching the papers from Matthew's hands. "Are you sure that just isn't when they found him?"

"Based on the condition of the body, we're looking at him possibly being killed by a vampire when the sun was still high in the sky."

"It also says here that the body wasn't completely drained of blood. He could have been bled to the point of death, then left to die, finally doing so around that time."

Matthew shrugged one shoulder. "Still, it would put the vampire in the sun to dispose of the body."

Warren lifted a perfectly arched eyebrow. "Or maybe we've got a vampire coven with human servants that do all of the dirty work. Maybe they dumped the body during the day?"

"That's likely, but wouldn't that still put the vampire up and awake to drain him to the point of death around, at least twelve or one in the afternoon?"

Matthew was making perfect sense and it was getting harder to counter his scenarios with other possibilities. "Shit, Matt. I think you're right." Warren continued to read the report. "Wait, you missed something … a few samples have been sent off to toxicology, Galen suspects a drug overdose as well."

"Where does it say that?" Matthew left his desk to stand over Warren's shoulder, reading what he'd missed. "Oh, I was just getting to that when you snatched the damn file from my hands. I didn't miss shit."

"Yeah, whatever." Warren gave him a playful smile. He still wanted to tease, knowing how thorough Matthew was when it came to giving attention to details. "We have to wait on the lab result on whether he had enough drugs in his system for that to be a factor in his death. That's going to take at least a day or two."

Matthew agreed. He went back to his own seat. "You know, I was thinking … this case, as far as we know has manage to pile on three bodies in a twenty-four hour period. The second victim, regardless of the cause of death, which I still think is blood loss, was murdered during daylight hours."

"Okay, what are you getting at?" Warren leaned forward.

"Well, I'm just thinking perhaps it's not a bad idea to get some help on this case. As far as we know, this is a night and day killer. We can't work twenty-hour hours straight and still think we're going to do our best, shifters or not."

"Are you actually suggesting we beg for help?" Warren snarled.

Matthew chuckled. "Or maybe Johnson had a point. Your pride is showing, partner."

Warren rolled his eyes. "I just think we can handle it on our own. We've never needed help before, and we don't need it now."

Matthew shielded his eyes with his hand. "Whoa! Your pride is shining even brighter than before. It's blinding!"

Warren slouched in his seat. "You know what? Fuck you."

Matthew belted out a hearty laugh. He hadn't laughed like that in over twenty-four hours. He was glad to know that he still could. "Don't be that way. Besides, you know deep down, past your seemingly impenetrable layer of arrogance, that I'm right on this one."

"I still think we can handle it on our own."

"Okay, fine … let's do this on our own. I just think it wouldn't hurt to have some help," Matthew said, smiling. "We need to call our-Richard and Xander." He almost said "Alphas".

Warren nodded. "Yeah, I was just thinking that."

"Hey, I forgot to ask you, what did Xander say about Marshall when you told him what happened earlier?"

# CHAPTER SIX

Darian decided to enter his mansion through the front door as oppose to the balcony he'd exited from. He walked into the living room where his entire coven was waiting for him. He'd contacted them all telepathically and told them he wanted to meet with them. They sat in their favorite spots on chairs and sofas. He took his seat in his favorite leather chair and began to tell them all of what he'd learn that evening.

"So this vampire is able to fly, does that make him as old as you?" Christopher asked. This was all very new to him; he'd been turned into a vampire almost two years ago, and hadn't had much experience dealing with other covens.

"Not exactly. Xavier can fly as well, but he's nowhere near my age. For instance, Gary is older than you, but you're much stronger. However, I'm not willing to disregard that this vampire may be as old as I am." Darian crossed one long leg over the other.

"Three dead bodies and one of them was a shifter. Do you think it's a message to us, or a sick idea of a good time?" Xavier asked.

Darian opened his mouth to speak when his cell phone started ringing. He answered it. After the initial introductions, he got the newest development in their situation. "A fourth victim?" It was the first time since he'd heard about the first dead body that the tone in his voice had shown any hint of distress. "I understand, thank you." He ended the call.

"We all heard. There's a dead body in Dekalb. Well we know one thing, they're able to move around easily without being detected," John said, reflecting on what was happening.

"Damn, why does it always seem like there's something going down," Natasha fumed to no one in particular. "Even the damn baby's starting to kick me right now." Her brows creased deeply in a frown. Her hand went to her stomach, massaging the area.

A few of the others chuckled in spite of themselves and the grim situation.

"So, are you going to Dekalb?" Tony asked his Master.

Darian nodded. "Yes." He rose, leaving the room.

Xavier followed him, pressing a hand on his back, gaining his attention. "Darian, what are you thinking?"

"Come with me."

"To the crime scene?"

"Yes, we can also talk in private."

Once they were standing outside of the mansion, Darian took hold of Xavier, pulling him closely. Seconds later, they were speeding faster than Xavier could have flown, toward the fourth crime scene. Once they reached their destination, they surveyed the number of media reporters, police and spectators surrounding the area.

"Too bad we can't get closer without having to do a lot of 'mental mojo', as Natasha calls it," Xavier said, wishing he could get a better inspection of the body. In the darkness, his vision was perfect. Unfortunately, he couldn't zoom in and out.

"If I need a closer inspection, I can go to the S.U.I.T. precinct with Warren. I don't need to get a better look to know that the same coven committed this murder. I can smell their scent on the body from here." Darian's eyes narrowed, conveying both predatory prowl and menace.

"Back to my original question, what are you thinking?" Xavier asked him, watching his lover with a keen interest.

"Right now, I have my suspicions, but I'm going to reserve them until I know more. There isn't a pattern to these killings, the shifter might have just been a murder done to prove that there isn't a pattern, that no one is safe."

"It's a *Challenge of Authority.*"

"Oh, I have no doubt that it's a challenge. What I don't know is if they want my territory," Darian replied.

Xavier didn't say anything, only turned to look at the body. They saw when Warren and Matthew finally arrived. Both of the shifters looked haggard, having been robbed of a good night's rest. From their bird's eye view, they watched the two detectives walk toward the crime scene, dipping under the S.U.I.T. tape. The two detectives began speaking to the coroner Darian had met earlier about this new victim.

***

"Same killers, Galen?" Warren asked, rubbing his hands over his face.

"I'm just getting here, guys. Give me a minute to converse with my team." Galen leaned over to hear what Janet had gathered, since she was the first of his team to arrive. He nodded every few minutes as more details were given. Once he'd gathered all that he could, he turned back to the detectives. "Okay, this person has been dead for approximately an hour and a half before it was discovered. Some kids leaving a keg party stumbled upon it-watch your step," Marshall warned, pointing to a puddle of vomit near the corpse.

Warren looked down just in time for his supernatural reflexes to save him from a minor disaster. "Shit, I knew I smelt something foul. I must be dead on my feet. My senses are completely off, just like my concentration."

Matthew looked at him, remembering his early request for assistance with their case, but didn't say anything as he knelt close to the body. He fought his hunger, using breathing and concentration techniques his Alpha had taught him. He was relieved to know that they were working. "So, would your expert opinion put this DB in the same pool as the others, killed by the same group?" he asked Marshall.

"I'm positive. The bite marks are identical. I've looked at enough of them in one day to know," Marshall confirmed. "Besides, Janet measured them already.

"Shit!" Warren hissed under his breath.

"That makes four," Matthew said, giving his partner a total body count.

"And that's four too many. We have to find out who these motherfuckers are, Matt." Warren looked down at the body of an adult Caucasian female, lying naked and cold on the pavement.

"Galen, have you found anything that can point us in any direction?" Matthew asked the medical examiner.

Marshall pushed his glasses back up on the bridge of his nose. "I'm beyond tired and I've looked at every detail on every corpse so much so, I'm seeing doubles. I'll look over this one more thoroughly, but as of right now, there's nothing that I can tell you that would lead you to this coven, Detectives. If I find-"

"Yeah, we got it. You'll let us know," Warren interjected. His tone wasn't angry, just disappointed.

They walked toward the group of young adults who had found the body. Both men flashed their S.U.I.T. IDs and badges at the group that consisted of three men and two women.

"Hello, I'm Detective Davis … " He pointed to Matthew, " … This is Detective Eric. We'd like to ask you a few questions. Is that all right with you?" Warren waited for their response before letting loose.

"Yeah, sure, I'll answer your questions to the best of my ability, shoot." One of the men said, the others nodded.

"We really appreciate your cooperation," Warren said, "Let's make this less complicated, what are your names?"

They began introducing themselves. The young man pointed to each person as they gave the two detectives their names. "I'm William Townsend," he said, being the last.

Warren nodded, jotting down everyone's names. "Excellent. Nice to meet you all," he said then he continued. "All right, at what time did you discover the body?"

"About two hours ago. We were leaving a keg party … we're all twenty-one and over, Officer, so it was legal," William lied, hoping to keep them out of trouble.

"Underage drinking isn't our jurisdiction and the least of our concerns, continue please," Warren said.

William continued. "Okay, that's good, cause I'll be twenty-one in two months," he confessed.

Warren smiled, he remembered those wild nights when he and Adrian, completely under-aged, would party hard at various bashes often coming home completely intoxicated, sometimes, even high from smoking marijuana. Xander had disapproved and put an end to their heavy partying, restricting them from drinking until they were old enough to handle it responsibly.

Warren listened as William recounted his tale. "So like, we were all pretty fucked up, ya know? And we kind of started playing tag and shit, you know, just being playful, havin' fun. And Melissa kind of like, tripped on something. I came over to help her up and that's when we saw the legs sticking out from behind the bushes."

"It was totally gross and disgusting," Melissa said. "I mean, ewww, I actually touched it," she shivered, showing her revulsion.

Warren refrained from reminding her that "it" used to breathe, laugh and cry just like her only a few hours before. He wanted to tell her to show some respect for the dead, then decided getting the information was more important than a sermon.

"Well, that's when Brian totally puked," William said, pointing to another male, who lowered his head, face reddening.

Warren was willing to bet his buzz was long gone. "Understandable, not every day one stumbles onto a corpse. Is this when you called the police? Did you touch the body?"

Collectively, they shook their heads. "No. Well, except for Melissa when she tripped over it, but we didn't move it. We've all seen enough movies to know that would just be stupid, drunk or not. We just called the police and waited for you guys to arrive. That's it," William said, still visibly shaken by the entire experience.

Warren nodded, both he and Matthew still jotting down information. "Okay, that's about all I'm going to need from you right now. Can you give Detective Eric your telephone numbers and addresses just in case we need to get in contact with you in the future?" It was more of a demand than a request.

"Sure," they said in unison, offering their information to Matthew as he wrote it all down. Warren went back to the body to chat with Marshall. On his way, he happened to look up and see Darian and Xavier perched on the rooftop of a nearby building. Bypassing Marshall, he approached the building. In the blink of an eye, both vampires were standing in the alleyway next to the building where the curious crowd couldn't see.

"Please tell me you know something I don't?" Warren pleaded.

"I wish I did, unfortunately, I don't," Darian said, leaning against the side of the brick wall.

"We overheard your conversation with those who found the body," Xavier said.

Warren nodded. "We know she was killed a couple hours ago, maybe three or four. The other victim died in the afternoon." He told the two vampires his and Matthew's speculation. "I personally think it was blood loss that killed him, but we won't know for certain if the drugs in his system had any play in his death."

"This coven could have a human servant assisting them, planting their victims in public locations in broad daylight. The other killings have taken place at night," Darian said. "That one corpse could have been drained by the human then left for dead to throw you off any patterns."

"That's as good a theory as any," Warren agreed, with a long, audible yawn.

Both Darian and Xavier eyed Warren's ragged condition. They'd never really seen the wolf appear so worn out.

"Are you okay, Warren?" Xavier asked.

Warren sighed deeply. "Ah, yeah … just fucking exhausted, ya know? I've been on my feet for damn near forty-eight hours." Right then, his cellular began ringing. Warren looked down at the number, recognizing it as his captain's. "Fucking hell!" He answered his cell. "Yeah Captain?"

"We've got another body, this one found floating in Wolf Lake. Listen, I'm going to assign you some help on this case, and I don't want to hear, 'we can handle it', because you can't. Detectives Johnson and Weinstein are already on their way to the fifth location. You four are going to work together on this." Before Warren could respond, she continued. "And don't think I didn't get wind of your 'my balls are bigger than your balls' competition earlier. We're a team, and this time, you two have two more partners. How's it going there?"

Warren sighed again, realizing he'd lost the fight. They were going to have to make nice with the other detectives if they wanted to solve this case as fast as possible. He gave her an update, which wasn't much.

"Whatever resources you need, they're at your disposal, I don't want this coven filling our morgue. You got that?"

"Yes, Captain."

"Good. Keep me in touch," she hung up.

Warren closed his cell phone. He looked at the two vampires. "We've got a problem."

"We've heard," Darian said.

"If this turns out to be a challenge against you, how do I keep our new partners away from this case? A vampire territory battle won't be within their understanding." Warren looked at Darian, awaiting his response.

"Don't worry about that now. Just do what you can," Darian told him, not wanting to stress the already stressed out wolf any more than he needed to be.

Warren nodded. He tossed a glance over his shoulder. "Look, I've got to get back, I'll call, or Xander will." He walked back to the crime scene, toward his partner.

Darian looked at Xavier. "Let's go to Wolf Lake, shall we?" He didn't wait for a confirmation. Taking his lover and second-in-command into his arms, he flew toward the fifth crime scene.

# CHAPTER SEVEN

"**W**ell it's about time we got some damn help!" Matthew was practically shouting upon hearing the news they were going to have to partner up with two other detectives.

"I didn't want to have to partner up with anyone on this, Matt," Warren said, frowning slightly.

"Why? Is your ego bruised? Because I have to tell you, I'm relieved."

Warren stopped at a red light. "Why do you assume I have a hero complex? Jesus, Matt! It's not about me!"

Sensing his partner agitation, Matthew apologized. "Warren, I'm sorry. I don't know… I guess you seemed kind of cocky talking with Johnson, earlier. I just assumed you enjoyed us being called the 'Golden Boys'."

"Well I don't … ," Warren paused, smiling slightly. "Okay, in all honesty, I do. But that still isn't the point. If this is a challenge to Darian's coven, it's going to be kind of difficult for us to steer the suspicions away from Darian. As a matter of fact, Johnson and Weinstein might try to make Darian a suspect. He is the Master vampire in Chicago. The S.U.I.T. for all its resources and knowledge knows nothing about our world. *Supernatural Etiquette, Safe Passages, Challenges of Authorities, Sanctuaries*, all of that, It's foreign to them and they won't understand."

"Give them and us some credit, Warren. Besides, we don't have a choice," Matthew said. He wanted to kiss his lover; he wanted to tell him everything was going to be fine, but he couldn't. Not out in the open. Pretenses were still important, even more so now than before.

"I need to let Xander know about all of this, you call Richard."

Matthew pulled out his cell phone, doing as Warren suggested. Richard answered in a groggy voice. "I'm sorry, were you asleep?"

"And enjoying it, what's happening now?" Richard asked. He wasn't annoyed, he simply wanted the updates.

For a split second, Matthew was jealous that his Alpha was getting a good night's sleep while he sat shotgun, exhausted with bloodshot eyes. He answered him. "We're leaving the fourth crime scene now heading back to the precinct. Also, they've just found a fifth body. Warren and I have been paired up with two other detectives and we have to share everything we have in this case with them,"

"I see. Make certain that both you and Warren are very careful about what kind of information you share, especially your sources. Make sure everything you share can be substantiated with solid facts," Richard cautioned.

"Yeah, Warren and I kind of touched on the trickiness of this pairing earlier. I'll pass that along."

"You sound exhausted, when was the last time you've slept... or eaten?"

"I haven't seen a pillow in two days and the last meal I had was a few hours ago."

"Matthew, you're not old or strong enough to test your nature. You need rest and real food if you plan on maintaining any amount of control," Richard's tone was measured but serious.

"I know, as a matter of fact, we're pulling into a *Nickey G's* right now."

Richard sighed. "I said *real food*, Matthew. You need a steak, preferably rare in order to sate your hunger, not a reprocessed burger."

"Oookaaay, we are currently pulling away from the *Nickey G's*, empty handed," Matthew informed.

Warren started chuckling in spite of his own fatigue. He was certain that Richard could hear him, and he didn't mind. It was funny to him.

"Tell Warren I said he should have known better than to take you there," Richard said, smiling at the foolishness of the two pups. At over three hundred years, almost every shifter he knew was a pup to him, especially those less than half a century old like Warren and Matthew.

"Tell him we're going back home to eat a real meal and get some real sleep. Shit, I'm fucking tired," Warren passed along.

Matthew pulled the cell from his ear. "I thought we were going back to the precinct?"

"We were, I changed my mind."

"Well damn, do I get a say in this?"

"What the hell, Matt? You want to try to solve this case as a zombie? Shit, I don't know about you, but I can barely keep my eyes open. We're shape-shifters, not fucking superheroes! We need sleep, we need to eat, we need to go the fuck home and deal with what we can later." Warren steered the car effortlessly along the highway heading home.

Matthew looked at him. "I guess it's good that our captain pulled in reinforcements, Mr. 'We-Can-Handle-This-On-Our-Own'."

Silently, Warren tossed him a look that said, *"Shut the hell up"*.

Richard listened to the two men argue. He wondered if they remembered he was still on the cell phone.

Remembering that his Alpha had been rudely put on hold, Matthew put the cell phone back to his ear. "Richard? I'm sorry about that," he apologized.

"He's right, you know. Call me once you've had a good rest and a real meal. Goodbye." Richard ended the call.

Matthew slipped his cell back into his pocket. He looked at Warren, who was smiling slyly. "Oh, wipe that smug-ass grin off your face."

"Don't be mad because he agreed with me."

"Getting help was *my* idea."

"Yeah, but going home was mine. Besides, your stomach's growling so loud, I think it might attack us." Warren laughed at his own sleep-deprived joke.

Matthew chuckled. "Yeah, you *really* do need to go to sleep. Whenever you come up with stupid shit like that, I know you're beyond tired."

Warren decided not to muster a comeback. Truth was, he was too exhausted. They drove home for a nice meal and a long sleep, not necessarily in that order.

\*\*\*

Darian and Xavier hid in the trees as they watched the fifth body being dragged out from the Lake. The coroner's team consisted of two fresh members and a very worn-out one; Galen, the leader. The man looked as if he was going to fall over at any second. He made a quick inspection of the body and left the rest up to his team. Darian read his mind as he walked away. Galen's suspicions were the same as Warren's; that the vampire was at least strong enough to stay awake during the day, if not strong enough to come out into the sunlight. It was perplexing to Galen because it was also impossible. All of the information given to them from the Council as well as what they'd gathered from the failed lab experiments years ago didn't reveal vampires had that kind of ability.

Galen was beginning to learn a truth he'd rather not been exposed to. Darian admired the human for his intelligence and loyalty. He did, however wonder how far it would go. Would he be able to handle the truth? And what would he do with that kind of information? Would he have to do anything at all? Darian believed that the S.U.I.T. would began to put the pieces of this puzzle together on their own if any more bodies were found murdered during the daylight hours. He and Xavier surveyed the investigation for as long as they could. They watched the two new detectives question the police helicopter crew who discovered the body of an African-American male floating face down in the lake. After two hours of observing the investigation, the approaching sun forced Darian and Xavier to retreat to their home. Darian decided he'd go out again, at sunset.

***

Barry finished getting all of the information he could from the officers who called in the body. He thanked them for their help and made his way to his partner who was speaking with Janet and Victor from Marshall's team. He stood beside his partner, taking in the rest of the information they were giving.

"So, you'll be able to tell me more later on, right?" Gabriel asked.

"After we perform our autopsy, we'll see what else we can come up with and let you know," Janet said before turning to leave, her partner following.

Gabriel looked at Barry. "Five victims in twenty-four hours! What the hell is this, some kind of game for these sons of bitches?!"

Barry shrugged. "I don't know, maybe. Are you happy you're on this case now?"

"Yes and no. If we don't catch these bastards, we'll be held accountable if they continue to kill. And if we do … correction, when we do, I'm looking forward to the credit we'll greatly deserve. Is that so wrong? To get a little recognition for what we contribute. I'm tired of Davis and Eric getting all of the high-profile cases, the media attention, the awards and accolades. It's not fair, like we can't do any better," Gabriel said, with a hint of agitation.

"Well, got that off your chest?" Barry smiled. "Don't hold back, let it all out."

"Man, fuck you. You get what I'm saying and you know I'm right."

"Yeah. Frankly, I just want to catch these bastards, I don't care what happens after that as far as accolades go."

"Call me greedy, but I want have my cake and eat it, too." Gabriel looked at the approaching sun. "I guess it's about five o'clock. We should head back to the precinct, catch up on the files, see what Davis and Eric figured out."

"Finally something productive besides bitching." Barry walked off in the direction of their car.

"I wasn't bitching," Gabriel protested, following behind him. The two climbed inside their squad car and drove to the precinct to go over all the files. They ordered breakfast, ate while they worked their case, bouncing ideas off each other. A few minutes later, they got another call. They looked at each other over their desks, then rose, heading to yet another crime scene.

# CHAPTER EIGHT

Warren flopped over Matthew's body, slapping the "off" button on the alarm clock. He slid off his lover, face first into the pillow.

"What time it is?" Matthew asked, stirring under the covers.

"Too damn early. What time did you set the alarm clock?" Warren asked, voice muffled by the soft cloth of the pillow.

"Seven."

"Like I said, too damn early. Set it again for ten."

"Warren, we should get started on this case."

"Matt, set it for ten," Warren wasn't giving his lover an option. He still felt exhausted, having had barely four hours of sleep. He didn't think another three hours would hurt, it would only help. Closing his eyes, he allowed himself to be taken back into a deep slumber.

Matthew looked at him, rolling his eyes. Tossing his legs over the side, he rose and collapsed back onto the bed; his willpower not strong enough to claim victory over his exhausted mind and body. Doing as his lover suggested, he set the clock for ten and went back to sleep.

Three hours later, Matthew turned off the annoying buzzer. "All right, It's ten now, we need to get up." Feeling much more energized, he climbed out of bed, heading into the bathroom.

Warren remained in bed, snoozing.

Matthew stuck his head out of the bathroom doorway. "Warren, get your ass up!" he shouted, jarring the other shifter out of sleep.

"Okay Matt, I fucking heard you the first time. Take your shower," Warren said, hoping he could buy himself at least another fifteen minutes while Matthew bathed.

Matthew smirked. "And here I thought you'd want to join me in the shower, you know, to wash my back." He stepped back into the bathroom, closing the door behind him.

Warren's eyes shot open, understanding the full meaning of Matthew's words. "You fucking tease," he mumbled as he climbed out of bed, heading toward the bathroom, pushing open the unlocked door. Matthew was in the shower, head thrown back as the water rushed over his muscular physique. Warren could feel himself hardening as he watched the water cascading over Matthew's skin. He climbed into the shower, purposely poking the other man with his hardened flesh.

Matthew tossed him a glance over his shoulder. "Do you have a permit to carry that thing?" He smiled.

"Nope, and it's way past the regulation size," Warren flirted.

Matthew's breathing began to quicken as his arousal grew. "So that's an unconcealed weapon you've got there. You know attacking an officer of the law is a serious offense."

"Arrest me." Warren pressed himself against Matthew, running his hands over his lover's torso, reaching down to stroke his fully erect member.

Matthew moaned as he pushed back against Warren. "We don't have time for foreplay ... ," he panted, unable to contain his lust any longer.

Warren understood what he meant. He agreed. Slicking himself up with the lubricant they kept stored in the shower, he slid himself deeply into Matthew, causing them both to shudder with indescribable pleasure. He loved having sex with Matthew now even more than before because he no longer had to hold back. With short quick thrusts, he pounded into his lover. Matthew braced himself, hands pressed firmly against the tiled walls. He moaned louder and louder as he felt his orgasm building. Warren followed suit, picking up the pace with a force that pressed Matthew completely against the tiled wall. Warren stroked Matthew skillfully with one hand, caressing his lover's sensitive areas as his other hand held firmly onto his left shoulder. Finally, their moment had come with a fierce intensity that caused them both to cry out in sheer ecstasy. Their eyes were closed tightly as their bodies rocked with their unified climaxes until neither man could give no more.

Warren collapsed against Matthew, pinning him to the wall as they both struggled to regain strength lost during their vigorous romp. It was a while before either man could move. Finally, Warren pulled away first, allowing Matthew to straighten himself.

"We really need to wash up now," Warren said, smiling boyishly.

"Yeah, I was trying to do that when you assaulted me!" Matthew joked as he began soaping his washcloth.

"Assaulted? That's not what I'd call it. Come here." Warren reached out, taking his lover into his arms, kissing him passionately. They broke the kiss several seconds later and began bathing quickly. Once they were finished, they began dressing.

"I don't know about you, but I feel very energetic," Warren declared as he tied the laces of his sneakers.

"I guess we really needed that," Matthew agreed. "Come on, we need to grab something to eat before heading in."

*** 

"Two more fucking victims?!" Warren exclaimed upon hearing the news that two bodies were found earlier that morning.

Detective Gabriel Johnson planted himself on the edge of his desk. "That's not the worst part," he said, pausing for dramatics.

Warren and Matthew looked at him, waiting.

"You gonna tell us or what?" Warren asked.

"It was an infant and a small child," Barry Weinstein answered.

Warren moved forward. "What the fuck did you just say?" He couldn't believe his ears.

"A five month old infant and a six year old child. They didn't just drain their blood either, they were flayed as well," Gabriel said, shaking his head in disgust.

"Oh my God!" Matthew gasped. "I've been a cop for a long time, I've never ran into anything like this."

"Same here," Barry said, slouching dejectedly into his seat. "We've been up for at least thirty hours. You two are fresh and ready to take over. This is what we've gathered so far." He handed Matthew a manila file containing several papers. "I think you'll find that interesting." He rose from his chair, grabbing his blazer at the same time.

His partner, Gabriel followed suit. "We'll be back in a few hours."

"Sure, get some rest, it's cool," Matthew said, somewhat distracted as he sifted through the papers.

"All right," Barry said and the two detectives left.

Warren and Matthew returned to their own desk, sitting down at the same time.

"A baby, Matt. A fucking infant! And this second child was younger than the first one." Warren ran his hands over his face, still horrified by the information. "We need to see the bodies."

Matthew's eyes scanned over the documents. "Yeah, I know," he said, without looking up. "Barry and Gabe might be onto something here. Apparently, a city in England has had the same string of occurrences that we're experiencing now. Yeah, see … " He passed the file and papers over to Warren, pointing to a spot on one of the sheets. " … About a year ago, seventeen bodies were found, some mutilated, some sexually assaulted, some drained, some all three. There was no pattern then, either."

Warren's eyes scanned the file. "These are still open cases."

"Yeah, I read that part, too. You know, this is just a thought, but do you think this could be the work of a copy-cat coven?"

Warren looked at Matthew as if to say. *"Give me a break"*.

"Hey, I'm just tossing out ideas; let's not close any doors, okay?"

"Matt, I seriously doubt that this is a copy-cat coven. Nor do I want to waste any time following dead-end trails."

"Don't knock it, Warren. For all we know, some crazy-ass coven could be looking at these other guys as role models. I'm just saying keep your mind open to the possibility." Matthew turned on his computer. "You'd be surprised by what inspires people sometimes."

"What are you going to do now?" Warren asked, looking at him from over the papers he was reading.

"I'm going to search for more cases that match ours, I don't think that file is all there is, but it's something. If we can establish a point of origin when these murders first started happening, we might be able to locate the coven," Matthew said, fingers typing furiously over the keyboard.

"Okay, hold up, you lost me … somewhat."

Matthew looked up at him. "I'm just trying something here, there's no telling if it's going to work. I'm figuring the killings had to start somewhere, right?"

Warren nodded slowly.

"Exactly, so maybe they started in the coven's own backyard, so to speak. Maybe they got bored killing in their hometown and started killing in other vampires' territories, the ultimate slap in the face for vampires, right?"

Warren nodded again, this time perking up at bit. "That makes a lot of sense, Matt. Shit, I'm sure Darian is quite pissed. It's a possibility, but we also need to take into account that they might not have started in their own backyard."

"Yeah, that, too... but we need to start somewhere."

"That's true."

Matthew went back to typing information into the computer looking up similar cases worldwide.

Warren rose from his seat. "I'm going to check with Marshall, if he's in. See what he's found out." Without waiting for a response from Matthew, he walked away, heading toward the morgue. Opening without knocking, he noticed that Marshall was there, with Janet. For a split second he was disappointed that he couldn't be himself, then felt sudden relief as Janet pulled off her gloves, apron and mask. She washed her hands in the sink then toweled them dry.

"Detective Davis." She nodded a greeting at him, that he returned as she walked past, exiting the morgue.

Warren looked at Marshall. "I heard the news, two children were drained and flayed."

"Yeah, well, that's not the worst part," Marshall said.

"I'm starting to think the worst part is hearing that fucking line. I've heard it more than I've wanted to in the past forty-eight hours," Warren replied with his characteristic dry sarcasm.

Unaffected, Marshall continued. "Well, you may want to brace yourself. Last night, I instructed Janet to go over the bodies; I wanted her to look for any special markings or for sexual assault. I haven't been able to perform thorough autopsies on the victims as I would have liked because I haven't been able to focus on one before another comes into my morgue."

"Is this you apologizing for giving me important, need-to-know information a day late and a dollar short?" Warren wasn't angry, but he was annoyed. However, he understood. Everyone involved in this case was pushed to their limits.

"As much as a flawless person such as I can apologize; yes." Marshall managed to crack a closed-mouth smile.

Warren smiled in return in spite of himself. "Okay, give me all that you have-that I don't already know," he added, as he looked at the tiny mounds now covered with white sheets on the stainless steel tables. He didn't want to get closer, but he did. Immediately he caught a very distinctive scent and it made him want to flee the room.

Marshall went on to explain. "Okay, all but one of the victims had been sex-"

Warren held his hand up, silencing the medical examiner. "I can already smell what happened to this poor child. What kind of a monster could do this? I …" his voice trailed off as he continued looking at the tiny body under the white sheet, knowing that a once innocent, vibrant and happy six-year old child now lay there lifeless.

Marshall nodded grimly. "A monster indeed. I took a look at his anus; there were several fissures in his rectum. The wounds also indicate it was done to him before they killed him. I can't imagine the horror and agony this child suffered."

Warren's mouth opened, but no sound came out. He walked away, his back to Marshall as he leaned forward against the sink. He felt sick to his stomach and thought he'd spew his breakfast if he didn't regain control over his emotions, and soon.

Marshall watched the detective struggle with himself. He had an idea of what Warren was thinking, because he was thinking it as well. Upon looking at the savagely molested and brutally murdered remains of the six-year old child and five-month old infant, he had almost felt at a loss. He allowed Warren time to recover from the horrendous news.

Several minutes later, Warren turned around. "I don't understand why I couldn't sense this on the victims. I should have known," he said, his voice low, somber.

"They must have done something to the bodies to mask or remove the sexual scent from their victims to throw you off, whatever that might be. Although, I'm sure they knew I'd find out during my examination. The infant was the only victim who wasn't molested. I don't know if our killers had a spark of humanity or whatever the case. Maybe molesting the infant was too much, even for them, who knows? But that's where their morals ended, the infant was killed at least five hours ago, around five this morning."

Warren walked over to the infant, pulling the sheet back to examine the body himself. The infant was a tiny mound of pale flesh, with dark veins running along its body. There was no blood or skin to be found, much like the first victim. He did catch a few scents that he was able to match to the other victims, but nothing more. "Anything else?" he asked Marshall.

"Nothing that you don't already know; same fang marks, no fibers, prints, or skin particles."

Warren nodded. He left the morgue, heading back to Matthew.

"What did you find out?" Matthew asked; his eyes still on the monitor. When Warren didn't answer him, he looked up, seeing his lover and partner's horrified expression. "Warren? What's wrong?"

Warren released a long, shuddering breath. He looked at Matthew. "The … ." He paused, struggling to find a less horrific way to deliver the news. "There was a sexual assault on every victim except the infant."

"So the six-year old … was it post-mortem?" Matthew asked.

Warren shook his head.

Matthew was suddenly realizing why Warren was wearing his emotions on his face. Finding out that all but one of the victims had been raped was emotionally damaging, even for a couple of hard-asses such as themselves. He was somewhat relieved to know that the infant wasn't molested, not that the baby fared any better than the other victims. Matthew really hated this coven more than he hated anything or anyone in his life.

"Matt, what are we going to do?"

"We're going to do whatever we can. Why don't you finish looking through that report? I'm still making a list of places with cases like ours."

"They raped another child, Matt." Warren fumed. "This one

younger than the first. Who's to say this isn't their pattern? That the next child will be younger than the one before? What if their other victims are just killed to throw us off that particular pattern?"

"God, I hope not. Lord knows we can't protect all of the children in this city. Not even their parents can … " Matthew paused, giving real thought to what Warren was saying. "But they didn't molest the infant. That puts a wrench in your theory, don't you think?"

Warren sat back, thinking. "No, they didn't." He sighed, rubbing his temple. "Shit, Matt, I don't know. Maybe they killed the infant to prove that they'll do worse. Just when we think they've done the most depraved crime ever, they've got another one ten times as bad up their sleeves."

"And as soon as we catch them, we'll make them pay for everything they've done. Stay focused, Warren. I need you focused. This case isn't going to get any easier or nicer for that matter, and you need to start hardening yourself now, or your emotions will only hinder us." Matthew looked at Warren.

Warren reflected on what Matthew said. He was right. Without further protest, he picked up the file Johnson had given him earlier and began reading it word for word. "Jesus Christ! Do you know where they found the baby?"

Matthew looked up from his monitor. "No, I hadn't gotten to that file yet. Where?"

"In a department store display lying in a bassinet."

"Oh my God!" Matthew covered his mouth, sickened. He removed his hand a moment later, shaking his head. "Stay focused," he whispered to himself. Diligently, he went back to work on his computer.

Warren's telephone rang and he answered it. "Supernatural Un-Yes Captain, what's up?"

"I need to see both you and Matthew in my office right now," Captain Michelle Lawrence demanded.

"Listen Capt', Matt's busy, I'll just come."

"Fine." She ended the call.

Warren replaced the receiver back on the base. "I'll be back." He rose and made his way to the captain's office. He knocked and waited for the "okay" to enter. When he heard her voice grant him entry, he did. "What's up Captain?"

"Please have a seat," she said, pointing to the leather chair in front of her desk.

Warren sat down and waited.

"When I first gave this case to you and Detective Eric, it was because you're the best I have on this team. You work hard and you've closed more cases than the others. But this time it's different. Seven bodies in twenty-seven hours is far too drastic a killing spree for me to leave it in the hands of four detectives."

"Captain, we're doing our best," Warren said in their defense.

She held her hand up. "You don't have to explain it to me, Davis, I know. However, we're in a race against time here. We never know when the next body is going to pop up somewhere and we don't know how many they're going to kill or why they're even killing. I'm putting this case on top priority. I've got the Infiltration Team out there looking for hiding spots a coven of vampires may be resting during the day. I've also enlisted the aid of two more detectives. They're coming in from California. I want you to pick them up at the airport at one o'clock."

"Captain, why the other detectives?" Warren was growing more agitated with each passing second. He didn't want Barry and Gabriel on the case and for damn sure didn't want outsiders on the case either.

"They were experiencing a rash of murders like ours two years ago. They might be able to give us some insight, and we could certainly use more officers on this case."

"They obviously didn't catch the killers in California, what makes you think they'll be able to do any good here?"

"Listen to me, Davis. I already know you're no closer to solving this case now that you were seven bodies ago."

"Seven bodies ago, I didn't have a case," Warren retorted.

"Now is not the time to be a smartass."

Warren nodded, but he still didn't like the new development.

The captain continued. "Now, I'm willing to ask for help and accept it to get the job done. All I know is, I don't want any more people to die. Now, you're going to work with these two detectives and I don't want to hear any more about it." When Captain Michelle

Lawrence put her foot down, it was down, or she'd put it up your ass.

Warren decided not to argue. What was done was done. "One o'clock, you say?"

She nodded. "That's right, *O'Lare* airport. I want to be working on this case around the clock."

"All right, I'll inform Matthew. Is there anything else?" he asked, unsuccessfully hiding his agitation.

"Yeah, a little less attitude from you. This isn't about you sharing your glory. This is about us catching a gang of ruthless, sadistic killers."

Warren wanted to explain to her it wasn't about his "glory" or "pride", but his nature. These murders were going down in his territory, but more importantly, it involved his Pack, and all of his friends and he didn't want or need the extra scrutiny. But he knew she wouldn't understand, so he allowed her to think it was his pride that was still stinging. "I'll adjust my attitude, Captain." He left her office, rejoining Matthew less than a minute later.

Matthew looked up. "What did the captain want?"

"Basically, we're leading the case, but the ITs are already in the field, checking out locations where the coven may be resting during the day.

"Okay, makes sense. We can't do it all." Matthew liked the newest development.

"Then you're going to love this. Two more detectives are flying in from California to assist on this case. Apparently, they went through what we're going through now and Lawrence thinks they may have some insight to offer."

"Oh, that does kind of suck considering our situation." Matthew agreed with Warren's annoyance.

Warren's telephone rang again. "Fuck, what now?" He snatched the receiver up. "What?!"

"Nice phone etiquette, Detective. I've got three people here who want to see you. Come around," the office desk cop said, hanging up the phone.

Warren hung up. "I'll be back; I want to see who these people are." He rose, heading toward the front desk. Before he made it around the corner, he recognized the scents of these three individuals. Rounding the corner, he was able to see Adrian, Daniel and Ignacio standing by the desk.

"Hey," Warren greeted.

The three men stepped up to him. "We were sent to help you out on your investigation, unofficially, of course," Daniel said.

"Shit, great," Warren said dryly.

"Is that good or bad?" Adrian asked.

"Huh? Oh! Good. Extra help is always good. Listen, did you guys sign in?" Warren looked at the three men.

They nodded.

"Great, do you have your passes?"

"Yeah, see." Adrian pointed to the white sticker plastered over his left pectoral.

Warren nodded. "Okay, let's go." He led them back to his and Matthew's desks.

"Damn your ass is unorganized," Adrian commented, looking at the messy stacks of papers piled up on Warren's desk. "Why can't you be more like your partner over there?" He pointed at Matthew's extremely organized desk where everything had its place.

"Because I'm not obsessive-compulsive," Warren answered, rolling his eyes.

"You're just messy, always have been," Adrian smiled.

"Whatever," Warren dismissed Adrian's comments. "Pull up some chairs."

The three men looked around for empty chairs, finding three they pulled them over and sat down.

"You're in a mood," Adrian commented, making himself comfortable in his chair.

"I've got good reasons to be. All right, I'm going to tell you guys everything we have on this case." Warren brought them up to date.

"That's some fucked-up shit." Adrian was the first to speak after hearing about the infant and the six-year old child.

"That's past 'fucked-up', Adrian. Shit, I don't know what it is," Ignacio said, his Italian accent thickening in his anger.

Matthew leaned forward. "What's more is, some Cali' detectives are flying in to assist on the case."

"Fuck. Just what we need, a bunch of noses poking around."

Adrian frowned, his aggravation was very apparent.

"Like it could have been avoided; seven bodies in twenty-seven hours. It was only logical they'd bring in more forces. Hell, I'm surprised the damn military hasn't been called in," Daniel said, running his hands through his hair.

"What are you going to do, now?" Matthew asked.

"Pretty much what you said the IT is doing. We're going to be searching remote locations where these vamps may be hiding. We're also going to search local hotels, motels and the like. And what I mean by local, I mean within Illinois," Ignacio said.

"Let's get out of here, place fucking creeps me out," Daniel said, rising from his seat.

The other two men did the same, saying their 'goodbyes'. On their way toward the front door, the three men ran into officers Kyle Ronen and his partner of four years, Lance Wilson. Ronen placed his hand on Daniel's chest, stopping the three men in their tracks.

Daniel looked down at the hand violating his body then his eyes traveled upward to the eyes of the hand's owner. "You wanna get your fucking hand off me?"

"What are you doing here?" Officer Ronen asked.

"I fail to see how that's any business of yours?" Daniel shot back.

"It's my business because I say it is. Now are you going to answer my question, or should I assume you were hunting in your little furry form just like before?" He looked at the other two. "You shifters, too?"

Neither Adrian nor Ignacio answered.

"I guess so." Officer Ronen removed his hand, tossing a glance to his partner. "I arrested this fucker several years ago when I caught him hunting off sanctioned grounds." He pointed to Daniel, who was now stepping up to him, so close their lips were almost touching.

A low, menacing growl bubbled up from Daniel's throat.

"What are you gonna do, freak? Rip my throat out?" Officer Ronen smiled.

"Doesn't sound like a bad idea," Daniel retorted.

"Daniel," Adrian pulled the shifter back.

Daniel allowed him to do so.

"We need to go," Ignacio said.

"I want to file a formal complaint," Daniel said, his eyes staring at the offensive cop.

"Go ahead, there's the front desk." Officer Ronen pointed at the officer behind the desk. "He'll take your complaint and file it with the others we get and flush it down the toilet with the rest of the shit." He slapped his partner on the arm with the back of his hand. "Let's go." He pointed at Daniel again, "I'll be keeping my eyes on you." The two officers walked away.

"Daniel, do you really want to file a complaint?" Ignacio asked. "I wouldn't. Let's just go."

With some gentle prodding, they were able to get the enraged shifter out of the precinct. Inside the car, Adrian asked Ignacio why he suggested Daniel not file a complaint.

"Because we could kill his ass later, and you don't want a complaint recently issued to be the first thing that connects you. That shit was uncalled for," Ignacio said.

Daniel chuckled. "The thought of me slowly ripping his head off his body is tempting, but I doubt Elise would allow me the pleasure of killing his ass."

"I'll do it for you. I don't think Richard would mind. Especially not after I tell him what happened," Ignacio smiled.

"I'm with you on that one," Adrian said. "Shiit, I started to fuck his ass up when he put his hand on you."

"It's good that we didn't. We can't be of much use in jail, awaiting trial for assaulting an officer. Even if the officer is an asshole," Daniel said, calming down. "Okay, where to first, boys?"

"First, I call my dad and tell him what's going on. You two do the same, next we hit up hotels and motels," Adrian suggested.

"You want me to call your dad, too?" Ignacio asked jokingly, hoping to calm Daniel down even more.

"Shut up," Adrian retorted, smirking. "You know what I meant."

"Yeah, I'll give Richard a call." Ignacio pulled out his cell. "We should have brought separate cars." He accelerated to pass a yellow light.

"Take me home, then and I'll get mine," Daniel said.

"Mine is at your house," Adrian said, gesturing to Daniel.

"Let's investigate Chicago, first. Then branch out from there."

Ignacio slammed on the breaks, unable to speed past a red light.

"I know I'll feel safer in my own car than with your crazy-ass driving," Adrian remarked.

Ignacio rolled his eyes.

"Wait, what if we find them?" Daniel asked.

"Kill them," Adrian replied.

"What if they can wake up during the day, even if it's for a split second? I don't think we should take the chance on going it alone. There's strength in numbers," Daniel pointed out.

"That's a good point, so no separate cars. Okay, when we call our leaders, let them work it out. We'll stick to our original plan and check out the hotels and motels … together," Ignacio said.

"I wish I had a helmet. Next time I'll bring one when I ride with you," Adrian told Ignacio, who tossed up his middle finger.

The three men laughed and began calling their leaders.

# CHAPTER NINE

Marcus ran his powerful, masculine hands through his lover's black shiny mane intertwining his fingers around the silky locks as his lover's head bobbed furiously over his groin. His lover's lips sealed tightly against his shaft, giving him the ultimate pleasure. The Master vampire moaned loudly as his orgasm rushed to the surface, shooting forth. His fingers locked tightly, gripping hair, pressing his lover's head against his groin as he thrust repeatedly until he had nothing more to give. His lover looked up with adoring eyes that gave him the smile his mouth was unable to.

Marcus looked down, grinning wolfishly. "Swallow."

Kiren did as he was told. "Did you like that?" he asked after the deed was done. His light brown, almond-shaped eyes peered closely at his lover, waiting for his response.

"What do you think?" Marcus asked, running fingers along the strong jaw line of Kiren's face.

"I think I enjoyed giving it more than you enjoyed getting it." Kiren smiled as he climbed onto Marcus' lap. "I love having you in my mouth."

Marcus chuckled deeply. "I love having me in your mouth, as well."

"Fuck me," Kiren panted lustfully, reaching between them taking hold of Marcus' penis.

"You know what to do," Marcus implied. He adjusted himself enough for his shape-shifter lover to slide him inside. A low moan escaped his lips as he began to work his hips in a thrusting motion, sending his lover into an ecstatic frenzy.

An hour later, the two men were breathless, panting as their sweat slicked bodies remained plastered together on the floor. Marcus pulled away after several minutes, relishing the sensation of his body leaving his lover's. The two lay side-by-side for a few minutes before they began to speak.

"Are we going to kill any more today?" Kiren asked, his fingers swirling patterns in the thin layer of blond hair covering Marcus' chest.

"Of course we are. I have to admit, this little city is proving to own up to its reputation. I haven't had this much fun in a while. It never sleeps and it thrives and throbs with energy, life, sex … reminds me of Los Angeles."

"Yeah, L.A. was a lot of fun. The S.U.I.T. there didn't know what the fuck was going on. The best thing is watching them chase their tails." Kiren laughed.

"I agree, watching the humans' little tin soldiers in such disarray is entertaining. But what I'm enjoying even more is watching this city's Master vampire scratch his head in bewilderment."

"You've seen him?" Kiren raise himself on one arm.

"Yes … and what a vision. I can easily see why he was chosen, he's magnificent."

"Describe him."

Marcus chuckled and began describing Darian's features. " … But, I think the most stunning feature this vampire possesses are his hypnotic forest-green eyes. I don't think I've ever seen eyes so vibrantly green before."

"Sounds like a real looker. I take it you've got plans for him?"

Marcus nodded. "I'm going to take my fill of his little territory and drain it dry."

"When can I have a little fun? I've had to watch you four feed greedily, when is it going to be my turn?" Kiren asked, feeling a bit left out of the festivities.

Marcus looked at him. "It's good that you've asked. I want you to have your fun today. But be careful."

Kiren smiled widely before climbing off the floor. "Thanks!" He jogged off toward his room. Two nights ago, when they had chased that Pride into the city, they had sensed the powerful aura of the supernaturals that inhabited the territory. At that point, Marcus wanted to settle down. After killing the owner of a three-bedroom townhouse in the suburbs, they set up their nest. There were five of them: four vampires and one shape-shifter. Three of the vampires shared one bedroom, Kiren had his own as did Marcus.

Kiren opened the window, allowing the afternoon sun to shine its bright light over his body and into the room. He stood there for a few minutes, soaking up the warmth before he went into the bathroom to shower and get dressed. The night before, they'd broken into a department store, stole a great amount of clothing and right before they left, Raven placed the skinless baby into the bassinet located in the display window. Imagining the horror-struck expressions of the humans walking past had filled her with devilish glee.

As it had been, she was right. The baby lay in the bassinet nearly two hours before anyone had even noticed what it was and called the police. Kiren and Marcus stayed up, switching TV channels looking for the breaking news report they were sure would be coming. Finally, around seven o'clock that morning, a news anchorwoman interrupted their cooking show to bring to light the "new disturbing developments in the grisly 'Reign of Terror'", as she called it, concerning the gruesome remains of an "innocent" baby in a department store display. Both he and Marcus laughed boisterously as the reporter recounted the witnesses' statements as well as the police and S.U.I.T. reports. An hour later, there came the other report of the horrendous discovery of a mutilated six-year old boy. Again, authorities were 'without suspects', had 'no leads' and were 'seeking any information'. They had recorded the news for Raven's benefit, knowing she would want to see the aftermath of her mischievousness. They also knew that Alicia would want to know what the humans thought about her little addition to the corpses, or subtraction, to be more exact. She did keep the skin of all her victims, making trophies of them. Kiren wished he could be in the morgue when they discovered Mikhail's handiwork on the six-year old's private area. Kiren didn't think he laughed as hard at Mikhail's antics before when he'd watched him violate the boy while the child screamed and cried.

He found what he wanted to wear, something bright. He pulled an orange t-shirt over his head and pulled on a pair of tan khakis. Leaving his bedroom, he walked up to Marcus, who was lounging lazily on the sofa, still naked.

"I'm going out now, anything you want me to do in particular?" he asked, smiling.

Marcus nodded. "Wreak havoc and have fun doing so."

"That's my kind of request." Kiren turned and left, heading out to put his own signature on the city.

It didn't take him long to find his victim. He chose an ice cream vender who was putting gasoline in his truck. He came up behind the man, covering his mouth with his hand, dragging him back into the truck and ordering the man to undress. Once the vender was naked, he ripped the man's throat open with his clawed hand. Blood spurted over his own shirt and khakis as he knew it would which is why he ordered the man to undress first, leaving the uniform clean. He watched the blood splatter his chest as it ran down in a flood over the dead vendor's torso. He wanted to feed so badly. The blood scent filled the truck with the most succulent aroma, but Kiren fought against it. He had no plans to feed his hunger with the man's flesh. Cleaning the blood off his body, he dressed in the man's clothes, making himself presentable. He was going to have to wait a while until the right time came before he could make his move.

\*\*\*

Warren and Matthew waited in the "arrivals" area for the two California detectives to come through the terminal.

"What good do you think these two will be able to do?" Warren asked.

Matthew shrugged. "Who knows what they might know. I just want all of this to be over with."

They waited for several minutes, holding a sign with the two detectives' last names on it before two men approached them. Immediately, Matthew and Warren noticed something familiar about one of the detectives, they wondered if his partner knew. Not sure if that was the case, they kept their mouths closed.

The taller of the two men greeted Warren and Matthew. "You must be Detectives Davis and Eric?"

The shorter man spoke, pointing to his partner, he said. "This is Detective Brian McNeary."

The first man who greeted them nodded.

"I'm Detective Colin O'Neal," said the shorter detective, extending his hand toward Matthew and Warren.

The four officers shook each other's hands.

"Why don't we gather your things and get the hell out of here," Warren suggested.

"That's the plan," Brian said.

Once they had their luggage, they climbed into Warren's SUV.

"Nice ride, barely street legal, though," Colin commented, looking at the girth of Warren's "little baby".

"I wouldn't talk about the truck if I were you, he's really sensitive," Matthew joked, breaking the ice.

The four men chuckled.

"Listen, the S.U.I.T. made arrangements for you prior to you guys coming here. You'll be staying at the *Xavier* hotel while you're in Chicago."

Brian whistled. "Wow, the *Xavier* hotel. Not sparing any expenses, I see." He smiled. He had heard about the luxury of that hotel chain, but had never stayed in one.

"The city and the S.U.I.T. like to make an impression," Matthew said.

"They must think we're supercops coughing up the dough for that kind of accommodation. Here I was expecting to sleep in one of the cells in the back of the precinct," Brian joked.

Warren chuckled. So far, he liked the two men. "The city has contracts with three of the top hotels that do business here. Whenever different officials, diplomats, etcetera, visit Chicago, they end up staying in the *Lendon*, *Esquire* or the *Xavier* hotels. The hotels get tax breaks and like Matt said, the city gets to make an impressive showing. The S.U.I.T. was lucky enough to establish a contract with this particular hotel."

"From what I've heard, a vampire owns it?" Colin questioned, somewhat disgusted.

Warren nodded. "Does that matter to you? If so, it's not too late to prepare your two cots at the precinct."

"Naw, no complaints from me," Brian said.

"I guess we don't have a choice. These fucking supernatural freaks got their claws in every damn thing," Colin commented with a sneer.

Warren and Matthew tossed each other a quick glance. Their question was answered. If that was how he felt about supernaturals, then they were certain he didn't know that his very own partner was one of the "freaks" he mentioned.

"We'll drop you off there so that you can get situated, then we'll take you back to the precinct to get you caught up," Matthew said.

"Okay, that's good, because I have to take a piss," Brian informed.

\*\*\*

Within an hour after arriving in the city, they were at the hotel, checked in and were in their room. Colin entered the bathroom when Brian came out.

"I guess it would have been too much to ask for separate rooms, eh? I've got to room with that snoring S-O-B in there," Brian joked, pointing toward the now closed bathroom door.

Warren chuckled. "As you know, the S.U.I.T. is generous, but not that generous. Mind if I speak with you in the hall?" he asked.

Brian nodded and followed Warren outside the room. Matthew stayed inside, monitoring Colin. In the hallway, Warren began talking.

"I know what you are, you know what I am, I just want to get that out in the open."

"I caught your scent right away, you and your partner. How do you pass inspections?" Brian asked.

"We have a friend who can pull all of the right strings. What about you?"

"Same here."

"What's with your partner?"

"He doesn't know about me. His family was killed by a hyena Pack, and he's hated supernaturals ever since."

"Shit. Ever think about getting another partner, one that's more open-minded?"

Brian laughed. "You ever tried switching a partner within the Team?"

Warren shook his head. Matthew was his soul mate; there would never be any need to look elsewhere.

"Well, let me be the first to tell ya, it ain't easy. Besides, it would get back to him that I wanted to switch partners. He's an excellent cop, one of the best and if I wasn't what I am, I couldn't ask for a better partner. But if I were to ask for a switch, that would raise questions, get what I'm saying?"

Warren nodded. "So you two get along?"

Brian nodded. "As well as can be expected."

"What about your once a month vacation day?"

"I've got a pretty tight excuse for those nights and no one has ever suspected." Brian slapped Warren lightly on his arm. "Thanks for looking out for me." He smiled.

"Don't mention it," Warren said, returning his smile.

The two men re-entered the hotel room. Colin was talking with Matthew as he checked the ammunition in his gun. When he saw his partner walk back into the room, he slipped his gun into his holster, preparing to leave.

"Are we ready to go?" Colin asked, wondering what the two men were discussing out in the hallway. They hadn't been in Chicago less than two hours and already there were secrets. He wasn't sure if he liked it. *Whatever Warren had to say to his partner, he could have said to both of them*, he thought.

"Yeah, let's go." Brian pulled his coat on and the four men left.

While in the car, Warren could sense the tension in the air radiating from Colin. He assumed that the other man was pissed off that he had a private conversation with *his* partner. He couldn't really blame him. Had another officer pulled Matthew off to the side, he would have to hold his territorial tendencies in check with all of his internal control to keep from attacking and reclaiming what was his. Or in a case like this, at least be included. Once they were at the precinct, Colin pulled his partner aside before they entered. Matthew and Warren watched the two men chatting in a corner. They could hear every word, even though Colin was trying to be discreet. Warren was right; he was pissed about the private conversation. Brian assured him it was nothing; he lied and said that the other cop was questioning their involvement in this case.

"Still, why didn't he come to both of us?" Colin asked.

"Because he sensed you were more confrontational, now can we go inside?" Brian looked at him as if to say, 'are you finished bitching?'

Satisfied with that answer, even understanding and agreeing with it, Colin nodded and they joined the other two men as they entered the precinct. They picked up their temporary I.D.s, and met with the captain before diving into the case. Colin and Brian looked over the paperwork and files matching their cases. Brian handed Matthew and Warren the information they had gathered when they were hunting down the same coven in California.

"Can we see the bodies?" Colin asked.

"I don't see why not," Warren said. He escorted them to the morgue where they found Marshall sleeping in two chairs in the far corner of the room. Warren chuckled, fully understanding why the busy man had finally fallen flat. He gently nudged him, slowly bringing him out of his deep slumber. Marshall opened his eyes and looked up.

"Jesus!" he flailed about until he was able to regain control and recognition of his surroundings. He looked around. "You scared the hell out of me. My goodness, was I just asleep?"

Still chuckling, Warren nodded. "And snoring."

Marshall wiped his eyes then stretched. "I do believe that is a first for me."

Warren shrugged. "It's understandable, you've only had what, six hours of sleep at the most?"

Marshall nodded as he rose. "Something like that." He took out his handkerchief and began wiping his eyeglasses. Once clean, he put them back on. "Whom do we have here?" he asked, looking at the two new detectives.

"Marshall Galen, this is Detectives Brian McNeary and Colin O'Neal." Warren gestured toward each man as he made introductions.

"Ah, nice to meet you gentlemen, I … um … hope you can forgive my indiscretion. Now, I take it you came to see the bodies, right?"

They nodded.

"Well, I hope you haven't eaten too heavily this afternoon, they're pretty disturbing." Marshall began revealing the bodies and going over the details of their demise.

Colin scratched the side of his nose. "So … are these the only bodies?"

"Shit, how many more are you expecting?" Warren asked.

"A lot more than seven," Colin replied.

"You haven't made it to the Second Phase, yet," Brian added.

Two sets of eyebrows rose. "The Second Phase?" Warren and Marshall asked in unison.

The two out-of-town detectives nodded. "I'm afraid so. So far, these DBs are the remains of the vampires, there's a shape-shifter, too. And he's a real sick son-of-a-bitch," Brian said.

Warren and Marshall tossed each other a look.

"Go on," Marshall prodded.

"If I'm not mistaken, he's the Second Phase; at least that's what we called it. And it was the only pattern we were able to identify. And if he's a creature of habit, he'll want to do the most damage that will be the most devastating. When this group was in LA, the Second Phase consisted of mutilated children, women, men, indiscriminate killing," Colin grimaced.

Matthew entered the morgue, joining the others. "I don't like the expression on your faces. What did I miss?"

"Apparently, there's a Second Phase to the killings," Warren informed Matthew of the new details.

"We've been going about it all wrong, then," Matthew said.

"How so?" Warren asked.

"We've been narrowing our search for murders committed by vampires, when we should have been widening our search for murders of all kinds," Matthew replied.

"I wouldn't beat myself up over it. We didn't know about the shifter at first until he left us the remains of his first victim," Brian said. "Even knowing about the shifter, we still couldn't find them."

Matthew rubbed his temples, hoping to ease the headache threatening to cause him hours of pain. "Maybe there is a pattern. We just weren't looking hard enough because the victims were so random."

"I'm listening." Warren watched the mental gears turning in Matthew's mind.

Matthew turned to the two detectives. "Who was the first victim in the 'Second Phase'?"

Now it was Colin and Brian who gave each other "the look". They were seeing where Matthew was going with his idea.

Colin nodded. "We need to get out there on the street. If you're going where I think you're going with this, his first victim or victims were children."

"Shit, let's go … we have to check out schools, playgrounds, anywhere kids congregate," Warren added. "Thanks Galen." He waved goodbye as he made his way to the exit with the other three men.

Marshall nodded then prepared his lab just in case. He hoped it wouldn't be necessary … hoped.

\*\*\*

Outside the morgue, once Matthew contacted the captain and told her their theory, he requested squad cars be sent to locations where there were plenty of children.

"You think this is a pattern," the Captain asked.

"I'm not sure yet, but it's worth a shot. I haven't had time to go over the other paperwork I have on this case and I don't want to waste countless hours doing so when the answer may be right in front of us," Matthew replied.

She could hear the desperation in his voice, even though he tried to mask it. If Matthew thought they had discovered the killers' next target, she was going to follow through. "All right, I hope you're right on this one, Detective. I'm going to call in reinforcements from the local police. There's no telling where this killer may attack and I think other cities need to be on alert."

"Great idea," Matthew agreed.

They ended their phone call.

"While you were on the phone, McNeary said that the first victim of this Second Phase was a seven year old boy found shredded to pieces and buried in a sandbox on a playground."

"So do you think we should be looking for playgrounds with sandboxes?" Matthew asked. "I mean, it would narrow down our search."

Brian shook his head. "The thing with these killers is that's too close to a pattern. During our investigation, we noticed that they liked to kill women and children, especially children. We figured they got off on destroying innocence and dominating authority."

Matthew raised an eyebrow. "That would explain the condition of the last victim and the fact that they're probably laughing their asses off as they watch us jump from one foot to the other."

The two other detectives nodded. "Although, most of the children were skinned alive in our case, some were molested as well. However, your situation is a bit different. When this was going down in L.A., no infants were murdered. Seems like they've evolved," Colin said.

"It's still like we're looking for a needle in ten thousand hay stacks," Warren started to slam his fist on his desk and caught himself just in time. Instead he rose from his chair, pacing.

"I'm going to call Weinstein and Johnson, get them here." Matthew picked up his telephone and dialed Weinstein.

When the other man answered, offering a groggy greeting, Matthew told him what they knew so far and what they were suspecting.

"What the fuck!" Barry Weinstein shot up in his bed, tossing back the covers. "Just hold it, we're coming in." He hung up without waiting for a response.

Matthew looked at the receiver, one eyebrow arched before placing it back on the base. "They're on their way here."

The four detectives continued to discuss their case until the other two could join them.

***

Barry called his partner's home number. There was no answer. Next, he called his cell phone; it rang with no answer. Getting worried, he dialed Gabriel's cell phone again; finally, there was an answer.

"What?!" Gabriel answered, highly agitated. His breathing was ragged and came in short gasp.

"Are you fucking?"

"Yes, Barry ... now what?" he asked once more, grunting a little as his mistress swirled her hips over his groin in a way to get him to give her all of his attention. "Ah, shit," he gasped as the pleasure hit him. "Can I call you back?" he asked between pants.

"We may have a break in the case, so I need you to meet me at the damn precinct, ASAP."

"A what? Hold on, what do you mean break-" He paused when his lover did. He looked down at her. "What wrong?"

"I'm not going to fuck you when I don't have your full attention," his mistress huffed as she slid off him, rolling over. Gabriel looked at her, clearly agitated by the entire situation. He put the phone back to his ear. "Barry, I can make it there in fifteen minutes."

"See you then." Barry hung up the phone, shaking his head. He didn't approve of his partner's secret life and he'd rather Gabriel be honest with his wife and just come clean, but he was his partner and friend and he'd keep his secret, besides, it really wasn't any of his business. He climbed into the shower.

\*\*\*

Gabriel looked at his beautiful mistress as she sat on the bed, pouting. "What's your problem? You know my job is demanding," he said coming out of the bathroom after his three-minute shower, hair still dripping wet. He was still upset that he never did get a chance to reach his climax.

She snorted. "Not just your job, Gabe. Your fucking wife is demanding, too! And your goddamn kids!"

"Now wait, hold it right there. Leave them out of this." He gave her a look that said he meant business.

"We've been through this before, when are you going to leave her?" she asked, arms folded across her pale, naked breasts.

Gabriel zipped up his pants then pulled on his shirt, buttoning it quickly. "Do we have to talk about this shit now?"

"I want to know where I stand."

He sat down in a chair as he put on his shoes, tying them. "I've been with my wife for ten years, Donna."

"That doesn't answer my fucking question, Gabe."

"I've told you what you mean to me."

"That's not enough anymore." Donna's blue eyes peered at Gabriel as he pulled on his jacket.

Finally losing his temper, he rose, storming over to the bed. "What do you want from me?! Want me to leave my wife and kids for you? Is that what you think is going to happen?"

She looked up, anger and disappointment spreading across her face.

He continued. "It's not. I love my wife, and I love my kids. I never agreed to anything more than this when we first met. I never made you any promises!"

"So, what? I'm just this piece of ass to you?"

He huffed. "You already know the answer to that question. Listen, Donna, I like you, we've had some good times, but that's all it is … good, raunchy times. Nothing more, I'm sorry."

"Get out! Get the fuck out!" Donna yelled, throwing pillows at him, which he nonchalantly batted away as he made his way to the door.

"I think it's best if I don't come back," he told her, opening the door.

"Fine! Don't!" Donna yelled.

In a final fit of rage, she threw the table lamp, which hit the door, shattering into bits and pieces. Gabriel was gone, on his way to the precinct. When he arrived, he ran into his partner, Barry in the parking lot.

"Glad you could make it," Barry teased.

Gabriel shook his head. "Don't start with me, please. I've been through enough as it is. What's this about a break in the case?"

Barry looked at his friend and partner, deciding not to pry. He began to tell him what Matthew said. " … And that's when I called you."

"Shit, at least it's something," Gabriel agreed. They met up with the other four detectives gathered around Warren and Matthew's desk. Introductions were made quickly. Immediately, the three shifters recognized that Gabriel had recently had sex, but was left unfulfilled. They also knew he had two female scents on him. Warren and Matthew knew one was his wife; the other more recent one was his mistress. They decided not to pass judgment, not knowing the full story, didn't seem fair.

"What should we do now?" Gabriel asked.

"These guys could be anywhere, but I think we should start with schools, which are now letting out. Captain's got patrol units as far as we could stretch them. We just need to join the patrol, maybe that'll make them too nervous to act," Warren suggested.

"I just thought I mention this, but these guys kind of like publicity and the more eyes on them, I think it makes the game more fun for them," Brian pointed out.

"We've got to do something," Barry said. "We'll patrol the north side."

Warren nodded. "We should break up. Colin, I think you should come with me, you don't know this city."

Colin nodded. "That's fine with me. Brian, you go with Matthew."

They made their teams and left to stake out their designated spots. Inside the car, Matthew called Adrian's cell phone. He answered.

"What's up?" Adrian asked.

"Where are you guys at now?"

"Glenview, why? Got something for us?"

"Yeah." He told them their plan.

"Really? I know that the others are kind of spread out around the state, I'll give my dad a call and tell him, thanks."

They ended their call.

"Your Pack?" Brian asked.

Matthew nodded. "Well, the man I was talking to is from Warren's Pack. But one of my Pack members is with him as well as another friend of mine. Our leaders are taking it upon themselves to assist in our investigation. We all want to stop these killers as fast as possible."

"Your communities work *together*?" Brian asked, eyebrows raised in astonishment.

Matthew shrugged as he steered the car. "Yours don't?"

Brian shook his head. "Not really. We're spaced out pretty far from each other's territories and don't communicate that much. There are four supernatural communities in California. My wolf Pack controls all of LA, the vampires run San Francisco, the hyenas run northern California, they have a pretty big Pack." He chuckled. "And the cheetahs run most of the southern/western territories. When we were going through what you're going through now, the vampires were the only ones who were actually trying to deal with it. Even my Alpha felt it was a vampire affair since vampires were the ones doing the killing. When the Second Phase hit, my Alpha got involved. But, for whatever reason, they left after leaving a cold trail of thirteen bodies. It just stopped after a three-day killing spree. I don't know if the same thing is going to happen here or not, but that's what happened two years ago."

"I don't want them to relocate, I want them to burn in hell," Matthew said through clinched teeth.

"My feelings exactly." Brian looked out of the window then turned toward Matthew again. "I hope I'm not being too forward, but I'm just curious, how did you two meet; you and Warren?"

"That's a long story." Matthew smiled.

"We've got a long drive ahead, why not?"

"I'll tell you mine if you tell me yours?"

"Sure."

Matthew began telling him how he and Warren had met and how they ended up partners on the S.U.I.T. force.

"I can tell you're a new shifter ... a coyote, how did that happen-if you don't mind me asking. Stop me if you think I'm being a nosy bastard." Brian tossed him a handsome smile.

"Naw it's cool. We're all in the same pool, right?"

"Yeah, your secret's safe with me."

Matthew told him he was attacked in a territory battle and that's how he was turned. "It's still taking some time for me to adjust, but I'm getting there. I think that's why Warren paired you with me."

Brian nodded. "I know how it is at first. I was born one, but of course, you can smell that can't you?"

"Yeah, it's a different scent, almost intoxicating ... definitely more animalistic. Nothing I would have picked up on if I was still human."

Matthew chuckled nervously. He was beginning to smell something else, and that was Brian's desire rising and knew the wolf was sexually attracted to him. Being flirted with by another shifter brought on an entirely different sensation, one that he'd only been familiar with through Warren. He could feel his own body reacting to the aura filling the car and was beginning to get uncomfortable.

"So," Brian began, his voice low, seductive. He knew that the younger shifter was reacting to the arousing waves he was emanating. "This thing between you and Warren, is it serious?"

"Yes!" Matthew exclaimed a bit too enthusiastically. "Very serious, I'm in love with him." He hoped he got the message through.

Brian settled back against the seat cushion. "Serious, eh?" He looked down at Matthew semi-erection. "Oookaaay."

Matthew knew what that meant, knew what the cop was referring to. He pulled the car over. Turning in his seat, he gave him his full attention. "Listen, Brian, I've got nothing against you. I'm actually flattered that you find me attractive, but don't let my reaction fool you. The only person I've ever wanted is Warren."

"Is that why you're sitting there with a rock-hard dick?"

"Semi-hard--thank you, and that's beside the point. Even if I was interested, and I'm not, I still wouldn't do anything with you. I'm loyal to Warren."

Brian laughed. He held his hands up in surrender. "Okay, okay … can't blame a guy for trying. I'm not going to hit on you anymore. Don't worry; I respect your loyalty to your partner. I'm not one to be a home wrecker."

"Good, I thought I was going to have to toss you from the car," Matthew said, chuckling.

Brian raised both eyebrows. "You think that you could have?"

"I don't know." Matthew shrugged with a smile. Maybe … maybe not."

"I would think not." Brian smirked. "Okay, let's go. I'm hoping we'll be able to catch his scent."

Matthew looked at him curiously. "Do you know his scent?"

"I smelled it on the corpses of the people he killed. I've never come face to face with him or the vampires he's associated with … "

Brian looked out of the window. " ... But I'd know it if I smelled it."

They drove on, with the windows down. It was worth a shot as far as they were concerned. "So ... how long have you and Colin been partners?"

Brian shrugged. "About three years."

"Is he trustworthy?"

"As far as I know, yes."

"Well, if you don't mind me asking, why haven't you told him what you are?"

"Did you know about Warren right away, did he come right out and tell you what he was?" Brian looked at him.

Matthew thought back to those days when he was left puzzled by Warren's amazing abilities and not having a name to identify them. He remembered the day he found out about Warren and the tension between them afterward. "No, he didn't come right out and tell me anything. I had to find out after he had been shot. I watched him heal right before my eyes."

"How did you take it?"

"I was fucking amazed at first. I couldn't believe it; I had had no idea what he was. Then he told me, and that was all I wanted to know for a long time. My partner, the guy I trusted with my life was a 'werewolf'. That's what I thought. But knowing that didn't make me see him any differently. The more I found out about his species, the more comfortable I became. I also know the term 'were'-anything is greatly frowned upon." He chuckled.

"Yeah, we find it insulting." Brian scanned the crowd as they drove past a school and its playground. "I don't trust my partner with my secret. He harbors too much resentment for our kind. I have to be careful every step of the way with him."

Matthew looked at the detective, feeling sorry for his situation. He wondered if Warren had ever felt that way about him?

"So, do you think these vampires can walk around during the day?" Matthew asked, changing the subject.

"Yes," Brian answered. "At least one of them can."

Matthew nodded, having his suspicions confirmed.

"To be honest with you, a vampire who can walk in the sunlight isn't one to fuck with, if you get my meaning," Briand stated.

Matthew nodded again, remembering Kysen; Darian's Maker. He was strong enough to control an entire state, not willing to share with any other supernatural. Matthew had met the Master vampire only once and still felt inferior whenever he thought about him. That was the effect of his presence, even though Kysen himself had tried to tone it down.

"I said that to tell you in all honesty, I don't know how far the resources of the S.U.I.T. will take us. From what I understand, the elders of our kinds don't fear the law, not in any form." Brian pointed to a spot where a lot of children where playing in a playground. "Think this is a good spot to stake out?"

Matthew pulled the car over, killing the engine. "As good as any." He had to agree with Brian. The resources of the S.U.I.T. may not help at all. The least they could do is point Darian and the others in the right direction. They waited, hoping to catch a sadistic killer. They knew the others were doing the same, each team hoping to get lucky.

# CHAPTER TEN

"**A**dan, do you honestly think this vampire can save us?" Stephanie asked, brushing the kinks from her long, auburn hair.

"He's the only vampire I know of that's powerful, Steph. I know we need help. I can't defeat this coven on my own; I've tried and almost died. Darian has managed to hang on to prime territory for over one hundred years. All of Illinois belongs to him, not just Chicago … that takes power and strength. This is our best chance if we want to survive." Adan, King of his lion Pride searched through the telephone book.

"What are you doing?" Stephanie asked, sitting down beside him.

"Last night, I went out and searched for him. As it turns out, he owns several businesses in the city, one of the most popular is a dance club called *Desires Unleashed*. I'm looking for the number." Flipping through the pages in the "Night Clubs/Entertainment" section, he finally found what he was looking for. "Here it is."

"Can he move around in the daytime hours like this vampire?"

"I don't know, but we need to get to him, now stop pestering me." Adan tossed her a look that showed his agitation with her.

"I'll join the others," she said, getting the point. She rose and left the little room.

Adan opted for a hotel room, hoping the pricey public location might throw the vampire coven off his trail, if only for a day. He hoped the vampires would think he'd stay lying low, as he had been doing. Somehow, that coven had always found them, no matter where they were. For a little more than a week now, he and his Pride had been moving from country to country, city to city during the day only when he knew that coven was resting, even if it's Master wasn't. The constant hiding and running … it had bought them time, hours only. The very night they arrived in Chicago, more deaths began to happen. He knew they were there. The same things happened in every city they ran to. Never in his life, had he experienced a group of supernaturals this bloodthirsty, this sadistic.

It angered and hurt him to know that his Pride doubted him. His inability to destroy their enemy had left many of them wondering if he was the leader they needed. In a heated argument, Tyler had called him a coward and gone against his wishes. He told the younger shifter to stay within the group, but frightened beyond all reasoning, he fled, hoping to find protection and solace within a cheetah Pride they had stayed with in Ireland. Adan was willing to bet the first body the Chicago S.U.I.T. had found skinned alive had been Tyler's. It was a message to him. Obviously, Adan felt guilty, more importantly, he felt helpless. Out of all the feline Prides, the lions were the only ones who depended on the male dominant to find them safe havens and be able to protect them. With his Pride being hunted and killed off one by one, he looked to be a weak King. He would be challenged; if not from within his Pride, then from other males looking to mate with his females. If he was to regain their confidence, he would have to save them and not allow anymore of his to die while he remained unable to prevent it. Needless to say, he was a bit stressed. His Matron walked into the room, climbing on the bed behind him. She began to massage his shoulders, relieving the tension.

"Breathe. Stephanie told me you almost bit her head off in here," Danielle said, her voice was calm and soothing.

Adan leaned against her, resting his head on her bosom. "She was pestering me. I've got enough people within our Pride doubting me silently. I didn't need to hear it out loud."

"No one doubts you. No one is fool enough to think you didn't do everything within your power. Even a five-hundred year old shifter cannot defend against the likes of this coven. No one blames you." She hoped she was helping ease his uncertainty.

He half turned, looking up at her. "Don't they? Tyler didn't believe in me, and now he's dead."

"We don't know that for certain."

Adan frowned. "Do you honestly believe the body they found outside of that nightclub wasn't his? That it was a message to us that they were still on our trail?"

"Logically thinking, I agree with you. Wishfully thinking, I hope not."

"Let's stick with logic right now," Adan said.

"Very well. If he is dead, it's because he was so confrontational. Sometimes testosterone is a man's worst enemy. You were wise to tell us to stay together. We're all alive because we did. He wanted to challenge you by defying your command. He failed. Do what your heart and mind tells you is right. Do not worry about what cannot be changed. Call this Darian Alexander if you think he will help us." She leaned forward, kissing him gently before climbing off the bed

"Thank you, Danielle."

"You're welcome, Darling."

"Can you send Stephanie back in here?"

"All right." With that, Danielle left the room.

Adan was happy she had talked to him; he was beginning to feel better already. He pulled his disposable cell phone from his back pocket, dialing *Desires Unleashed*. When the operator answered, he asked if or when the owner was coming in. The operator didn't know, but said she'd take a message. He gave her his cell phone number and told her to have Mr. Alexander call him as soon as possible. The operator took the message and they ended the call. He leaned back against the pillow, concentrating on his next move. He knew that the vampire coven that hunted his Pride was an old and dangerous one; he only hoped that Darian would be able and willing to help them.

Stephanie poked her head into the room slowly; hoping Adan's "little talk" with Danielle had cooled some of his temper. "Danny said you wanted to talk to me?"

He looked up. "Yes, I'm going out to get something for us to eat, I would like for you to come with me." He rose, stretching his muscles.

"Sure, let me just put on my shoes." Stephanie went to do just that, returning wearing pair of brown leather sandals to match her khaki capri pants and shirt.

"What do you want to eat?" he asked as they made their way to one of their rental cars he paid for under an alias.

"Pizza is quick and filling." Stephanie looked out of the window as they sped by hundreds of people and buildings. "Adan, I've been trying not to think about it, but I'm really scared."

Adan winced. Her feelings of fright stung like a gunshot wound. He had never wanted his Pride to feel fear. He'd promised to always protect them, and now it was looking like he wasn't going to be able to. He knew he had to do something quick, he hoped Darian would help him not only save his Pride, but save face as well. "Don't worry, Stephanie. I'll die before I let anything happen to any of you. You know this." He maneuvered the car between two towering SUVs in the parking lot of a well-known pizzeria restaurant.

"I know. I trust you. I just hate that we're in this situation, fucking asshole coven," she snarled.

Adan chuckled softly, agreeing with her sentiments. "Let's go get something for us to eat." They exited the car and entered the restaurant.

*** 

"God, that tastes horrible. Jeez, who do you have to arrest to get a decent cup of coffee around here?" Colin groaned after swallowing a mouthful of lukewarm coffee, which lacked the amount of sugar and cream he desired.

"Hey, you want gourmet, you're going to end up paying at least three dollars more," Warren commented. He peered out of the window at the children finally happy to see the end of the school day, eagerly climbing into their parent's automobiles. Each child's face featured smiles and all were unaware of the danger that may be lurking nearby. They wanted to catch this killer before any more lives would be put into jeopardy.

"When this coven ran amok in California, it was really fucked up. The entire city was scarred shitless and no one knew when the killings would end. The thing is, you don't want them to end just because the killers got bored; you want them to end because the killers got caught, know what I mean?" Colin asked. He made certain to keep his eyes on all of the children and their comings and goings.

"Did you ever think you guys were close to catching them before they left?" Warren asked, curious to know if they had a chance.

Colin was silent for a few seconds; ashamed of the answer he was going to have to give him. "No."

"No? Why not?"

"They can kill every hour on the hour, if they wanted to. Shit, they damn near did."

"So, in other words, it was a blessing when they got bored with California and moved on?" Warren wasn't sure how he felt about the sentiment. He didn't want them to be able to "move on". He wanted them *dead as hell!*

Colin continued. "I'm not happy about it either, but for lack of a better explanation, yes, you can say that I was somewhat relieved when they moved on. I had hoped someone would be able to take them out if they slipped up. I've never seen anything like the carnage they caused, and the S.U.I.T. for all intent and purposes was powerless against them, just like we are now."

"You don't have any faith in us?" Warren was shocked to hear that from a S.U.I.T. officer. Most officers he knew believed they were the end-all to all supernatural criminals. Needless to say, most S.U.I.T. officers had God complexes.

"I'm not stupid, or idealistic. I know when I'm fighting a battle I can't win. From all of the knowledge we've manage to gather about vampires and shape-shifters, at no point did we ever discover a vampire who can kill during the daylight hours, am I right?"

Warren nodded. The human world did only know so much and the supernatural Council was hard-pressed to expose anything else.

"What about human servants?" Warren asked, fishing to see if he would agree with another scenario.

"What about them?"

"Could it be possible for a human servant to keep a victim alive long enough to dispose of the body during the day?" Warren asked.

"I guess anything is possible. We never found any trace of human involvement, but that's not to say there isn't any."

"I just don't want to rule it out."

"No, I wouldn't either, but some of the victims we found would suggest otherwise. Now, I'm no expert dealing with vampires, but I'm willing to bet my hairy left nut that one would have to be pretty fucking old to kill under the shining rays of the sun."

Okay, human or not human, Warren was impressed by his deduction. "I would have to agree with you, based on what I'm seeing so far."

"Exactly. I don't know what your hardest arrest or take down was, but Brian and I almost died taking out one vampire who we caught feeding on prostitutes. I honestly don't know how we survived. Brian was amazing and quick on the draw; he was the one who killed him. But that vampire only killed during the night and was pretty terrified when he realized he was caught; that tells me he was young probably just turned. People who think they are above the law don't get panic attacks. I'm willing to bet an older vampire would fit into that category."

"How come none of this was reported?" Warren asked, wondering why that bit of information had been omitted.

"A lot of that was kept secret during their reign. We were instructed to keep a lid on that so as not to cause public panic. Not to mention, the government's invested a lot of time and money into the S.U.I.T. We're supposed to be the final word in supernatural justice. If the public knew just how useless we were made to look, that would really hurt the bottom line, know what I mean?" Colin looked at Warren.

"That would explain why the media is being heavily monitored right now." Warren thought about the light media coverage in spite of the extremely public crime scenes. It was all starting to make some sense now.

"Yeah, seems like a repeat of L.A." Colin pulled out his cell phone, "I'm going to contact Brian, see how things are looking on their end."

Warren was shocked at how much Colin suspected. He also wondered how much the government knew to be a fact about supernaturals, even though the Council only confirmed so much of the information that was previously gathered six years ago. He listened to the conversation between Colin and his partner. Apparently, things were looking quiet on their end as well. He hoped that, with the help of their leaders and respective covens, Prides and Packs, they would have success where the others failed.

***

"Fuck, I'm tired as hell right now," Gabriel said, rubbing his eyes with the palm of his hands.

Barry chuckled. "Should have taken your ass to sleep instead of getting your rocks off."

"You just had to bring that up, didn't you?"

Barry looked at him. "Why don't you divorce Melinda instead of sneaking around with random broads?"

"It's complicated, Barry. Melinda and I have been going through a rough patch right now. We haven't slept in the same bed in over six months. She doesn't even want me to touch her," Gabriel said, finally confiding in his friend.

"Maybe you two need to talk to a therapist, it worked wonders for Leanne and me. Here, let me give you the number of our therapist, Dr. Amelia Watson … you'll love her, trust me."

Barry wrote down his therapist's number on a piece of paper and handed it to Gabriel, who took the paper, looked at it and slipped it into his front side pocket.

"I'll try anything right now. I really want to open the lines of communication with my wife." Gabriel took a sip of his mocha cappuccino.

"What do you think caused the riff?" Barry returned his attention back to the little children who were playing in the park, swinging on swings and sliding down slides.

"She hasn't been the same since … ." Gabriel's voice trailed off.

Barry finished his sentence for him. "Since the car accident?"

Gabriel nodded. "I don't think she believes I still find her desirable. She's been pushing me away ever since. Hell, for all I know, she might resent the fact that I walked away virtually unharmed when she didn't. I even think she blames me for the accident. I keep going over all of these reasons why my wife has grown so cold towards me … any one could be an answer or all of the above, ya know?"

Two years ago, Gabriel had been driving that rainy night, when he swerved to avoid a drunk driver and ending up ramming their SUV into a tree. While he survived the accident with only a few cuts and bruises, his wife suffered broken bones in her face and torso so severe, it required multiple plastic surgeries to restore her features and limbs as close to their natural state as possible. In the end, her confidence was not so easily restored.

Barry turned back toward his partner and best friend. "Do you?"

"Do I what?"

"Still find her desirable?"

"I love her."

"That may be, but do you still find her desirable. I mean, I saw your piece of ass on the side, she looks like a poster pinup model, and that's even without the fake tits."

"She was easy, she scratched an itch, and most importantly, she's old news. I broke it off today."

"Got too clingy?" Barry chuckled softly.

Gabriel chortled. "Yeah, she wanted me to leave my family for her."

"You still didn't answer my question?"

"Oh, I thought I did. Yes, I find her desirable. Every time I try to get intimate, she comes up with an excuse to put distance between us. This has been going on for almost two years, to the point now, we don't sleep in the same bed, like I said."

"Call the therapist, it's worth a shot. I know you don't want a divorce."

Gabriel shook his head. "The kids would be devastated. But shit, enough about my problems. I'm more interested in catching these killers. What they did to those people, especially the last two children … fucking sick sons-of-bitches."

Barry nodded. "Truer words … While you were in the john, I called Davis and Eric, everything's quiet on their end as well."

"They'll slip up soon enough, we'll catch them, I'm sure. I'm kind of happy the captain put us on this case, too. It gives us a chance to prove that we're just as good as her 'Golden Boys'."

"You've got to admit, Gabe, Warren and Matthew are excellent detectives."

Gabriel shot a glance at him. "Whose side are you on?"

Barry snorted. "I'm merely stating a fact. It's not like they haven't earned the right to be considered two of the best, Gabe. Besides, we're on this case because we're just as good; our record is second only to theirs in the department. I'm just giving credit to where credit is due. I'm sure there are others who complain about us, like those assholes Ronen and Wilson."

"Kyle and Lance can kiss my ass, for all I care. Worst fucking cops on the S.U.I.T., if you ask me. I don't know why they're still there."

"Because they fly under the radar low enough to escape disciplinary action." Barry leaned forward, peering more closely through his window. "Look at this guy right here, watch him. He came from that car over there which has been parked there for thirty minutes."

Gabriel leaned over, watching a man dressed in a white t-shirt with a black windbreaker jacket with a sport's team emblem on the back. His dark blue jeans were frayed at the cuffs and his black work boots were a bit worn at the toe. "Yeah I've got him in my vision. Do we wait for him to make a move, or approach him now?"

"If this is the guy, we don't want to get him without allowing him a chance to give us the evidence we need to nail his balls to the concrete. If he goes for one of these kids, we take him down fast," Barry said. "You better call the others just to tell them we have someone suspicious lurking about the playground."

Gabriel did just that, notifying the other two teams of their current status. The two detectives continued to monitor the mysterious man who was watching the children. After another twenty minutes, the man decided to make his move, making his way into the frenzied group of playful children. The two officers continued to observe as the man pulled money out of his pocket, handing each of the five children who were still gathered around him a dollar. He offered to buy them all ice cream. Once each of the children had their frozen treats, he continued to seduce the children with more goodies. The two officers climbed out of their car, making their way over to the man from behind. They heard him offer the children more candy. Two of the children decided to go with him. He took their hands and turned, coming face-to-face with the two detectives, badges bared, which stopped him dead in his tracks. He let the two children go as he dashed to the side, feet hitting the pavement at top speed, running as fast as he could with both detectives hot on his trail.

When they finally closed the distance between them, Gabriel lunged forward, tackling the man to the ground in the middle of the parking lot of a grocery store.

Barry came around, gun pointed at the assailant. "Stay down! Don't fucking move! Now, slowly, put your hands-palms down on the ground ... I said slowly!"

The man did as he was told. He dared not move as the other officer locked a silver cuff around one wrist, then wrenching his other arm around his back, doing the same to that wrist. Gabriel pressed the barrel of his gun against the man's spine, jabbing him slightly, causing a bit of pain.

Gabriel wasn't sure if this guy was a part of the gang of killers they were chasing, he knew he was human; a shape-shifter was often too fast for them to catch on foot. Not to mention, the silver handcuff were having no effect on him. Nonetheless, it was time to ask a few questions. For all he knew, this guy might be their human servant, if they had one, out collecting victims for them.

"What were you doing at the park? What were you planning on doing with those kids?"

"Nothing," the man lied. "I was just buying them some treats, that's all? I swear."

"Cut the bullshit, don't fucking play with me, I do have a license to kill on the spot." Gabriel poked him with the barrel once more.

"You can't do that, Police can't kill on the spot! You have to find me guilty of something, and you didn't!" The man shot back, certain that he was correct in his understanding of standard law and police procedures.

"Police can't. S.U.I.T. can. All I have to do is suspect you're a supernatural up to no good, and I'm already at that point. Now, do you want to help your case by answering my questions, or are you going to continue to piss me the fuck off?"

Barry watched his partner's interrogation. He looked around, making sure no one interfered.

The man on the ground swallowed hard then nodded. "Don't kill me, I'll corporate, I promise. Please let me up," he begged.

"I'm still waiting for an answer." Gabriel was thankful that the procedures that govern the S.U.I.T. allowed him a great deal of leeway, since they were the judge, jury and executioner in certain matters dealing with various suspects. Humans however were a trickier matter entirely. In the past, humans suspected of being supernaturals had been killed on the spot. As long as it was proven that S.U.I.T. officers were justified, no disciplinary action were taken. Knowing he was bluffing somewhat, Gabriel chose to keep the man under duress, hoping he'll be more willing to answer his questions honestly.

The man beneath him  began to mumble and sob profusely.

"Speak up, I can't hear you," Gabriel ordered. Apparently, his plan was working better than even he had anticipated.

"I'm a bad man. I'm a sick man ... I need help," the man sobbed. "I wanted those kids ... I ... I wanted to touch them. I'm sorry. I'm so, so, sorry!" He sobbed even more, snot running freely from his nose.

Gabriel looked up at Barry; neither man said anything to the other. They knew that they hadn't caught their target, but they had caught a predator none the less. Gabriel climbed off the man then hoisted him to his feet. They escorted the suspected child molester back to the squad car, shoving him in the back seat.

"Call the PD, tell them we've got one of theirs," Gabriel told Barry, who did just that.

Gabriel called Warren and told him what had transpired.

"Well, at least you took down one scumbag, keep your eyes open," Warren said.

"Yeah, same to you," Gabriel replied, before ending the call.

The two S.U.I.T. officers waited for the police to come get their suspect. Once the exchange took place, Gabriel and Barry drove to another location, believing that their current stakeout was now compromised. If the killer was there, chances were, he wasn't going to attack. They parked outside the After-School Community Center where kids of all ages congregated for activities and tutoring.

"The quest continues … " Gabriel mumbled, watching the center.

"You did well back there, I just wanted to tell you that," Barry complimented.

Gabriel smiled. The two detectives continued to search for their killers, hoping to get a break sooner than later.

# CHAPTER ELEVEN

Kiren devoured as much of his victims as he could eat, and now he sat in the back of the ice cream truck in his half beast form, licking their blood from the palms of his hands. Finally, he transformed back into his human appearance, burping loudly. He smiled down at the bloody, gnarled and grotesque remains of his meal, relishing the memory of their fears, their cries and screams and how no one could have helped them by stopping him. He made certain to leave little pieces of flesh attached to each mutilated corpse so that the S.U.I.T. would be able to identify the bodies of each kid, but he didn't make it easy.

One corpse had half a face. One, the tip of a finger still had a piece of skin attached. Another had an eyeball still in the socket, and the last had its full facial features, but the skull was completely shattered, disfiguring the appearance of the child. What was left of the remains was piled high inside the freezer. Dressing quickly, he exited the truck, smiling to himself. His lover would be proud of him. He would delight in recounting how he managed to sway the children to him. It was easy, he'd tell him. The cheerful tunes from an ice cream truck always bring out the children. Once he found his victim, he snatched the child inside; making sure no one saw him. Then he would drive to another location and do it all over again. He made certain to let many children go away happy, with their ice cream cones. He did notice the increase in police and S.U.I.T. patrol and he found it hilarious. No matter how many cops they put on the street, he was certain none would be able to stop him. He was right. Once he had captured the children he wanted, he parked his truck in front of a church. It was at that moment he indulged himself, savoring his "meal". *Yes, his lover would be so very pleased.*

He watched the truck, waiting for his little playthings to be discovered. After waiting for the sun to set which wasn't too much longer, his lover and Master appeared, settling down silently on the rooftop beside him.

"Having fun?" his lover asked.

"I'd be having even more fun if the law officials would actually pick up on my set-up," Kiren complained. "You know how impatient I can be."

"Want my help?"

"Would you?"

"For you, anything." Marcus smiled as he mentally searched for a child nearby walking with his mother. He controlled the two, forcing them to walk toward the abandoned ice cream truck. Then he planted suspicion in their minds and left them to their own devices. "There, that ought to do it."

"Thanks. So what were you doing earlier?" Kiren asked.

"I was watching the other shape-shifters who occupy this territory. They work together, which is odd. I can honestly say that I hadn't anticipated this manner of unification. The last time I saw more than two species living together in harmony, was … maybe three hundred years ago in Beijing. For the most part, we are all very territorial and oftentimes, each other's domain is not breached by the other. However, these supernaturals that live here are not only sharing this entire territory, but they are friends and lovers. I'm extremely intrigued." Marcus looked down at his lover, his long blond lashes practically brushing his cheeks.

"Well, it's an anomaly, no denying that. What about the vampire Master here?"

Marcus smiled. "He started early this evening, searching the cities. I've taken great pleasure in spying on him. I don't know how old he is, because I do not wish to alert him to my presence by invading his mind. When I am ready, I'll do so, but not now. He also left instructions for a few of his coven vamps to search for us in teams of twos. Only he is searching alone, oh, and he's left the rest of his coven to watch over his humans."

"Should we pay him a visit, kill his humans?" Kiren asked, wanting to perform yet another bold move.

"Not yet... all in good time, my impatient one. Right now, I want to watch him sweat. I want to watch all of them sweat and I want to smell their fears rise from beneath the surface."

Marcus stepped behind his lover, wrapping his arms around the shifter. He leaned forward, burying his face in the other man's neck, sinking his fangs. Kiren gasped, arching against his lover's chest. He moaned in ecstasy as his blood rushed through his veins toward the vampire's thirst. Reaching up, he pressed the back of Marcus' head closer to him, pushing the fangs deeper into his flesh. The vampire's mouth widen, taking in more blood. Finally, the moment came that they were both waiting for. Indescribable pleasure coiled inside of them, working its way toward the surface. Marcus covered Kiren's mouth with his hand, muffling the shifter's screams of his sexual release as their orgasms exploded; one dry, one wet. Once, he was done, he pulled away, retracting his fangs. He held Kiren against him as the younger man's body shook in the aftermath.

"Can you stand?" Marcus asked once his lover's body ceased its erratic movements.

Kiren nodded weakly. "Please," he panted.

Marcus smiled, knowing full well what the shifter wanted. "Please what?"

"Let me taste you, I want it … I need it!" Kiren begged, desperately.

Without making him suffer further, Marcus ran a razor sharp nail across the blue vein beneath the skin of his wrist, opening it. Blood bubbled up from the wound, and Kiren dove for his wrist, instantly locking his mouth around the fount, sucking greedily. Falling to his knees in front of Marcus, Kiren's mouth remained fastened to the wrist he held firmly in his grip. He sucked harder and harder enjoying every drop. In the distance, he could hear Marcus moan and he knew he was the reason for the Master vampire's pleasure and that excited him even more. Time seemed to stand still; he only became aware of it when Marcus pried his wrist free from him.

Kiren looked up, dazed and still under the effects of the vampire's blood. He groped for Marcus' wrist, reaching behind him for it. "Please! More!"

Marcus pushed him down and immediately pressed his foot on the shifter's chest, pinning him to the tar-covered roof. "Gain control, Kiren, or we'll not do this again." His voice was low, but commanding, forcing the other man to come to his senses. He knew it was a struggle for his shape-shifter lover to do so, but he was satisfied when he finally did. Once Kiren had regained his composure, he removed his foot.

"I'm sorry," Kiren apologized, looking up at him.

"Do I have to wean you off my blood?" Marcus asked with both eyebrows cocked.

Kiren shook his head. "No. I'll do better next time. I won't act that way. It was just, earlier I fed so much … the blood, it only added."

"I'll let it slide this time, but do not behave this way again." Marcus held his hand out, offering to help Kiren to his feet.

Once the shifter was standing, both men watched as a police squad car pulled up next to the ice cream truck.

"Ah, finally, things are starting to pick up," Kiren said, smiling. He was still buzzing from the blood flowing inside of him as well as from being bitten. His face lit up with glee as he watched the officer approach the ice cream truck with a flashlight, peering into the windows.

***

The officer walked around the truck, examining every detail. He called in the license plate number and waited to get a reply. When he heard back from dispatch, it was as he suspected. That ice cream truck was the same one reported missing along with the driver only a few hours earlier. The cop continued his investigation, using a handkerchief to open the unlocked door. Stepping inside, he looked around, guiding the flashlight over the compartments of the truck's interior. The first thing he noticed that was out of the ordinary was the large puddle of blood that covered the floor. He immediately called for back-up. The blood trail led to the freezer, which he followed, carefully stepping around the blood as not to contaminate the evidence. Using the same handkerchief, he opened the freezer door, peaking inside. He closed it quickly, fumbling backward, bumping into a shelf. He stepped into the puddle of blood in his haste to exit the truck. Once outside, he ran toward his squad car as he fumbled with the radio attached to his uniform. He called in a code 1-8-7 and he was in the middle of reporting what he'd seen when a violent wave of nausea caused him to lurch forward. He vomited a filthy stream of a half-digested combination of cheeseburger, fries and milkshake on the ground beside his car.

Once he was done, still shaking from his entire ordeal, he continued to report back to dispatch. Within a matter of minutes, two more blue and white squad cars pulled up, not fully aware that the initial report was now confirmed to be a S.U.I.T. matter. The four officers got out, immediately checking on their fellow officer. He told them what he'd seen and two of the officers went to investigate for themselves. One cop had the same reaction the first officer had, vomiting in the alley beside the church. The other criticized the first for leaving a footprint in the blood. He told him the bloody footprint led from the truck to his squad car.

"I didn't expect to find what I did, okay! Fuck!" Officer Brown cursed as he ran his hands over his buzz cut. Sixteen months on the Force, he'd never seen anything like what he saw piled in that freezer.

"Let's just hope the S.U.I.T. doesn't try to chew our asses for it, that's all I'm saying." Officer Nicholls said then he turned toward his partner. "You okay?"

His partner, Officer Beals nodded. "I'll tell you what, I'm glad we don't have to deal with this shit. Anyone who can do that to children needs to be fucking skinned, burned and buried alive."

"So now what, we just wait on them?" Officer Townsend asked, another rookie, six months new to the Force.

"Yeah, that's how this kind of thing works," his partner Officer Whitney confirmed. Several other squad cars pulled up, the police maintained the scene blocking it off with the official S.U.I.T. tape they were provided with, keeping onlookers from getting too close as they waited for the S.U.I.T. to arrive.

*** 

"Well, that was entertaining," Marcus said, chuckling.

"Yeah, their reaction was funny, but I really want to see what the S.U.I.T.'s reaction is going to be." Kiren was impatient; he wanted to see the next stage of law enforcement's reaction to his handiwork. "By the way, what are the others doing?"

"They're feeding and searching for my little lion Pride that we tracked here."

"Adan and his women … I can't wait to get my paws on them." Kiren smiled wickedly.

Marcus tossed him a look. "I'm sure."

"Shouldn't be too hard to find them," Kiren speculated.

"We always do, no matter what tricks he comes up with. I will admit, he's a crafty one, and he's making the chase very exciting. It's because of him that we found this interesting little territory. Eventually, I'll have my way with him and the inhabitants of this city. For now, we haven't even begun to turn this place upside down."

The two men waited for the S.U.I.T., which they knew were on the way.

***

Sitting in their cars in separate locations, the S.U.I.T. detectives assigned to the case all received simultaneous calls. They answered their cells and dispatch gave them the information. Once they had the location of the newest victims, they each raced to the scene. Warren and Colin were first to arrive. They entered the truck, viewed the carnage, and exited. Both came out, taking deep breaths, each for different reasons. Warren's hunger was growing as was his disgust and Colin was fighting the nausea that swirled in his stomach as well as his own repulsion for the way the children were murdered. When Matthew and Brian arrived, they both had the same reaction as Warren, Matthew struggling a lot more to contain his animalistic urges and hunger.

"My God … my God!" Brian hissed, unable to hide his emotions as he leaned against Warren's car.

"I take it they've increased their creativity when it comes to how they murder their victims from when you had to deal with them?" Warren speculated, judging by both Colin's and Brian's reaction, he knew he was right.

Brian shook his head. "Nothing like this."

Colin nodded. "Nothing," he added.

Clicking his cell phone closed, Matthew gave everyone the update. "All right, Marshall's team is on their way, should be here in the next fifteen minutes. We need to talk with an Officer Brown, since he was the one who first discovered the bodies, also, it's his bloody footprint that contaminated the evidence." He wanted to keep everyone focused.

"We'll speak with the mother and son who called in the abandoned truck," Colin said, tapping his partner on the arm, getting his attention. The two walked toward and patrol officer who pointed out the woman and child standing behind the red and white S.U.I.T. tape. Brian nodded in return and they headed in her direction. By the time Warren and Matthew were done questioning Officer Brown, Barry and Gabriel had arrived. Pulling in behind them was Marshall and his team in two Sidewinder S.U.I.T. SUVs.

Barry and Gabriel approached Warren and Matthew as the two detectives were making their way around the ice cream truck.

"We got here as fast as we could," Gabriel said. "How many victims?"

"Four. From what I saw, they're all little children," Warren answered.

"Jesus Christ," Gabriel hissed. Exasperated, he rubbed his hands over his face, palm covering his mouth as he struggled to maintain his emotional control.

Barry patted his partner on his back. He looked at the other two detectives. "Whose shoe print is that?" He pointed to the bloody shoe print trail leading away from the truck.

"Don't get too excited, it belongs to a PC who fucked up the scene after viewing the bodies. He ran from the truck and puked his guts out somewhere over there," Warren said, gesturing toward the cop's patrol car.

"Shit, how bad did he fuck up the scene?" Gabriel asked.

"Just the shoe print. Marshall and CSI should be able to work around it. He said he didn't touch anything and used a handkerchief to open all of the doors," Matthew answered.

"At least he did that part right," Gabriel remarked.

"What else do you have?" Barry asked.

Warren shrugged one shoulder. "It's disappointing, because it isn't much. What you see here, is what we've got, nothing more," he said, handing Barry his note pad.

The two detectives were going over the other's notes when Brian and Colin joined them.

Brian filled the others in on what they found out. "She doesn't know anything. She said her and her son 'suddenly wanted ice cream for some reason'. They looked over and saw the truck, approached it and saw that no one was inside. She then called the company to report an abandoned truck. She said she wasn't quite sure why she did any of it. What do you guys make of that?" he asked the others.

Warren and Matthew gave each other knowing looks. They were thinking the same thing … they suspected that woman and her child were under vampire manipulation. Warren couldn't wait to call Xander and report this; all he needed was a minute alone to do so. He decided he should excuse himself at that moment. The other detectives nodded, not fully concerned about where he was going as they continued their own speculations.

Warren pulled out his cell phone and called Xander. When his Alpha picked up, he began telling him everything.

"My God," Xander said, appalled. "I'll get back with you. First I need to make some telephone calls."

"Sure thing, I'll keep you posted." Warren closed his flip cell and returned to the others. The detectives waited around for Marshall's preliminary report. They kept watch as Marshall and his team along with CSI meticulously worked the scene as they continued their own investigation. However, they weren't the only ones watching.

\*\*\*

Kiren and Marcus watched and listened to the controlled chaos below, each pleased with the outcome.

"This is the beauty of it, they don't know when it's going to end, they don't know how to stop it, and they don't know anything more than what we want them to know. They are completely in the dark … all of them," Kiren said, smiling.

"And it's right where I want them," Marcus agreed.

"The wolf called his Alpha, this should be interesting."

Marcus looked at him. "Why? Why would it be interesting?"

"Because, the Alpha, this Alexander … he's going to call the Master vampire and maybe the other leaders and I think we should stick around to see if they come to see for themselves; my artistic contribution," Kiren replied.

"Oh, they'll come … but I'll be the one waiting for them, not you."

Kiren's gaze shot toward Marcus. "I want to stay. I want to see their fucking faces. Why do I have to leave?"

Marcus took hold of his chin, applying a bit of pressure, silencing the shifter. He tilted his head upward so that their eyes met. "I realize that I allow you to take certain liberties and I'm not as strict with you as perhaps, I should be. But never forget who and what I am. Never forget that I don't have to answer to you. I don't have to explain my reasoning to you. Have I made myself perfectly clear?"

"Yes." Kiren nodded with some difficulty. "Perfectly. I'm sorry."

Marcus released him. "Good. In addition, to emphasize my meaning, I'll refrain from explaining my reasons for why I don't want you here. As a matter of fact, leave now."

Kiren frowned, but he dared not argue anymore. Instead, he leaped from the rooftop away from prying eyes and ran faster than any mortal or shifter in the area could see. As Marcus watched him retreat, he smiled. The last thing he wanted was for their target to zero in on his shifter, his lover and occasional "pain in the ass". Cloaking his aura, which helped him contain his scent, he blended into the curious crowd effortlessly. A younger vampire wouldn't be able to pull such a stunt off as they don't have the ability. He did and he was intrigued and wanted to see the others when they arrived.

\*\*\*

Xander ended his final call for the moment. He'd called Darian, Elise, and Richard, alerting them of the newest developments. Darian and Richard were going to go to the scene. Elise decided to drive around with Sergio, patrolling the city. She shared the others feelings of anger, pain and frustration. The coven killed people in various locations throughout the state, but she believed that their main hideout was Chicago and she wanted to see if they would be able to track them down from there instead of running around the entire state as they had done earlier. For some reason, Elise believed the coven felt it would be a greater insult to hide right in the very heart of the city, right under their noses. Xander suspected that they might be in the nearby suburbs of Chicago, simply hovering over the city to keep from being easily detected. Both ideas were acceptable so he decided to send Adrian and Nagesa to one suburb. Tatiana and Justin were sent to another while he investigated one on his own. Elise sent Daniel and Carmen to search the north and south side of Chicago, while Miranda searched the west side. It was worth a shot, of that, they were certain.

# CHAPTER  TWELVE

Darian thought that their plan was practical, as best as any he'd be able to come up with. He traveled to the location of the most current crime scene, noting a shifter was involved. He met up with Richard who was standing nearest the truck in question.

"Richard," Darian greeted, cutting past his usual pleasantries.

The other man looked at him. "Darian," Richard replied in the same fashion.

"Were you able to gather a distinct scent?" Darian asked.

"Yes. The shifter is male, and he's a lion … which means he's extremely territorial, more so than other male shifters. His scent inside of the truck is hours old, but the scent I smelled when I first arrived was fresh, had to be no more than twenty minutes old. He was just here. I'm suspecting he claims this scene as his territory and most likely wanted to see the commotion he created," Richard replied.

"So, it's just the one scent, then?" Darian noted. He was keeping track of how many were involved. So far, he had four vampires and one shape-shifter … more then he'd like.

Richard nodded. "Just the one … at this scene, that is. This is the 'Second Phase' Matthew told me about. I haven't had a chance to speak with him yet, he's over there." He gestured toward his young Pack member standing next to Warren and two other detectives.

The two men stayed silent as they listened to the gossip around them, in hopes of gathering more pertinent information. Apparently, four children had been brutally slain. Their bodies had been partially eaten and mutilated; body parts dismembered in some grotesque fashion, completely deliberate. Darian listened to Marshall speaking with the six detectives, giving them his report. The medical examiner said he'd never seen anything quite like what was in the freezer. He told them that the children looked to be between the ages of five and eight, no more than ten based on the size of the bones and skulls. He mentioned how intricate details were left on the remains from what he could see.

It was at that point when Warren stated; "it was left on purpose so that we could find out who the kids were". Adding to that, Matthew said; "they needed to get in contact with the police throughout the state to see who had filed missing persons' reports and in which city". The detectives decided one team needed to stay to continue the investigation while the others should head back to the precinct in order to make those numerous telephone calls. Warren noticed Darian and Richard among the observers and once again, he excused himself, which seemed to make two of the other detectives curious. They watched as Warren made his way over to the crowd.

Darian and Richard stepped closer to the tape as Warren drew nearer. They had heard everything that was said and believed the officers were on the right track, but now both men wanted to know exactly what was on his mind that he couldn't say to the others he was with, with the exception of Matthew. They also acknowledged that one of the other detectives was also a shape-shifter, a wolf. Both Darian and Richard found that interesting.

Once Warren was standing face-to-face, he began to speak. "Okay, I'm sure Xander told you about the mother and son and how she somehow felt compelled to buy ice cream. Then when she noticed the empty truck, how she called the company to report it. The owner said that the driver never did check back in to report locations, and he had begun to worry. When she called him, he called the police because it was the end of the driver's shift and he hadn't returned the truck or signed out. That's when Officer Brown came out here. Now I think there was some vampire manipulation going on here. I just want to know something… can you guys hypnotize people in your resting state?" Warren asked, performing an analysis of checks, balances and elimination.

Darian shook his head. "No, when we're under a full resting state, we are not respondent. However, more powerful, ancient vampires no longer have to succumb to the resting state unless they want to. They can rest to regain energy, strength, but they are never completely under."

Warren nodded. "How do you defeat a vampire that old?"

Darian held his hand up, silencing Warren. "This isn't the place to discuss such things."

"I agree. We may not be alone and we should be careful about what we say from now on," Richard agreed.

Warren kind of understood what they were saying, but he was still slightly confused. "I get that you're concerned that someone may be eavesdropping, but wouldn't you be able to sense or smell them?" he asked.

Darian gave Warren a look that meant more than any words could have expressed. Basically, he wanted Warren to remain quiet.

"Never mind," Warren said, getting the hint. He suspected that Darian didn't want their enemy to know how much he knew about them. "Listen, I'm heading back to the precinct. You've got my number." He walked away, rejoining the others and a few minutes later, four detectives drove away in two cars, leaving Gabriel and Barry to complete the investigation.

Darian looked at Richard. "We'll keep in touch." He walked away, taking flight once he was away from curious onlookers.

Richard decided to stay, just in case the lion came back to his "territory."

*** 

Darian flew toward downtown Chicago, landing on top of the highest skyscraper the city possessed. He scanned the minds of all of the vampires he could sense in the area, seeing if any of them knew anything or happened to be a part of the coven he was tracking. After several minutes, his cell phone rang. He answered it.

"Mr. Alexander, this is Lisa from *Desires Unleashed*. A man called for you earlier today and left this message." She gave him the message Adan had left with her.

Darian memorized it and thanked her before ending the call. As he was dialing the number Adan had given him, he felt the aura of another vampire. He looked up in time to see a beautiful man at least six-two, with cobalt blue eyes and long blond hair flowing past his shoulders, standing only twenty feet away from him. Then the man vanished instantly. Darian turned around, looking in all directions for the vampire. The appearance of the vampire was so instantaneous, one second he was there and the next, he wasn't. He did note that the man was wearing a white shirt and black pants and shoes. He scanned his memory and realized that he remembered the man. He was at the crime scene amidst the crowd. At that time, he was simply another face amongst many. Granted, it was an exceptionally handsome face, which may be the reason why Darian remembered him so well, but a random face none the less. Now, he was no longer just another person in the world. Now he was a recognized member of this coven, possibly the Master himself.

Darian suspected the vampire didn't try to attack because it's all a part of some form of entertainment for him. He already knew the vampire Master was stronger than he was by the time of death of one of their victims. Now he knew what he looked like and figured that was just another game the ancient vampire was playing: revealing himself to prove that he wasn't afraid of him. Darian was deep in thought when he remembered about Adan's message. He dialed the number, still looking around carefully. He knew now that he couldn't sense this vampire unless the vampire wanted him to; which disturbed him greatly.

Adan answered his cell. "Hello?" he asked, tentatively.

"Hello Adan," Darian responded, recognizing the shifter's voice instantly, "You wanted to speak with me."

Adan exhaled, relieved to have finally made contact with him "Yes, Darian … I need your help, desperately. I wouldn't have contacted you otherwise."

"Does this have anything to do with the vampire coven terrorizing my domain?" Darian asked, slightly annoyed.

"I'm afraid so. I'm sorry for bringing this threat to your territory. I swear, it was not my intention, but as I said, I was desperate. Trust me, Darian, it wasn't the least bit easy for me to come to you, but I have to ask, will you help me?" Adan asked, then he waited for a response.

Darian didn't think he'd have much of a choice either way. "Yes, I'll help you. Come to my home." He gave him the address. "I'll be there after I'm done here, but someone will let you in just in case you make it there before I do."

"Thank you, Darian." Adan said, "I won't forget this."

"Don't thank me yet, just meet me there," Darian said, before ending the call. He contacted Elise and Xander, using his nifty three-way dialing technology. He told them only that he needed to see them and their entire communities at his mansion as soon as possible and left it at that. He wanted to wait until they were all there so that all cards could be placed on the table. He then contacted Richard and told him he wanted him and his Pack to be there as well.

"I'm afraid I won't be able to make it, but I'll send my Pack," Richard said. "I don't want to leave this scene … I have a very good feeling that the shifter will return and when he does, he'll have me to face."

"If that is your decision, I want Xavier to be there with you in case you'll need assistance. He'll be there shortly," Darian suggested.

"Good, I'll be here." Richard ended the call.

Darian, with the use of telepathy, contacted Xavier, who had just put their son to bed and told him what he wanted him to do. Without protest, Xavier left the mansion, leaving Natasha in safe hands with members of their coven. He flew toward Richard, traveling as fast as he could. Darian continued to mentally search a few more beings looking for information a little while longer before he returned home. When he walked through the door, he was greeted by Natasha, who wanted to know where Xavier had gone to. Darian took a seat in the living room, relaxing a little as he waited for the others to arrive. He looked at her as she waddled to a chair, taking a seat. He smiled at the sight and then answered her question.

"I have a task I want him to perform. He'll be back soon. Shouldn't you be resting?" he asked, concerned about her pregnancy, and the amount of stress she was under. He didn't want her stress to be increased any more than it was, but he wasn't so sure if he could prevent it.

"I've rested enough for one day, now I want to be with you. I can tell that you're upset, feel like talking about it?" she asked.

"I will soon. I'm waiting for everyone to arrive."

"I already know it's got something to do with these vampires. I just heard on the news that four children were found murdered, their bodies left in the freezer of an ice cream truck." Natasha was horrified, as was Xavier when they first saw the report on the television. It made her hold her son closer, thankful that he was unharmed. She felt nothing but sorrow for the parents who would have to endure the aftermath of that senseless and brutal crime.

"You would be right," Darian said in confirmation. He closed his eyes and leaned his head back against the cushion of the chair, calming himself.

Natasha watched him, but stayed silent. She figured he had a lot on his mind and wanted to get a moment to clear his thoughts. Fifteen minutes later, the doorbell rang. Billy answered it. A few seconds later, several members of Elise's Pride and Xander's Pack entered the living room. They greeted Darian and Natasha. Within an hour's time, everyone who could make it there, were waiting for Darian to speak. Several of them looked at Adan, wondering who he was and why he and his Pride were there.

"I wanted you all here because we have information you all need to know," Darian said, gesturing toward Adan. "I'm sure you're all aware of the four children slain this afternoon."

Several of them nodded, each horrified.

Darian continued. "Good, we're all on the same page. I have seen who I suspect is the Master vampire of this coven … tonight."

The room lit up, everyone wanting to ask him questions at the same time.

Darian held his hand up, silencing everyone.

"Are you okay?!" John asked, shocked.

Darian nodded. "I'm fine. He didn't want to fight me. I believe he was simply toying with me, showing me that he wasn't afraid of me … or any of us for that matter."

Xander nodded. "Were you able to sense him?" he asked.

Darian exhaled slowly. "No. And that bothers me more than I'd like."

"It means he's stronger than you," Natasha said, her stress levels rising.

Darian looked at her. "Perhaps you shouldn't be here listening to this," he said. He could hear her heartbeat increase its palpitations and that worried him. He didn't want anything to put her and their unborn child's health at risk.

"Please don't start that. Hiding the truth from me won't help in this case. Especially since the news keeps such good track of their activities," Natasha said.

Darian nodded. "Very well, he's either an ancient or old enough for ancient blood to give him the power he has."

There were several gasps around the room. Mainly because they were all wondering how they were going to defeat a vampire stronger than Darian. The last time they met a vampire of considerable strength, she was a little over three thousand years old. Even then, Darian had to pull out everything he had to defeat her, they all did. Many were considering a time before that, dealing with Kysen, when Darian had strongly advised them not to trespass on the Master vampire's land because he would destroy them. No one had doubted him, especially since Kysen held dominion over the entire state of Montana. So now, Darian tells them that this vampire is stronger than him. There was no telling how strong the shifter was or the other members of his coven were.

Darian allowed them a few moments to gather their thoughts then he continued. "I asked Adan to come here to address us all. He may have information which can help us." He looked at Adan, opening the floor to him.

Adan nodded. "First of all, I would like to apologize for bringing this threat into your land. I really had no other choice."

"Wait a minute, it's because of you he's here?!" Christopher asked, greatly irritated.

"Christopher!" Darian growled, silencing the young vampire immediately. He shocked the others as well; no one had actually seen Darian reprimand one of his vampires in such a manner. They did have to agree, Christopher was out of line.

Christopher looked at Darian, but remained silent, not wanting to anger his Master anymore.

"Trust me; the last thing I wanted to be is a catalyst for the creator of death and carnage. And the last place I want to be is here, pleading for help," Adan said, hoping he'd set the record straight. "Fact of the matter is, it was only a matter of time before this coven made its way into this territory. They've been chasing my Pride for the past week or so. I've only managed to escape them because of my own perseverance. When I first encountered him, he had accosted me on the streets of Bombay. That city doesn't have a Master vampire, because I won't allow it and those who have come to challenge me for the territory haven't been strong enough or smart enough to defeat me. So when he came to me, I took it as a challenge. I told him to leave my land or die. He only laughed at me-"

"Were you able to sense his aura?" Devin asked, cutting Adan off unintentionally.

"Only a little, only what he wanted me to sense. I thought he was young like the others who'd come before him. I had no idea he wasn't interested in my territory at all, but my Pride. I told him again to leave. I told him that I didn't want to see him again. It was then that he released his full aura, blasting it at me strong enough to slam my body against a nearby brick wall. At that point, I knew I couldn't defeat him, I had never felt a vampire's aura with that much power. I knew then it was either take my Pride and leave or die."

"Did you try to fight him?" Justin and Devin asked at the same time.

"Will you two let the damn man speak?" Sergio and Adrian said in unison. Both men looked at each other, surprised.

"Sorry," Justin said as Devin nodded.

Everyone's attention returned to Adan.

"To answer your question, I didn't want to initiate a fight with him at that point, Sometimes displaying bravado isn't the best decision. Understand I'm not a coward, but I'm not stupid, either. I know which battles I should pick and I have a greater responsibility to my Pride to protect them at all costs. My dying there in the streets wouldn't have done them a bit of good. Regardless of that fact, he attacked me. He was on me before I could get back to my feet. His nails were embedded in my neck when his hand closed around my throat. I could feel my blood oozing from the wounds. I remember him leaning forward, licking the blood, I heard him moan … it was eerie. It was then that he kissed me, forcing his tongue into my mouth. I tried to push him away with one hand and free my throat from his grasp with the other, he was immovable." Adan paused.

Danielle placed her hand on his knee, wanting to comfort him. He looked at her, smiling sadly. He turned to the others.

"When he pulled away, he said, 'You're no good to me alone.' Then he let me go and vanished. At that point, I knew I had to get home, but I didn't know what I was going to run into when I got there. I didn't know if he would be waiting for me to reunite with them to kill us together, but I had to take the chance. When I got there, I told them what had happened." He placed his hand over his Matron's. "Danielle suggested we wait until the sun rose to make our escape. I didn't know when the vampire would come for us, but he didn't come that night. When the sun rose, we fled the city. Boarding a plane to Pakistan, I had gotten permission from the Pack Alpha there to take *Sanctuary*. As soon as we exited the plane, I felt his aura."

"My God!" Madeleine said, unable to contain herself.

"My thoughts exactly. My guess is he'd been watching us the entire time, cloaked. He watched as we left the mansion and boarded the plane. He then followed our plane, landing when we did. It was only his aura I felt and he wanted me to. He didn't attack us until that night, hours later. It was almost sunrise when he and his coven converged on us, killing several members of Donovan's Pack. They were very precise. It was as if they wanted to torture them for allowing us *Sanctuary*, and they wanted us to know this. The rising sun forced his coven into retreat. He went with them. I believe he joined them only to protect them. Donovan blamed me for bringing the threat to his doorstep; we fought ... I won."

"Did you kill him?" Natasha asked, completely engrossed in the tale.

"Yes. I didn't want to, but I was challenged to the death. I knew we couldn't stay there, I also knew that I would have to violate many territorial laws because I didn't want to involve any other community in our situation. I didn't want any others to be punished for granting us *Sanctuary*. I suspected and hoped that no harm would come to those who weren't in cahoots with us, so to speak. I took my Pride through city to city, only running into the occasional Alpha or Queen who bothered to stop us to find out why we were there. When I told them, they offered to help, only to get us out of their territory as fast as possible. Although, each leader was grateful that I did tell them that there was a threat." Adan shrugged one shoulder. "It was what I would have wanted someone to do for me. I soon realized that he would only attack us during the evening, when his entire coven could participate. I made certain that during the evening, we were either hidden, or in a public place where he seemed to be less incline to attack."

"Did he kill any members of your Pride when he would attack you?" Elise asked.

"No, he only injured us, some almost to the point of death. It would have been very easy for him to kill us, even on his own. But it wouldn't have been that much fun for him and his coven. Do you understand?" Adan looked at the others' expressions, seeing that they comprehended what he was saying.

"He's a cat and you're the mouse," John said. "That explains why he left your Matron alive to heal you after the attacks."

Adan nodded.

"Tell them about Tyler," Carrie-Anne spat out, her words laced with accusation, anger and sadness.

He looked at her, slightly annoyed. She turned away from his irritated gaze.

"Who's Tyler?" Sergio asked.

"He was the only other male within my Pride. I believe he's dead now. I had wanted to keep my entire Pride together. He accused me of being a … how did he put it, "punk-ass", and challenged me. We fought. Carrie-Anne interfered, not wanting her lover to die. He didn't want to follow my orders, and I told him to leave. He did. Carrie-Anne went to join him and discovered that he was missing and that Marcus had killed the entire Pride he tried to seek shelter with."

"We suspect that Tyler was the first body the S.U.I.T. found in front of that night club," Danielle said.

"If so, I believe it was a message to us," Adan added. "Unfortunately, I can't prove it because I didn't want to expose myself to see if it was true. But it makes perfect sense. Marcus would want to let me know that he was still tracking us."

"Not to mention, he wants you all together. He killed Tyler to prove there was no escape and for you to play this game by his rules," Xander said.

"What the fuck?" Ignacio shook his head, hands waving in front of him. "Hold up, hold up, hold the fuck up. I'm seeing a pattern with this fucking coven, and I'm not liking it."

"Yeah, we've established that you're the target. It's real fucked up this coven kills anyone who interferes with them chasing you," Adrian said, growing even more unnerved.

"Except none of you are dead yet and it's been forty-eight hours since we first arrived," Stephanie commented.

"That may only be because we haven't been helping you," Carmen said. "None of the other communities were killed when they didn't help you."

"Are you suggesting we leave?" Stephanie asked; raising one eyebrow.

"Now that you mention it …" Carmen shot back.

"Ladies, this is counterproductive. Besides, it's too late for a retreat at this point. This coven is now toying with us as well," Xander pointed out.

"It would seem that way from what I experienced this evening," Darian added. "This, Marcus, showed himself to me, wanted me to know him. He was also at the crime scene, I noticed him there but had no idea he was a vampire. He's probably been watching us from the very moment he arrived."

"I'm almost certain that was the case. I don't think he knew where we were, which is why he started killing. He and his had to find their pleasure somehow, someway," Adan said, sadly. "Although, it would have only been a matter of time before he found us."

"Jesus," Sergio said, shaking his head. "Well, if this son of a bitch didn't know where you were, I'm willing to bet he does now. We should stick together. There's no sense in us being divided, making it easier for this motherfucking coven to attack us."

"I'm all for that idea," Devin agreed, not wanting to be an easy target. At that point, he was kind of happy younger vampires were down for the count when the sun rose.

"I agree with Sergio," Elise said, looking at the others. "We've proven that we're more powerful together. You've come to us for help, there's no turning back now. We're going to have to face them together … it's our only chance."

"I'm sure we will be able to take them out," Tatiana agreed.

"I hate to be the one to have to bring this up, but I'm going to anyway. This vampire has to be at least what? Five-thousand years old in order to walk around in the sunlight, right?" Natasha asked, looking at Darian.

"Yes and no," Darian answered.

"Huh?" She looked at him, confused.

"Remember what I've told you about vampires drinking from old vampires and gaining in strength, power, abilities and their age levels?"

"Yes."

"He has to be at least three-thousand with the blood of an ancient vampire flowing through his veins. Or he could be an ancient vampire at five-thousand years or older." Darian hoped that gave them an idea of what they were going to have to deal with. "Not that it matters. He's more powerful than I am and that's the reality of it all."

"I think I just shit myself," Sebastian said, looking at the others. He was trying to grasp the situation and what his role was going to be in it. His father had wanted to include him in this meeting. He'd told him that at nineteen, he was becoming a man, nearing his age of maturity, and it was time that he became a part of the Pride's dealings. He would have to learn how to defend his Pride and their territory.

Sergio looked at his son. "I hope that was just your way of saying you're scared and not to be taken literally."

"I don't smell anything, so I guess so," Devin added.

"Damn Devin, that was just gross. I'm just saying this is some scary shit!" Sebastian said.

Devin shrugged. "Hey, you're the one who said you 'shitted yourself', I was just saying … ."

Sebastian smirked. "Yeah, still though, gross."

Devin shrugged nonchalantly once again.

"In other words, Sebastian, welcome to the big leagues," Justin said.

"What are we going to do?" Sebastian asked genuinely curious as to how they could defeat a juiced-up vampire who's at least three-thousand years old and his psycho gang of bloodsuckers and a crazy, brain-damaged, flesh-eating sidekick.

"I still say strength in numbers, we stick together. When the sun rises, we don't leave you guys alone," Nicole suggested, pointing to John and gesturing toward the other vampires.

"We can't stay holed up in Darian's mansion, as nice as it is … we still need to track them down. Hunt them instead of the other way around," Devin said.

"That's all fine and dandy, but you forget, we've been doing that," Daniel said.

"Perhaps we've been going about it the wrong way," Ryan spoke up for the first time that evening.

"Go on," Xander encouraged, wondering what the young coyote was thinking.

"Okay, I've been tracking the news and listening to everything I've been hearing about this coven. Bottom line is, we can't save the people they're killing. There aren't enough of us to spread throughout the city and do you really want to? Teams of two or three are going to stretch us pretty thin. We've just found out that this coven killed an entire Pride, there's no telling how many members there were or how strong they were," Ryan paused in case anyone had anything to say.

They didn't. They only waited for her to finish stating her thought.

She continued. "I think we should stay here, like Nicole said, and they'll come for us since who they've been chasing is here with us. We bring them to us instead of chasing them around, playing their game."

"Valid point, but who's to say they'll take the bait? They might continue to kill, knowing it's a direct insult and challenge to us. If we stay here, it'll give the impression that we're afraid of them, that we're weak. News will spread about our *perceived* cowardice, and we'll be fighting for this land constantly, never getting a break because we'll be presumed as easy targets," Sergio pointed out.

"Especially if they get bored and leave, like they did in

California," Carmen said.

"I can't say for certain if this played a part in them leaving California, or not. However, my gut tells me they got who they came for when they ran amok in California. I did the research. They chased a Pack of hyenas there, terrorized the city, and killed the Pack. After the Pack was annihilated, they left," Adan informed.

"Trust me, they got bored before they decided to kill who they came for. That's why they killed them. As long as you're providing them entertainment, they're allowing you to live," Sergio replied.

Adan remained silent, reflecting on what Sergio had said.

"Okay, this is really fucked up." Carmen sunk a bit lower in her chair.

"We're going to have to find a way to take them out one by one, that's just it. There's no other way around it," Miranda said.

"Yeah, that sounds good in theory, but from what we now know … they're never apart," Ignacio pointed out. "Marcus never strays too far away from his coven, and I'm sure when he's not there the shifter is-" He paused, thinking he answered his own question.

"We need to take out the shifter when Marcus isn't there," Ryan finished Ignacio's thought, seeing where he was going with it. "That way, we'll be able to kill the resting vampires a lot easier."

"Yeah, that's what I'm thinking. We need a diversion!" Ignacio smiled at his own brilliance.

"Wait, I hate to be a bubble-buster-" Devin began.

"So don't be," Carmen said.

"I'd be remiss, as Elise would say, if I didn't bring this up. We're going on and on about this attack plan, but we don't know where they stay during the day." Devin looked at the others.

"We know that. Once we find out where they're hiding, we're going to need a plan. And that's what this is all about," Nicole said.

"Again, I'm going to bust that bubble," Devin began. "What if when we discover their resting place, the vampire and shape-shifter are both there. That other plan just focuses on if the shape-shifter is the only one there. All I'm saying is, maybe we should have a plan if both of them are there."

"We're trying to avoid that. That's where the diversion comes in at, Devin. Since the Master vampire tracks down Adan's Pride, he'll have to leave his own coven. That's when we can strike," Carmen answered.

"I think I see where Devin is going with this and I'm beginning to see that the plan is heavily flawed," Darian said.

"How so?" Carmen asked.

Darian went onto explain. "This plan you're discussing is based on some fantastical notion that this ancient vampire will be unaware of our intentions. Even if by some unexplainable circumstance, we catch him off guard, finding his resting place is going to be difficult. Even if the diversion tactic works, we'll only have one time to execute the plan and in order for that to happen, we'll already have to know where his resting place is."

"Shit," Sergio groaned, slouching dejectedly in his chair. "He's right. This bastard can watch us twenty-four hours a day if he wants to, and we'll never know. So the moment he sees us searching for his home and if we're lucky enough to find it, he may attack us, or move his coven before we can form our attack."

There were several moans from the others in the room as they were beginning to see they were back at square one.

"Well, we have to think of something," Tatiana said as she held her sleeping daughter, Nyah in her arms.

"I agree." Xander nodded.

They began to discuss the best way to separate a psychotic Master vampire from his resting coven.

***

"What?!" Gabriel yelled into the receiver, probably shattering the eardrums of the officer on the other end. "Are you sure?"

"Not entirely, but one of the victims found in that truck does match the description she gave us, Detective Johnson," the officer said. "The mother reported her child missing five hours ago when she was expecting him to get off the school bus. When he didn't come home, she got worried and called *Jayden Parker Elementary* school to find out what happened." the Forrest Park Police Officer recited the report she'd written early that day. "As the law dictates, we put out a description and APB immediately. The S.U.I.T. dispatch gave us the information we have now, and we have to ask the mother to confirm if the child is her son or not." The cop dreaded having to be the bearer of such horrible news. She decided to share her innermost thoughts with a fellow officer of the law. "There's no solace coming either way. If it's not, her child is still missing. If it is, her child was taken away from her forever."

Gabriel felt the sting of those words more than he wanted to. Being a father himself, the loss of a child was something he didn't think he could bear, especially having one of his children murdered. He needed to call his wife immediately and looked for a way to end his phone call in a polite manner. "I want to thank you for your help," he said.

"Anytime, Detective," the officer replied. "Catch those bastards."

"We will, take care." Gabriel ended the call. He immediately contacted his wife. When she answered, he wanted to make sure his children were still at home, safe, and not playing outside.

"Yes, Gabe, they're here … what's wrong?" Melinda asked, suddenly frightened. This was the second time in a matter of hours that her husband had called, worrying about their children.

Gabriel released a long breath. "Do me a favor, baby, I might not be home tonight. Let's keep the kids out of school for the time being, all right?"

"Is this because of the four children they found murdered in that ice cream truck?"

"Yes. I've just found out that one of them was abducted from Wesley and Rhiana's school. It could have been one of our own as easily as it was that other poor child. I don't want to see my kids on the ten o' clock news. Keep them home where they'll be safe." Gabriel couldn't have been more serious.

"Oh my God!" Melinda's hand covered her mouth, shocked to discover how close her own children had come to such a fate. "Gabe, please be careful."

"I will, baby. We have to catch these fuckers, and we will. I love you. Kiss the kids for me, okay?"

"I will." Melinda paused. "Gabriel?"

"Yes?"

"Nothing."

"Are you sure?"

"Yeah, just try to make it home soon, the children miss you."

"Be safe and I'll be home as soon as I can." Gabriel hung up the phone. He looked at the receiver on its base for several seconds, stunned. His wife didn't respond in a way that he'd hoped. He had wanted to hear her say the words "I love you, too", but never did. He hadn't heard her say those words to him in months and was beginning to wonder if she did still love him. He shook his head, clearing his mind, trying to keep his focus on the job.

Barry came up behind him, slapping a hand on his shoulder. "Are the kids okay?"

Gabriel nodded. "Yeah, they're fine."

"Okay, since we didn't find out anything more from our investigation with the ice cream truck, what was that all about?" Barry asked. He and Gabriel had just returned from the last crime scene and neither wasted time before working their leads, hence the telephone call.

Gabriel told him what the police officer said about the missing child.

"Sounds just like the same report we all got. The kids were all last seen running to get ice cream. The truck was gone before anyone realized the kids were missing. Also, no one had suspected the ice cream truck right away, if they did, they didn't report it." Barry sat at his desk, rubbing a finger over his brow, displaying his frustration. "My fucking head is killing me."

"Pop a pain killer," Gabriel suggested.

"I did, about an hour ago, hasn't done shit yet."

Gabriel smiled slightly. He leaned back into his chair, running his fingers through his dark brown hair. "I've got to be honest with you, Barry. I really don't know what to do next. We can't track this coven and now we have a shifter involved. The pattern that *looks* like it may be developing leaves us unable to pinpoint their next targets … I just don't know what else to do. Got any fresh ideas?" His blue eyes studied his partner.

"I'm in the same boat you're in and it's sinking. We're both fucked." Barry tossed his notepad on his desk, followed by his ink pen.

The other four detectives joined them. "I take it you two got the same story we did?" Warren asked.

Both Gabriel and Barry nodded. "What's next?" Gabriel asked.

"In California, the second victim was another shape-shifter," Brian stated.

"Another? So, they *are* following some sort of pattern? In both of our cases, at least one shape-shifter was killed. Was your shifter skinned?" Matthew asked him.

Colin and Brian both nodded. "He was a hyena, and they killed him in full animal form, taking his pelt."

"Don't they have to wait until the full moon to do something like that?" Gabriel asked, wanting a confirmation.

Warren, Matthew and Brian gave each other knowing looks. The Council had been mum concerning shape-shifters. Because the senator who had been turned wasn't a Natural Born, he had no idea that a born shifter could change at will and was the only one who could transform partially. Slowly, but surely … the truth was leaking through.

Colin answered him. "Apparently not, because this shifter was killed with only a quarter moon in the sky."

"Shit!" Barry and Gabriel said in unison. "Why are we just finding out about this?" Gabriel asked, his brows furrowed in anger.

"Because, like I told Warren earlier, we were told to keep a lid on our case and to only let certain details leak to the press, nothing more. Nothing that would jeopardize the mission of the S.U.I.T. or rich people's pockets," Colin answered.

"You don't say." Gabriel looked at the other three detectives. "Did you know shape-shifters could change forms like that?"

Warren and Matthew looked at each other, feigning bewilderment.

Warren shrugged. "No, I didn't. This is news to me," he lied.

Brian wanted to steer the conversation in another direction, hoping to confuse the insightful humans. "Perhaps they found a way to change him. Maybe they used torture tactics to cause enough pain for them to turn. We know that can happen from our research." He shrugged. "Anyway, it doesn't matter. That's not important. What is important is catching this cov-"

"What the hell are you talking about? How is that detail not important?" Colin asked his partner. "In both of our cases, we're discovering more and more about these supernatural freaks than we ever knew. Everything we learn is important, Brian."

Brian cleared his throat, thinking about a way to correct his faux pas. "You know what, you're right. I didn't mean that it wasn't important, it's just, how does knowing that help us now? Not to mention, we don't even know for certain what we think we know, if that makes any sense. We need to spend our energy on what's tangible."

"Then let's not ignore what's so obviously 'tangible'... like for instance, vampires that might be able to fly and go out during the day," Colin shot back.

"Can we not argue amongst ourselves," Matthew intercepted, hoping to calm the rising tempers in the room.

"That's fine with me," Brian agreed, hoping to cease Colin's line of questioning. He brought their attention back to the case. "Now, maybe we should have a chat with the media, put out a bulletin for everyone to be on guard. We should alert the public of their next possible target."

"That's just it, we don't know who their next victim will be. The shape-shifter was the first victim in our case, not the second," Matthew said. "We don't know if the next victim is going to be a child or not, or if it's going to be killed by a vampire or the shifter."

The six men were silent as they pondered their scenario. Each one was trying to come up with a solution with little success.

"They must be laughing their fucking asses off. The government's "best" scratching their heads and asses," Colin remarked, angered by their lack of options and ideas.

They all were.

\*\*\*

Back at Darian's mansion, they were still at a stalemate on the perfect tactic to deal with this new threat.

"Well, we haven't heard from the S.U.I.T. yet, I guess the killing has stopped for the time being," Justin said.

"Marcus is probably watching this mansion right now. It's very likely he could be reading our thoughts, hearing our voices," Darian commented, crossing one long leg over the other.

"Well shit, what's the point of us even trying to think up a plan anyway?" Sergio asked, irritated by the entire situation. "You can't feel this motherfucker's aura, so we don't know if he's listening or not."

"I'm with Sergio, if we happen to come up with a plan that doesn't completely suck ass, he'll know about it," Adrian added.

Darian shrugged one shoulder. "It doesn't matter. This vampire is smart. I'm sure he already knows we're trying to come up with something. That's just common sense. We should continue plotting under the assumption that he'll know about our plan."

"How is that productive?" Tatiana said, exasperated.

Darian sighed. "Well for one reason, it's far more preferable than sitting here staring at each other in dumbfounded silence. Another reason is, we may brainstorm enough to come up with a plan that might work whether he knows about it or not."

Natasha pointed frantically at Darian, he watched her, confused. Her mouth was a perfect "O" as she struggled to get the words out in her excited state.

"Calm down, take your time," he instructed.

She did, taking a deep breath. "Sorry. I just had the perfect thought! Okay, you're having a hard time tracking this vampire and you can't read the shifter's mind. You got me to thinking when you said Marcus-" She cut herself off, looking at Adan. "Are you sure that's his name, this vampire?"

Adan nodded. "It's the name he gave to me the night we first met."

"Do you know the other coven members names?" Natasha asked.

"Why do names matter?" Stephanie asked.

"Woman, hush!" Adrian told Stephanie, who rolled her eyes, but remained silent.

"I believe the shifter's name is Kiren. I heard him call him during one of our battles," Adan answered.

"What's with the tidbits of information you're dealing out?" Adrian asked, frowning as he was growing more agitated.

Adan raised both eyebrows. "I was interrupted with questions, if I remember correctly, then you all simply took over ... I let you, because it seemed more ..." He looked at Tatiana, nodding at her. "... Productive to talk about solutions instead of the problem."

"If I may continue," Natasha blurted out, frowning at Adrian.

"Go on, I'm just ... I'm fucking tired, that's what I am," Adrian replied.

"We all are." Natasha continued, "if we can somehow steal something personal of theirs, I may be able to see what they're doing even before they do it."

"How are you going to steal something of theirs?" Devin asked. "It's not like they're leaving shit at the crimes scenes."

"I'm not dumb, I know that. I was basing this on the fact that they may attack us or Adan and his Pride again. Since they keep letting them live, and us for that matter. They may attack us and at that point we can take something from them I can use."

Adan perked up as well. "You can *do* that?"

Natasha nodded. "Yes, I can do that, and I don't have any reasons to think it won't work. My ability isn't magical or supernatural, it's mental."

"Do you think he'll be able to block her?" Elise asked Darian.

"Yes," Darian replied, honestly. "But it may be worth a shot, we may be successful, we may not. Even if Natasha sees a glimpse of their location that may be our only chance to strike. I believe the shifter is the best candidate for this. He doesn't have the ability to block Natasha from seeing his future."

"Then, let's hope when they do attack us, we survive," Xander said.

"I'm not looking forward to this plan at all," Sergio groaned.

"I don't think any of us are," Elise agreed.

It was true, no one liked the plan, but it was the best thing they could think of at the moment.

\*\*\*

Back at the precinct, the six detectives were still brainstorming.

"Listen, I have a completely outrageous idea, but it's better than nothing," Brian began. "It's completely unorthodox, but we're out of options. Why don't we petition supernaturals within the city for help?"

Colin was flabbergasted. "What?! That's fucking insane!"

Brian shot him a look. "Why is it insane, Colin? Maybe a vampire or shifter can track this coven in a way we can't. The S.U.I.T. is an amazing force, I'm not denying that, but even we have our limitations."

Warren and Matthew gave each other another knowing look, not quite certain if the plan proposed was a smart one, or bad. They certainly knew their respective communities were taking their own initiative, but they didn't want to involve any outside supernaturals, who may complicate matters.

"Are you saying we should enlist the services of say … a supernatural private investigator?" Gabriel asked. The idea both intrigued and frightened him.

Brian nodded. "Yeah, something like that, why not?"

"I don't think the S.U.I.T, would allow that," Barry said, not sure if they would or wouldn't.

"Why not? When I was on the Force, we hired outside professional help all of the time. Psychic, clairvoyants, psychologists, hell, even other fucking criminals to give us the inside info," Brian protested.

"Yeah, but they weren't supernaturals," Colin argued.

"Psychic … clairvoyant," Warren whispered, immediately thinking of Natasha. "I think you may be onto something." Excited, he ran to his telephone, dialing Natasha's cell. She didn't answer. He then dialed Darian's home number.

John answered. "Hello?"

"John, this is Warren, listen," He began to tell them what they were discussing. "Think Natasha would be up for it?"

"You have no idea just how perfect your timing is. Natasha just volunteered to use her abilities. We just need to get something of theirs she can link to," John informed.

"That's going to be difficult, they didn't leave anything behind,"

Warren said.

"We're hoping they attack us and we survive long enough to snatch a belonging for her to connect with."

"What the fuck? How is that a good idea?" Warren was incredulous.

"It's not, but it's all we have for now."

"Why would you think they'd attack you?"

"There's a lot of shit you don't know about. Let's just say that they may attack for fun, like a cat taking a playful swat at a mouse. If they do, that's our plan of action," John said.

"When we get the time, I want you to fill me in on everything. For now, I'm wondering if Natasha will be able to connect with the vibes these bastards may have left behind."

"Well, there's a thought." John was surprised they hadn't thought of it themselves.

"Think she'd be willing to visit a few crime scenes and possibly touch a few bodies?" Warren asked.

"I honestly don't know … that's something you're going to have to ask her."

"Can you put her on the phone?"

"Yeah, one minute." John passed the telephone to Natasha. He told her who was on the other end.

"Hey Warren," she greeted.

"Hey Tasha, listen, I was wondering if you wouldn't mind coming to one or two crime scenes with me, possibly viewing a dead body or two. You know, to see if you'll be able to see something, some kind of residual vision?" Warren asked.

"I'm not sure if that'll work. I've never had a vision of someone after they've died. Maybe my clairvoyance might pick up on a few vibes left at the crime scenes, but I wouldn't expect much. I'll do whatever I can, though. I was just talking to everyone about using my ability to help. If you want, you can swing by … Hold on," she interrupted her conversation to listen to what Darian was saying to her. "Warren, don't worry about coming to get me, Darian is going to take me to the scenes, but we'll meet you back at the precinct, okay?"

"Sure, I'll be here, and thanks." Warren ended the call. He was excited by the new prospect of getting a little "psychic assistance". Whatever Natasha could see might help them.

Matthew came over to him. "Any luck?"

Warren nodded. "Yeah, she's heading to the crime scenes with Darian then they're coming here."

"Good," Matthew smiled.

A few minutes later, their telephone rang, they answered. They had three new crime scenes with three dead bodies. They got the information they needed.

Gabriel, with Barry in tow, approached Warren, Matthew, and the other two California detectives. "We're going to investigate the DB on Grand. Which ones are you four going to tackle?" Gabriel asked.

"Brian and I have the DB on Chicago Ave., Matt and Colin have the one on Belmont," Warren said, pulling on his coat. "We'll call you guys once we get there, tell ya what we know. I'm sure Galen's on his way there. I feel just as sorry for him as I do for us."

"Well, the good news for him is, at least he's got two teams. They can take shifts. These bastards are making sure to keep all of us on our toes, literally," Gabriel said, adjusting the collar of his jacket.

The six detectives split off into three teams, heading in the three separate directions. Warren figured the coven knew that there were six detectives on the case, why else would there be three crime scenes instead of one? Or was this just another stitch in a pattern they couldn't see. He wondered just how much they knew about them. He wished he could get back to his Pack and friends to brainstorm with them. He contacted Natasha's cell phone, this time she answered. He told her where he was going, and asked if they could meet him at the new crime scene. She agreed, letting him know what Darian said about the Master vampire being able to read their minds, and the key details they discussed. She also told him the Master vampire's name.

"His name is Marcus? How do you guys know that?" Warren asked, shocked.

"Adan told us. Warren, we're getting ready to leave, so we'll meet you at your crime scene in a little while."

"Who's Adan?"

"He's a friend of Darian's that we're helping out. It's a long story, and I'll have to tell you later."

"All right, see you soon."

"Okay." Natasha ended the call, and gave Darian the address.

"Three new crime scenes," Darian said, not really needing her to confirm, he already knew.

"So it seems," Natasha said, pulling on her coat, buttoning it over her expanding belly.

Darian frowned, eyebrows creased. "I don't want you going there,"

"Darian you need me to gather inform-"

"That's not my point," Darian interjected. "If we are to hold on to this plan that we have, we need to not raise suspicions, and that's assuming he doesn't already know. If he doesn't, you going to this most recent crime scene, and touching items there, will no doubt raise their suspicious ... and their overall interest in you. We'll stick to the original plan. I'm willing to bet they aren't monitoring their past scenes."

Now understanding what Darian meant, she had to agree. "What if they are following us?"

"It's the chance we're taking. However, my guess is they want to watch the police try to figure them out. While they are preoccupied with that, we can do what we need to do." Darian closed the car door behind her then climbed in behind the wheel.

"I've got a question, if they're split up, viewing three crime scenes, wouldn't now be a good time to attack them?" Natasha asked, believing she was seeing a weakness.

"I was thinking that as well. Although, I'm not sure if they are split up, and even if ... I wouldn't want to take the chance that one of them will alert Marcus, nor do I know how strong his other members are. We don't want to be overpowered," Darian said. "Let's pretend they are split up, for the sake of argument. Xander and his Pack converge on one, how quickly will our enemy be able to combine their forces and turn the tables, attacking them before any of us can get there? Not to mention the public attention it will draw seeing a full on supernatural battle take place."

"At this point, I could care less about the media attention. Can't you read Warren's mind now, you're strong enough to keep tabs, right?"

"I can, but how many will die before I reach them? Are you willing to take that chance?" Darian asked her.

"I don't like our options, but I think it's worth a shot," Natasha said.

"There's something else, they're able to hide their auras very well. It's a good chance they could be among them and our companions wouldn't even know it."

"So have members of Adan's Pride join each team, that way, they should know what they look like, right?" she asked, hoping she was actually offering good ideas and not just being contradictory.

Darian cracked a smile. "You've put a lot of thought into this, haven't you?"

"Just kind of came to me. I don't know if it would work, but who's to say it won't?"

"You're right. If Elise, Richard, Xander and Adan are willing to take that chance, so will I," Darian said, finally agreeing. "Why don't you call the mansion and give them your idea."

"Me?"

"Yes, you. Your idea, you tell them."

"I'm just so used to you or Xavier doing all the... Okay, I'll do it." She decided not to finish her first thought about how he and Xavier always take control of every situation. She pulled out her cell phone and called the mansion. When Miko answered, she told her the plan.

Miko was impressed, but also a bit leery. "Does Darian agree with this?" she asked.

"Yes. He says it's tricky, but he thinks it's worth a shot."

"All right, I'll tell the others. I'll call you back and let you know if we decide to do it."

"Okay." She ended the call, turning toward Darian. "They'll let us know what they're going to do."

Darian nodded as he steered the car effortlessly to the crime scene where the third victim was found in a parking lot.

# CHAPTER THIRTEEN

Miko went to the other leaders and told them what Natasha told her. They seem to think about the idea, weighing their options and other possible scenarios. Once they decided they were going to do it, Elise called Richard, explaining to him the situation. He too, thought it was wise and gave them permission to take his members with them.

"So are we ready to go?" Elise asked.

"Yes," Xander replied. "Why don't you decide who among your groups will take each crime scene."

The other leaders agreed, joining their groups telling them the plan. Without wasting any more time, they drove out to the three separate crime scenes, searching for their target. To the other observers, they just looked like curious bystanders trying to get a closer look at the scene.

Matthew had been looking over the body when he felt a familiar presence. He looked up to see Ignacio coming near him. He turned, seeing other members of Xander's Pack scattered around the area, but still staying relatively close together. After about an hour had passed, he walked over to Ignacio. "Did Richard send you here?" he asked.

Ignacio nodded. "Yeah." He told Matthew about their plan.

"I haven't sensed anything. With younger vampires, I can get a vibe from them that tells me what they are and how close they are to me. But I don't feel anything now, do you?"

Ignacio shook his head. "No. I'm wondering if Elise or Adan are having better luck."

"I wonder if this coven is even here?" Matthew pondered.

"Maybe they are and we just don't know where to look. I can't fly, so there's no way I can scan the area. We aren't supposed to split up just in case they are here, because we don't want to weaken our defenses. This is just fucked." Ignacio ran his fingers through his silky black curls.

Adrian joined the two men. "Hello Matthew."

"Hi Adrian, any luck?"

Adrian shook his head. "I'll tell you what; these bastards are good at what they do. That's why I wasn't even trying to sense for an aura, I figured they'd be masking it. And they aren't in the crowd either, because I've been sniffing for anyone with the smell of blood on their body and I got nothing."

"Yeah, I did the same thing," Ignacio said. "Too bad you can't smell that hint of decay on a vampire when they're animated. It's only when they're resting when you can get that scent."

"Damn it, I know. That would totally help us out," Adrian agreed.

"I've been trying to find people with the scents I've smelled on the bodies, no such luck there either," Matthew said.

"What I find amazing is that other vampires seem to be avoiding this crime scene," Adrian said.

"Perhaps they're scared of being targeted, or maybe they're scared we'll target them," Ignacio stated.

"You've got a point. I sure would have snatched the first vamp I sensed out of the crowd," Adrian agreed, chuckling a little.

"What are you going to do now?" Matthew asked.

Adrian shrugged. "I don't know … search a little bit longer. If we still don't have any luck, I'll go back to the mansion, call Natasha, tell her the plan was a bust."

"There's nothing like delivering good news," Ignacio commented sarcastically.

"To bad we don't have any to deliver," Adrian said, he looked at Matthew. "Keep in touch with us. Call us after you get all of the details about this murder."

Matthew nodded. "Expect a call soon."

Both Ignacio and Adrian turned, heading back to Xander and the others as they continued to scope the area. They all exchanged words about not being able to find anything. Xander called Elise to check in on her. She was having the same predicament, as was Adan. The three leaders decided to head back to the mansion, unsuccessful.

\*\*\*

Natasha and Darian arrived at the fourth crime scene having done all they could at the third. Natasha walked around, with Darian by her side. A year ago, she'd drank Darian's blood one more time and like the two instances before, she felt her psychic and clairvoyant abilities expand, growing more powerful … more acute. She was still able to get visions in her sleep, and she was able to touch an item and see a past event connected to that item, but now she was able to feel stronger psychic waves in a concentrated area if she focused hard enough. If she was able to do that, she would get a vision, sometimes just foggy images seconds short, telling about the most recent event that had taken place in that area.

She continued walking around, brushing her fingertip along leaves, stones, trees, until she felt a tingling sensation vibrating throughout her body.

"I think I've got something," she whispered. With both eyes closed, she continued to concentrate until snapshot images began to flash inside her mind's eye. "Oh my God," she gasped.

Darian only watched her. He didn't want to interfere now that she had a connection.

"It was four vampires … two men, two women … one of the women looks Asian, the other woman and one of the men are black, and the last must be Marcus. They killed her here, in the bushes … Oh my God! She was so scared!" Natasha jerked her head sideways as if to shield her eyes from the visions. Her lids were shut tight as her eyebrows creased from the pressure. "They raped her." She began to cry. Witnessing this woman's death, even in mental fragments, was difficult to endure. "The men took turns. They wanted her to enjoy being raped … they bit her … they drug her body … that's it." She opened her eyes. "The vision is over, and thank God."

Darian approached her, wrapping her in his embrace. He held her close, comforting her. He could imagine what she'd seen and felt and hated putting her and their unborn child through any of it. He looked down. "Are you all right?"

Natasha nodded. "I'll be fine." She wiped the tears from her eyes as they ran down her cheeks. "It was just … so graphic, like I was there watching the whole thing. Darian, they're crazy. I mean really psycho, sadistic crazy. It wasn't enough that they were raping her, they wanted her to enjoy it, making her body respond to them. Then when they drained her, they made sure that it was painful so that she couldn't enjoy the way … you know."

Darian nodded. "The way it normally feels to be fed upon. I'm going to peek into your mind; I want to see what you saw."

She nodded, giving him permission. He entered her mind, searching for the image of them killing their victim. He found it. He could see their height and body frame, but their facial features were a bit blurry. He suspected they would be, it was still enough to go on. He broke his connection. "I'm taking you home."

"What about the morgue?"

"What about it? There's isn't anything more you can gather there, that you didn't get here."

"But, maybe I can get a better vision of their faces."

"They are already dead … the residual kinetic energy isn't there that would help you see another vision."

"But what if they have clothing there I can touch?"

"All the victims were found naked, Natasha. Even so, your abilities are not that advanced. We wanted you to get a vision and you did. There is nothing more you can do. I'm taking you home." Without waiting for another response, Darian took her by the hand, leading her toward their car. They drove back home where he hoped he could keep her safe. On the way, Natasha contacted Warren and told him what she saw.

"I was wondering what was taking you so long to get here. I started to call you."

"Oh yeah, sorry about that, I should have told you we deviated from the plan."

"It's all right, as long as we were able to get some information."

"What about DNA? Did you find any semen or sweat, ya know?" Natasha asked.

"Yeah, we did on some of the victims who still had skin, but it's going to take a while to match the DNA to its owner and I seriously doubt these bastards are in the system anyway. I'm guessing they were born before its time."

"Yeah, I didn't think about that."

"I've got to go, Tasha, I'll call you later."

"Okay, let us know what's going on with the three victims," Natasha reminded before they ended their phone call. She looked at Darian. "What are you going to do once you take me home?"

"Hunt."

"But you said this vampire was stronger than you. Won't you need help?" she asked, concerned.

"I'm not hunting for him. I'm going to join Richard; hopefully he's right in his assumptions that the shifter will return to the scene. I want to make sure you're safe at home before I go."

"Oh, all right." Natasha looked out of the window as they sped past farmland, then buildings then residential homes as they entered Evanston where they lived.

# CHAPTER FOURTEEN

Richard and Xavier stood far enough to monitor the area without being detected. They waited for the shape-shifter to return to the scene of his heinous crime.

"Are you sure he's coming back to this scene?" Xavier asked, having waited hours for this shifter to make an appearance.

Richard nodded. "I'm sure. Now that the last of the media has left, he'll want to come back, smell the lingering scents of fear and uncertainty. He might even want to mark this as his territory; he won't be able to help it, not his kind."

"If you don't mind me asking, what makes this male shifter any different from you or another male shifter?"

Richard leaned his back against a tree. "With all canine species, the males run the Pack with a female Matron who works as his second in command. Her position is strictly domestic, you could say. The Alphas handle the finances, territory, and disputes. They decide who stays and who leaves the Pack, and so on. With the feline species, the Queen is the leader, and the male king works strictly in a protector capacity. He makes sure their territory is safe from trespassers. The Queen is responsible for all matriarchal and domestic duties. With lions, however … it's slightly different."

"Go on, this is interesting. I figured out as much, but wasn't sure." Xavier was enjoying the conversation as they staked out the scene.

"With lion shifters, there's really only one male, sometimes two within the community. The alpha male… the King controls the entire Pride, much like Alpha males do within their Packs. He's extremely territorial and usually doesn't allow other males within his Pride. Even their sons which they have with any female within their Pride are sent off on their own once they've reach their age of maturity. Their Matrons take on the domestic role, responsible for making sure everyone is happy at home, food is on the table, children are raised properly, etcetera. The King chooses his Matron, not the other way around as it is with other Prides. If the King feels as though his Matron is weak or compromises his Pride, he can get rid of her a number of ways, it's his right. I do believe they are the only shifter community that functions in that fashion … it's natural for them."

"I see. Is the King's position a hierarchy?" Xavier asked.

"No. The strongest wins control over the Pride. If he is defeated for the control of the Pride, the new King can either choose to keep the current Matron or pick another one. So you see, male lions are very territorial, he's going to want to come back …" Richard leaned forward, smiling wickedly. "I think we may have our shifter."

Xavier turned in time to see an Asian man approaching the scene. He was extremely handsome and looked to be in his late thirties … possibly early forties, and very well built. His outfit covered his muscular physique perfectly. The man walked gracefully around the area, which was blocked off by S.U.I.T. tape. Stooping under the tape, he approached the spot where the truck had once been. Tilting his head backward, he inhaled deeply, a look of pure satisfaction spread across his face.

"Let's go now before he gets away," Richard whispered.

He converged on the shifter, who saw him coming. Kiren dodged Richard's attack, stepping back several paces.

"Too slow, motherfucker!" Kiren taunted.

Richard was able to maintain a straight face in spite of being completely blown away by the shifter's speed and agility. He decided to go for the shifter's pride. "Are you too scared to stand and face me? Why run?"

Kiren laughed. "Scared? Don't be ridiculous. Why would I be afraid of you or that vampire you brought with you for back-up … the one that's waiting for the perfect moment to attack me." He looked up into the trees, spotting Xavier instantly. "I seeee youuuuuu." He smiled.

Now it was Xavier's turn to be shocked. How did the shifter even know he was there? He was perfectly hidden and nowhere near enough for him to get his scent. He didn't bother to get any closer; he figured his position would still be a cause for alarm for their target.

Richard took a step closer, noting that this shifter before him didn't make a move to retreat. He figured he knew why. This shifter was strong! He could feel his presence and realized it was nothing like his own … it was more powerful. Richard knew now that every move he was going to make had to be precise, flawless. He couldn't let his emotions hinder his strategy. He hadn't anticipated the shifter to be so strong, yet so young. He had no idea how a shifter could be so formidable and not age appropriately. He looked to be too young to possess this level of strength. No, this wasn't going to be a usual challenge.

"Are you interested in this territory?" Richard asked.

Kiren shrugged. "Maybe, maybe not … big city life has its perks, though."

"You should have picked a different city," Richard shot back.

"Really? I don't know, I kind of like this one," Kiren taunted.

"This city is already taken." Richard was sizing him up, trying to wait for the perfect moment to attack. Any miscalculations could end in his death, this he knew.

"Yeah, it's taken … by us. This city and everything in it is ours. Allow me to show you what I mean." Kiren approached Richard, who stood his ground. He unzipped his pants, removing his penis and began urinating on the other shifter's shoes, marking them as his territory, insulting Richard in the most horrendous manner. He paused, smiling wickedly.

Richard looked down at his shoes, then back up at the shifter. His jaw tense has he gnashed his teeth together, not wanting to make a mistake that would get him killed. He knew that Xavier was waiting, ready to make a move when he did. He believed that this shifter was stronger than both of them. They had to be careful on their defense since it was just the two of them. He wasn't going to lose his temper now, even though he wanted to rip the shifter's penis from his body.

"You've ruined a perfectly good pair of shoes," Richard commented, calmly, not wanting to reveal how much that truly enraged him.

Kiren zipped himself up. "*My* shoes now, I'll do with them what I like. You know ..." He stepped up closer to Richard, sniffing him. "I'm stronger than you are. Right now, that brain of yours is trying to figure me out and you can't. But the best part is how sexy you look to me trying to stand here and act tough."

"I'm not acting."

"Then attack me? Or are you trying to wait until I make a move that you feel will give you the perfect opportunity? Maybe you just want to fuck me?" Kiren wanted a rise out of this one! He wanted him incensed. He wanted them both standing before him. The vampire in the tree, waiting, bothered him a bit ... they were both bothering him just a bit. He figured if the shifter attacked, the vampire would too and he could kill them both. If they didn't make the first move, then he would.

Richard decided he'd better take the initiative, he hoped it would throw the shifter off enough for them to capitalize. He leaned forward, kissing the shifter full on his mouth, startling him, as that wasn't the sort of "attack" he had been expecting. Xavier came up from behind, latching onto the shifter immediately, draining him as fast as he could. Richard's nails elongated and he slashed them across the shifter's throat.

Kiren had been taken by surprise. He bucked and managed to throw Xavier off him, sending the vampire catapulting toward a tree. Richard was attacking again, relentlessly. Kiren fell victim to the second blow, but managed to counter the next. As fast as he could, he morphed into his half-beast form, catching the other shifter off guard. Before his opponent had time to follow suit, Kiren grabbed him, burying his teeth deeply in his enemy's neck. Xavier regained his baring and attacked again, stopping Kiren from ripping open Richard's throat. Xavier bit down hard, trying to rip out the shifter's jugular. Kiren raked a clawed hand down's Xavier's face, nearly ripping out the vampire's left eye. Xavier growled in pain, his bite loosening and Kiren took that opportunity to wrench him away from his neck. He punched Xavier several times, breaking ribs in the process. Richard regained some of his strength, but was still badly wounded. He managed to rise, but Kiren caught him by his throat, claws digging in. He was ready to make his killing blow on both men when the powerful hands of another being stronger than him, took hold of his head. He felt the hands press and twist as if they were trying to remove his head from his shoulders. Kiren released his enemies and maneuvering in a way only a feline can manage, he twisted around to see another vampire in front of him. He slashed out, but was too slow, and the vampire with the long jet black hair was behind him. Before he could react, the vampire punched him, sending him several feet off the pavement. He hit the ground hard, knocking the air out of his lungs. Before he could gather his senses, this vampire was on him again, slashing at his throat and abdomen, weakening him. Then the other two men joined him.

Kiren thought he was going to die. This other vampire overpowered him in every way! He held his hands up, trying his best to block their attacks, making sure to protect his vital areas at all cost, but he was losing the battle. All of a sudden, before his enemies could deliver their final blow, they were tossed from him, flying in separate directions. His Master and lover stood before him, visible signs of rage plastered all over Marcus' face and he knew why. He wasn't supposed to be there ... he had disobeyed him and it almost cost him his life.

Darian rose to his feet, his back ached from the contact he made with a thick tree trunk. Xavier was also just climbing to his feet, dizzy. The bloody wound on his face had healed and he was able to see clearly. Richard leaned against the wall he'd hit, unable to move. Two of his broken ribs protruded through his torso and four vertebrae on his spinal column had been shattered. He sat there suffering intense pain waiting for his injuries to heal, hoping they would. The three men looked on as Marcus gather his shifter in his arms.

Darian decided to attack again before they could get away. He raced forward toward the shifter, who was severely injured. He never saw the fist that send a blow so devastating, it catapulting him backward sending his body crashing into a nearby boarded up building. Several bricks shattered under the impact, which crumbled on top of him. He never saw when Marcus flew away with his shape-shifter lover. Dimly, Darian became aware of his own injuries. Blood ran freely from his nose and lips, he could taste it in his mouth. His head spun and tilted when he tried to rise and he placed a hand on the side of the building to steady himself. When the world stopped spinning, he could see clearly and noticed Xavier kneeling over Richard's body. Instantly, he was over there. Richard was still alive … just barely. Darian lifted the shifter up and both he and Xavier flew to his mansion. Darian contacted John, informing him of their condition, stating that he would need help once they arrived.

John took the message to Elise and Tatiana, knowing their blood would help heal Richard enough for the shifter to be able to heal on his own. When the three returned, both women came to Richard's aid. Darian laid him down on the leather cushions of his sofa. Elise opened the vein in her wrist ready to donate blood as she was both older and stronger than Tatiana and she wanted to heal him quickly before it was too late. She pressed her bleeding wrists to Richard's mouth forcing him to drink. He began to swallow her blood as Tatiana and Ryan began licking his numerous life-threatening wounds.

"I swear, the only reason he's still alive is because he's old and powerful," Xavier panted, exhausted after his fight and the flight home. "What's going on? I've never faced a shifter that strong before."

Darian collapsed in his chair, wiping the blood from his nose and lips with the sleeve of his shirt. "Neither have I," he said, absently as if his mind was elsewhere.

"Darian, what's going on?" Xavier asked once again, wanting to get any updates that he may have missed. He couldn't help but notice the new people sitting around their home.

Darian told him everything he and the shifters had discussed. He introduced Adan and his Pride. He told him what Natasha saw in her vision and about the other bodies discovered that evening.

"Oh my … ," Xavier whispered, suddenly relieved that he survived the encounter with a vampire so powerful and his *freakishly* strong shifter. He continued to watch Elise and the others heal Richard, hoping the shifter would be all right.

"Are you two okay?" Natasha asked, sitting beside Xavier who appeared to be under a lot of stress.

"Yes, I'm just hoping Richard pulls through," Xavier said, tossing a glance toward the sofa where the shifter lay. The three women around him moved away, allowing him room to maneuver.

With considerable effort, Richard sat upright. "I'm fine, thanks to all of you."

"My pleasure," Elise said, rising to her feet with Sergio's assistance.

Tatiana sat beside her husband on the other sofa. "How old do you think the shifter is?" she asked. She was shocked that this shifter was able to gain advantage over both Richard and Xavier. Furthermore, she was unnerved by how much trouble Darian had with the shifter as well.

"I'm three-hundred and thirty-seven years old. He had to be far older than me to have that kind of strength," Richard said, rotating his neck straightening out his newly healed muscles, which had been shredded by teeth and claws.

"He wasn't the least bit afraid, either. That is, until Darian got there," Xavier said, remembering how the shifter "marked" Richard's genuine leather shoes. He was sure the others could smell the shifter's scent very well, but everyone remained silent about it, until Sebastian spoke up.

"Well, at least we'll be able to track him better since he marks territories. One of you guys must have stepped in his piss," Sebastian said, hoping he could add something. He smelled the scent of urine strongest on Richard's shoes; but he felt he was being tactful by not pointing out whom.

Sergio looked at his naïve son. He wanted to fuss at him about etiquette, but decided he was the last person to complain about someone's tact. He left it up to Madeleine, and she proceeded.

"Sebastian, there's a lot you need to learn about shifter etiquette now that you're coming into maturity. We understand that your senses are becoming more acute, but certain things need not be said. Nonetheless, what you stated makes perfect sense," Madeleine chastised lightly.

"But Mom, I was just trying to help. What did I say that was wrong?" Sebastian asked in his defense.

Madeleine opened her mouth to speak, but Sergio interrupted.

"We can all smell the piss, Sebastian. You didn't need to bring that part up."

A few of the others snickered at the innocence of the situation. Elise lowered her head at Sergio's tactlessness, but said nothing. She only smiled. *He was who he was*, she thought to herself

Sebastian's face reddened. "Oh," he said, finally understanding his blunder.

Madeleine turned toward the others. "Getting back on track, chances are he's marked the territory of where they're staying. Now that we know what his scent smells like, we can target those areas during the day. We should split up in teams of two."

"I see where you're going with that. I've been thinking about something as well. We need to get information from Warren when these people were killed," Sergio added.

"Why?" Adrian asked.

"Because, maybe it will help us target their location. The distance traveled by them and the time it took for them to kill their first victim," Sergio answered.

"That won't work," Devin said.

"Why not? Sounds like a good idea to me," Justin asked.

"Because they can fly very fast covering great distances in a little amount of time. It would be impossible for us to be able to determine how long it took them to get to their first victim," Devin answered. "Also, there's no way for us to be able to judge how fast they can fly because we don't know how old they are. It's not like we can send Darian out on test runs."

"Besides, how would we be able to tell what direction they came from anyway?" Adrian asked, finding another hole in Sergio's plan.

"What if Marcus kidnapped their victims earlier and then killed them later at different locations or at their hideout?" Devin added.

"Can't a vampire fly fast or slow?" Adrian asked, further dissecting Sergio's idea.

"You two got any more parades you need to rain on?" Sergio asked, frowning. He was even more irritated because they were right. He hadn't factored into his equation Marcus' "freedom in the daylight", or a vampire's flying abilities.

Devin made a face. "Sorry. Jeez, I'm just trying to help. We need to have all bases covered if we're going to face off with these guys."

"Wait," Annabelle leaned forward. "I think Sergio is onto something. We may not be able to pinpoint their location based on how long it took them to get to a crime scene. However, we may be able to pinpoint an area where they're staying based on how long it took for them to get to safety before the sun rose."

"What do you mean?" Adrian asked.

"Well, there was a victim found that had been left there right before sunrise, right?"

"Yeah, the baby in the department store, and the body that was dumped right in front of the *Eclipse* night club," Devin said.

"Well, we can't count that one really because Marcus obviously did that," Annabelle said.

"How do we know that Marcus didn't do all of them?" Carmen asked.

"Because his coven enjoyed killing, too, and they found multiple bite wounds on most of the victims," Danielle said, finally contributing to the conversation.

"She's right. In my vision, they were raping the victim, taking turns. They would want to have something to do with displaying their victims for people to find," Natasha added.

"It doesn't matter. Devin was right, it's impossible to gauge their location based on flight patterns for all of the reasons mentioned," Darian said.

"Well, shit. I'm out of fucking ideas," Sergio said. He looked at Adan. "Anything you want to add? You know more about them than we do, after all."

"Great brainstorming. You have a point. When they were chasing my Pride, they would do so until time became an issue, and they had to retreat," Adan said.

"How does that help us?" Devin asked. He turned toward Darian. "I've seen you guys take flight, you're fast as hell and I'm sure you can cover great distances in a few seconds."

"It tells us one thing, it gives us an idea how powerful the other vampires are in his coven," Xander said.

"Hm?" Devin was confused.

"Remember Devin, vampires all must rest at different times

depending on how powerful they are," Justin stated.

Devin nodded. "Oh, that's right. So if they retreat before the sun rises, it's a good chance that they aren't as strong as, say, Darian?"

"That's the theory," Sergio said.

"Adan, were you able to gather a time when they would retreat?" Xavier asked.

Adan nodded. "They would leave before the sun began to rise over the horizon, when the sky was still a pale morning shade of blue." He gave them the hours of sunrise in the various locations they were in.

"That's something. That means that at least one member of his coven is under five hundred years old. Sadly though, I think that's all we can gather from that information. Even a vampire as young and powerful as Xavier is can cover a fair distance in a matter of minutes," Darian pointed out, bringing them back to square one.

"So basically, you're telling us to simply wait it out … wait them out. Either they attack or they'll leave?" Sergio asked.

"We really don't want them to leave because they would be a lingering threat, but we may not have any other options. They are cunning, powerful, they've done this many times and I'm willing to guess they don't make a lot of mistakes. Tonight, with the shifter might have been a mistake on their part, but even then, we couldn't capitalize on it," Darian answered.

"I see one other option … But I don't know if it'll work," Natasha said, gaining everyone's attention.

"Go on," Darian encouraged.

"Why don't we have Adan and his Pride leave our territory, after we station our people in the so-called 'new' territory, so when Marcus attacked, we'll be there to help?" Natasha looked at the others. "He might not be expecting an ambush."

"Where were you at when your most powerful vampires got their asses whooped by that guy? And another thing, I don't fancy being the decoy either," said Shannon, a member of Adan's Pride. She had grown irritated by the human and their current situation.

"Shannon!" Adan growled, giving her his only warning.

She looked at him then pouted.

"Hey! Lay off Natasha. At least she's trying. What have you

contributed besides bringing us into your problem?" Devin fussed. He didn't appreciate hearing someone insulting his friends.

"At least I'm listening to the conversation and not 'contributing' stupid ideas!" Shannon shot back.

Adan growled before springing forth from his chair and slapping Shannon hard across her cheek, causing her to yelp. "Apologize, now, to those you've insulted."

Hearing the commanding voice of her King, she had to control her temper. She nodded. "I'm sorry for being rude," she said softly to Natasha, Darian and Xavier.

Darian regarded her with one eyebrow cocked. Xavier nodded.

Natasha didn't like her, but was willing to accept the "forced" apology if it would smooth things over. "Apology accepted. Do you have any ideas that might work?" she asked. In a way, she wanted to put the other woman on the spot, since she was so negative. On the other hand, she wanted to know if she did have any ideas that might work.

"Does it even matter what we think. If this vampire is monitoring our conversation, then he already knows what we're going to do before we even get a chance to do it. I say we just wait them out. Perhaps we should carry little pagers or something to hit a panic button whenever one of us encounters them alerting the others. Maybe then we can all meet up and have a chance," Shannon said.

"This is fucking demeaning. We've narrowed down our options to cowering in one location and panic buttons," Sergio said. "God, I'd love to face off with this punk-ass coven on a battle field."

"I wouldn't count on that," Xavier said. "Be careful of what you wish for. What got me was that the shifter looked to be the same age as Richard. How did he get to be so strong?" He looked at Richard to see if he had any ideas.

"I have my suspicions," Richard said.

"And they are?" Xander asked.

"This is just a rumor, although I've never seen anything that could prove the rumor a fact until tonight. It's not necessarily far-fetched either, but I think this shifter is powerful because he's consumed the Master vampire's blood." Richard looked at the others.

"You think it made him stronger? What else could drinking

vampire blood do to a shifter, besides getting them highly addicted to it?" Justin asked.

"According to ancient tales, it could prolong their life expectancy, increase their strength and heighten their senses even more," Richard said, leaning back against his chair. "I didn't think it was true, and the fact is, most shifters steer clear of vampire blood because it's highly addictive. I've never met a shifter who had drank a vampire's blood and had gained from it."

"So how old do you think he really is?" Xavier asked.

"There's no telling. He could be anywhere between four hundred years old or a thousand," Richard said.

Xander leaned forward. "I've heard of something like this before, but like you, I'd never seen any evidence of it. In ancient times, vampires who kept shifters as slaves often rewarded them with their blood. It was done so to keep the shifters in line ... loyal."

"If that's the rumor, how come we don't know of any shifters who lived past the age of five-hundred?" Devin asked.

"Maybe shifters who've drank vampire blood to live longer don't tell other shifters about it. I mean, it's not like the guy revealed his secret to Richard. If I'd done something like that, I wouldn't tell either and I wouldn't reveal my age simply for the sake of taking the advantage in battle. It's best to let your enemy underestimate you," Ignacio said.

"I guess it would have to be a really old vampire for that little trick to work?" Ryan asked, not sure.

"I would think so. No offense intended, but I don't think my strength would increase if I drank from John," Ignacio speculated.

"None taken," John scoffed. "So Richard may not be able to take out this shifter, but Darian can. I think Natasha was onto something. Maybe we don't need to know where their nest is. Adan and his Pride might have to be the decoy, whether they like the idea or not. Since they were this coven's original target, chances are Marcus will follow them just to keep tabs. Some of us will go with you. Hopefully, you'll draw out Marcus and him alone. We all gang up on him and kill him. I don't think he'd be able to take us all. His death may draw out his coven then we can take care of them, too."

Sergio shrugged one shoulder. "It's an enhancement on the other plan, might work. We were so focused on finding their hiding place, we didn't really think about it that way, so I'm game."

"That might be the only chance we have left," April said.

"Hold on, wait a minute. I've seen this vampire in action, and I don't think your plan is going to work either," Shannon said, a frown on her face.

"Why is that?" John asked, growing annoyed with Shannon as well.

"Well because he can spy on us and never attack. Your plan is based on if he attacks us," Shannon said, punching a hole in John's plan.

"Well then maybe you should all sit out in the open at a park and if he attacks you, push your little panic button and we'll come in a jiffy," Carmen remarked.

"I see you have time for jokes. Glad you find the humor in this situation," Shannon retorted.

"I think I speak for everyone when I say, there's nothing funny about this shit. We didn't ask for this über-powerful fuck to start threatening us, killing in our territory, but you brought him to us. It's time for you to hold up your end to solving your own problem," Adrian said. "You have yet to offer anything but complaints."

"You know what, if it wasn't us, it could have been you," Shannon argued.

"It is us, now, thanks to you!" Christopher blurted out in frustration.

"Besides, he may want to toy with you, just to prove he can. I'm still hoping we can get something from them I can connect to," Natasha said.

"And he may not, your ideas are stupid," Shannon said, holding onto her resolve.

"Bitch, you've got one more time to insult us and Marcus is going to have one less shifter to kill," Nicole threatened.

"Enough! Mon Dieu! Can we stop the arguing!?" Elise silenced everyone.

Sergio looked at Elise; he knew whenever she slipped into speaking French she was extremely upset and frustrated.

"The plan won't work … ," Darian's voice trailed off.

"What's the problem, Darian?" Natasha asked.

"If Marcus feels as though he's being overpowered, he could simply fly away. Or if he sees the others with you, he could choose not to engage you in battle as Shannon stated," Darian said, "Marcus is as wise as he is sadistic. And even if we escort you safely out of town, what does that mean for the rest of us? Marcus may choose to stay, or may choose to continue to hunt Adan's Pride down, or he may-"

"Okay, I think we get it," Sergio said. "Well, are we back to square one?"

"I think so. It was a long shot to begin with. Marcus probably would have sensed it as a trap in the first place," Xavier said. "Besides, he doesn't attack in the daytime remember? And at night, he's with his coven."

The others looked at him, dejected.

"Great, just great! That makes me feel *much* better." Shannon threw her hands upward, relieved.

"So we're back to sitting it out and waiting?" Devin asked.

"Looks like. Besides if we leave to escort and aide Adan and his Pride, who's to say Marcus won't take the opportunity to slaughter Darian and his coven while they rest?" Tatiana stated, breaking her long silence.

"Yeah, yeah, you're right, bad idea, baaad idea," John said, nodding in agreement. He did not like the possibility of being killed in his resting state, once was enough as far as he was concerned.

Shannon began to cry. "What are we going to do?" she sobbed.

Adan rose from his seat making his way toward her. He placed his hands on her shoulders, urging her to look up at him. She did. "Shannon, I know you're scared, and it's okay. However, none of us can afford to have you breaking down right now. The time has come for us to fight. I need you strong, do you understand?" His eyes were locked on hers.

Shannon wiped her tears with the back of her hand. She nodded slowly. "All right"

"Good." Adan nodded, inhaled, exhaled then turned toward the others. "We can't keep running, I won't keep running. Tomorrow we'll make our stand. We'll go to an area where we won't be in the public eye, if he chooses to attack us there, then so be it."

"That's practically suicide!" Justin exclaimed.

"It's a challenge, not suicide. It's something I should have done before instead of bringing you and many others into this," Adan said, feeling guilty about his role in the deaths of so many.

"This isn't your fault, Adan. Your Pride wasn't the first community this coven attacked and if we don't find a way to stop them, it won't be the last. I mean, who's to say we wouldn't be next after he had killed you in India?" Nicole said, putting in her opinion. "Although, I do sympathize with those who wish this wasn't happening, I don't think it's fair for us to blame you because it is."

"That's true. They were in L.A. two years ago, so who's to say we weren't next. All right, if we do this, it's got to be as a team," Daniel said.

"Adan, why don't you and your Pride go on with your plan? Elise, Xander and Richard, you should send members to accompany them, in case Marcus does attack. Others should stay here, just the same. That way, all of our bases will be covered. Like Darian, I don't believe that he will attack you, he seems to like to do so when his coven is with him, but let's just see where this takes us," Xavier suggested.

"My Pride is in," Elise said.

"Likewise," Xander agreed.

"Very well." Darian rose. "It's decided then."

The others sat around, looking from one person to the next. Each person was wondering what was on the other person's mind. The silence of the room was broken by the loud musical rap ringtone on Adrian's cell phone.

Adrian answered it. "Yeah, Warren, what's up?"

"Tell Xander the bodies were in the same fashion as the others. These guys are really showboating, rubbing all their shit in our faces."

"Yeah, we figured that much. Listen, you and Matt need to get to Darian's mansion as soon as possible."

"What's wrong?"

"We came up with a plan, you may not like it, but it's the plan."

"We'll get there as soon as we can. We're still trying to wrap up this crime scene."

"Just get here," Adrian said before ending the call. The others began discussing fighting strategies for the best way to take out an ancient vampire.

"Darian, any ideas?" Sergio asked.

"The most effective way would be decapitation," Darian answered.

"What about fire? We might can get some blowtorches," Justin suggested.

"If he's as old as I think he is, fire won't have much effect on him, at least not from a blowtorch," Darian said.

"What about a rocket launcher?" Sergio asked.

"Do you even *have* a rocket launcher?" Adrian asked him.

"No, but maybe Warren might have access to one. He and Matt are S.U.I.T., don't they have access to all kinds of weaponry?"

"And what if you miss and blow up somebody's house?" Adrian asked, looking at Sergio sideways.

"Then their house is going to be all fucked up and I hope they aren't home. You know what? I'm tired of all the 'what ifs' being so negative. What if I hit his ass with it, then what?" Sergio looked at Adrian, then Darian questioningly.

All the others turned toward Darian, awaiting an answer.

"Would a rocket launcher work?" Sergio asked.

"I really don't know. A rocket is supposed to be extremely powerful, it may be able to dismember him … I don't know … I doubt it." Darian was curious to see if modern technology would have that kind of effect on a vampire as powerful as this one.

"Well, that's an option. Call Warren up, tell him about it, see what he says," Tatiana said.

Adrian decided to make the call.

\*\*\*

Warren felt his phone vibrating in his pocket and he answered it. "Rocket launchers? What the hell do you need with rocket launchers?" he asked Adrian.

"We're trying to get whatever weapons we can to kill these

vampires. See if you can get your hands on some flamethrowers, too."

"Shit, I'll see, but I can't make any promises."

"That's good enough for me. See you when you get here."

They ended their call.

"Was that Adrian?" Matthew asked. He and Brian had finished their investigation and had decided to join Warren and Colin at their scene.

"Yeah, they need us to go to Darian's home after we're done here," Warren said. "Sounds like they're planning to take on a bunch of terrorists."

"Yeah, I heard the list of weapons they wanted. Do they have a plan?"

"Yeah, but they said we're not going to like it." Warren scratched his eyebrow. "Listen, we need to see if we can get our hands on some weapons."

"I see." Matthew was standing beside Warren when his cell phone began ringing. "Yeah, Captain, what's up?"

Their Captain sighed. "We have another body, multiple vampire bites, partially mutilated. Marlon's there now, says the victim's been dead for about half an hour. I need someone there on the scene. How's your investigation coming along?"

Matthew was saddened to hear about another murder. This whole situation was far too out of control for his taste. "To be honest with you, Captain, we're no closer to solving this case than we were forty-eight hours ago."

"Damnit. I'm giving you all of the resources I can. I don't know … " She was beyond frustrated. Her superiors had been pestering her to remain quiet regarding the facts in the case. She had been told to keep a lid on how many bodies were found if possible, as to not alarm the public. It was important to her superiors that the S.U.I.T. was to keep up appearances that they were in control. She however cared very little about the bureaucratic red tape and more about saving lives. However, she did do what she could to keep the media frenzy down. " … Maybe I can petition for more S.U.I.T. officers from other precincts, see if anyone can spare some teams. Missoula, Montana may be able to send help over. They're always outsourcing their officers."

"I don't think it would matter, Captain. This coven doesn't have amateurs. They know exactly what they're doing. If they don't want to be found, they aren't going to."

"So are you telling me we should give up trying?" she asked, agitated.

"No, of course not, I'm just saying that it may take some time closing this case no matter how many people you put on it." Matthew suspected adding more S.U.I.T. officers to the case may be what their murderers wanted. The extra attention seemed to be fueling their killing spree.

"All right, we'll play this your way. I won't bring in anymore officers for the next twenty-four hours, but if you're still shooting blanks, I'm going to do what I have to do."

"That's fair."

"Get to that other crime scene."

"We're on our way," Matthew said, ending his call.

"I heard everything."

"We need to tell them." Matthew gestured to the four men coming their way.

Brian, Colin, Gabriel and Barry approached them; each man looked physically drained, frustrated and angry. Like Matthew and Brian, Gabriel and Barry had decided to rejoin Warren and Colin when they had wrapped up their crime scene investigation. Having all of the detectives who were on the case in one spot made it easy to go over new developments and strategies.

Gabriel stopped in front of Matthew and Warren. "I'm about ready to get a few raids going. You know, shake down a few supernatural joints," he suggested.

"That's a plan, you should do that. Meanwhile, Matthew and Colin, you need to get to our newest crime scene," Warren said.

"*Another* fucking one?" Gabriel asked, his face contorting in outrage.

"Yeah," Matthew answered, telling them the address. He turned to Colin. "We should get going, come on." The two detectives left.

Brian looked at Warren. "Do we have the authority to raid supernatural businesses?" he asked.

"I'm sure we will," Warren said, dialing their captain. When she answered he told her their plan, asked for permission.

"I'll call a judge and get the paperwork started. It shouldn't be a problem," Michelle said.

"Thanks, Captain." He closed his cell phone and waited. Several minutes passed before his captain called back. He answered. "Tell me something good."

"My pleasure, you have permission. Come and pick up the paperwork," their Captain informed.

"Excellent." He ended the call and turned to Brian. "We're all good. We need to swing by the precinct for the paperwork. Let's go."

# CHAPTER FIFTEEN

A t the eleventh crime scene, Matthew listened to the initial report from Marlon.

"Wait a minute, are you fucking telling me that this may be a copy-cat killing?" Matthew asked, both eyebrows arched.

"That's exactly what I'm telling you. None of the fang or teeth marks match the ones from the other victims. You have another group of supernaturals trying to make a name for themselves. The good news is … they're not half as sophisticated as the originals. They've left saliva, footprints and a host of other clues. CSI lifted several fingerprints off her car," Marlon said, still stooping over the body finishing up his initial examination.

"Shit, this is something we don't need," Colin said. Both his hands resting on his hips as he looked down at the mutilated body of a young African-American woman who looked to be in her early twenties.

"Listen, Marlon, if you find anything else, let us know right away," Matthew said. "Let's go talk to some of these people, see if anyone saw anything."

The two detectives questioned everyone still standing around the crime scene. After a few minutes of somewhat gentle prodding of one of their witnesses, the man finally admitted to seeing the three men and one female drag the victim from her car and began feeding. Immediately, Matthew ushered the witness to their car. They drove back to the precinct to continue their line of questioning. Matthew sat the eighteen-year-old male at his desk, offered him a soda to keep him calm.

"I understand how difficult this is for you. I hate to put you through this, but we need to know what happened, please start from the beginning and anything you can give us will be helpful,"

Matthew said, gesturing for the teenager to give a recount of the attack he witnessed.

"Yeah, dude, sure. I want to help. Man, I've got to tell ya, I've never seen anything like that shit before. They just jumped in front of her car, broke her window and dragged her out. She was kicking and screaming, begging them to let her go. I wanted to help her, I *did*." The young man looked at the two detectives, his bottom lip trembled. He stared at them with wide eyes filled with a mixture of sorrow and shame.

"Please go on," Colin urged.

"You don't believe me, do you? That I wanted to help her? I did, but I was just scared. I mean, they're vampires ... super strong and shit. What could I do against them?"

"Were you the one who called the S.U.I.T.?" Matthew asked.

The young man nodded.

"Then you did all that you could do and you have no reason to be ashamed," Matthew said, hoping to ease the young man's conscience.

"I guess," he said softly, not sure if that answer was enough to assuage the guilt he was feeling. "They killed her. The female with them was the shifter, when she started eating her legs ... ." The young man's voice trailed off.  "I was so scared, I just ran. I ran so fast, I didn't want to turn around to see if they were behind me. When I thought I was safe, I called you guys."

"Can you describe what they look like? We're going to get a sketch artist in here, think you can give pretty good descriptions of her attackers?" Colin asked.

"Yeah, I can. I'll never forget their faces."

"Hold on," Matthew said, holding up his right hand. "Going back to your story, you said there were four of them, right? Three vampires and a shape-shifter ... the shifter was the female?"

The man nodded. "Yeah, really pretty, too. It's too bad she's a killer. When I saw them standing their talking, I was trying to work up the courage to talk to her before they started attacking that woman."

"How old did she look?" Matthew asked.

The man shrugged one shoulder. "I don't know, about twenty,

no more than twenty-two."

"Thanks." Matthew called the sketch artist, requesting his services. "David will be here in a few minutes to make the sketches. I'm going to the bathroom." He rose from his chair and left. When he was alone, he called Warren's cell. When his partner answered, he told him what was going on. "Warren, the DB we found on North Ave., was a copy-cat killing and I think I know who might have done this one."

"Who?"

"Remember that little gang of vamps and their female shifter we busted last year for vandalizing the *Slayer's Lair* nightclub?"

"Yeah, think they've beefed up their criminal acts?"

"To the highest level. They've taken the recent killings as inspiration. We have a witness that said he saw three vamps and one female shifter attack and kill a woman. They fit those descriptions, and they're always hanging out together. We need to find them and fast. They should be in custody while we wait for forensics to prove them guilty or innocent. Right now, the witness is giving David their descriptions."

"Good, you keep to that. We don't need any second rate hacks fucking up this investigation. Right now, I'm on my way to shake down a few supernatural businesses, see if anybody knows anything. If I see them, I'll bring them in personally."

"Okay, we'll be here." Matthew ended the call. He called Richard, giving him an update. Once he was done with that, he returned back to their witness.

***

"A copy-cat killer!" Brian stated, surprised. "You know, at least have the damn decency to wait until after the original killer is caught or dead before you start treading on their territory. They might actually piss off the real coven."

"Not before pissing me off first. Matt and I have an idea who did the killing. If I see this gang in one of these clubs, I've got a good mind to bypass their 'legal rights'," Warren said, speeding toward *Desires Unleashed*. He reached into his pocket, removing his cell phone. "I need to make a call." He called Darian.

"Hello Warren," Darian greeted.

"Darian, I just thought I'd call and let you know, we have to do a sweep of supernatural-owned businesses. I'm heading to yours right now."

"I understand. I'll call my staff and inform them to assist you upon your arrival."

"Thanks." Warren ended his call.

"Who's that?" Brian asked.

Warren tossed him a look. "The Master vampire of the city."

"And you have his personal number?"

"We have history."

"I see. If I'm not too out of line for asking, I'm sure he's aware of what's going on in *his* city … what's he doing about it?"

"Whatever he can. Listen, I'm going to tell you something only because you're one of us. Can I trust you?"

"We've just met, so I hope you can. I won't tell anyone, I swear," Brian replied.

"Okay. Darian's already had a run in with the Master vampire of the coven." Warren felt he could be honest with Brian.

"I feel like there's more to that."

"I don't want to use the word, damn-near 'indestructible', but that's the vibe I got when they told me of the encounter he had. The Master vampire's name is Marcus and we already know he's a powerful son-of-a-bitch, but even the shifter in his group is stronger than Matthew's Alpha, who is over three-hundred years old, and that's a brand new bag of trouble."

"Holy shit! The S.U.I.T. really doesn't have what it takes to take out that kind of power."

"Don't you think I know that? Fuck! I feel like I'm just out here keeping track of their kills. I feel fucking helpless. Our ultraviolet bullets can't do shit to this vampire," Warren said, slamming his fist on his steering wheel.

"But our silver-nitrate bullets can take out the shifter."

"If we can get him into the position for a straight shot, yeah."

"Do your leaders have a plan?" Brian asked, suddenly wishing he were back in California and not anywhere near this "super coven".

"They do. I've been trying to get home for hours now to see what it is, but I just haven't had the opportunity." Warren pulled the car in front of the club. Several S.U.I.T. squad cars pulled in behind him. All of the officers climbed out of their cars. Warren stood in front of them, one hand raised high, while the other held tightly to his automatic handgun loaded with ultra-violet bullets.

"Remember, we just want to pull in our regular rule breakers. Let's spread out and search the clubs along this strip. Brian and I have this one. Move out." Warren led the way.

The bouncers were aware of their "raid". The doorman stepped to the side. He looked at the two detectives. "I've got to tell ya, Warren, I thought all of them were coming in here. I mean, that's a lot of brass in one place."

"They did too, but I don't want to disturb Darian's business unnecessarily. I'm just looking for four people. Did a group of three male vamps and a female shifter come by tonight?" Warren asked.

The bouncer shrugged. "I haven't seen them, but you can take a look inside anyway."

"Thanks." Warren nodded toward the entrance. "Let's go," he said to Brian, who followed him inside. He knew there were only two sections of the club that were opened to the public. The dance section and the strip club section. They searched those areas quickly realizing that the group wasn't there. He and Brian made their way toward the backroom for members only. Immediately, it hit them. The air was thick with the scents of sex and blood, desire and ecstasy. They could hear what was going on even before they opened any doors.

"Jesus! You guys know about this place? It's illegal!" Brian said. He swallowed hard, as he wiped away a bead of sweat from his forehead. He was beginning to feel hot under the collar, his own arousal rising like an erupting volcano.

"The S.U.I.T. doesn't 'officially' know … if you catch my drift. That is why it's just you and me in here. Are you going to be able to keep yourself together?" Warren asked, smiling slyly as he witnessed Brian struggling to regain control.

"Ye-yeah. I'll be fine. Let's go," Brian said through heavy pants.

Warren approached the two shifter guards. "Hey." He flashed his badge and they stepped to the side. The two detectives went into the middle room all the way in the back of the hallway.

Brian reached out, stopping Warren from opening the door. "Wait. Um, who are we looking for in there?"

"We're looking for anyone who may have seen them tonight. I don't think they've been here. It would be pretty fucking stupid of them to show their faces in the club of the Master vampire after they broke one of his rules. They wouldn't be able to get past the shape-shifter bouncer without setting off alarms. He would smell the scent of death all over them and alert Darian. I'm just looking for someone who may be able to lead me in their direction."

"Ah, I see. Okay, let's go."

Warren nodded then opened the door, releasing the full blast of the sexual essence that clouded the air.

"Oh shit," Brian gasped. His knees went weak and he had to grab a hold of the doorframe to keep from falling to the floor. His body quaked several times as he panted breathlessly.

Warren watched him, not saying a word. He knew what to expect and had prepared himself as best he could. The first time, when they were still together, he and Adrian went to the backrooms, and they had both ended up just like Brian. He smiled to himself at the memory.

"Fuck, I can't believe I just came," Brian whispered once he was able to gather his footing.

"It wouldn't be the first time this area had that effect on people." Warren licked his lips. He took several deep breaths, hoping to keep control of himself long enough to do his job. He was glad he had prepared himself for the overwhelming energy the room produced. He knew that Brian had no idea what was behind that door, so it was no surprise to him that the shifter climaxed.

Warren waited for Brian to get his baring before he continued searching the room. It was becoming increasingly difficult for him to deny the urges raging through his own loins as he made his way through the withering bodies of dozens of people moaning in ecstasy on several dark red pillows. The two men could smell several shifters who happened to be in "heat" at the moment. As they passed by one, she reached out, hand cupping Brian's groin.

"Fuck me," she begged with pleading eyes. Her hand began to caress his second growing erection. She opened her legs, allowing him to catch a fresh scent of her longing.

Saliva gathered in his mouth, Brian had to swallow before he drooled. Unable to stop himself, he sunk to his knees falling onto her. He began kissing her as she quickly unzipped his pants pulling him free. He entered her without hesitation, moaning loudly as he pushed himself into her to the hilt.

Warren turned when he noticed Brian was no longer behind him. He quickly located his temporary partner, finding him in the arms of a female wolf. "Fuck!" He hissed under his breath, understanding what was happening. It was the same thing he wanted to do. It was the same thing he felt like he needed to do, but now was definitely not the time. He ran over there, reaching down, prying Brian away from his conquest.

"Let's go, we've got work to do, another time," Warren said, pulling Brian to his feet.

"Damn, I'm sorry," Brian said, his chest heaving. "I've never been in this kind of environment before. This place is driving me insane. It's got all my senses tingling."

"Yeah, I figured. However, I need you focused. There's someone I want to talk to right now, come on." This time Warren made sure Brian was in front of him as they made their way across the room toward a male shifter enjoying the oral pleasures of a younger male vampire who happened to be feeding at the same time. Warren pulled the vampire away, angering both men.

"Hey, what the fuck?!" The vampire hissed. He stopped his complaining abruptly when he saw the barrel of Warren's gun and Brian's S.U.I.T. badge directly in his face. "Shit, hey, I was just having some fun," he began to explain as he wiped away the few drops of blood that had spilt.

"Don't worry, you're not who we want anyway. Find someone else," Warren said, gesturing for the vampire to leave. He did. "Now, as for you, Vinny... where are your friends?"

The shifter sat up against the pillows looking at the two detectives. "What friends?" he asked, hand reaching down to caress his bloodied erection, eliciting a moan.

"Don't fucking play with me tonight." Warren grabbed him by his hair and began dragging him toward the door. Vinny cursed as his hands instinctively tried to pry his hair out of the detective's grip. Outside of the room, the three men were able to chat without as much temptation clouding their judgment.

"Ow! Let go of my hair, fucker!" the younger shifter cursed.

"Are you trying to piss me off?" Warren asked. He released Vinny's hair then slapped his palm against the shifter's forehead causing him to hit the back of his head against the wall.

"Ow! Shit!" Vinny rubbed his head. "What do you want?" He looked up at them, features distorted with a mixture of anger, disappointment and fear.

"The three vamps and the female shifter, you know who I'm talking about. I think her name was Emily … something … ," Warren said, trailing off so that Vinny could fill in the blanks.

"Yeah, I know them; Emily, Eric, Jake and Andre. I haven't seen them tonight," Vinny said.

"Do you know where I could find them?"

"What's in it for me if I tell you?"

"I won't kick your ass, or have you forgotten, the S.U.I.T. has a license to kill? I'll shoot you and swear I found you eating children for dinner. Are you going to work with me or not?" Warren threatened.

Vinny sighed, not liking the other option one bit. "I'll help you, but you didn't get this information from me. They find out I told you the location to their hangout … they're stronger than me, they could hurt me."

"They won't find out … that I can promise you."

"Okay. You should be able to find them on Belmont, right off of Halsted." He gave them the apartment address. "Apartment number three-fourteen on the third floor. Remember, you didn't hear it from me."

"Fine. Is this their only hangout?" Brian asked.

"The main one. They also like to hang out around the Human-Only district and fuck with the humans leaving there."

"Thanks for your cooperation. You can get back to your evening activities." Warren and Brian left the club. He told the other S.U.I.T. officers who checked in with him where they needed to go, sending them to patrol the Human-Only district for their suspects.

"We're going to their home?" Brian asked, climbing into the passenger seat beside Warren.

"Yeah, it's in Boystown. I'm just hoping they're home." The two detectives made it to the address in less than ten minutes. They approached the apartment as quietly as possible. Without a warning, Warren kicked down the door, gun pointed at the four people inside scrambling for weapons preparing to attack.

"Don't fucking move, or we'll shoot. You know we won't miss," Warren warned.

One of the vampires was crouched low in a springing position. After hearing Warren's warning, he decided not to lunge forward. He rose to his feet. The other three followed his lead.

"What do you want, wolf? Does the S.U.I.T. even know they've got two mutts working for them?" the apparent leader, Jake, asked arrogantly.

"I don't even have to ask if you killed that woman on North Avenue. I can smell fresh blood all over you. You smell like death," Warren said.

"We don't know shit about some dead bitch on North Avenue. We fed tonight, but that's it."

"Bullshit," Brian said. "I can smell the same human blood all over her and she shouldn't have the scent of human blood on her." He gestured to Emily, the shape-shifter.

Emily stepped back, toward the window.

"Fuck this!" Warren shot the leader before he could move, taking him by surprise. The ultraviolet gel bullet exploded inside his chest, turning his skin to ash from the inside out, killing him instantly. The others attacked, having witness their leader's execution. Warren fired his weapon several times, striking another vampire in the arm, killing him. Brian shot Emily as she was trying to escape out the window. He hated that he had to shoot her in the back, but he wasn't going to let her get away. The last vampire tried to rush past Warren to get through the door, but Warren punched him hard across the face, knocking him to the ground before putting a bullet into this head. Both detectives watched as the ultra-violet gel glowed underneath the vampire's skin, working its way through the bloodstream burning the vampire from the inside-out. The vampire twitched several times as his flesh rapidly turned into black ash leaving a darkened stain in the shape of his body that blew away with the gust of wind that came through the window.

Warren looked around the room at the minor carnage. His gaze settled on Brian who was nodding at him. "You make a pretty good partner," he said, complimenting the other shifter.

"You, too… I've got to say, it's good to take out some bad guys. I haven't had this feeling of satisfaction since I landed here," Brian said, holstering his gun.

"Yeah, unfortunately, the real threat is still out there and we're not one step closer to stopping them." Warren snapped his gun back into place in its holster. He called in the shooting, reporting directly to his captain.

"Let's hope they're the copycat killers. I'm sending the forensics team to your location along with someone from Marshall's team to finish your investigation there and retrieve the remains. When they arrive, I want you two to come back here to go over David's sketches. I want you to make certain those were actually the killers our witness said he saw," Captain Michelle Lawrence said.

Warren knew he couldn't tell her the truth. That he already knew he had the killers because he could smell fresh blood all over them, or that they smelled of a fresh kill, so he agreed. "Sure thing."

Captain Lawrence sighed. "Good. In other news, we're still gathering details from several people we were able to pick up during the raids. We still don't have any information as to where these other killers are."

"I figured as much. These guys are pros at what they do, they're not likely to leave a bunch of trails, that includes consorting with insignificant supernaturals who'd rat on them for a free pass," Warren said.

"Still, we need something. We need to catch these psychopaths Warren, there's no telling how many more people they're going to murder."

"I know. We'll see you soon." Warren ended the call. He looked at Brian. "The first S.U.I.T. employee who walks through that door, we can leave."

"Works for me," Brian said. "By the way, before we head into the precinct, can we swing by the hotel so I can change my clothes?"

Warren chuckled. "We probably should. I wouldn't want Matthew to get the wrong idea." He remembered Brian's sudden "reaction" back at *Desires Unleashed.*

"He'd think you'd be unfaithful?" Brian asked.

Warren shook his head. "It was just a joke. He's knows me, knows I'd never cheat on him, even though you're hot. I'd never do anything to hurt him."

"Well, that's love. It's good that both of you know there isn't anyone who's going to come between you," Brian said, remembering how miserably his earlier seduction of Matthew had failed.

Warren smiled to himself. "Yeah, it is."

Brian chuckled. "I do think before I leave here, if we solve this case ... I'd like to go back to *Desires Unleashed.*"

Warren gave him a sly smile. "Unfinished business?"

"You could say that," Brian said with a wink.

The two men chatted casually about their case and other topics until two team members from CSI arrived on the scene. They updated them on what had taken place, as planned and then left. Warren stopped by the hotel so that Brian could change his pants and freshen up, then they continued on to the precinct. They met up with the other four detectives on the case and confirmed with their witness and the sketches that the supernaturals they killed earlier were the ones they had been looking for.

"I guess this is what they mean when they say, 'open and shut case, Johnson'," Barry said, nodding knowingly at his partner, whose last name happened to be "Johnson".

"I'd like the phrase better if I could actually apply it to the bigger case," Gabriel said.

"Yeah, well, we're working on that," Colin said.

"I'm just glad the sun's almost up," Gabriel stated.

"That would mean something if all of these vampires slept during the day, but they don't," Barry said.

"What haven't we tried?" Warren asked. "I mean, we've done

stake-outs, raids, patrols, every one of us has spoken to our CI's. What's next?"

"I'm having a hard time believing that they were able to kill all of those people and not have one person who saw them do it, at least witness them disposing of the bodies," Brian said. He ran his hands down his face as he released a long sigh.

Colin patted him on his back. "Relax, Brian."

"I can't! Fuck, none of us can until this is over, Colin," Brian said. He looked at his friend and partner. "I'm sorry. I didn't mean to take my frustrations out on you."

"It's okay, I understand." Colin turned, looking at the other four men. "What do we do if a witness does step forward? Aside from getting a possible description, how are we going to track them down?"

"One step at a time, Colin … one step at a time," Warren said.

The six detectives decided to take shifts while the other four left to go home, eat, sleep and restore themselves. Barry and Gabriel volunteered to take the first shift. Warren and Matt dropped Colin and Brian off at their hotel before heading toward Darian's mansion. The sun was rising over the horizon as they pulled into the winding driveway. Inside the mansion, they knew that all of the vampires were asleep as well as several shifters. Both men sat down in front of their leaders as they were told the details of the plan.

"I don't like it, but there's really no safe way to play this out," Warren said.

"Let me get this straight … are each of our entire groups going?" Matthew asked.

"No," Xander answered. "I'm taking six members from my Pack, Elise is taking four from hers and only Richard is joining us."

Matthew turned to Richard. "You don't want me to come with you?"

"No. You need your rest," Richard said.

"I want to argue with you about that, but it's true. I'm exhausted," Matthew agreed.

"I know. I can see it in your eyes. You are as well, Warren. The two of you need to sleep, in case this doesn't work out as planned, we're going to need you at full strength." Richard eyes panned over the faces of both men.

"I understand," Warren said, rising from his chair.

"Call us if you need us," Matthew said.

"We will. Darian set aside a room for you, he figured you'd both be exhausted and would appreciate a warm, comfortable bed," Elise said.

"Well, he was right," Warren replied, chuckling.

"Follow me." Elise led the two men to Natasha's old bedroom. They undressed and climbed into bed. A few seconds later, they were both asleep.

# CHAPTER SIXTEEN

"**D**ad, I'm actually surprised you're all for the use of weapons this time around," Adrian said, as he was checking over his handgun loaded with silver bullets.

Xander looked at his son, whom he'd chosen as an enforcer for their Pack for a reason. He smiled. It wasn't that he was opposed to using weapons at all. He felt the use of weapons were ideal in certain situations, like now. "Why wouldn't I be? This situation calls for it. We're not in a battle for our territory. This has everything to do with survival, and we should be prepared for whatever may come."

"But isn't this still about us defending our territory? What about the 'integrity' of it?" Adrian asked, remembering his father's words to him.

"Because this is our territory, yes, we are defending it. However, no official *Challenge of Authority* has been issued. We are not the only ones being attacked. We must eliminate this threat by any means necessary. I don't think there's a community in existence that wouldn't understand our methods and use them if they were in our predicament," Xander answered.

Adrian nodded, understanding his father. "This is our best shot, I think. He may be able to hurt us one on one or even three on one, but I don't think he'll be able to defend himself against thirty to one. I just wanted to make sure you weren't disappointed in your decision."

Xander nodded. "Whether or not this is the best course of action to take, is irrelevant. It's our only option at this point."

Richard entered the den, looking at the two shifters conversing. "Are you both ready?"

They turned toward him. "Yes," Xander answered.

"All right, everyone is outside getting into the automobiles." Richard turned, exiting the mansion.

Adrian looked at his father. "Let's do this."

Both men left, climbing into a new black Sidewinder SUV with Richard, Elise, Sergio and Daniel. The two SUV's carrying Adan's Pride were followed by two SUV's with Elise and Xander's members in them. They drove through Chicago, heading into Oak Forest, They continued driving, wondering if they would soon be attacked by Marcus not wanting Adan's Pride to flee the city. Another hour passed along with another city and still, there was no attack. Devin, who was driving the first SUV pulled over along the road, the others followed. The leaders of the three groups climbed out to see why he pulled over. They walked over to the SUV.

"Devin, what's wrong?" Elise asked.

Devin shrugged. "He told me to pull over." He pointed at Adan.

"Why?" Elise asked, now looking at Adan.

"Because," Adan began, giving them a sad smile. "I really can't ask for more than what you've all tried to do for me and my Pride. None of us can guarantee this is going to work. You should return back to your family and friends, we'll-"

"Enough with the death wish, already. You go off on your own, you're as good as slaughtered," Sergio said. "You came here for help and you might as well stay and fight, win or lo- Naw, fuck that, we're going to kick ass when the time comes." He was not willing to even imagine a predicament that ended in defeat.

"I'm not afraid to fight or die. I just want to protect my Pride. Many of them have never seen battle, let alone had to fight for their lives," Adan said.

"Maybe it's time. I know that in your Pride, things run differently, but now is the time for your females to step up," Sergio said.

Adan nodded thoughtfully. "That's true. Another thing is, I don't think going to another city within the state is enough to draw him out."

"Why didn't you say that before we drove all the way out here?" Devin asked.

"Just thought about it, that's why," Adan said.

"None of that matters. We all knew it was a long shot to begin with. How about this," Sergio turned toward the others. "We head back but we stay separated, keeping a short enough travel distance between our two locations. Let's see if they attack us that way. Our best option is to keep them divided. They'll either split up to attack us, or team up to attack one location in which we can alert the others in time for them to join us to combine our forces. This is, of course, a contingency plan in case they bother attacking us at all."

"I think that is a pretty decent strategy," Xander said, nodding. "In fact, I'd like to elaborate on it. Perhaps, we should gather three or four members from Darian's coven and take them to our second location. That way, our strength can be as equally divided as much as possible. Also the vampires can telepathically connect with each other in the event of an attack."

"That works for me," Devin agreed.

Elise smiled, so proud of her king and lover, father of her children. "I'll inform Darian when he rises. The only thing that's still troubling me is the age of Marcus' entire coven, I really wish I knew how powerful they were."

"I know, right now, we just have to do what we can. Let's head back," Xander said.

They all decided to follow Sergio's plan and headed back to Evanston. Some stayed at the mansion, while others went with Elise and Richard. The second team left after gathering John, April, Gary and Tony from Darian's coven, and drove to the hotel Elise had rented which was less than ten minutes traveling distance, possibly two if you break all speeding laws, from Darian's mansion. Each team waited it out to see what would happen next.

***

A little after noon, Warren pulled into the parking lot of the S.U.I.T. precinct. He and Matthew picked up Brian and Colin along the way. They went inside, meeting up with Barry and Gabriel, who were looking over paperwork.

"Anything else happen that we need to know about?" Warren asked.

Barry looked up from his paperwork. "No. Everything's been quiet so far. I don't know what's going on, what they have planned.

But it's been at least twelve hours without a body being reported."

"I don't know if that's good news or bad," Gabriel said.

"Well, we'd know about a body if there was one. This coven likes to brag about their kills," Colin stated.

"You two need to head home, get some rest. We'll take over the watch from here," Matthew told Barry and Gabriel.

"Good idea," Gabriel said, yawning as he stretched his limbs. "Let's go, Barry." He rose to his feet, pulling his jacket from the back of his chair and slipping it on. Barry did the same and both detectives left.

Warren looked at the other three men. "Let's do some patrolling, see what we can find out."

"Okay, we'll take the south side, you take the north, keep in contact," Matthew said.

Warren and Brian headed north, while Matthew and Colin headed south. They patrolled the neighborhoods, speaking with other supernaturals to see if any of them had information. No one knew anything that could help them solve their case, but they continued to search for answers.

***

Kiren lay panting breathlessly beside Marcus, his chest heaving as he struggled to regain his composure. Marcus lay on his back, his eyes closed as he relished the sensation of his lover's blood warming him as the last waves of his fleeting orgasm subsided. The tingles began to vanish until there was nothing left but the memory of their lovemaking.

Kiren rolled over, watching him. "Are you still mad at me about last night?"

Without opening his eyes, Marcus answered him. "Yes."

"I couldn't help it, I wanted to see them. I wanted to watch them try to figure me out."

"I don't care. You were careless and you almost died because of it. Had I not come when I did, Darian would have killed you," Marcus said, finally turning his head to look at him.

"He took me by surprise. I'm sure on any other given day, I

could have killed him."

Marcus laughed. "And then you'd really piss me off. That beautiful man is mine. I have plans for him. Besides, you couldn't kill him even if you wanted to. He's stronger than you'll ever be. But that's not to say you still can't have fun. His lover and second in command is weaker than you. In addition, they have the woman, their son and she's pregnant with their second child. This makes her very special."

"Think he'd surrender if we took her hostage, threaten to kill her?"

"No. He's a Master vampire; he has much more at stake than his human lover if he surrendered. As a matter of fact, I'd think him weak if he did. No, this one would never give in so easily and I think that's what's exciting to me. He knows I want him, yet he's not running as many others have in the past."

"Just like that pussy, Adan?"

Marcus chuckled. "You're incorrect. You mistake his fleeing as a sign of weakness. He is powerful and brave, but he has obligations to protect his Pride, his women. He knows his death would most likely mean theirs and he's trying to prevent that."

"Do you still want Adan and his Pride?" Kiren was curious. He knew his lover had struck a gold mine per say when he'd met Darian, Elise, Xander and Richard.

"I do, even more so now than before. He has joined forces with the other supernaturals in this state and I'm intrigued to see where this is going to go. I've never come face-to-face with a situation such as this where separate communities are working together. Also, they have members within the S.U.I.T., which I wasn't expecting, so intelligence is coming in from all angles." Marcus smiled wickedly. "As a matter of fact, I want you to do something; we need to raise the bar on this one."

"I thought we already had," Kiren said, running his fingers down the length of Marcus's chest down to his muscular abdomen.

"Killing the infant and the others is nothing compared to the hell we're going to bring forth."

Kiren sat up, intrigued. "What is it that you want me to do?" His eyes were bright with anticipation.

"This S.U.I.T. organization needs to be roused a bit more. I've enjoyed watching them chase their tails in trying to figure us out. They've failed and they know it. These humans have no idea who they're dealing with." Marcus caressed the side of Kiren's face. "You'll enjoy doing this."

"The anticipation is killing me; what is it you want me to do?!" Kiren was growing more impatient.

Marcus chuckled. "There are two detectives who were flown in from California to help. One of them I sensed is a shifter … a wolf. The other is human. I want you to turn the human. Remember, turn him not kill him. Then I want you to turn the other two human detectives who are working the case as well. I think it'll be fun if we change the S.U.I.T. around a bit, don't you."

Now it was Kiren's turn to smile; only his bared a more sinister appearance. "A little change here, a little change there, I'm enjoying the possibilities. Can I do this thing my way?"

"Have all of the fun you want to. There's nothing those other shifters can do to stop you."

Kiren's smile grew wider as he planted a kiss on his lover's lips before climbing out of the bed. He began to dress quickly, not bothering to shower.

"You're not going to shower first?" Marcus asked, knowing the answer.

Kiren shook his head. "No, I want your scent all over me."

"I figured as much. Good decision by the way. My scent being on you is quite complementary."

"I think so." Kiren chuckled. "Do you have any idea where I can find these humans?"

"Of course I do. I formed a mental link with them the moment I realized they were handling the case." Marcus told Kiren where he could find his targets. "Have fun," he said before his lover left.

Kiren was beyond excited. No one had ever dared to destroy the S.U.I.T. organization before. The concept was forbidden. The Council; which consisted of eight supernaturals, both vampire and shape-shifter, had long ago decided that the humans should have their police Force in order to keep the peace. They decided the humans should have their laws and their justice; everything reasonable to make them feel safe enough to sleep at night. In order to co-exist with mankind, the S.U.I.T. was a necessity and therefore it was agreed that no direct attack would be taken against them for the sake of maintaining that peace.

Master vampires and various leaders of shifter communities all agreed to allow the S.U.I.T. to protect the humans from those of their kind who broke the four laws. Many didn't agree with the new system, but none dared to overstep the ruling of the Council. Not until now. What Marcus was planning was a direct insult to the Council. Kiren wasn't surprised by Marcus' plan. His lover had never had much respect for the Council. Many felt that the Council had given in to the humans all too easily, which allowed the humans to think they were still in control. Others, however, had felt the Council was wise in their decision, which allowed supernaturals more power over the humans than they ever had before.

Then there were those, like his Master, who did what they wanted to do, whenever they wanted to do it. They didn't obey a set of rules made up by people weaker than themselves. They ruled their own world and this attack was a message to all who dared to press their ideals onto them. Kiren would make his Master proud. He pulled his car in front of a red brick home. The lawn was trimmed in pretty flowers and there was a child's bike lying on its side next to the rose bush. He climbed out of the car, walked up to the front door and knocked.

Gabriel's daughter, Rhiana answered, looking upward at the very tall man who stood before her. "Hello, can I help you-"

"Rhiana … ," her mother came up behind her, taking over the introductions. "Sweetie, go and play with your brother, okay."

"Okay, Mommy," Rhiana said, running upstairs.

Her mother returned her attentions back to the stranger. "Hello, how may I help you?"

"Is your husband home? I have some information for him about his case."

"Yes, my husband's home. Please wait right here." Melinda closed the door, locking it in place. She called to her husband who came out of the kitchen at the sound of his name.

"Yeah, babe?" he answered.

"There's a man outside, he says he has information about your case."

Gabriel's eyes widened as he quickened his pace toward the front door, he opened it. "Who are you?"

"Someone with a message." Kiren pushed Gabriel hard knocking him backwards to the floor. Moving faster than the two humans could see, he punched Gabriel's wife, rendering her unconscious before returning his attention back to Gabriel who was scrambling to his feet. Kiren smiled as he advanced on Gabriel, pushing him back onto the floor. "You're not going anywhere."

"What do you want?!" Gabriel asked, his face reddening with anger and frustration.

Kiren tilted his head sideways. "Isn't that the million dollar question? What do I want? What do we all want? Great sex, a hot meal, a bank full of cash and a lot of fun ways to spend it... am I right?" He chuckled.

"You're the shifter, aren't you, the sick son-of-a-bitch who killed those children?" Gabriel questioned.

"I am," Kiren said before straddling Gabriel and pinning him against the floor. "We're going to have a lot of fun together."

"Fuck you!" Gabriel growled as he struggled in vain to toss the shifter off him. He looked over toward his wife who was now bleeding from the open gash on her forehead. "My wife! What did you do to her?!"

"You're ballsy for a human. I like you. Don't worry; she's not dead... concussed, but not dead. There might be some brain damage, but that's not really my concern. Now, those two adorable kids of yours, I could have some fun with them."

Gabriel stopped struggling as he locked eyes with the shifter. "Leave my children out of this."

"I'm feeling pretty charitable today, so maybe I will, then again, maybe I won't. Tell you what; I'll let it be your decision if I involve your kids." Kiren's smile widened, revealing his pearly whites. His right hand held both of Gabriel's wrists to the floor, while his left slid down his captive's chest, past his stomach, finding his groin. "Niiiice. Have you ever fucked a guy before?"

"Don't even fucking think about it, freak!" Gabriel began to struggle again against his captor.

Kiren frowned as his grip tightened on Gabriel's groin causing the man to grimace as sharp pains shot through his sensitive flesh. "That wasn't a nice thing to say at all. It certainly wasn't smart. You must want to watch me devour your precious kids in front of you. You know I can."

"NO! Please, don't hurt them!" Gabriel ceased his struggling.

"Are we willing to be cooperative now?" Kiren asked, his hand beginning to massage Gabriel's groin.

Sickened by the shifter, Gabriel swallowed hard. "What do you want from me? You want me to back off this case?"

Kiren laughed outright. "No, nothing so easy as that. I don't care if you work twenty-four hours straight on this case, makes no difference to us, you'll never stop us even if you did. No, we have other plans for you and I have a few of my own ideas of what I want to do to you."

Gabriel didn't want to mention what he thought those "ideas" were. He didn't want to think about what this shifter was going to do to him. But he knew he needed to ask, so he did. "What are you going to do to me?"

Kiren unbuttoned Gabriel's jeans then unzipped them.

"Fuck! Stop it, please!" Gabriel begged.

Kiren ignored Gabriel's pleas, slipping his hand underneath the waistband of the other man's underwear, fingers finding the soft flesh. "You know, I get a lot of pleasure making men like you bend to my will. Right now, you're soft, but I can make sure you don't stay that way."

"Men don't turn me on; you're wasting your time." Gabriel hoped he could dissuade the shifter from taking him against his will.

"I don't think I'm wasting my time, unless of course, you want me to let your kids take your place instead."

"You son-of-a-bitch! I swear to *God* you touch my kids I'll find a way to personally rip your *fucking* heart out of your *fucking* chest! You *fucking* freak!"

"My, my! You kiss your kids with that mouth?" Kiren laughed. "I guess you do. It is the same mouth you eat pussy with, right?"

"I'm not fucking playing with you; leave my kids out of this!"

"Like I said, that depends on what you do and what you don't do." Kiren pulled Gabriel's penis free and began stroking it in a slow motion. "I know this feels good. You need to stop fighting me. I'm not the kind of man you want to piss off. You've seen my handiwork, haven't you? Remember the ice cream truck?"

Gabriel's eyes widened. "Those kids … you're psychotic." He was struggling to maintain his calm, but his groin was beginning to respond to Kiren's masterful fingers. He hated that his flesh was growing harder with each stroke. But he knew this killer wasn't bluffing. The last thing he wanted was to see any harm come to his children.

"Yeah, I know. I had fun, too."

"So are you going to rape me?"

"Rape you? Hell no. You can't rape someone who gives themselves over to you willingly. That is what you're doing, right… giving yourself to me?"

Gabriel thought about his innocent children playing upstairs, completely oblivious to what was happening downstairs. He looked at his wife, who he wanted to run to. She needed emergency medical help she wouldn't get until he gave this shifter what he wanted. He looked back at the man on top of him. "Yes."

"See there, I knew we could come to an understanding." Kiren smiled as he snatched Gabriel's pants down, removing them. He unbuttoned his own pants, pulling himself free.

"You promise not to hurt my family?" Gabriel asked one last time.

"For a piece of your hot ass, I promise." Kiren positioned himself between Gabriel's legs.

"I hope you burn in hell for this shit."

"Ooooo, I love when you talk dirty," Kiren said before plunging himself deeply into Gabriel's opening. The shifter moaned loudly as he began to stroke inside him.

Gabriel bit down hard on his bottom lip drawing blood as he struggled to keep quiet, not wanting to bring alarm to his children. He closed his eyes to shut out the horror. Nonetheless, he was aware of what was happening to him, although some part of him was still in denial. He could feel the shifter's weight on top of him, grinding. He could feel the shifter's hardness gliding in and out of him roughly. He hated the feeling of this shifter's breath coming in labored gasps against his skin. He turned his head away, not wanting to look at the face of the beast on top of him. He wanted to not be there. He wanted it to all be over, the pain, the humiliation, the horror. It seemed like it would go on forever and he didn't know how much longer he would be able to endure what was happening to him. Relief finally came in a final thrust, a loud moan and one last tremor. He felt the shifter pull out leaving him in intense agony. He knew he was bleeding and would need emergency care. What he didn't know, what he wasn't prepared for was the sudden plunge of sharp feline teeth sinking into his skin. Not meaning to, he screamed as the searing hot pain shot through his shoulder, all the way to the bone. He opened his eyes, to see Kiren pulling back, licking his lips, his long incisors were retracting.

"Now, I'm done with you," Kiren said, smiling.

Gabriel could hear his children coming down the stairs as they called for their daddy. "Stay where you are!" He shouted back to them. He couldn't let them see him like this, he just couldn't. He looked at Kiren. "Please… don't leave me like this," he managed to say through fevered gasps. Sweat began to pour profusely from his pores. He began to feel cold chills racking his body causing him to shiver uncontrollably. A vicious wave of nausea rushed through him and he rolled over onto his side in time to vomit a foul stream of half-digested food onto the floor.

Kiren watched him for a few seconds. "I like you. I don't normally give in to requests, but for you … Just this once." He pulled Gabriel's pants on, buttoning and zipping them. "If you live through this, your life will never be the same. Consider it a gift," he whispered in his ear before leaving.

Gabriel's children, no longer able to stay away, made it downstairs to the horrible scene that awaited them. Their mother lay unconscious in a corner, bleeding from a head wound while their father was sweating, bleeding, trembling and vomiting, unable to move. They began to cry, frightened, not fully understanding what was going on. Wesley ran to the telephone, remembering what his father had once told them about home safety and emergencies. He called 9-1-1, gave them their address. Emergency personnel made it to their home, rushing both Gabriel and his wife to the hospital. Police took the children to the hospital as well, calling Gabriel's mother along the way to take custody of the children upon her arrival.

***

Barry just finished arguing with his new neighbor who allowed his French poodle to defecate on his manicured front lawn. Harsh words were exchanged, but in the end, the neighbor apologized the very moment he saw a glimpse of the detective's silver and gold S.U.I.T. badge attached to his belt buckle. Barry accepted the apology, but was satisfied when the man finally walked away with his dog in tow. Just when he was turning to go back inside his home, he heard someone call his name. He turned around.

"Do I know you?" Barry asked.

"No, but you will. I've just come from visiting your partner, Gabe. Now, you're not as handsome as he is, but I'm wondering if your ass is as sweet as his," Kiren said, smiling wickedly.

Without hesitating, Barry pulled his gun from his holster and began firing. Kiren managed to dodge every bullet with ease. To Barry, it looked as though the shifter wasn't moving at all! As Kiren dodged the bullets, he advanced on Barry faster than the man realized. Within an instant, he was standing in front of him. Kiren grabbed both of Barry's arms, painfully pinning them behind his back as he began to elongate his teeth, baring his incisors as he'd done with Gabriel. Barry roared in rage as he struggled vainly to break free; a second later, long, sharp teeth pierced his skin, splattering his own blood across his neck and cheek. He cried out in both rage and pain as the shifter retracted his teeth. A second later, the shifter was gone and he was lying on his side. His limbs grew heavy as his muscles grew weaker. He found himself unable to move as an ice-cold chill rushed through his body, followed by a vicious wave of nausea. His vision began to blur and grow darker as the fever took hold. Like his partner, the contents of his stomach purged, splattering over his award-winning lawn.

His wife, who had been in the backyard gardening, heard the gunshots and her husband scream. She was now at his side, terrified. It had all happened so quickly and was over in a matter of seconds! There was so much blood! Barry's gun lay on the ground beside him and he was unresponsive, but still alive. She pulled her husband's cell phone from his pocket and called 9-1-1. Within minutes, an ambulance and two police cars pulled up and rushed them to the hospital.

***

A second call came over the police scanner. A second S.U.I.T. officer was attacked at his home fifteen minutes after the first attack. The address of the first and second attack was given.

Warren looked at Brian, shocked. "Fuck! Barry and Gabe!"

"Those are their homes?" Brian asked, swallowing the last of his coffee.

"Yeah! Shit! We need to get to the hospital to see if they're all right." Warren shifted the car into gear and headed for the hospital Barry was rushed to. They arrived at the hospital seventeen minutes later. With a flash of his badge, both he and Brian were allowed past the posted police guards.

Their captain, Michelle Lawrence was standing beside Barry's wife, Leanne, who was in tears as the doctor spoke about her husband's chances for survival. His chances were slim, the fever was high and they were unable to break it at this point. They had run a blood check on him, and it was quite apparent that the shape-shifter gene was mixing with his DNA, transforming him. The doctor informed them if Barry was able to survive the fever induced by his transformation, he would be a shape-shifter when it was all over and done with.

"We're going to do everything in our power to insure that your husband pulls through, Mrs. Weinstein," the Doctor said, hoping to reassure the distressed woman.

"Thank you, Doctor," Leanne said, wiping the tears from her eyes. She wanted to be by her husband's side, wanted to hold his hand and talk to him so that he knew she was there. However, she wasn't allowed inside, not yet.

Captain Lawrence hated hearing the bad news about two of her best cops. Already, she had received two telephone calls from the Director of the S.U.I.T. organization inquiring about the two detectives' condition. She knew why he'd called her, knew the reason why he was so "concerned" about their condition. She had told him she'd find out and get back with him. She was delaying making that phone call. Instead, she laid a comforting hand on the sunken shoulder of Barry's wife, attempting to give her some hope.

"Barry's strong, Leanne. He's going to pull through this, don't worry," Michelle said, giving the woman a slight smile.

"He'd better. He knows I love him too much to lose him. Besides, I was making his favorite dinner tonight, he's not going to want to miss out on that," Leanne said, making a joke to ease her fears, boosting her own morale.

Captain Lawrence smiled and nodded. She looked up to see Warren and Brian standing beside the nurses' counter, watching them. She approached the two men.

"What happened?" Warren asked, genuinely concerned.

"Both Gabriel and Barry were attacked. Gabriel's wife was attacked also; she's in the same hospital as Gabriel, recovering from a concussion. Gabriel's in worse shape. He was bitten, like Barry was." She refrained from telling the two detectives about the sexual assault Gabriel had endured; thinking he wouldn't want that information known.

"Fuck!" Warren growled. He stopped himself from punching the wall in his outrage.

"So if they pull through this, they'll be shifters?" Brian asked, already knowing the answer, but wanted to see her expression.

"Yes." Michelle's expression was sad, disappointed.

"So, what does that mean for them?" Warren asked.

"Let's not discuss that right now. I still need you two out there searching for this shifter. I've contacted the other officers of the S.U.I.T. and informed them of the attack. We should all be on alert right now. I don't want to say that we are under attack as a whole. This might be an isolated assault on the detectives who are on the case specifically, and it might be something else entirely. Just beware and keep in touch with me at all times," Captain Lawrence patted Warren on the shoulder as she passed by him on her way back to the precinct.

"I want to catch this fucker, Brian," Warren said.

"You and me, both."

Warren walked over to Leanne, who was sitting in the waiting room. Squatting down in front of her, he placed his hands on top of hers. "It's going to be all right, Leanne. Barry's one hell of a guy, he's a fighter. He'll be up and about and looking for that dinner you cooked within twenty-four hours, you'll see."

Leanne chuckled. "I know. Thanks Warren."

"Anytime. Listen, we have to go, but I'll come back and check in on you."

"Thank you."

Warren rose and Leanne grabbed his hand. He looked down at her. "What's wrong?"

"Warren, I want you to be careful. Promise me you'll be careful."

"I promise."

Satisfied, she released his hand and watched as the two detectives stepped onto the elevator, disappearing as the doors closed. Inside the elevator, Warren called Matthew.

"Did you hear about Gabe and Barry?" Warren asked.

"Yeah, Colin and I just left the hospital where Gabe's at. He's in bad shape Warren. They don't think he's going to make it. He was also sexually assaulted. I overheard the doctor talking to Gabriel's mother," Matthew said.

Warren was silent for several moments before responding. "And his wife?"

"She's going to be all right. She has a mild concussion, and should be up and talking later on today."

"What about the kids?"

"They're fine… unharmed. They're with Gabe's mother right now."

"That's good … That's good. Where are you right now?"

"Just grabbing a few burgers before we head over to the Ravenswood area, what about you?"

"I don't know yet. Listen, I want you to be extra careful. The captain thinks this may be an attack on the S.U.I.T. or just an attack on the detectives assigned to the case. Either way, watch your ass out there."

"I was already thinking that and we're keeping an eye out for anything suspicious. I wish I knew what this motherfucker looked like. Darian gave a great description, but it's still hard to pinpoint a face out here, ya know?"

"Yes, I know. Listen, we're getting ready to head downtown. I'll call you later." Warren ended the call as he and Brian climbed into their car. He told Brian what Matthew told him.

"He was turned, on top of being raped? That's fucked up."

"Tell me about it."

"At least his wife and kids weren't killed," Brian said.

"That's the only good news there is. Not that I'm not happy about that, but I am wondering why he didn't hurt them, you know?" Warren asked. He couldn't help but wonder why the shifter decided to show a sliver of kindness now, considering all of the damage he'd done.

"Maybe he didn't want to, or maybe he was told not to, or maybe it's more fun for him to know that he's changed their families forever. Who knows what going on in his demented mind?"

"I see your point. It's evident that this is just a big game to them and we're the pieces."

Brian nodded. "We should get a move on. We're going downtown, right? What are you looking for there?" he asked.

"Right now, I don't even know. I suppose I'm looking for any man who's Asian and smells like a lion."

"So we'll be hitting the bricks. Sounds good to me, I'd like to stretch my legs, do a little walking."

"Then it's decided." Warren headed downtown to walk the streets hoping to catch a whiff of the shifter.

\*\*\*

"Did you get my burger with extra mayo?" Colin asked.

"Yeah, here." Matthew handed the other man his cheeseburger

and fries.

"Is all that yours?" Colin asked, amazed as he looked down at the two triple cheeseburgers, large fries and onion rings Matthew had.

"Yeah, I haven't eaten anything all day, I'm starving!" Matthew thought he was being modest. He really wanted to order four burgers, but settled for two as to not alarm the human detective.

"You must have a great metabolism, just like Brian," Colin said, unraveling the foil from his burger and taking a huge bite.

"Yeah, and an elastic stomach, or so my mom always told me," Matthew lied. He remembered how he used to look at Warren the way Colin was looking at him whenever they sat down for a meal. Warren's plate would be piled high, while his was the "normal" serving of food. He had no idea the hunger a shifter felt and he wished he hadn't teased Warren as much as he had in the past. Lucky for him, his lover was always a good sport about it.

The two detectives were enjoying their meal as they sat in their car parked in the lot behind the restaurant. Matthew was devouring the last of his second burger when he was surprised by the shattering of glass from his driver's side window. French fries flew in all directions as the two detectives jumped in their seats. Before Matthew could react, he felt the other shifter's fist striking his jaw, jarring his brain. He was hit two more times before he was knocked unconscious. All of it happened within a matter of seconds. Colin managed to pull his gun from his holster, getting off one shot that passed through the roof of the car. Kiren grabbed hold of his wrist, twisting it until the bones broke from the pressure. Colin screamed from the pain, but he continued to defend himself. Leaning back against the passenger door, he raised both feet, kicking with all his strength. He managed to make contact with the shifter's face, jerking his head backward. Unfortunately, it was not enough to force the shifter to release his broken wrist. Kiren climbed into the car, over Matthew's unconscious body toward Colin. As he had done with the others, he elongated his incisors as he moved upward Colin's legs, pausing over the struggling man's groin. He lowered his head, sinking his teeth into Colin's genitals, biting into the flesh. He loved the gut-wrenching scream that came from his victim; it was music to his ears.

A second later, Kiren pulled away and smiled as he watched the human began to suffer from the effects of the fever. "I bet you never had someone love your dick as much as me," he said, laughing wickedly. He looked up as the sounds of police sirens drew nearer. "Someone must have heard that gunshot you let off, and called them. As impressed as I am at the response time, I can't help but feel a little annoyed. Well, that's my cue to get the hell out of here." He ran off, jumping into his car, speeding away.

When the police arrived, they saw what had happened to the two detectives. By the time the ambulance had arrived, Matthew had been roused and refused medical treatment, but insisted on traveling with Colin. He called Warren en route toward the hospital.

"Warren, we were attacked!" Matthew said in a rush of words when his lover answered the cell.

"What the fuck?! Are you okay? What about Colin?"

"I'm fine. I was just knocked out. Colin's in bad shape. The son-of-a-bitch bit him right on his groin and he's bleeding pretty badly. The paramedics are trying to stop the bleeding now." He gave Warren the address and name of the hospital they were heading to. "Meet me there."

"We're on our way." Warren ended the call. He looked at Brian. "It's Colin, he's be-"

"I heard," Brian said through gritted teeth.

"Let's go," Warren said as both he and Brian made a mad dash toward their car.

Brian looked out the window as the car sped through traffic, watching the city pass by in a blur. His mind was swamped with concern about his partner. Would he pull through? How will he feel if he does? Would they still be friends afterward? Would Colin ever trust him again? He tried to clear his mind of those thoughts. Whatever happens would happen no matter how much he worried about it, of that, he was certain. They arrived at the hospital minutes later. Both men met up with Matthew in the waiting room.

"Is he still alive?" Brian asked Matthew.

"Yeah, he's still alive. The doctors are working on him right now. I called the captain and told her what happened," Matthew said.

"Well if there was any doubt that the officers on the case are under attack, this should take care of that. Another thing I've put together is this shifter only attacked the human detectives on this case. I'm sure he could have kill Matthew; instead he just knocked him out. They're toying with us by turning three officers," Brian said, piecing together certain events.

"I'm calling Xander," Warren said, and did just that. He contacted his Alpha, giving him all of the information he had up to that very moment.

"My God," Xander said under his breath after hearing about the attack on the three officers. "I have to tell the others. Right now, I want you three to stay together, do you understand me? As a matter of fact, come here." He gave Warren the address of their hotel.

"We'll be there in a little while."

"Please hurry."

"Will do." Warren ended the call. He looked at Brian. "Matt and I are going to meet up with our Packs. Do you want to stay here with your partner, or come with us?"

"Hard decision. I want to stay beside my partner, but I also want to help catch these sons-of-bitches," Brian said, not sure which choice to make.

"Here's the thing, the doctors aren't going to let you in there until he's out of the woods. While you wait for that to happen, you can come with us. If you don't you'll just be sitting in the waiting room for hours," Matthew said, bringing things into perspective.

"You're right," Brian agreed. "But I'm coming back here after we're done."

Warren nodded and all three men left the hospital, heading toward the hotel. The sun would be setting soon and they had no idea what would be next. They made it to the hotel. Warren made the introductions, making sure everyone knew who Brian was and vice-versa. Once everyone was settled into various chairs and sofas in the room, they continued to discuss their predicament.

"What do we do now?" Devin asked, looking toward Elise for an answer.

"There's nothing we can do, Devin. They don't want to be found, and searching around aimlessly has gotten us nowhere,"

Sergio said.

"So we just have to wait, is that what you're saying?" Devin asked.

"Do you have any other ideas?" Carmen asked.

Devin huffed. "No, not really… I just hate this … not knowing what to do. I hate being a sitting duck. I hate not being proactive in our defense."

"I know how you feel. Trust me, I hate this shit, too," Sergio agreed.

The others nodded, as they all felt the same about their situation.

# CHAPTER SEVENTEEN
## SUNSET

Kiren burst through the door, climbing onto Marcus' lap, kissing him passionately. "I had so much fucking fun!" he said, once he broke the kiss.

"I take it you got to all three targets?" Marcus asked, his hands massaging Kiren's buttocks.

"All three."

"I can smell one of them was a little more fun than the other two?"

Kiren smiled wickedly. "He was the sweetest. I took him right there next to his wife who was out cold. His kids were upstairs and had no idea what was happening downstairs."

"Do you want him again?"

Kiren shook his head. "No, he was nice, but I don't want him again. I have my eyes on Adan. He's beautiful and powerful. Bringing him to his knees will please me greatly."

"Then he's yours."

Kiren held his head upward, ears twitching at the sound he was hearing then he smiled. "The others are up now."

"They are."

"So, what are we going to do tonight?"

"Nothing. We let them stew in their fear and confusion. I want to see what they are going to do, especially the S.U.I.T. organization." Marcus smiled widely.

"Aren't you four going to hunt?"

"Yes, we are. But we aren't going to kill."

"Well, that's no fun," Kiren whined, pouting.

"That's my decision, and you'd do well to follow my orders." Marcus looked at him, one eyebrow raised sardonically.

"I won't disappoint you again, I promise."

"Good."

The other three members of Marcus' coven emerged from the bedroom, fully dressed.

"Are we hunting tonight?" Mikhail asked.

"Yes, but no killing," Marcus said.

The three of them nodded and left the apartment to search for their evening meals.

***

Outside, standing on the corner, Raven frowned. "I don't see why we can't kill tonight, what's Marcus up to?" she asked.

"It's not up to you to question him. Let's just hunt, feed-without killing and head back in," Alicia said, scanning a group of young people as they walked down the street, unaware of the danger that was lurking near.

"It better be something good," Raven complained. "Let's eat them real quick and head back."

"No, that's stupid. They're too close to where we're at. We don't know if this Master vampire of the city is scanning minds, and we don't want him to lock on to some stupid human who's nearby. Let's hunt the suburbs," Mikhail suggested.

The other two agreed and that's what they did, feeding greedily and making it back home while the night was still young. As politely as they could, they asked their Master about his plans. Marcus spoke to them, told them of his strategy, of what was done to the three S.U.I.T. detectives earlier that day. Told them of the games he had in store for Darian and the others. It was then that Raven had a question.

"Master, what if the Council tries to retaliate for our attack? They have powerful allies."

"They also have powerful enemies and I do not fear the Council. They are a group of eight politicians given supernatural gifts undeserving. The deals they made with the human government were one of human interest. Any supernatural worthy of their gift would never submit to the laws that govern us, nor would they cower before toy soldiers. If the Council dares to confront me, I will destroy them. They know this, which is why they've been silent and will remain silent. There is nothing they can do, nothing they will do." Marcus reclined his chair, settling even more comfortably against the cushions, confident about his notions.

"You are all powerful, Master, I was wrong to doubt you," Raven said.

"All is forgiven," Marcus said, smiling. They waited out the night, leaving their enemies untouched and bewildered.

***

In the privacy of his bedroom, Darian slowly paced the floor. His mind ran rampant with ideas. He was struggling to find out what Marcus and his coven were up to. He didn't want to admit it to himself, nor to the others that he was beginning to feel out of his league with this Master vampire. Still, he had hope that together, they might have a chance at defeating their enemy, once they were able to lock onto them and their overall plan. He was very distraught after hearing about the three men who were bitten that day and he wondered what the future held for Matthew and Warren because of it. Xavier entered the room, closing the door behind him. He watched Darian standing in the middle of the room.

"You can't blame yourself for any of this, Darian," Xavier said, stepping closer.

"I don't. I just wish I could stop it."

"We will, together when the time is right. We need for them to make their move and when they do, we'll be able to act. Just sit tight." Xavier was hoping to ease his lover's anxiety. He'd never seen Darian so upset; he didn't like it. But he understood it. When Darian sat on the edge of the bed, Xavier took the space next to him.

"Have you fed tonight?" Xavier asked him.

"Yes."

"Did you get any relief from it?"

Darian turned to Xavier. "No, not really, which is rare."

"I could do something about that, might help you to relax," Xavier said, imploringly.

"You think I need to relax? Do you think I can?" Darian was

intrigued.

"I think you should, yes. I've never seen you so distraught, and quite frankly, I don't know if you're able to concentrate as well as you could if you had a level head. This is true with anyone, be them human or supernatural, young or ancient."

Darian caressed the side of Xavier's face, gazing into his beautiful lover's gray eyes. "I love you, my beautiful *Inamorato*."

Xavier smiled. "I know." He slipped his hand between Darian's legs, gently massaging his groin causing his lover to moan.

Darian's breathing quickened. He closed his eyes, leaning his head backward. Xavier undid his lover's pants, freeing him. In the privacy of their bedroom, on his knees in front of his lover, he relieved Darian of his stress, releasing his tension along with the last tremor of pleasure.

Xavier rose, running the back of his hand over his mouth. "Feeling any better?" he asked, smiling.

"Much." Darian returned his smile.

"We should join the others."

"All right."

Both men joined the others who were lounging and discussing their situation and other interests. Earlier that night, they decided to give it another chance and searched the state, hunting their enemy, but were unsuccessful. Finally, just two hours before dawn, they gave up and returned to their separate locations. Only now, Richard was with Darian instead of Xander and Elise. They knew all they could do was wait … wait to see what was going to happen next.

# CHAPTER EIGHTEEN
## TWO DAYS LATER

Captain Lawrence sat in her office with the Director of the highly esteemed S.U.I.T. organization sitting in the chair on the other side of her desk. His silver and gray hair was parted on the side and slicked back. He had taken the position nearly three years ago after the last director died in a plane crash. No one knew that the last director had become the meal of the very supernaturals he and eleven others were trying to hunt. Either way, it was good news to Milton Cunningham, who was known throughout the organization for being a ruthless, heartless bastard and now, sitting in front of her, Michelle finally understood why.

"I don't think I need to tell you why you have to fire those two men," Cunningham said, shifting lazily in his seat.

"They both just managed to pull through after a vicious attack and you want me to go into their hospital rooms, while they're lying in bed recuperating and tell them they no longer have jobs?" Michelle asked incredulously.

"Please, spare me the sentimentality. They knew what they were getting into when they agreed to join the S.U.I.T. Every officer employed within the organization knows there's a chance they could become infected while on the job, just like every soldier knows they could get killed in war. It's a chance you take."

"Don't give me that bullshit 'there's always casualties in war' speech. These men have dedicated their lives to this city, to this country! They deserve more than a kick to the curve!"

"I didn't make up the policy, I just enforce it. And if you want to keep your position here, I suggest you do your job and follow through with protocol. This is not up for negotiation. Also, I would *highly* suggest you keep a lid on the secret internal investigation we've arranged. We would hate to discover any leaks," Cunningham said as he rose from his chair. "I'll be expecting your final reports and termination papers on those two detectives on my desk tomorrow morning, Captain Lawrence." With that, he left.

"'*Highly* suggest' my ass," Michelle mumbled to herself. She knew what his version of "*highly* suggest" meant. It meant that it was a direct order he expected her to follow without question. She rose from her chair, walking over toward her window overlooking the busy downtown streets below. She dreaded what she was going to have to do, but it's what she had to do.

She made it to the hospital a half hour later, deciding to give Barry the bad news first. With a flash of her badge, the officer guarding Barry's room nodded and stepped to the side allowing her entry. Inside she saw that Barry's wife was sitting beside his bed, smiling at her husband. Leanne rose cheerfully and approached Michelle when she saw her and gave her a big hug. Michelle returned the embrace before making her way over to the bed where Barry laid.

"Hey Captain, thanks for stopping by. I heard about Gabriel, is he okay?" Barry asked.

"He's awake now, and his wife is all right, too," Michelle said.

"Good, good." Barry released a long sigh of relief.

"Listen Barry, I had to come here today to deliver some bad news."

Barry adjusted himself sitting up straight in his bed waiting for her to continue.

"I got a visit from the Director of the S.U.I.T. this afternoon, and … as much as I hate this, I have to follow protocol."

"Just spit it out, Captain," Barry said. He was beginning to understand what she was trying to say.

"We're going to have to let you go. The rules of the organization-"

Barry held his hand up. "I know about the damn policy. Is there anything you can do about this decision?"

Captain Michelle Lawrence shook her head. "I don't think so, but I want you to know that I'm going to try my best. I'll be looking for a way to reverse the decision."

"Hold on, let me understand what you're saying," Barry's wife,

Leanne interjected. "Are you telling us that you're firing him after his years of dedicated service? Barry has been serving this country for twenty years! What happened to him isn't his fault. He was a victim. You don't throw excellent cops out on their ass when they become victims of vicious criminals. You give them solace! Support!"

"Leanne, I know where you're coming from, trust me. I hate that this is happening, I do. But I have a job to do and rules to follow, I'm sorry," Captain Lawrence said in her defense.

"Bullshit!" Leanne threw her hands up in the air. "This is bullshit. Baby we don't have to take this laying down. I'm going to call my brother, Aaron." She put her hand over her husband's, offering him support. She looked up at Michelle. "And you can tell the Director of the S.U.I.T. that he can kiss our ass, and to expect a lawsuit shortly."

Michelle didn't bother to argue, as a matter of fact, she didn't blame them for their response to such horrible news. She nodded and left before they officially kicked her out.

*\*\*\**

Michelle drove to her next location, to visit Gabriel. He was bright-eyed and speaking with the nurse in an attempt to get more food.

"But I'm still hungry, I'm starving! It's not like I'm loving this hospital shit, but I just want a little bit more, please. Listen, I'll pay for the cafeteria food if you can get me two sandwiches," Gabriel pleaded. He could still feel his stomach rumbling.

"I'm sorry, but the rules are the rules. I'll bring up another plate at five o'clock this evening," the nurse said.

"Don't bother, I'll be checking myself out of this hell hole in an hour, just get out," Gabriel spat out, gesturing toward the door.

The nurse turned and left, walking past Michelle on her way out. Michelle approached the bed.

"How are you doing, Gabriel?" she asked.

"I don't even want to talk about how I'm feeling right now, Captain. Is there a reason why you're here?" Gabriel skipped the pleasantries; he wasn't feeling in a chipper mood.

"All right, I'm going to cut to the chase. The reason why I'm here is because I have to follow policy."

"I thought you said you were going to cut right to the chase."

She exhaled. "I have to let you go."

"You came all the way down here to tell me that shit?"

"I felt you deserved to hear the news from me in person."

"Oh yeah, that makes it all a little bit better. This is bullshit, Captain!"

"I have my orders, Gabriel."

"I don't give a shit about some fucking protocol! I put my life on the line for the S.U.I.T., for this government and now you're telling me you're tossing me out on my ass?!"

"I'm going to try to do what I can to reverse this decision." Michelle couldn't really blame him for being upset; she just hated being the bad guy in the equation.

"This is fucked! I'm not disabled … shit, maybe I'd be better off if I was. You wouldn't be able to fire me if I was. I can't help what that motherfucker did to me, Captain. I was doing my job, I don't deserve this!"

"I know. I'm trying to help you."

"What am I going to do now? What about my pension?"

"Policy doesn't honor pensions for officers who are terminated." Michelle actually looked away, not wanting to bear witness to the expression on Gabriel's face. It was the look of someone who had been terribly betrayed.

Gabriel chuckled. It wasn't the chuckle of someone who was happy. It was the chuckle of someone who was at the end of their rope, someone who was beyond frustrated. "This is a piece of work, right here. What about severance pay? You know. Something I can use to feed my fucking family while I look for another job?"

"That, I am going to do for you. I'll start up the paperwork this afternoon." Michelle turned to leave, stopping in the doorway. "You can clean out your desk anytime this week, whenever it's convenient for you. I really am sorry." With that, she left. The least she could do was make sure they got one final payment for their services if nothing else.

Gabriel sat on his bed, fighting back the tears that threatened to roll down his cheeks. It was too much, too much at one time and he felt lost. Real men don't cry, his father always told him that when he was a little boy. So, whenever he got a skinned knee, or a bloody cut, he had choked back the tears. He had wanted to prove to his father just how much of a man he was. However, sitting in his narrow hospital bed, his whole life seemed to be crumbling apart before him. He felt helpless, out of control. Images of his attack flashed through his mind, the violation followed up by his transformation. He shook his head, in an attempt to clear his brain. Reaching over, he picked up the telephone, calling the nurse. He wanted to check out. The nurse came to his room and he told her his wishes.

"That's perfectly fine, Mr. Johnson. There are just a few more tests we want to perform. Don't worry. The doctor will release you shortly."

"Are you deaf? I said I wanted to get the hell out of here. I don't want the doctor to 'release me shortly' which in hospital terminology, could mean 'hours later'. I want to go now, or do I still have rights in this fucking country?" Gabriel asked, climbing out of bed.

The nursed backed away, frightened by his anger as well as his new found strength and ability.

Gabriel looked at her, he could smell her fear rising and it both unnerved and enticed him. He felt the desire, the need almost to hunt her, rip her throat out and then feed. He turned away from her, swallowing hard, trying to regain his control. "Get out, please."

The nurse was all too willing to do just that, rushing past Warren as he entered. Gabriel immediately caught the scent of another shape-shifter. The scent was distinctive and obviously canine; his new instincts told him that. The aura of this shifter was stronger than his and he found himself spinning around sharply to see who had entered the room. He fell back against his bed when he saw Warren standing before him.

"He got to you, too?!" Gabriel asked, thinking Warren was a victim as well.

Warren shook his head. "No. I was born what I am."

Gabriel looked confused, as if it was all too much information at once. "I don't understand?"

"Both of my parents were shape-shifters; I was born one. You're different from me because you were turned into one."

"Did they fire *you*?" Gabriel asked, his overwhelming feeling of resentment laced his words making them sound cruel, harsh.

"I heard about what happened to you guys. When I called in to check on Barry, his wife told me that you two were fired." Warren stepped closer.

"Yeah, they fired us. That's the thanks we get for doing our fucking jobs." Gabriel ripped off the hospital gown. He reached into his overnight bag his mother had packed for him, pulling out a clean outfit and began dressing.

Warren looked at the hospital bag that contained Gabriel's old clothes, they were bloody and torn. He managed to catch the scent of the shifter who attacked Gabriel. That and the blood raised Warren's bloodlust and his need to hunt. "You should call your wife, tell her to come pick you up," he suggested.

Gabriel began to laugh, but it was sad. No sounds of joy came from him. "My wife, yeah, that's fucking rich. She's taken the kids to her mother's house. She's fucking terrified of me now." He turned, facing Warren. "You know it's almost funny. If she wouldn't touch me before I was attacked, why should I expect her to want to touch me now?"

"Gabe ..." Warren had never seen the man so unhappy. He suspected that Gabriel was feeling like he was the loneliest man in the world at the moment.

"It's true. I've lost everything, Warren. My fucking job, my wife, my kids, my manh-" He cut himself off, not wanting to reveal too much, although he expected the truth to start circulating around the S.U.I.T. precinct soon about his sexual assault since it was a crime.

Warren was silent for a few moments, wondering if he should extend himself to Gabriel or not. He knew that the ex-detective's life was now upside down, but he also knew that his new life needed guidance. If he didn't get control of himself and his instincts, he could die.

"Gabriel, I know right now you must feel like shit, but there's something I need to talk to you about," Warren said, taking the first step.

Gabriel finished tying his shoes. He looked up at him. "You know what you could do for me; you really want to help me, Warren. Tell the captain about you, what you are."

Warren was taken aback, not expecting him to say that. "Why? What good could that do?"

"Don't play dumb with me, Warren. You know damn well what good that can do. All of this time, you've been getting the special cases, the title of the best cops on the Force, even before you and Matthew became S.U.I.T.. All of this time, you've been the best and now I know why. All of this time you've been superhuman doing superhuman shit to get the job done. You're the best in the precinct; everyone knows it. That's fucking leverage, can't you see?"

Warren shook his head. "Gabriel, if I come clean, it won't only affect my job, but Matthew's too. Hell, every officer in the S.U.I.T. will be suspect!"

"Can you honestly stand there and tell me you don't think that's already going to happen? I wouldn't be surprised if the next time you sign in to work, you get greeted with a blood and urine test."

Warren was quiet. He had thought about that and did suspect the testing was in the works. Xander followed his better judgment and had called Sara Wyant in an attempt to get the jump on any test date so that Warren and Matthew would not be caught off guard. Unfortunately, Sara had no knowledge of any tests in the future, but said she'd keep them informed.

"If I come clean, both Matt and I will be fired," Warren said.

"Then you're a fucking coward, Warren." Gabriel turned to walk out of the room when a wave of dizziness came upon him. He fell against the door, knees buckling. Warren was beside him within an instant, with his arm around his waist, supporting him.

"Gabriel, I know what happened to you sucks big time, but you have to let me help you," Warren pleaded.

Gabriel looked up at him, panting slightly. "I'm starving … and weak."

"I'll get you something to eat on the way to the hospital to visit Barry."

"Fine."

Gabriel checked himself out of the hospital against doctor's wishes and he and Warren left. They stopped at a burger fast food restaurant and ordered several combo meals, which Gabriel ferociously devoured along the way. He'd never been so hungry in his entire life! It was as if he couldn't swallow fast enough. His stomach felt as if it was an empty pit and only after the third triple bacon cheeseburger, did he start to feel fulfilled. Warren had been relatively quiet in the car, waiting to say what he needed to when he could have both Barry and Gabriel in the same room together. When they finally arrived in Barry's hospital room, the two partners reunited, thrilled to see each other alive after their ordeal. Leanne hugged Gabriel, offering him her support. She immediately told him about her lawsuit, which she'd already put into motion.

Warren watched them converse for a few minutes more before speaking. "I'm going to have to interrupt you, I have something important to say. Barry, I'm sure you realize I'm a shape-shifter, just like you are now."

Barry looked at Warren then nodded. "Yeah, I sensed that. I'm still getting used to smelling other supernaturals. There are two male nurses here who are shape-shifters, too. I'd be lying if I didn't say I was shocked when I caught your scent, though."

"Yeah, I bet. Listen, what I'm going to say now is only for your benefit and Gabriel's. You've entered a different world since becoming shifters. You were bitten by a lion. You're going to have to learn what that means. I have someone willing to take you into his Pride-"

"Hold on, what the hell are you talking about?" Gabriel asked, confused.

"You're new, okay. You haven't learned how to control your urges, your instincts. You have no idea just how powerful you are now. You're going to need someone to teach you all of these things." Warren watched both men as he spoke.

"What if we don't want to enter into any Prides?" Gabriel asked, somewhat stubbornly.

"Don't be stupid, Gabe. Like I said before, this is a whole new world for you and trust me, you don't want to be in it alone," Warren said.

"Go on, Warren," Barry said.

"You're actually going to buy into this?! I'm sorry, but the only help we needed from him is for him and Matt to stand up for us and he refused!" Gabriel fussed, pointing a finger at Warren.

Barry looked at Warren, both eyebrows raised, shocked. "Is that true? You won't stand by us?"

Warren lowered his head, rubbing his fingers over both his eyebrows. "I don't know, Barry." He looked up at them. "I don't know. It's not right what happened to you, but Matt and I put a lot of work into covering ourselves."

"Oh, really? How nice for you. We, unfortunately, didn't have that opportunity. All I know is you're going to stand by and let us get screwed. I guess it's okay as long as it's not you," Gabriel said. He turned away from Warren, obviously upset.

"You know what, Gabriel? I've had as much of your sanctimonious bullshit as I can stand. I didn't see your ass banging on doors demanding equal rights for supernaturals when you weren't one!" Warren shot back.

Gabriel turned around to face him.

"And now, because your ass got bit, you want me to ruin what I've worked so hard for to help you out. Would you even do the same for me if the shoe was on the other foot?"

Gabriel stared at Warren, thinking about his answer. He wasn't sure if he'd risk his job for the other shifter. He looked away.

"I guess I've got my answer. Look, like I've said, I hate what's happening to you, but let's just keep our heads cool and we'll see what we can do." Warren looked to both Gabriel and Barry.

"Warren, if there's anything you can do to help them, please let us know," Leanne pleaded with him.

"It's not going to be easy. Look, we have some connections; we might be able to help them without exposing ourselves." Warren wasn't sure if he could help them, but he was going to try.

"We've already been fired," Gabriel reminded him, turning to face Warren. "What help could you possibly provide to get us our jobs back? Just because I've lost my job as a detective, doesn't mean I've lost my ability to detect bullshit when I hear it. If you had these so-called powerful contacts, then you wouldn't be so fucking scared to come forward yourself."

"Gabe, take it easy," Barry said, trying to calm his partner down. Gabriel looked at him then turned away again, facing the window. Barry looked at Warren. "Tell us what we need to know."

Warren stared hard at Gabriel before giving his attention to Barry. "If you think you can survive without a Pride, you're wrong. Others will seek you out, pick on you. Some may even try to kill you because you'll be considered rogues, strays or orphans. None of those titles come with good news. You'll be outsiders. Not only that, the Alphas of this state have the right to kill you if they so choose."

"They can't just kill us, it's against the law," Gabriel said, turning back around.

"What part of 'Brand. New. World.', don't you fucking get, Gabe?!" Warren shouted, finally reaching his boiling point. "Human laws don't apply!"

"Can you stop fucking shouting, it's too loud!" Gabe said, matching Warren's tone.

"Can the both of you shut the fuck up right now?! You're both too loud," Barry said, covering his ears. His senses were powerful, more than he'd ever expected. He hadn't gotten control of them and was hearing sounds and voices from all around the hospital. He suspected Gabriel was going through the same thing. All he understood was that he wanted some type of control over himself, with or without his job.

Warren didn't yell, he knew what affect the loud sound of his voice had on them. "Sorry about that, Barry. In time, you'll learn to regulate your hearing. You have to understand when I say, you're not human anymore, guys. The first thing you need to do is accept that. Next, you need to accept the fact that human laws don't apply to us. We have our own rules, our own laws of nature. Trust me when I say that leaders of Prides and Packs have the right to kill you. In our world, it's perfectly legal and expected."

"So, joining this Pride you mentioned will spare us this extra trouble?" Barry asked.

Warren nodded. "Yeah, it will. Joining this Pride is beneficial to both of you. Don't shit on this opportunity."

"Fine, take us to this Pride," Gabriel said, grudgingly agreeing.

"Okay. Barry you check yourself out before this hospital runs any more tests. The next thing you know, they'll want to perform an anal probe on you," Warren said.

"That's just what I said," Leanne commented, looking at her husband.

"All right, all right, I'm getting out now." Barry climbed out of the bed and began dressing in the clothes his wife had brought from home. Within minutes, he was dressed and waiting for his official release. Fifteen minutes later, there were heading toward Elise's hotel. Warren was driving his car with the three of them traveling behind him in Barry's. They arrived at the hotel and made it to the room. Sergio opened the door, allowing them entry.

Warren stood beside Barry, Gabriel and Leanne. "Hey everyone, these are the two officers I was telling you about, and this is Barry's wife, Leanne." He made the introductions quickly.

"Shitty thing that happened to you, but happy to hear that you pulled through," Sergio said to the two new shifters.

"Yeah it was, thanks," Gabriel said, feeling very uncomfortable surrounded by so many unknown supernaturals. He looked around the room at the various faces and thought about Warren and Matthew and how they knew these people. He could feel the auras of Xander, Adan, Danielle, Sergio and Elise. He suspected that they wanted him to feel their power, to understand who and what they were. They were the leaders of their shifter communities. He could sense the differences between their species and knew some were wolves, others, lions, leopards and coyotes. His nose itched and he scratched it, feeling instant relief.

Adan stepped forward. "You've been turned into shape-shifters, lions, to be more exact. I'm the leader, the King of my Pride. This isn't up for negotiation, I will be training you. Unlike most communities, felines more importantly, we are different from the rest and your instincts are different as well."

"We weren't turned by you," Gabriel began.

"No, but if you don't want to be eliminated by other shifters, you'll listen to what I have to say. You need to learn how to hunt on and off *Lunar* nights. You need to learn control of your instincts, or you'll end up killing your children by accident." Adan looked at Barry. "Or your wife on any given day, especially if she's menstruating."

Barry shook his head. "I would never hurt my wife, I love her."

Adan laughed. "You won't be meaning to, but you could."

"I don't agree with you. Right now, I don't feel at all out of control." Barry wasn't one to be stubborn, but the thought of killing his wife by eating her unnerved him.

Adan smiled sadly, nodding. He gestured toward Sergio, who nodded in return. He walked toward a closed door and opened it, motioning for someone to step forward. Patricia, a lion from Adan's Pride emerged from the room. She had been put in there in anticipation of the new shifters' arrival. Adan had thought it wise to put her there for their safety and hers as she was in the height of her heat. Instantly all of the males in the room senses heightened, becoming acute, in tune to the female. When Adan motioned for Patricia to come closer to him, she did. Both Gabriel's and Barry's eyes were fixed on her, unable to look away. Their breathing became ragged, growing urgent along with their need to have her. Both men approached her, circling, drawing closer to smell her. She stood there, allowing them to do so. Gabriel growled low, the sound vibrating off his throat as a warning to his friend that the female was his. Barry returned the growl as he reached out for her. Gabriel punched him, knocking Barry off balance. He then grabbed Patricia, kissing her deeply as he reached for her breasts, massaging one.

Patricia's passion grew, her body yearning for what Gabriel was offering. Barry advanced on Gabriel, pulling him from the female, snarling as he did so. Leanne started to rush toward them, but Xander held her back, shaking his head. She looked at her husband, growing jealous as she witnessed him fighting his best friend over a woman he didn't even know simply to see who would have sex with her first. Tears began to run down her face as she slowly began to realize what becoming a shape-shifter meant for her husband and herself.

Before the face-off grew out of control, Adan separated the two men, asserting his dominance, pushing both men sending them crashing into separate corners. Danielle ushered Patricia back into the room, away from the warring males. Gabriel shook his head of the cobwebs, as did Barry. Their hormones were settling back down as their hardened erections began to soften ever so slowly. Both men looked at each other, then back at Adan.

Gabriel was the first to rise. "What just happened?" he asked, completely confused by his actions.

Warren assisted Barry to his feet. "You okay?"

Barry nodded. "Yeah," he assured, wiping blood from his now healed lip with the back of his hand.

"As I tried to tell you, your instincts are out of control, even more so because you were turned, not born shifters. You could easily take any female willingly, or against her will or eat them during that special time of the month if you don't get control over your nature." Adan looked from one man to the other.

Gabriel's breathing was still coming quickly. He was still aroused by the lingering scent in the room. "I wanted her so badly! I … I couldn't help myself." He was completely bewildered.

"We know," Tatiana said. "It's that way with us all. But if you noticed, you two were the only ones who were going for her, while the other men in the room remained where they were."

Both Gabriel and Barry looked around the room. Tatiana was right, none of them seemed to be affected at all by the aroma of the female the way they had been.

Barry nodded. "Okay, I'm convinced."

"I know a smart man *would* be. I've always felt that seeing is believing and one step from seeing is experiencing, which is why I allowed you two to have that interaction," Adan said.

"I see why they made you the boss," Barry said, smiling slightly.

"We didn't make him boss," Devin corrected, slightly insulted.

"It's just a saying," Barry clarified himself, not wanting to be misunderstood. "I didn't mean to offend."

"Oh," Devin said, settling back into his chair. "I knew that."

"Down boy," Carmen teased the younger shifter. Devin rolled his eyes, but remained silent.

Barry looked at his wife, who was still standing beside Xander. "Darling, I'm sorry … I … ." His voice trailed off, unable to explain his actions. He felt ashamed over his lack of control.

Leanne walked over to her husband, slipping her arms around his neck. "It's okay, I think I understand. I have watched the Animal Discovery Channel. From what I saw, it was very raw ... in a way, natural. Not that I liked seeing what I saw, but, I think I understand."

"I don't ever want to hurt you in any way. I ... I think ... ." He shook his head, his voice trailing off in confusion. He was wondering if the next thing he was going to say was a smart decision.

His wife, knowing her husband very well, seeming to read his mind, finished his sentence. "You think it's best if you stayed away from me and the kids right now, don't you?"

Barry looked at his wife, their eyes locked. "I do. What just happened was an eye-opener for me. There's so much I don't know, and hiding my head in the sand hoping it will all go away isn't going to help. Do you mind?"

Leanne shook her head. "If you need to learn control so you don't screw any other strange females in heat, or eat the kids and me ... I'm good with that."

"Arrrg, don't remind me." Barry leaned forward, kissing her gently.

Warren turned toward Gabriel. "Gabe, what about you? Are you willing to stay with Adan?"

Gabriel looked at the others then he nodded. "Yeah. To say I don't have much of a choice is an understatement."

"You have a choice, but the alternative isn't the wisest choice one could make in your situation," Adan said.

Gabriel nodded. "I get your point. Thanks for helping me."

"Besides, if you want any chance of getting your jobs back, or any job at all, you're going to need his help," Sergio said, pointing at Adan.

"As far as I'm concerned, you two are the least of our worries. We still don't know what the fuck's going on with Marcus and his coven." Adrian said.

"Yeah, they've been playing nice for two days now. Do you think they're still here?" Devin asked.

"Is Marcus the name of the Master vampire we're looking for?" Barry asked, getting back into his detective swing.

"Yeah, we've been trying like hell to take him out, but it's difficult. He's ancient and the shifter in his gang, the one who bit you is one powerful son-of-a-bitch," Adrian said.

The others watched Gabriel's expression at the mentioning of the shifter who attacked him. They could all still smell Kiren's sexual scent all over him. They suspected Gabriel was sexually assaulted, but none dared to bring it up, understanding all to well what a sensitive subject that was. They could still see the pain and humiliation in Gabriel's eyes, even as he lowered his head. Barry could smell the scent, too and knew it was sexual. He had suspected Gabriel was violated when they reunited at the hospital, but neither man said anything. He figured, when Gabriel was more comfortable with the subject, he'd talk when he was ready.

"Where are you now with your investigation?" Barry asked.

"For the first time ever, we're right were the S.U.I.T. is. We don't know where they are or even if they're still here," Sergio said.

"The good news is, there haven't been any more attacks against the S.U.I.T. or civilians," Warren said.

"That's not to say they've gone," Adan added. "The question is, do we stay?"

Elise looked at him. "You're going to have to stay, at least for the time being as you train these two." She pointed to Gabriel and Barry.

"Besides, you abandoned your territory, do you think it's still there for you to reclaim?" Sergio asked.

"There's no way for me to tell right now. It's a possibility that another community has already taken over," Adan said.

"It's kind of funny, shifters are almost like hermit crabs in the way we move into others' territory," Sebastian comment.

"You *would* bring up something like that," Devin said, chuckling.

"Enough you two," Madeleine said, quieting the two young men.

"What are we going to do?" Gabriel asked, looking around the room.

"I wish I could tell you that we're going to do something spectacular, but the truth of the matter is … nothing," Sergio said.

"We're trying to see what's going to be their next move. We

don't think they've left, but we're not sure. So we wait," Elise added.

"Oh," Gabriel looked at Warren. "Are you going to work, now?"

Warren nodded. "Yeah, Matthew's already there-" He was interrupted by the ringing of his cell phone. He answered it. "What's up Matt?"

"We've got a problem, I'm on my way to your hotel now," Matthew said, sounding extremely nervous, which was rare for him.

"Matthew, calm down, what's going on?"

"The shit's hit the fan. I just got off the phone with Brian. He's just been fired! They tried to arrest him, but he got away."

"What the fuck? Why? What happened? How'd they know?"

"Colin outted him."

"Why? Did he do it on purpose?"

"Brian said it was an accident. He went to visit him once he came to, and Colin recognized him for what he was. Unfortunately, he blurted out, 'He got you, too?' in front of their captain."

"Shit!"

"There's more, I just snuck out of our precinct in time before they could perform a saliva and silver test on me. They don't even know I'm gone, I got out through the morgue thanks to Marshall's help."

"Those kind of tests are new. We're not going to be able to avoid this, Matthew. If we don't take the test, we're going to be suspected of being shifters, and if we do, they'll know for sure that we are. Fuck!"

"What do I do?"

"Get back here. If we go in there and get tested, they'll arrest us like they tried to do to Brian. Speaking of which, where's he now?"

"I'm on my way to pick him up. He said he can't go back to their hotel. He sounds scared and I think he's waiting for his Alpha to come or send someone to get him."

"We can't go back to the precinct until Sara knows what's going on?"

"How can she switch the results when they're instantaneous? None of us can pass a silver stamp test."

"I know, I know."

"Okay, wait, calm down, Matt. Pick Brian up and get back here, try not to speed, we don't want to give any cop the reason to report your whereabouts." Warren hated that one of his worst fears was now happening and it was completely out of his control.

"We'll be there soon," Matthew said, ending his call.

\*\*\*

Matthew was trying not to speed as he headed to pick Brian up at a fast food restaurant.

Matthew pull in front of the restaurant and Brian climbed into the car. "Thanks for picking me up," he said, closing the door behind himself.

"Not a problem. Where's Colin?"

"I had to leave him at the hospital. I can't believe this shit's happening. Two hours ago, I was a decorated S.U.I.T. officer, now I'm a fucking fugitive," Brian said, his face was contorted with rage and confusion.

"I'm guessing this is what Marcus wanted. Pure panic and us off his ass," Matthew said.

Brian laughed. "Were we really a threat to him? All we did was find the bodies. We were no closer to ending their killing spree here than we were when they were in California. I agree with you, I bet they're all just sitting back laughing at our asses."

Matthew didn't say anything, although he felt the same way Brian did. "What are you going to do about Colin?"

"He's safe. He was a human who was turned into a shifter while on the job. I, on the other hand, was a shifter masquerading as a human. I submitted fraudulent information on federal documents. I lied under oath and everything I've done in the past will be brought up for questioning. They're going to want answers. I don't know what they're going to do to me. When our captain ordered the other S.U.I.T. officers to arrest me, I just ran."

"I don't blame you. For a human who scammed the government, they have jail time; for us, there's no telling. I know firsthand that the government has killed our kind for less," Matthew said, driving the car into the hotel parking lot. When both men made it to the hotel room, Warren let them in.

Brian looked at Gabriel and Barry. "Hey guys."

"Hi. I can't get over just how many shifters were in the S.U.I.T.," Gabriel said.

"It's enough of us, you just don't know we're there. Well, at least you didn't before," Brian said, settling on the sofa.

"Can I ask you why? I mean, if it's such a big risk, why do it?" Gabriel asked.

Warren looked at him. "Because innocent people need protecting, it's a universal belief. We have the abilities to help, so we do. I know that's why I joined the S.U.I.T., to save lives."

Gabriel was watching Warren, seeing the sincerity in his expression. He was beginning to understand why Warren didn't want to turn himself in to help Barry and him out, not that he wasn't a bit bitter about that.

"When I got off the phone with you, I got a page from the Captain, I'm sure she wants us to come in for testing. We both know that's not going to happen," Warren told Matthew, getting back to the main discussion.

"She's probably suspecting something by now. Especially since I haven't returned any of her phone calls," Matthew added.

"When I was waiting for you to pick me up, I got a call from one of my friends back at the S.U.I.T. precinct in California. They're conducting tests there, too. This is probably happening all across the country. Seems like this was planned from the moment Colin and you two were attacked," Brian said, pointing to Gabriel and Barry.

"Holy shit! There's no telling how many shifters have been exposed because of this," Devin said.

"Probably all of them," Warren said.

"When it rains, it pours," Tatiana stated.

"I think it's best that you accept the fact that you might be fired from the S.U.I.T., especially if you refuse or avoid taking the test," Xander told Warren and Matthew.

"Shit," Warren turned away, walking towards a window overlooking downtown. "I've worked too hard to get this far."

Matthew came up behind him, rubbing his shoulders. "It's going to be all right, we'll bounce back, Warren."

Warren turned, facing him. He pulled Matthew close, kissing him deeply.

"Whoa, wait a fucking minute! You two are gay?!" Gabriel asked, shocked. He never would have thought the two men were homosexual, not to mention, lovers!

Both men turned toward him. "You're just now figuring that out? Didn't you catch his scent on me?" Warren asked.

"You're his partner, didn't seem unusual from what I've been experiencing lately. Besides, I've had a lot on my mind and that was before all this shit happened, worrying about your love life wasn't a priority of mine," Gabriel admitted.

"Well, I guess I don't have to tell you not to tell anyone else at work. We may be out of a job soon," Matthew said, stepping away from Warren. His cell phone rang, catching his attention. "It's Galen."

"Answer it," Warren said.

He did. "What's up Galen?"

"It's not looking good for your guys. The official word is about sixteen shifters have been arrested and are now awaiting a trial, and at least forty-seven others are like you, and are staying clear."

"Fuck. It's what I feared, what can we do about this?"

"As I'm sure you already know, Michelle and I are together, we trust each other, so I decided to tell her about you," Galen said.

"What did she say?"

"She's on your side, but she has to play it safe. She agrees with me when I say the S.U.I.T. could benefit from employing more supernaturals. For now, stay incommunicado, and I'll keep you all up to date."

"Thanks for looking out for us," Matthew said, grateful to have a friend still within the S.U.I.T.

"You're two of the best cops and men I've ever met, you don't deserve what's happening any more than Gabe and Barry deserved what happened to them. Something needs to be done about this ridiculous policy, maybe now is our window of opportunity." Galen said. "I have to go, but I'll keep in touch."

"Thanks." Matthew ended the call. "You all heard what he said."

The others nodded.

"This is the last thing we need right now," Brian said.

"Or maybe not," Justin began. "If we can take out Marcus and his coven, it'll look good in your favor."

"*If* we can. We don't even know where to look," Devin said, sinking back against the cushions.

"We stick to the plan, let them make the next move and take it from there," Xander said.

"So be it," Elise agreed. They waited for the sun to set, hoping Marcus and his coven would strike soon.

"We should go to Darian's mansion and stay together. Our plan to remain separate in preparation for his attack is proving to be fruitless," Danielle suggested.

"That's a good idea. I miss the others anyway," Devin said, gathering his coat. They checked out of the hotel and headed toward Darian's mansion.

# CHAPTER NINETEEN

**"M**aster, how long are we going to let the night slip away? Please tell me we're going to have some fun tonight?" Raven asked.

Marcus chuckled. "Yes, we will have fun. I want Darian and his coven. Tonight, I'll get what I want."

"You said they were separated, what do you want us to do?" Mikhail asked.

"They are no longer separated. Earlier today, they rejoined the others at Darian's mansion." Marcus sat in his chair while Kiren sat on the floor beside him. The Master ran his fingers through the shifter's hair lovingly, lightly stroking the strands.

"Why did they pull that stunt anyway is what I want to know? You'd think it'd be smarter for them to stay together," Alicia commented.

"It was a smart plan, had it worked," Raven said.

"What do you mean?" Alicia asked.

"Well, they were probably hoping that Marcus and Kiren attacked them during the day," Raven answered. "Especially since these circumstances are different. We haven't run into a vampire coven willing to help Adan and his Pride before."

"The coven has a powerful Master and to attack while the vampire is resting, would be a smart plan … if that's your plan, anyway," Mikhail said.

Marcus continued, "Exactly. It's something I would have done in their position. I would have tried to tempt my enemy away from his hiding place by offering him something I knew he wanted. Then I would have my people gang up on him, allowing myself to have a second attack planned to take him out when he was alone, or at the very least, without his full arsenal."

"That's why you left them alone?" Mikhail asked. "I don't mean any disrespect, Master, but-"

"I already know what you're going to ask me and the answer is 'no'," Marcus interjected. "They couldn't have prevented me from killing Adan and his entire Pride if I wanted to. Understand, I want them off their guard. I want them guessing and wondering what we're going to do next? Or even if we're still interested in hurting them."

"I want a piece of Darian myself," Kiren growled.

Raven laughed. "Yeah, I bet. I heard about what happened to you, seems to me you brought it on yourself."

"Fuck you! Still doesn't take away from the fact that I'm going to make him pay," Kiren spat back.

"No, you won't. I've told you this before, Darian's mine. Deal with what happened to you, get over it," Marcus said, giving his lover a stern stare.

Kiren lowered his head, nodding slightly, dejected.

"How are we going to go about doing this tonight?" Raven asked.

"I'm sure they're expecting something calculated, stealthy." Marcus laughed. "On the contrary, I'm in the mood for a 'snatch n' grab' tonight. Kill whomever you wish, take whomever you want."

"Just so I know what's what ... Darian is off limits, anyone else?" Mikhail asked.

"Yes. Xavier, Christopher and John are also to be taken. Don't care if you harm them in the process, they'll heal."

"I want Adan," Kiren said. "And Richard, at least he'll pay for setting me up."

"Very well. I have my eye on Miko, Nagesa, Sergio, Adrian, Ignacio and Miranda," Alicia said.

"Child's play. I'm taking the remaining leaders and I'm going to make them humble. That would be Tatiana, Elise, Danielle and Xander," Raven stated.

"Yeah, but the ones I'm going after are born warriors, their birthright is to fight to the death and kill anyone in their way. Politics isn't their forté. You point in the direction of a battle and that's where they excel. I want to bring them to their knees," Alicia explained.

"Ah, I see why you chose them," Raven said, smiling.

"I don't know who I want. They're all so … I don't know, what's the word … Powerful, independent, headstrong? Any one of them is a treat," Mikhail said. "I suppose the one who puts up the strongest fight against me will be my pick for the evening."

"Are we done yet?" Marcus asked, slightly annoyed. "This conversation closely resembles what one would have at thanksgiving dinner and who gets which parts of the holiday turkey."

Mikhail chuckled. "Just pour some gravy on mine and we're all good." His smile widened when he noticed Marcus turning away, smiling.

"Let's go," Marcus said. "I'll fly, you four drive."

"Wouldn't we get their faster if we all flew?" Mikhail asked.

"We would, but then where would we put our bounty?" Marcus asked, sarcastically, being slightly annoyed by the younger vampire's question.

"I'm sorry, Master. I get it now." Mikhail refrained from asking any more questions as they headed toward the door.

***

Darian returned home, sitting in his chair. At sunset, he had gone out searching the city for their enemy. After a few hours of hunting and being unsuccessful, he decided to called it a night. He looked at the two newest shifters in his home. Both men seemed to be in complete awe of him. They had seen him once before when he was held in lock-up at the S.U.I.T. precinct a few years ago, but never up close. They could feel his aura and they knew he was powerful.

"I do hope you take Adan seriously when he says you need training," Darian said.

Gabriel swallowed hard. He felt as though he'd choke on Darian's aura if he hadn't. Never in all his years on the S.U.I.T. had he felt power so intense, so absolute. He nodded. "Yeah, after what happened earlier, we'd be crazy not to."

Darian smiled slightly. "Good… wise decision." He looked at Adan. "If this coven hasn't attacked by now, maybe we should start looking at other cities to see if they've chosen another target."

"I wanted to do that earlier today when I went into the precinct, but I had to get out of there fast because of the tests," Matthew said.

"Ahh, that's right." John nodded. "Perfect timing, the S.U.I.T. resources could have really come in handy right about now."

"When all else fails, we can use the internet to look up that information," Natasha said.

"I did that, already," Ignacio said. "There's nothing that resembles what happened here. There were some bombings overseas. A few rapes, gang-related violence, other random murders that have always plagued the news and a shape-shifter was killed on the spot at a murder scene, but nothing more. There wasn't even a mention about what's going on with the S.U.I.T. right now."

"I'm sure the S.U.I.T. is using all its political pull to keep it under wraps as much as they can at this point," Warren said.

"Yeah, if that got out, it would be more chaos than it already is," Matthew agreed.

"Back to the point, where the fuck are they?" Sergio asked to no one in particular.

Xavier stepped forward, addressing Darian. "I don't think they've left. Perhaps we need to-"

The sudden shattering of glass from four windows interrupted Xavier. Using his quick reflexes, he raced to Natasha, protecting her from the shards of glass that flew inward. Others took cover to avoid getting slashed by the countless shards that sprayed the room. The front door imploded with a force that shook the mansion, sending wood splinters shooting into the parlor and down the hallway. Kiren stood in the doorway, in half beast form. His animalistic eyes focused on his prey and he revealed a mouth full of razor sharp teeth in a menacing grin.

"Shit!" Sergio cursed as he began changing forms himself.

The others who could followed suit, changing into their half-beast forms as fast as they could. Darian was on his feet instantly advancing on Mikhail. Marcus saw him. He knew if Darian were to land a hand on his coven member, it would take less than a second for him to kill him. He advanced on Darian, grabbing him from behind, tossing him sideways, and sending his body airborne through the brick, plaster and drywall into the next room.

Xavier turned and gasped at the site, shocked to see his lover and Master flying over his head. He turned when he saw Natasha holding their son, hiding under the table behind the sofa where he had put her. Tears streamed down her face as she cuddled their child. Not wanting to waste another second, he ran to her.

"Natasha, come with me!" He grabbed her hand, knowing she and their children were his priority as Darian had instructed. She climbed out from underneath the table with Xavier's assistance. As she cleared the edge, rising to her feet, Sergio's body landed on the table, smashing the wood into splinters. He groaned as he struggled to rise from the debris. Once he climbed to his feet, he rushed back into the battle, his claws slashing Alicia down her back, preventing her from attacking Elise. The female vampire turned, punching Sergio, knocking him into Elise, sending both crashing to the floor.

Xavier watched what happened to his two friends. "We need to get all of the younger ones out of here," he told Natasha.

"The children, they aren't protected!" she said, panicking.

Xavier mentally contacted Gary and Sebastian along with their human servants, ordering them to gather the children and follow him. In the mist of the chaos, the supernaturals managed to gather the children and younger members as Xavier had commanded. They were all following him when Mikhail attacked Xavier.

The stronger vampire wrapped his hand around Xavier's throat. "Where do you think your ass is going? The party's just started." He smiled.

"Yeah, but it's a dud," Xavier shot back.

"Oh, trust me; it's getting better each second. Besides, I don't want you to go."

Xavier looked past Mikhail to see his lover rising. "Life's full of disappointments," he managed to say through gasps.

Darian climbed to his feet, shaking the mental cobwebs from his mind when he noticed Mikhail's fingers were locked around Xavier's throat. He advanced quickly, grabbing Mikhail from behind, plunging his fangs deeply into the vampire's artery. Viciously, he pulled back, ripping away the vampire's throat, splattering blood on both Natasha and Xavier. Mikhail released Xavier, giving the vampire a chance to escape with the others. Darian began to change forms taking on his full demon visage, while at the same time he drove his claws through the vampire neck. With a powerful pull, he severed the vampire's head from his body, killing Mikhail instantly.

Tatiana and Elise were both busy healing the shifters who were gravely wounded. They ran from one body to the next, opening their veins for whomever needed help. Marcus saw Tatiana healing Xander. He ran toward them, at that point, yanking Tatiana to her feet. Holding her by the back of her neck with one hand, he stabbed his clawed hand through her back, shattering her ribs, piercing her lungs. Tatiana screamed as Marcus pulled his hand from her torso. Again he moved to attack her. Xander struggled to rise, fighting against his own weakness and pain. Before Marcus could stab her again, he lunged forward, pushing Tatiana against the Master vampire, preventing him from plunging his arm through her chest. Marcus tossed Tatiana away from him, sending her body crashing through Darian's seventy-five gallon fish tank, shattering the glass into tiny shards. Dozens of exotic fish spilled with the flow of water splashing on Tatiana as she lay there struggling to live.

With Xander on his knees, Marcus reached underneath his chin, pulling him to his feet. "I'd kill you if you weren't already a marked man. That doesn't mean I can't have fun with you, though." Before he could do the Alpha any more harm, Warren shot him in the arm. Marcus turned around with a smirk. He made certain to have Xander in front of him. He looked at Warren, smiling. "You do know that I let you shoot me just so you can see how useless your ultraviolet bullets are against me."

"Really?" Warren asked, not really caring if what he said was true or not. He knew the only reason he responded was to buy the others time so they could attack. He watched the ultraviolet gel ooze down the side of Marcus' arm. Underneath the skin, the gel seemed to evaporate, having no effect on the vampire whatsoever.

Ignacio and Justin saw what was happening to Xander so they rushed toward him and Marcus, combining their attack. The Master vampire used Xander as a shield and weapon, swinging his body in all directions, using him to knock the other two shifters into separate directions. Adrian dove forward; dodging his father's flailing legs.

He managed to grab hold of Marcus' legs, and he bit down hard. His teeth sliced through skin and bone. Marcus grimaced in pain as he looked down at the shifter attached to his leg. He threw Xander across the room, sending his body crashing into the fireplace. Bricks broke apart, falling in a dusty heap on top of Xander's semi-conscious body. Before Marcus could focus his attack on Adrian, three other shifters converged on him, each hoping to keep him from killing the others.

Raven had Rachel pinned against the floor. The female shifter struggled to throw the vampire off, but was unsuccessful. She screamed in rage and frustration, gaining Stephanie's attention. She ran to Rachel's aid, attempting to pull Raven off of her. The vampire lashed out, slashing her claws across and back again, slicing through skin, muscle and bone. Stephanie's eyes stared forward in shock. They bulged out of their sockets as a thin line of blood appeared across her throat. Blood began gushing from the opening, splattering the women as the head tumbled over her shoulders to the floor, rolling several inches to a stop. Stephanie's decapitated body crumpled to the ground next to her severed head. Blood continued to gush from the gaping wound.

"Your turn, now," Raven growled in Rachel's ear. Without waiting another second, she drove her nails into Rachel's shoulders, severing tendons and cutting through bone. With a wicked smile, Raven yanked her arms outward, ripping away Rachel's arms, sending the two limbs in separate directions.

At that same moment, Elise was thrown to the ground by Kiren. White-hot pain shot through her body, but she turned when she heard Rachel's scream. She gasped when she saw what Raven had done. Rolling away from Kiren, she ran toward her Pride member.

Raven sensed Elise coming nearer and she rose, bringing Rachel to her feet. "Any last words?" Raven asked her.

"Die bitch!" Rachel spat out through gritted teeth. The intense pain she was in was unbearable. She could no longer fight, blood gushed from the ragged, gaping, shredded wounds. White bone jutted from the torn flesh where her arms had been, making the shifter weaker.

Elise lunged forward, but it was too late. Rachel fell into her arms, sending both women to their knees. Elise looked up seeing that Raven had disappeared. She looked down at Rachel; her friend and Pride member's eyes were blank, void of all life. Elise checked her, not wanting to believe she was dead. As her hand ran across Rachel's back, it dipped into a bloody hole in the middle of her spine. She now knew how her friend had died. Gently she laid her down on the carpeted floor. There was no time for mourning … that would come later if they survived.

Kiren advanced on Richard, who was attacking Alicia, trying to keep her from hurting Miko. He grabbed the Alpha coyote from behind, wrapping his arms around his neck, cutting off his air supply. Richard struggled in Kiren's grasp, but was unable to break loose as the shifter's furry vice-like grip tightened around his throat slowly cutting off his air supply.

Across the room, Darian witnessed Kiren rendering Richard unconscious. He charged toward him, his long nails slashed down Kiren's back, forcing the shifter to cry out and turn around. At that point, Darian's other hand swiped at his throat, nails ripping away flesh. Marcus heard his lover's gurgled scream. He turned; releasing Ignacio, who was bleeding profusely from a wound in his throat where Marcus had fed. The ancient vampire ran toward Darian punching him hard across his jaw, jerking the younger Master vampire's head backward. There was a snap of bone and Darian stumbled, his head leaning to one side. Marcus followed up with a backhanded slap, which propelled Darian upward against the wall with an impact so powerful it cracked the plaster. Before Darian could hit the ground, Marcus caught him in midair; punching him twice and knocking him unconscious. He dropped the vampire to the ground, staring down at him with a mixture of malice and lust. Annabelle ran toward the two vampires, stepping in front of Darian's unconscious body. Enraged, Marcus grabbed her, not giving her a chance to make her move. He took her by the throat, nails digging deeply into her flesh. Instinctively, her hands went to his, trying to force his grip away. Without further hesitation, he punched through her torso, his fist breaking through bone and shredding organs along the way. Wrapping his fingers around her still beating heart, he snatched his arm back, ripping her heart through her now shattered rib cage.

Miko crawled to her feet in time to see her lover fall lifeless from Marcus's hands. She saw him toss her heart onto Darian's chest. Her vision turned crimson as she ran toward the ancient vampire, screaming out in rage. She never saw him turn or his hand strike out. She only knew her body ached from the hard landing and the room was spinning.

While Marcus was preoccupied with Miko, Adan stealthy finished off what Darian had begun, crawling toward Kiren, who lay on the floor, struggling to heal himself without the blood of a Matron. Using his claws, he ripped and shredded the muscles, bone and flesh, disconnecting Kiren's head from his body. "Marcus!" the lion King yelled, getting the Master vampire's attention.

Marcus turned to see the lion King holding his lover, Kiren's head in his hands. "What have you done!" he growled, his eyes burning red.

"Just as I suspected, he really does give great head," Adan quipped, intent on enraging the Master vampire. He wanted to distract him long enough to allow the others to escape. It was working … for the moment. Alicia was busy battling Miranda, Adrian, Sergio and Nagesa.

A low, menacing growl rumbled through Marcus chest, up toward his throat. He snarled as he advanced toward Adan. He stopped short as several ultra-violet bullets whizzed past his face. He turned, to see Gabriel firing away. Effortlessly, Marcus dodged every bullet. Gabriel was so busy trying to land a shot, he had no idea that Raven was behind him. Her mouth was bloodied, her claws extending as she slashed them across the back of his neck, nearly severing his spinal cord. Gabriel released gurgled gasps as his hands went to the back of his neck, trying to stop the bleeding. He fell to the ground, pressing his back against the wall. Never had he been in a battle like this! Marcus looked around the mansion, noticing that Adan had taken advantage of the mere seconds he spent dealing with Gabriel and had escaped his wrath. He smirked, thinking about how crafty the lion was and how he'd pay him back tenfold for killing his lover. He took in the carnage; two of his coven lay dead amongst the many wounded. He was also pleased to see others whom did not belong to him lying dead as well. He was disappointed that he hadn't killed more before they escaped.

Raven stepped over Rachel's mangled and mutilated body. "We should have come to kill them all. We shouldn't have tried to spare any!" She growled, angry and hurt that Mikhail was dead.

"It's done. We'll make the survivors pay for what they've taken from us," Marcus said.

Alicia stood over Sergio's prone form. He lay gasping for air, desperately clinging to life. "Should I kill him?" she asked.

Marcus looked down at the injured shifter. "No. We take the survivors. Simple death is too quick of an ending for them." He reached down, taking Darian into his arms and tossing him over his shoulder. "Bring them!"

He left the mansion, tossing Darian into the trunk of his SUV. Alicia and Raven began loading the trucks with the survivors. They laid Sergio on top of Darian and Adrian beside him. Both women were angry that Elise and Tatiana managed to escape in the confusion of the battle. They wanted to hunt them down; they would ask their Master if they could at a later time. After two more trips back into the mansion, they now had Gabriel, Christopher, John and Miranda in their possession as well as the remains of the members of their coven. Raven drove toward Darian's private jet. They were going back to their own territory with their bounty. Where they were going, the sun would be high in the sky; the vampires would be forced to remain asleep.

It's what Marcus wanted.

# CHAPTER TWENTY

Stopping to catch their breath against the side of a building in an alley, a few of the survivors looked at one another. Some wore clothing that was ripped during the battle, while others were naked.

"What are we going to do now?" Devin asked Elise as she leaned against the wall, struggling to catch her breath.

"I don't know, Devin. Oh my God, I don't know! I need to think!" she snapped, not really meaning to. She looked at Devin who hadn't deserved her anger. "I'm sorry, darling. I just need to think."

"We need to reunite with the others and get dressed. When the shit actually went down, I just kind of ran in whatever direction I knew they weren't going in. I didn't want to run in the same Xavier took the others in, because I thought it best we separate," Daniel said. He was supporting Carmen who now slunk against the wall. Both were naked.

"Does anyone have their cell phone on them?" Elise asked.

"I do," Billy said, handing it to her.

"Momma, I'm scared," David said, wrapping his arms around Madeleine's leg tighter than ever before.

"I know, baby, it's going to be all right." She tried to reassure him, even as she rocked her toddler, Mia, trying to calm the wailing child.

Elise held on to her son, Cicero. She was relieved that Danielle was holding her daughter, Annette-Natë. With her free hand, Elise dialed Xander's cell phone, hoping he still had it. There was no answer. She dialed five other numbers she knew; the fifth number had an answer.

"Who is this?" asked Warren, obviously on edge.

"Warren, this is Elise. Listen, we need to meet up, where's a good place?"

"Shit … Um … How about that hanger Xander owns?"

"You don't think they'll check there?"

"They might, but where else can we meet up? We don't have cars and most of us don't have any clothes. We need to get somewhere close by."

"True. It's as good an idea as any. We'll meet you there in an hour." Elise ended the call.

"We heard, sounds like a good place to regroup," Daniel said. "Xavier and the rest of Darian's coven are going to need someplace void of windows since the sun's almost up."

"Now that you've mentioned that, we're going to need to get coffins. Maybe they'll be some at *Desires Unleashed*. We need to pick some up before we get to the hanger," Devin said. He was a nervous wreck. He wanted to know if John was still alive, or if he was waiting it out somewhere like they were. He tried to keep his lover by his side, but his daughter was his first priority and he had to get her to safety when the moment came for them to flee. He hated not knowing if John was all right or he was dead.

"Let's hope so, we're taking a big risk going there and it's out of the way, so let's hope it's not in vain." Elise hailed two cabs that were going in opposite directions. Both drivers slowed down, hesitating. "Please, we need transportation. We were attack and need to get somewhere safe. We'll pay you whatever you want," she pleaded.

The cab driver eyed her nakedness with a mixture of curiosity and lust. His gaze scanned the others and by their tattered and bloodied appearance, he believed her story to be true. He allowed her to climb in beside him in the passenger seat. Four others climbed into the backseat. The other cab driver decided to do the same when he saw the money Madeleine waved at him and he pulled over to pick up the remaining members of the group.

They gave the drivers directions to the popular club. While inside the cab, Elise continued to call the others. When she reached them, she told them of the meeting location.

"Why don't we just meet at *Desires Unleashed* since you're heading there now?" Adan asked.

"Don't you think it's too *exposed*?" Elise asked, not thinking the club was the safest place for them to be.

"After tonight, do you really think there's any place in this city were we can hide?"

"You're right. Fine. We'll meet you at the club." Elise ended the call.

Within an hour, they arrived at *Desires Unleashed*. Xander and his Pack along with Adan and his Pride were already there. The three groups did a check of who was present and who wasn't. They weren't sure what it meant if someone was still missing.

"Has anyone been able to contact Xavier yet?" Elise asked.

Justin nodded. "He contacted us fifteen minutes ago, spoke with the manager, told her to let us in. He said they were on their way here."

Elise nodded. "Good, we need to regroup."

Ten minutes later, Natasha, Xavier and the remaining members of Darian's coven entered followed by Richard and the rest of his Pack. Matthew was already there. He hugged each member of his Pack as they entered, thrilled to see they had survived.

Xavier was exhausted from the battle and the retreat as were the other members who were with him. He looked around the room, taking count of all the familiar faces. "I'm glad to see so many of you survived."

"And those who didn't?" Elise asked, somewhat apprehensively.

Xavier shook his head. "I went back because I wanted to see if anyone was still there."

Devin stepped closer to him. "John?" His voice trembled with the fear he felt.

Xavier looked down. "He wasn't there. Neither were Sergio, Christopher, Darian, Miranda, Gabriel and Adrian."

"They took them," Xander said softly to no one in particular.

"How many were left?" Elise asked once again, still not really wanting to hear the truth. She already knew her Pride had suffered a loss with Rachel, despite her efforts to make sure every one of her Pride got out safely. When it looked as if she wouldn't survive, Sergio had sacrificed himself for her, taking the blow that Kiren dealt. She had had to leave him behind; it was the toughest decision she'd ever had to make. For hours, she struggled to remain calm, to not break down in tears, not knowing what had happened to him. She had to be brave for her Pride, for their children … for Sergio. Now that she knew he was not among the fallen, she had hope once again.

Xavier continued. "We lost Troy and Annabelle," he said, turning to see Miko walk away. Her cheeks were stained with trails of dried tears she'd shed over the loss of her lover. She had cried so much, she no longer felt any more pain or sadness. The only emotion she felt now was hatred fueled by the thoughts of revenge in her heart.

"I'm so sorry," Elise said to her, offering her most sincere condolences. "Miko … I'm sorry."

"Her death will not go unpunished, even if it kills me, that asshole is mine!" Miko growled, unable to be consoled.

Elise understood her anger and decided not to push any further.

Xavier continued. "Rachel is dead, so are Stephanie, Patricia, Lori, and Philip." He looked at Xander, Elise and Adan, whom had suffered the biggest loss of life. "I am sorry for your losses."

Xander nodded. "As I am sorry for yours."

Elise nodded as well, but remained silent.

"Thank you, I too, am sorry to hear about your loss as well," Adan said.

"Xander, are you all right?" Justin asked, worried about his Alpha.

Xander looked at him. "Yes. I'm all right, just thinking." He thought about his actions during their battle when he ran to save his wife from Alicia's attack. His wife was almost onto death from the attack; he had to get her to safety, share his blood with her and hope that it was enough. Now, knowing that his son may still be alive, he knew he could count on him to be strong enough to stay alive long enough for them to save them.

Tatiana felt a sense of relief knowing that her son had survived the initial attack, at least, that's what she was hoping for. If he wasn't among the dead, he may still be alive.

"What do we do now? If they have them, we need to save them, right?" Devin asked, wanting to rescue John and the rest of his Pride and friends.

"Hell yeah, we save them! I've had about all I can take of this sick fuck!" Barry said, feeling a bit anxious. He wanted to save Gabriel, his partner and best friend.

"Feeling a bit fired up, are you?" Brian asked, still nursing a wound in his stomach.

"I just want to save my friend. What about you? Are you okay?" Barry asked.

Brian nodded. "Yeah, it's just taking a while for this to heal. The fuckers actually sliced through my intestines. Without my Matron here, it takes longer for me to heal.

"I can help with that," Tatiana said, approaching the younger shifter.

"You don't mind?" Brian asked.

Tatiana shook her head. "No. Besides, if we're going to get our members back, we're going to need all of the healthy, strong help we can get." She offered him her wrist, which he took.

"Thank you," he said before biting her, tearing a small wound. He began drinking her healing blood.

Barry watched the interaction, amazed by how quickly he was healing, how healthy his skin was beginning to look. "Wow, I didn't know you could do that."

"You can do that, too, nowadays," Warren reminded.

"I suppose I can," Barry said.

"Listen, I don't mean to be rude here, but just what the fuck are we going to do now?! How are we going to get them back?!" Devin asked, his voice rising with his anger.

"I'm with Devin. We couldn't track their asses down before they attacked us, there's no telling where they're at now," Justin said. "How are we going to find them? We shouldn't have fucking ran away. They probably think we're some cowards now."

"I don't give a damn what they think of me, I just want our friends and family back!" Nicole said. She feared for Adrian's safety as well as the others and it was bothering her immensely not knowing where they were or if they were still alive.

"We had to run away, Justin, we didn't have a choice," Ryan said.

"We should have combined our forces like we first planned, we had them!" Justin argued.

"Don't be stupid, now is not the time," Ignacio said, silencing the ranting shifter. "They were playing with us, couldn't you tell?"

"We killed two of their members," Devin pointed out.

"*No*, we didn't. *Darian* killed one and injured another one good enough for Adan to kill him. *We* didn't do much damage at all," Ignacio said. "And I'm willing to bet if they were taking their attack more seriously, more of us would have died, if not all of us."

"I saw the opportunity, I took it. That's all we really had tonight, little slivers of opportunity," Adan agreed.

"That's true. Besides, we needed to protect the children. Can you imagine what would have happened to them?" Natasha asked both shifters.

Devin put his head down. He didn't need to imagine what they could have done; he'd seen their idea of "child's play".

"But ... we left them," Justin said, his voice breaking as tears ran down his cheeks.

"It's what Darian wanted, for us to get away so that we could regroup. Ignacio's right, if Marcus wanted to really kill us he could have done so easily. This wasn't about them killing us... it was about them toying with us. Perhaps they wanted to take prisoners, and were only planning to kill whomever they didn't want. I think they underestimated us and I'm counting on them to continue to underestimate us," Xavier said.

A few of the others nodded, agreeing with his assessment.

"So how are we going to get them back?" Justin asked.

"We need to find out where they are," Elise said.

"Natasha, can you connect with Darian?" Madeleine asked.

"I've tried that. All I'm getting is blackness, like there's nothing there," Natasha said, feeling sadden by the fact that she couldn't reach Darian.

"Could he be dead? When you don't see anything but blackness, that normally means the person is dead, doesn't it?" Warren asked.

"Normally, yes; but with Darian it's different. Our connection is stronger than that. I'd feel if he was dead," Natasha clarified.

"I would, too. He's not dead. I believe Marcus is controlling his mind," Xavier said. "Forcing him into a resting state."

"He can do that?!" Sebastian asked, shocked.

Xavier nodded. "He's more powerful than Darian. An ancient vampire can do many things a younger vampire can't. For instance, he can probably control shifters' minds … something neither Darian nor I can do."

"But I thought Darian could read our minds?" Devin asked.

"Not everyone, you … Yes and even Warren, but he can't read Elise, Sergio or even Ignacio's. And he can't control your thoughts or actions, not yet at least, he's not strong enough," Xavier explained.

"No wonder vampires are so fucking arrogant!" Ignacio said under his breath. He looked up at Xavier. "No offense to you intended."

"None taken. I have an idea, it's the same one I was going to mention before we were attacked," Xavier began.

"What's that? I'm open to all ideas," Ignacio said.

"We go to Darian's Maker. He's powerful, ancient … he might help," Xavier said.

"Whoa, hold up. I don't know, Xavier. Out of the frying pan and into the fire. That guy scares the shit out of me!" Justin said, remembering the last time he'd seen Kysen.

"He seemed cool at Darian's party," Natasha said.

"Yeah, he was 'cool', but I got the feeling he was only tolerating us for Darian's sake," Justin stated.

"We may not have a choice. The only reason two of their members are dead is because of Darian," Xavier said. "Now he's not here with us-"

Ryan interjected, unintentionally. "Yeah, I agree with what Ignacio said earlier. We *were* kind of just cannon fodder. I hate to think of us like that, but that's how it felt. I just remember running around trying to keep them from ripping my throat out. They were so powerful, so fast! Most of us didn't stand a chance."

"I like to think we helped Darian," Shannon said, not liking the 'cannon fodder' comparison.

"You're fooling yourself," Ryan retorted. "Those five bastards were kicking our asses! Adan only finished off what Darian started by ripping off Kiren's head, thank goodness. And I don't think you did much of anything at all, except maybe get thrown around a lot."

"Like you took out one of them," Shannon shot back. "I still think we did a good job, that's why so many of us survived."

"Bitch, we ran, that's why we survived!" Carmen said, finally growing annoyed with Shannon.

"Who are you calling a *bitch*?!" Shannon shouted.

"Enough! Damn it!" Elise shouted, glaring at Carmen, giving her a silent warning. Carmen nodded, remaining so. "I want to rescue our friends and family and I don't have time for petty arguments about 'who kicked whose ass'!" she said that last statement mockingly, purposely chastising Ryan, Shannon and Carmen.

"I was going to say that," Xander remarked. He turned toward Xavier. "If you think going to Darian's Maker is our last good resort, then we need to get going. The sun will be up soon."

Elise nodded. "I'll arrange for my jet to take us, you do the same, Xander. While we're doing that, Xavier, you should call Kysen, request permission."

"I would if I could, I don't have Kysen's personal information, all I remember is where he lives," Xavier revealed.

"Oh shit, now I'm really worried. Kysen will be totally pissed if we enter his territory without permission. He may try to kill us before we even get a chance to ask for his help!" Justin blurted out, nearly panicking.

Xander grabbed hold of his shoulders, forcing him to face him. "Calm down, Justin! Carrying on isn't helping our situation, be brave."

Justin looked at his Alpha. "I'm scared, Xander. I'm trying not to be, but God help me, I am. I'm scared for all of us."

"I know. It's all right to be afraid, but we must stay proactive. Going into hysterics isn't going to help us at all."

Justin nodded. "I'm sorry."

Xander caressed the back of Justin's neck lovingly, hoping to reassure him. He released the younger wolf. "We'll go anyway; this is the chance we're going to have to take."

The others agreed, seeing it as their only choice. Those of them who were naked were able to dress in a few costumes that they found in the dressing room of the employees who stripped at the club. Afterward, they took several cabs and made their way toward the two different airstrips. Xander and Elise made traveling arrangements along the way. Those who went with Elise boarded her plane and those who went with Xander boarded his. Both airplanes took off towards their destination.

Shannon looked around Elise's jet. "I hope this plane doesn't plummet to the ground because of overcrowding," she said.

"Well, to lessen the load, we can always toss your ass out," Carmen remarked.

"Can we not joke about plummeting planes while we're ten thousand feet in the air," Natasha said, looking at the two women.

Adan rose from the floor he'd been sitting on. "Shannon, come with me." He made his way toward the bathroom.

Shannon sense that he was upset with her and didn't want to follow him, but she did … he was her King. She rose from her chair and walked into the bathroom behind him. "Yes, Adan?" she asked in her sweetest voice.

Adan turned around quickly, backhanding her at the same time, knocking her to the floor. She cried out, clutching her now bruised cheek.

"Get up!" he ordered.

Trembling, she rose to her feet.

"You will keep your attitude in check. I've had enough of your smart-ass comments. Your constant badgering of our companions is insulting to our Pride."

"I don't like how they make us look weak," she said in her defense.

"They don't make us look weak. We need their help if we're going to survive this. We're all in this together and no one needs your attitude." Adan was stern, finally fed up with her behavior.

Shannon lowered her head. "I'm sorry, my King. I'll behave."

Adan gently touched the side of her face where he had struck her. She put her hand over his, lovingly.

"We're going to pull through this, Shannon. Trust when I say everything I've done and will continue to do is for our best interest," Adan said.

"I know."

"Let's join the others." He opened the door and they stepped out walking back into the area of the plane where the others were. Some were napping, others were talking and some were eating. Adan, feeling the hunger pangs, was more than ready for his meal.

"I can hear your stomach growling all the way over here," Danielle said. "Let me make you a plate." She rose preparing him a feast from the food that was recently served. She handed him the plate and he ate greedily, devouring every morsel.

Barry watched them, realizing that Carrie-Anne, another member of Adan's pride, had made his plate. He was starting to see the differences in how the two Prides functioned. He was seeing that in the lion Pride he was in, the males were revered, the females submissive. He watched Elise and her Pride and saw that she controlled her Pride and the males followed her orders. He thought it was interesting. He also realized that he and Barry were the only males other than Adan who were in his Pride, which made him immediately think about all of the animal behavior/habitat shows he'd seen in the past and was witnessing the distinct similarities.

"We should get some rest before we land. We'll be there in less than three hours now," Elise said.

"Can you rest?" Madeleine asked.

Elise shook her head. "No." She chuckled. "I wish that I could, but I can't. That doesn't mean you shouldn't try."

"I can't sleep either," Madeleine admitted. She held her daughter Mia in her arms; David was laying asleep, his head in her lap.

"Daniel, are you all right?" Elise asked, knowing exactly how he felt. Marcus and his coven kidnapped both of their lovers.

Daniel looked at her. "I'll be fine once we save Miranda, Sergio and everybody else."

Elise nodded. She watched over the others waiting for the moment when their plane reached its destination.

\*\*\*

The early morning sun was rising and only Raven, who was sitting next to Marcus on the jet, was still awake for the time being. The ancient vampire sat in a chair telepathically piloting the aircraft with ease. He watched Darian rest, and at the same time, he blocked his mind, preventing any connection his coven tried to make with him. He had underestimated the younger vampire and his comrades. Of this, he was certain. Never had he encountered several groups of supernaturals who were so willing to die for each other. Who were so in tune with each other, to the point in which they functioned as one cohesive unit. *Their* attack was calculated, stealthy. It angered him that the younger Master vampire, who was now lying helpless on the sofa before him managed to kill one of his coven members. Not to mention, injuring his lover, weakening him enough for Adan to kill him. He had no intentions of allowing any members of his coven to parish. They were to play with their victims as they always had. They were to torture them as they ran screaming in blind fear. Then, once they killed the ones they didn't want, they would take their bounty for later. Darian was the only supernatural in their midst who had the strength to battle the members of his coven, but Darian was no match for him … This he knew. He sat there, puzzled, trying to figure out how the younger vampire succeeded in doing what he did.

"Master, are we going to hunt down the others … Make them pay?" Raven asked.

"We won't have to hunt them down; they'll come for us … When we want them to. We have their members, they're not going to give up trying to look for them," Marcus said, still staring at Darian. "He's so young, how did he do it?!"

Raven knew that he was no longer speaking to her, but more to himself. She looked at Darian as well. "He had help, Master. Many of them ran like the cowards they are, leaving others to sacrifice themselves. We hadn't expected that."

"Make no mistake, Raven. They didn't run out of fear … They fled out of necessity, taking the weaker members with them. I wanted to kill their human lover. I wanted to rip their unborn child from her womb. They worked so well, keeping me distracted and occupied enough for them to escape, even if it meant their lives."

"Don't worry, Master. You'll get to do everything you want to do soon enough," Raven said, hoping to reassure her Maker.

"I know, and I'll make sure they watch when I do it." Marcus turned from Darian, looking out of the window, relaxing as he watched the wisps of white clouds float by. His mind was still swimming with images of their battle, recounting the events as they happened. Trying to figure out how the others worked so well together.

"When are we going to bring the rest of them to us?" Raven asked, looking at him anxiously.

Marcus turned facing her; his jaw tightened showing his irritation. She was beginning to enrage him with her questions. "When the time is right, do not ask me again," he said, glaring down at her.

"Yes, Master," Raven said, deciding to remain quiet.

Time passed as the sun rose higher in the sky, it forced Raven to rest. The vampire being only 2000 years old could no longer stay awake. Marcus looked at all of the sleeping supernaturals lying about the jet. He turned when he saw movement in the corner of his eye. Sergio began to stir on the floor where he laid, finally coming to. He opened his eyes, immediately becoming alert. He looked around, freezing instantly once he saw Marcus sitting in a chair watching him.

"You're awake. I was wondering how long you were going to lay there," Marcus said, giving the young shifter a toothy grin.

"Where are you taking us?" Sergio asked, knowing they were on Darian's airplane. He looked around the room again, seeing Darian resting along with John and Christopher. He saw that Miranda was still asleep and healing from her wounds, slowly. Gabriel and Adrian were both still unconscious and healing from wounds inflicted during their battle. He looked down at his shoulder, which was still sore, but healing well. His arm was nearly ripped off in a fight with Kiren. If it weren't for Richard coming to help him, he didn't know what he would have done, or what would have happened to him. During the battle, he remembered being somewhat confused, expecting their enemy to attack them more viciously. He thought they'd want to massacre them, but that didn't happen. Instead, Marcus and his coven seemed to be playing with them at first. It seemed that they wanted to scare them, torture them, hurt them, but not kill them. Then as the battle progressed, it seemed as though Marcus and his coven wanted only to kill certain members of their group. Sergio remembered how swiftly Raven murdered Stephanie and Rachel, as if they meant nothing to her. Yet, she toyed more with Elise and Miranda. He was beginning to understand that their enemy was picking and choosing who they wanted and killing those they didn't. Sergio turned back toward Marcus, waiting for an answer.

Marcus hadn't answered the young shifter, he only observed him looking around the room. He watched him contemplating their situation and knew what the shifter was thinking. Sergio was right, he wanted only to kill a few, take those he desired and leave others to search for them. To extend the game of 'cat and mouse' he enjoyed so much. Even still, he was looking forward to playing it, in spite of losing two significant members of his coven. One thing he knew for certain, he would make both Darian and Adan pay for the death of his lover.

"Where the fuck are you taking us?" Sergio asked again, this time more assertively.

Marcus cocked his head to the side. "Why should I tell you? What good would having that information do you now?"

"I just like to know where I'm going. If it's someplace I've never been, I may want do a little site-seeing, take some pictures, you know," Sergio retorted.

"I don't believe you'll be seeing much of the sites."

"Is that right? What are you going to do, kill us?"

"Eventually, but not until I can do it in front of your love ones who'll no doubt come looking for you."

"You tried this plan before, it backfired. By the way, how's your boyfriend?"

Marcus' eyes narrowed slightly, astonished by the shifter's audacity. "I'll make sure to sate my desires with your mate when she comes looking for you." He rose from his chair, closing the distance between them faster than anything Sergio had ever seen. He took hold of the shifter's chin, digging his nails into his flesh. Bringing their faces closer together, he whispered to Sergio. "Darian made her come harder than you ever did. She'd slick his dick up with her juices. Ooohhh, you should have seen them, how they devoured each other. Too bad you'll never have his skill, you'll never hear her scream your name like she screamed his." He released the shifter, slamming him back against the floor.

Sergio refused to rub his aching jaw. He knew he was bleeding from the nail marks which had cut into his skin. His anger kept him focused. He tried hard not to growl or snarl at Marcus, not wanting to give the vampire any satisfaction. He didn't want him to know just how much his words cut into him. It was no secret that Sergio was extremely protective of Elise and their relationship. However, every once in a while, he wondered about the relationship Elise had had with Darian, but he'd never let it consume him. Never would he allow doubt to creep into his mind if he was completely satisfying his lover or not. Not until this moment, at least. *Is what Marcus said true or did he say it to hurt him?*

As Marcus stood over the shifter, he began to laugh. "Look at you. You're obsessed! You can't take not being the top dog, oh, correction; top pussy. You think about it, don't you? You think about the nights when she'd run from you, into his arms. You remember his scent all over her don't you? He also bit her and you know, a vampire's bite is undiluted ecstasy, there's nothing on earth like it. You're right to doubt yourself... you just can't measure up to that man over there." He pointed to Darian resting of the sofa.

"Fuck you!" Sergio said through gritted teeth.

"Face it, you won her by default." Marcus laughed.

Enraged, Sergio lunged for Marcus, fist curled up. The Master vampire stepped to the side, easily avoiding the angry shifter. Sergio's momentum propelled him, sending him crashing into the side of the plane. Before he had time to recover, Marcus had him again, nails digging into his throat. He lifted Sergio up, leaving his feet dangling a foot from the floor.

"I admire your strength, so I can see why she *settled* for you. The other members of your pathetic Pride paled in comparison. She really didn't have much of a choice to begin with." Marcus punched Sergio's abdomen, knocking the wind out of him. He slammed the shifter hard on the floor then stepped on his throat, applying pressure a little at a time, cutting off Sergio's airway, denying him oxygen. "After Darian dumped her, who did she have to go to? Devin? Daniel ... Sebastian?" He laughed heartily.

Sergio's hand turned into claws as he prepared to defend himself. Marcus saw when he raised his hand to rip his leg and he stopped him, grabbing hold of Sergio's hand, crushing it. Sergio screamed, unable to keep it in. His hand was afire, lit with pain pulsing up his entire arm. His free hand grabbed his now injured one. Marcus climbed on top of the shifter, prying his hands apart and pinning them over his head to the floor.

"Go fuck yourself!" Sergio said through pain-filled pants, spitting directly in Marcus' face, his saliva landing on the vampire's cheek.

"Now that was just rude. How would you like it I was to spit on you? Here I am, trying to be a good friend, telling you the truth about the woman who claims she loves you and you spit in my face for my efforts."

"Well, calling you a sick fucking bastard just didn't roll off my tongue as smoothly as that did," Sergio said, smiling at him.

Marcus sat up, straddling him. He wiped the spit off with the back of his sleeve then he reached behind him, taking hold of Sergio's groin.

"What the fuck are you doing? Don't fucking touch me!" Sergio began to squirm, trying to wiggle away from the vampire, to no avail.

"I think you know by now that I'm going to do whatever I want to whomever I want." He slipped his hand inside Sergio's pants, his fingers finding the shifter's penis. "Ah, cut; why am I not surprised." He began stroking Sergio's shaft, his fingers expertly massaging the sensitive flesh with the skill he'd acquired over the span of six thousand years. He smiled to himself as he felt the shifter respond to his touch.

"You don't want to do that," Sergio warned.

"Why not, already I can feel you becoming hard."

"You better get your hand off me!"

"No. I'm horny and you're getting there. I don't see why we can't have f-" Marcus was interrupted by the hot stream of urine Sergio released. He pulled his hand away as if he had been burned.

Sergio began laughing. "I warned you, warned you twice."

Marcus growled. With a hard backhanded punch, he knocked Sergio unconscious, even loosening two of his teeth. He rose to his feet and leaning over, he wiped the urine from his hand onto Sergio's shirt before entering the bathroom to wash thoroughly. He cursed to himself, agitated by the shifter's actions. He stepped out of the bathroom, looking around the plane at their captives. His eyes stopped on Christopher, the youngest of Darian's coven, the most impressionable. At the far end of the plane, he saw Adrian stir.

Adrian opened his eyes. Much like Sergio had, he looked around, taking in his surroundings. He saw Sergio laying on the floor, zipper undone and a wet urine stain on the front of his pants. He didn't want to think about what happened to his friend to explain why he was in that state. He saw Miranda rolling over, coming to. When she woke up, he asked her if she was all right.

"I'll be fine," she answered, rubbing her leg a little. The wound was healing nicely, in spite of her not being able to drink Elise's blood to heal faster. Both of them turn toward Marcus, who had been watching them.

"So, are we your bargaining chips?" Adrian asked.

"No. Leverage … temptation, and outlets for my desires and aggravation, but not at all bargaining chips." Marcus unfolded his arms and began walking closer to them. "See, in order to be bargaining chips, the people I would be bargaining with would have to have something I wanted. Something I couldn't get unless they gave it to me. I *take* what I want, as you can see." he made a sweeping motion toward the unconscious bodies.

"You talk too much," Gabriel said as he came to.

"Welcome to the party," Marcus retorted.

"See what I mean?" Gabriel sat up, back against a coffee table. "Where are you taking us?"

Marcus chuckled as if he was in disbelief. "What is it with you people? Why would I tell you where I'm taking you? What sense would that make?" He had to admit to himself, this group of supernaturals were far more entertaining to him than many others he'd come in contact with over the centuries. Their conspicuous candor was refreshing to him.

"You've already proven that you take what you want. You've said no one can stop you. What difference would it make our situation if we knew?" Adrian asked, attempting to gather the information they needed.

"Cute. Your mind games won't work on me, but it was a nice try. I would have done that myself if I were in your position." Marcus stepped a bit more closer. He was enjoying their wisecracks, which were far more entertaining than the 'pleading for their lives' he'd gotten from others. Although he had to admit, he had not enjoyed Sergio pissing on him. He'd make the shifter pay for that offense later.

"And what position is that?" Adrian asked, wondering what their fates were going to be.

"If my Pack and all of my friends abandoned me, including my mother and father, leaving me in the presence of the very man they knew I could not defeat … An extremely powerful vampire who would probably kill me, I'd want to know where I would die, too." Marcus sat down in a chair next to where Sergio's laid.

"You must be pretty bored with immortality," Gabriel said. He looked around the plane. "Wait a minute, who's piloting this fucking plane?!"

"I am," Marcus answered. "And don't try to analyze me. There's nothing I find more thrilling than living forever, growing more powerful as time goes on."

Adrian rolled his eyes. "I'm sure," he scoffed.

"And just how the hell are you piloting this plane?!" Gabriel asked, incredulously. He couldn't help but notice the Master vampire was not in the cockpit where he should have been.

"He's using telepathy, Gabriel. Powerful vampires can do that easily," Miranda said.

"Oh," Gabriel said, surprised. He was starting to realize just how little humans really knew about the supernaturals. How their world really worked and he really didn't appreciate the crash course he was forced to take to gain that knowledge.

"Your partner, Barry ran with the others. He didn't stop to wake you up when you were knocked unconscious. Funny, you'd think he wouldn't leave you alone. You know that's what you are, don't you? Alone. No one here really knows you and probably won't care if you died," Marcus said, watching Gabriel's reaction. He didn't get the response he'd hoped for which disappointed him. Gabriel only shrugged.

"It's not their fault I'm here, it's yours," Gabriel said, keeping a brave face.

Marcus undeterred, continued to play his mind games. "Must suck being alone. Your mistress no longer wants to sleep with you. Your job, for which you've dedicated your life to-fired you. Your wife dumped you, your children are afraid of you, of what you've become, and your best friend aban-"

"Shut the fuck up! You don't talk about my family, you psychotic son-of-a-bitch!" Gabriel barked, unable to control his anger, even though he knew he was being provoked.

"You have no more family, Gabriel. Didn't you realize that when you woke up in the hospital room all alone," Marcus asked, feigning sympathy, one eyebrow cocked.

"Go to hell!" Gabriel shot back. He could feel his temperature rising to a boiling point. He wanted to lunge at the vampire, to rip his throat out.

"Gabriel, calm down," Adrian said, knowing Marcus wanted to antagonize them, he wanted to torture them and a good deal of that "torture" included what he could do to them mentally.

The younger shifter looked at Adrian. Gabriel nodded, understanding what he meant. He had to keep his calm, even if it was *damn near impossible*.

Marcus turned his attentions to Adrian once again. "Yeah, I guess you would know a thing or two about being dumped also. You couldn't even keep your best friend happy as a lover. Maybe you were too afraid to be on the bottom because that's where you knew you belonged. Isn't that right, Adrian?" he said, rising from his chair.

"I'd tell you to 'suck my dick' if I didn't think you'd take me up on the offer," Adrian said, settling back against the cushions. "Is the remainder of this boring ass flight going to be you pulling these preschool antics trying to get a rise out of us?"

"There are other ways to get a 'rise' out of you," Marcus said smiling. "For now, however, I'd like to rest for the remainder of the flight."

Adrian smirked. "Maybe, *I* want to talk now, I've got so much to s-"

"Sleep." Marcus said, exerting his mental power over them. The three shifters fell asleep instantaneously, slumping over to their sides. He sat in his chair again, watching all of them slumber. He was almost excited for what he was planning on doing to them and couldn't wait to return home.

***

Once the two jets landed at the airstrip, they all deplaned. Six trucks were waiting for them as Elise and Xander had arranged. Once they were on the road, the other five trucks followed Xander's SUV as they sped toward Kysen's Mansion. When they arrived, everyone climbed out, except the vampires, who were thoroughly protected from the sun's harmful rays by tinted windows, jackets and blankets as they were unable to find coffins at the club.

Xander turned to address them. "Some of you should stay in the trucks to look after the others. Those who want to come inside, follow me."

"I think I'll stay with Xavier," Justin said, climbing back into the truck. Several others followed his lead, climbing back inside while the others followed Xander as he led the way toward the front door, which opened before he could knock. Kysen's human servant greeted them.

"My Master sensed when your planes landed. He's expecting you," the servant stepped aside, allowing them entry. Once they were inside, the servant led them to the den. "Please wait here," he said, before turning to leave.

They looked around the room, marveling at the lavish luxurious decorations. They waited feeling their nervous tension mounting, some of them were more nervous than the others.

"I hope he helps us," Devin said.

"Why wouldn't he?" Sebastian asked. "Darian's in trouble."

"I don't know … I just hope he helps us," Devin repeated.

"I don't see why he wouldn't. Aren't vampires loyal like that?" Sebastian asked. He was excited to meet Darian's Master, his Maker; the vampire who brought him over. He'd been impressed with Darian ever since the first day he'd met him. He regretted not being allowed to go to the birthday party Natasha threw for him, which Kysen had attended. He'd heard so much about him when the rest of his Pride returned home, he was just itching with anticipation to see if he was a being who could measure up to the hype.

"In my experience, I've seen some who are loyal and some who aren't. The blood bond they share doesn't always instill loyalty, remember both Tony's and Christopher's histories with their Makers," Elise said.

"Oh, I see," Sebastian said, nodding.

Several minutes passed before Kysen entered the den, dressed in a cream button-up shirt, matching flat-front pants and sandals which complemented his dark chocolate complexion. His long braided hair was tied behind his back, revealing his beautiful almond-shaped golden brown eyes. He crossed the room gracefully as if his feet didn't touch the ground. He made his way toward his favorite chair, settling into the cushions comfortably, crossing one leg over the other, with both hands clasped together resting in his lap. His eyes scanned over the many faces peering back at him, noticing that the face of his child, Darian, was not in the crowd. After scanning all of their minds, he now knew why. He could sense that they were in fact, tired, weary, and afraid and in pain. He could smell their fear in the air and it made his mouth water. It was a scent that always awakened the predator within. He welcomed that scent when he hunted, it enhanced the entire experience, made it more intoxicating ... primal.

Letting his eyes scan over them, he spoke. "Very rude of you to enter my territory without my permission." His voice reverberated throughout the room, sending chills down the others' spines.

"We apologize for the intrusion, however, we didn't have a choice," Elise said, stepping forward.

Kysen studied her closely. He remembered her from Darian's birthday party. She'd been pregnant then and radiated a certain glow that he had found mesmerizing. Now she appeared to be a bit worse for wear. Her hair was uncombed, clothes torn, bloodied. Her eyes were weary, sad. As far as he was concerned, that was no way for a woman of her stature to appear.

"Go on." Kysen made a gesture for her to continue.

"Xavier only knew your address, and little else, so we couldn't have called to request permission. We need your help," she said, locking her aqua green eyes to his golden brown. She couldn't help but stare at his exotic beauty. It never ceased to amaze her just how gorgeous many of the vampires were. She would have to agree with Sergio when he mentioned vanity was their motivation for turning only those who they deemed pretty. She knew that Darian was guilty of this as well, although, she wasn't sure if Xavier would be interested in making one solely out of beauty.

"I know why you need my help. Fine mess you've gotten yourselves involved in," Kysen said.

"Will you help us?" Elise asked, getting to the point.

"No." Kysen rose from his seat, approaching them.

"Why not?!" Devin blurted out, not really meaning to.

Kysen turned slightly, addressing him. "Because, I have no interest in cleaning up your mess."

"But Darian needs your help!" Devin continued.

"This is his mess as well."

"Wrong. This is your mess and others like you," Adan spoke up.

Kysen turned sharply, one perfectly shaped eyebrow arched, looking at him. "Come again?" He'd never met this shifter before, and he didn't appreciate him speaking out of line. But he did have to admire his stunning beauty. His golden amber eyes were truly something to behold. He studied Adan, waiting for him to respond.

"This vampire who attacked us is ancient, like you. I'm sure you've seen all of the carnage he and his coven have caused, yet you sit idly by and watch people suffer when you have the power to put an end to it. This is not our mess," Adan stated.

"Is that so?" Kysen smirked.

"You know it's true, what I say," Adan replied.

"Kysen, I think I speak for all of us when I say that we're all very tired, it goes without saying that tempers will flare," Elise said, gaining the ancient vampire's attention. She continued. "The reality is, we need your help, I don't see why we have to go through this in order to get it. You love Darian, why not help him?"

"What I do or choose not to do for him is my business," Kysen said, giving them all a stern glare.

"One could say that it was a mistake coming here. However, I don't believe that," Xander said. Kysen turned, looking at the Pack Alpha. "You're powerful, I can sense your aura, I'm sure that you want me to. You're more powerful than Marcus is. He has Darian captive … At least that's what we believe. If so, my son, her lover and others are with him. He could be doing God knows what to them. Darian is yours, by all rights. At the very least, what Marcus has done is an insult to you. We want to rescue them, but we need you. Will you help us?" He hoped he was appealing to Kysen's love as well as his overall possessiveness toward Darian.

Kysen stood silent for several moments, thinking about what they said. He smirked. "Perhaps had you not fled your territory in such a cowardly manner, Darian wouldn't be in need of my help."

"You can tell yourself that, but before us, there were others. Countless others, whom Marcus tortured and murdered. Eventually, he would have found Darian. And my Pride 'fleeing' our territory was not done out of cowardice. Unlike you, I protect what's mine, with no questions asked, no prodding needed. I did what I thought I had to do, to make sure they survived," Adan shot back.

Four younger shifters, who had been standing near Adan, began to step back, not wanting to be near him if Kysen were to strike out. They remembered Darian's apprehension when coming face-to-face with the older vampire, in spite of their strong bond. Many believed Kysen would kill Adan, since the two men shared no bond whatsoever. Elise and Xander stood their ground. They were going to continue to persuade Kysen to help them, even if it meant incurring his anger.

"But you *couldn't* protect them on your own," Kysen continued. "You've failed them anyway."

"At least I tried. You won't even do that for Darian."

"There are no consolation prizes for failing at being a leader. *'Trying'* isn't doing. Why do you care what I do for Darian? Had he stayed with me, he wouldn't be going through this anyway."

"Is that what this is about? You're teaching him a lesson?" Elise asked, incredulously.

"If that's how you want to see it," Kysen answered.

"Why are you being petty? This is childish behav-" Adan's words were cut off by powerful fingers tightening around his throat.

Kysen's face was less than an inch from his. "Speak not of what you do not understand! I should kill you for what you say."

"You know I'm right," Adan managed to say between labored gasps.

The two men stared at each other.

"Kysen, could you live with yourself if Darian were killed?" Elise asked, hoping he'd let Adan go and bring his attentions back to the matter at hand. He didn't.

"Out of my home! All of you!" Kysen growled.

Devin wasted no time in leaving. Others followed his lead. Nicole gestured for Elise, urging her to follow them.

Elise told them to go then she turned, stepping toward Kysen until she was standing beside him. "Please let Adan go," she said.

"No. He stays," Kysen said, still holding Adan, but not aggressively. He was no longer choking him; his hand now pressed the younger shifter against the wall. "I have something I want to discuss with him."

"It's all right, Elise. Go with the others," Adan said.

Grudgingly, Elise decided to go, leaving the two men alone.

Kysen released Adan, stepping back, taking in his appearance. He could sense the lion's aura as well as his pride. He smiled. "You've got nerve, I'll give you that. Perhaps it wasn't cowardice that sent you to my Darian. Nonetheless, they feel as though you brought this onto them."

"I can see why they'd feel that way," Adan said, rubbing the soreness across his throat.

Kysen reached over cupping Adan's cheek. The shifter stood still, keeping his eyes locked on the vampire, who smiled. "You remind me a great deal of him. Your boldness, even if it's rather imprudent."

"It seems to be the only language you old ones appear to understand."

Kysen leaned forward; his lips were inches away from Adan's, who allowed him to make that approach. "You're bleeding."

"You made me bite my tongue," Adan explained. His eyes softened as he looked at the ancient vampire. He was beginning to sense Kysen's attraction to him.

"I see," Kysen said. He pressed his silky, full lips to Adan's, kissing him passionately. He slipped his tongue inside, licking the blood that was spilt. When he pulled away, he licked his own lips, savoring the taste of the young shifter.

"Vampires," Adan snorted.

"I hate to see good blood go to waste."

"Then save Darian and the others," Adan said, forcing Kysen to stay focused on more important matters.

Kysen tilted his head slightly, admiring Adan. "And you and your Pride?"

"It's true. In saving Darian, you'll be helping me by killing Marcus. Is that why you don't want to help us?"

"I did not say that."

"Then, was Elise right when she said you're trying to teach Darian a lesson? Hoping he'll come back to you?"

"You are *beautiful*," Kysen said, changing the subject, throwing Adan off guard. "Positively exquisite."

Adan huffed, growing frustrated. "Stop changing the subject," he complained. "Why are you being so nonchalant? These are important matters."

"Important to you."

"I can see that you don't care about what happens to us, but don't you care about what happens to Darian?"

"You keep mentioning his name to me as if I'm supposed to hop on my white steed and race to his rescue, with my sword raised high." Kysen chortled.

"You'd come to his birthday party, but not to his rescue?" Adan questioned sarcastically.

Kysen laughed outright. "One does seem more trivial than the other, doesn't it?"

"You're wasting time. Will you help us or not?" Adan asked.

"The sound of your voice is delightful to me, as well as your accent." Kysen's eyes trailed over Adan once more, drinking in his beauty.

"Don't look at me that way."

"In what way?" Kysen asked, smiling slyly.

"Need I remind you of your recent outburst, which ended with me shedding blood?"

"As I recall, it was you who bit your own tongue. Besides, you had that coming. As far as I'm concerned, you were out of line. Being a leader yourself, I'm sure you've … *disciplined* those beneath you before."

"Is that what you call it? Is that what you think I am … '*beneath*' you?"

"Don't act so surprised." Kysen flashed him his most captivating smile. "Besides, I'd rather like the idea of having you beneath me," he said imploringly.

A surge of desire rippled through Adan sending chills down his spine. "You're pretty sure of yourself, aren't you?"

"Of course." Kysen could sense the shifter's arousal growing and was pleased.

Adan snorted. "I see where Darian gets it now."

"Oh, don't be so sure. My Darian was very arrogant long before I brought him to me. You remind me of him … His passion … His valor, especially in your comments toward me."

"I've simply grown weary of playing the games of beings who are old enough to know better." Adan knew he was pushing it by being so direct. He also knew that it was working. Pleading with Kysen didn't seem to be the answer. He didn't blame Elise and the others, they were being respectful, something they would have wanted in return had the situation been reversed. He however, owed this vampire nothing and he was far too exhausted to be respectful. All he knew was that he wanted to save the lives of those who were now in danger as well as his Pride. If insulting this vampire could get a rise out of him, then so be it.

"I'll save Darian and the others, not because you unskillfully attempted to goad me."

Adan chuckled. "Then why?" *Still with the games*, he thought. *How bored are the old ones when this seems to be their entertainment?*

"Does that matter?"

"You seemed very adamant to teach him a lesson, I'm just curious as to why you've changed your mind?"

"Because, Darian belongs to me. He always has, he always

270

will."

Adan's eyes narrowed. "You were going to save him all alone, weren't you?"

Kysen smirked. "Yes, once I read your minds and knew what had happened to him."

"Why all of the games, then?"

"Because I could." Kysen walked away, sitting in his chair. "And I wanted to see what you'd all say." He called for his servant, who entered the room.

"Yes, Master?" the servant said, bowing.

"Tell the others they may park their trucks in the garage and come inside," Kysen said, still watching Adan from across the room.

"Yes. Master." The servant left, following Kysen's orders.

Adan approached Kysen. "When you go to save him, I want to come."

"Think you, that I need your help? Honestly, you will only hinder me. Look at what your assistance did for Darian."

"That's not fair."

Kysen studied the shifter for a few seconds then he spoke. "Why do you want to come? What help could you possibly be against them?"

"I owe Darian my life."

"As he once owed you his?" Kysen asked, making reference to Adan's past.

"It's true. I did help Darian a hundred and forty-eight years ago."

"Hunters."

"They attacked him and his coven right before dawn. Like me with my Pride, he was trying to protect his coven. One of his members had made the mistake of being caught feeding, led them right to his home which the hunters had set fire to, leaving them without shelter from the sun.

"Darian did manage to kill the hunters?" Kysen asked.

"He's your child isn't he? He did. But that wasn't his problem as you know."

"You gave him shelter."

Adan nodded. "Even though we hadn't met before, I felt he

could be trusted."

"A man of integrity, indeed," Kysen remarked.

"I'll have you know, I never reminded Darian of the debt he owed to me when I came to him for help."

"You never had to. Darian remembered. He's honorable that way."

"I still feel as though you'll need help if you're going for them. Marcus is ancient, like you and those within his coven are powerful as well. They may make it difficult for you to attack him," Adan said, trying for reason.

Kysen pursed his lips and cocked a brow as contemplated. "Perhaps, you're right."

Kysen's servant entered the room again. "Master, our guests are inside now, where should I send them?"

Exhaling a long sigh, Kysen relaxed in his chair, crossing one impressively long leg over the other. "You may send them in here."

The servant bowed and left the room, returning with the others trailing along behind him.

Elise entered the room, looking at Adan, she then turned her gaze toward Kysen. "Is everything all right?"

Adan nodded. "Yes."

Kysen watched all of the supernaturals and humans pour into his den. He looked at their torn, dirty, and bloodied clothing and frowned. "Although, you are guests in my home, I do not want you sitting or touching anything here. Not until you've bathed properly. You are all offensive to my senses and this just won't do."

A few of the others looked down at their attire, no one said anything, many agreed, and wanted to clean up and change clothes, but just hadn't had the opportunity. Others however, didn't take too kindly to Kysen's insult, but still remained silent.

Elise decided to question Kysen, to see where he stood. "We need to know if you're going to help us. If not, we need time to come up with another plan."

Kysen arched an eyebrow. "Fiery, aren't we? I admire that trait in a woman." He ran a finger over his full-shaped bottom lip. "I will help Darian, and the others."

"Now?" Elise asked, stepping forward.

"As soon as I am able to contact him," Kysen answered.

"I thought your connection to him was strong, why can you not reach him?" Xander asked. He was worried for his son as well as the others. He had no idea what Marcus had planned, and he certainly didn't want the others to suffer any longer than they had.

"This vampire is powerful … he has Darian's mind blocked along with the others. However, I can sense his general location," Kysen informed. "I could break his hold on Darian, but I don't want to alert this, *Marcus* to my presence. I want this insolent vampire to believe he's still in control."

"What is their general location?" Xander asked.

"Europe … quite possibly near the Mediterranean."

"Italy? Greece?" Xander suggested.

Kysen nodded. "Most likely, Italy. I won't know for sure until I get closer to that area. Unfortunately, I'm sure some of you will want to accompany me, which will hinder me significantly."

"Then we should leave now," Elise suggested. "I will be traveling with you."

"As will I," Richard said.

"It goes without saying, this vampire has my son, I'm going," Xander said.

Kysen rolled his eyes, exasperated. "Shall we wait for nightfall for Xavier and the rest of Darian's coven to declare their heroics?"

"Kysen, please, there's no need for insults. We just want to help in any way that we can. Remember, our loved ones are also there, they need us as well," Elise said.

"Who's insulting? I'm simply putting things into perspective so that you all won't have any delusions. The very fact of the matter is, you couldn't help yourselves. Yet, you're so very confident that your presence will help me. Forgive me, but from what I've gathered from your minds, you may be going to your deaths," Kysen pointed out.

"I'm not afraid to die," Richard said. "And since we are allowing each other the courtesy of bluntness, may I point out that you may very well be going to your death by facing them without assistance. Marcus is extremely powerful and you'll only be ambushed by him and his coven. You're powerful, but not invincible against one who's almost equal to your own strength."

Kysen pursed his lips. "So you'll be my cannon fodder, as they say?" he asked the four leaders, whom he knew had much to live for.

"Part of being a leader means putting yourself in a situation like this. Whatever happens, will happen. I've never shied away from dangerous situations and I don't plan on doing so now," Xander said.

"Can we go now?" Elise added.

Kysen eyed the four shifters, secretly admiring them for their bravery.

"Very well. The remaining members of your groups are free to stay here. I would highly suggest that someone stronger than them …" He pointed to the other shifters in the room. "… Should stay here to protect the others in case Marcus or one of his should decide to track you down."

Richard looked at the others then nodded. "You make a valid point. I'll stay. I'm the second strongest here. In my stead, you should take Xavier with you."

Kysen turned, looking at Xander. "Do you agree?"

Xander nodded. "Xavier is strong, besides, he'll want to be there for Darian. I'm sure you understand the bond they share."

Kysen chuckled softly, catching the hint. "Very well. Go and fetch him."

"We don't have a coffin to place him in, do you?" Elise asked, wanting to protect Xavier from the harmful rays of the sun.

"I do," Kysen said. Telepathically beckoning his servant, the man entered, awaiting his Master's command. "Follow him… he'll take you to my storage room where you'll find several coffins. Bring three. There's one I want you to bring in particular, it's solid gold with encrusted jewels. I'm sure you'll spot it right away."

"For Darian?" Elise asked; one eyebrow arched.

"Yes," Kysen responded.

"I should carry that one, seems like it'll be heavier than the others," Richard offered.

"Thank you." Elise motioned for two of her members to follow the servant and Richard toward the storage room.

Kysen looked at them, he shook his head slightly. "Feel free to bathe properly before you lounge on my furniture. There's plenty of clothing for you to choose from. My servants will give you anything that you'll need while you are here." He turned to Elise, Xander and Adan. "The three of you should also bathe and change clothes before we go."

"Do we really have time for that? I want to leave as soon as possible," Elise said, stepping forward, not at all caring about her appearance.

"Make time," Kysen said, not relenting on his request for them to be presentable and most of all, appealing to his senses. The scent of blood, in general, didn't repulse him. However, the scent of decaying blood did. And there was plenty of that on their attire.

"Where should we go?" Adan asked.

Kysen turned toward him, smiling sardonically. "If you weren't friends of Darian's, I'd spray you down in my backyard. However, you may use my guests' bathrooms. My servants will take you there." Again, he mentally called for more servants and they came.

The three shifters were led in separate directions toward three bedrooms. Richard, Daniel, and Devin returned with the three coffins, placing them on the floor. Kysen walked over to the gold and jewel-encrusted coffin, leaning down, he ran his fingers lovingly over the polished top. The others stood in the room, silently watching him. He rose, looking around, pleased that most of the shifters were gone, cleansing themselves. Several minutes later, Elise, Xander and Adan returned each wearing a fresh change of clothes.

Natasha came down as well; just in time to see them placing Xavier inside a black lacquered coffin. She had been quiet earlier, her body felt sluggish, and she was exhausted. She watched the intense interaction between the supernatural leaders, hoping Kysen wasn't as big of an *asshole* as he was leading them to believe. She'd met him only once and had mixed feelings about him. She was happy that he finally decided to help them. She wanted Darian and the others to return safely, and didn't want to think about what could be happening to them at that point. She didn't want to imagine them being killed or tortured.

"Kysen," she began, catching the vampire's attention, he turned toward her.

"Yes, Natasha?" he answered.

"Thank you for helping us."

"Your gratitude is not required. I'm only helping Darian, in doing so, the rest of you are benefiting from my intervention," Kysen said.

Natasha huffed. "Can't you just say, 'you're welcome'? Why do you have to be this way?"

"What way? I'm simply telling you the truth. You seem to believe that I should care about your fates simply because Darian does … I don't."

"Well, thank you anyway, for whatever it's worth," Natasha said before turning to take a seat on the sofa with her son.

Kysen looked at the child in her arms, he walked over to them. "Has Darian enjoyed being the father of this child?"

Natasha's eyes focused on him. "Yes, very much so. He loves being a Dad and he's excited about his second child, too."

"He's more domesticated than I would have ever guessed."

"Is that a problem?"

"It's weakened him." Kysen turned toward the others. "It's his love, his concern for you that has put him in this predicament."

"You can complain to him once we save him, can we go now?" Elise asked once again.

"Very well." Kysen led the way, leaving the shifters to carry the three coffins.

Elise carried a redwood coffin, following Kysen.

"I'll take this one, you take the other," Xander said, hoisting the gold coffin onto his shoulder with a slight level of difficulty.

"Nice how he left us to carry the load," Adan groaned to himself as he lifted the black lacquer coffin containing Xavier onto his shoulder. He left the mansion followed by Xander carrying the coffin meant for Darian. They loaded the coffins on two trucks, Darian's coffin being the only one inside a huge Sidewinder SUV. The sun was shining brightly as they made their way toward Kysen's private jet. Once on board, they settled comfortably as Kysen mentally piloted the aircraft toward Darian's location.

"What if he senses us coming?" Xander questioned.

"He'll be expecting you, I'm sure. He won't be expecting me. I'm going to mask my aura until I need it to locate Darian's exact location," Kysen said.

"I see," Xander said, nodding.

"What if he kills Darian when he feels you prying for their location?" Adan asked.

Kysen turned sharply, glaring at him. "And what if none of this ever happened? So many unnecessary questions! They're becoming more than a little annoying."

"It seems as though you are now the one who doesn't want to face a possible reality," Adan said.

Kysen chuckled. "'A possible reality' could be so simple as this aircraft suffering engine failure and falling out of the sky sending you to your fiery deaths."

"I disagree. That won't happen with you piloting."

Kysen rolled his eyes again. "Whatever. Can we not discuss Darian's hypothetical demise?"

"Very well, what would you like to discuss? Do you have any questions for us?" Adan asked, giving Kysen his attention.

"As a matter of fact, I do. You and Darian … he was your first, am I correct?" Kysen asked, smiling lustfully.

Adan jerked, the question catching him off guard. "What a thing to ask at a time like this. Besides, don't you already know the answer?"

"*You* are tense in this situation, not me. And no, I do not know. I hadn't bothered to pry that deeply into your memories," Kysen answered.

"Why ask that of me, though?" Adan asked; feeling slightly embarrassed. The question was rather intrusive and intimate and they were not alone.

"I'd prefer to discuss matters not dealing with torture, deaths and 'what ifs'." Kysen crossed one long leg over the other, his eyes remaining on Adan as if Elise and Xander were not there. He was intrigued by the young lion as well as attracted to him. His beauty was exotic, much like that of Darian's and his personality was spirited. He stared at Adan's golden amber eyes and his beautiful brown complexion. He watched Adan's full lips part as he prepared to respond to him.

"Forgive me, but I'm finding it difficult to think about anything other than saving the others at this point. I don't want to discuss …

certain things," Adan answered.

Kysen smiled. "Is that the reason your pulse quickens when you look at me? Why your blood flows faster through your veins? Even now, I can smell pheromones emanating from you. You're attracted to me, yet you're fighting that attraction. Why?"

"Perhaps, I'm struggling to figure out what is it about you exactly, that I could possibly find attractive." Adan raised an eyebrow.

"Touché. I suppose I haven't been the most gracious host. It really isn't my nature."

"What is your nature then? So far as I can tell, you're rude, arrogant, jaded, disconcerting … and ultimately repulsive." Adan knew he was taking a chance in saying what he said. He was even more shocked when Kysen's smile widened.

"You forgot to mention vain."

"I was hoping I wouldn't have to add that to an already astonishingly long list of undesirable attributes."

Kysen laughed outright, tickled by the shifter's brazen responses. It had been a while since he'd met anyone quite like him. He enjoyed pushing Adan's buttons, playing with him … seducing him.

"I'm going to the lady's room," Elise announced, rising from her seat.

The three men rose from their seats as she walked past.

"I see you're a gentleman … for the most part," Adan said, noting how Kysen rose from his chair.

"She is a lady of high standards, is she not? I can respect that," he said, settling back into his chair.

"Do you need to feed?" Xander asked. "You're going to need all of your strength to defeat Marcus."

Kysen opened his mouth, preparing to refuse the offer, but then he glanced at Adan, then back at Xander, changing his mind. A shifter's blood was indeed a delicacy, but most of all he wanted Adan.

"I will need to feed before we make contact with them, yes," Kysen lied, turning toward Adan. "Will you be donating?"

Adan snorted. "I don't remember making the offer. No."

"Well, as I am eradicating your initial problem, the very least you could do would be to make sure I'm at peak physical condition when I do so," Kysen prodded.

It was now Adan's turn to laugh. "Who would think you had moments when you're not at the height of your ability?"

"Well, I could face this vampire and his coven with hunger pangs distracting me. If that's the chance you're willing to take," Kysen said, his mouth curled slightly at one end.

Adan cocked an eyebrow, watching Kysen suspiciously. "I wouldn't put it past you to be manipulating this situation just to feed from me. I bet you're not even hungry."

Kysen laughed. "I could be manipulating you, but then what if I'm not?"

Adan sighed. "You don't have to play games with me, if you want to drink from me then fine. If it'll give you the added strength you'll need to defeat our enemy, I'll be more than happy to donate."

"Much appreciated," Kysen said.

"I'm sorry, but I must ask, why are you not the least bit concerned about this other vampire?" Xander asked.

Kysen turned toward him. "Because I plan on killing him. He's insulted me by taking what's mine, by hurting what's mine. His ill-guided action towards Darian are unforgivable and I plan on making him suffer for what he has done."

"Don't underestimate him, please. Darian didn't and still we were not prepared," Xander said, hoping Kysen's over-confidence didn't cloud his judgment. He wanted to succeed and believed there was no room for errors.

"Understand, I am neither Darian nor you. I will kill this vampire. As a matter of fact, he would probably already be dead had I not had to drag the lot of you along with me," Kysen said through tight lips.

"Can we not discuss that again? I want to save my lover and my friends. I feel as though you'll need us, even if you don't. The only time we wasted was getting you to help us," Elise said upon exiting the bathroom.

"Please, enough hostilities. We're in this together. There's been more than enough fighting for one day, don't you think?" Adan said, looking at the others.

Kysen sighed as he settled back against the cushions. "Very well, we still have a long flight ahead. Why don't you all rest?" His voice was gentle as he spoke, revealing yet another layer of who he was, or could be to his companions.

"Thank you," the three shifters said in unison and did just that.

Adan laid down on the sofa, feeling comfort and relaxation for the first time in over a week. He felt safe on their airplane knowing that Kysen would protect them ... Well... he hoped Kysen would protect them. He opened one eye, looking at the ancient vampire from across the plane.

Kysen chuckled softly. "Don't worry... no one will be attacking while I watch over you. You can rest easy."

Adan sat up, propping himself on one elbow. "You love Darian very much, don't you? And it's not because you believe he is your property?"

"I do, and he does belong to me. Not as a suitcase would to the person who purchased it, but as a child to a parent. My blood flows through him, giving him life everlasting. My knowledge has guided him. The lessons I've taught him as sustained him for over sixteen centuries. Our bond is stronger because I created him out of love."

"I care for Darian as well. To answer your earlier question, yes, he was my first sexual experience. But that's all I want to say on the matter."

"I hope it was memorable, in a good way," Kysen said, curious as to why Adan seemed so reluctant to discuss the interaction.

"It was. That is why it was so difficult for me to part with him at that time."

"Ahhh, you were in love with him."

"I was young."

"You still are. You are only ... What? Less than two-hundred years old?"

"A hundred and sixty-six, to be exact."

"And still so much more for you to experience. Your Pride holds you back. I must say, being the leader of a shifter community does keep one grounded. If you go somewhere, your entire community must travel with you because at any time, you can become a target if another sees a moment of weakness."

"As my understanding, it's not much of a difference for Masters of vampire covens."

"That is why I refuse to keep a coven. I'll choose a companion and together we experience all that this world has to offer." Kysen was enjoying their conversation. As he spoke with Adan, he realized that he was hungry for that contact, the intimacy. He needed it, actually. Even if he didn't want to admit it, he missed being with someone.

"I'm sure a vampire of your age has experience so much already," Adan said, sitting up a bit more. He was being drawn deeper into the conversation, growing more curious and intrigued with Kysen.

"It's almost always new when I'm traveling the world with a companion who is amazed by it," Kysen said softly, reflectively. His eyes stared forward, distant as if he was remembering a fond experience.

Adan studied him for a few seconds, wondering what Kysen was thinking about. He finally decided to ask him. "What are you thinking about?"

"The first time Darian and I traveled to America, how almost childlike he was, wanting to see, touch and taste everything. This was, of course, before it was called 'America'." Kysen smiled fondly.

If you don't mind me asking, how old was Darian when you met him … I mean, turned him?"

"When we first met, he was twenty-six. I turned him when it was his time, when he was in his prime, when everything about him was perfect. He was twenty-eight."

"How interesting," Adan said, words slightly distorted due to a massive yawn.

Kysen chuckled. "You should rest. Go on, there's only a few hours before we land."

"How fast are we going?"

"Very. You could say, I'm not using this jet's conventional functions."

"I see." Adan nodded slowly as he lay back down on the sofa, eyes closing, almost against his will. Within a matter of seconds, he was in deep sleep. Kysen continued piloting the airplane. He used his mental ability to sense Darian's aura, but only the surface, not wanting to break through Marcus' hold over Darian … that would come soon enough.

# CHAPTER  TWENTY—ONE

Nightfall had fallen over the horizon two hours ago. Marcus knew Darian was trying to awaken, so he forced him to remain in his resting state, as he had the entire time. He didn't want the vampire to see any landmarks which could give him a hint to their location as well as to where his mansion was. Alicia and Raven had chained the shifters and John to the wall of their dungeon. The chains, which were made out of silver, kept each shifter pinned tightly against the stone wall, making it impossible for them to break free. Next, they had laid Darian and Christopher on the cold, hard stone floor.

Marcus entered the room, standing over them, looking down.

"Master, what do we do with them now?" Alicia asked.

"Now, we do what we intended," he answered, releasing his telepathic hold over all of them. The shifters awoke to the searing pain of thick, heavy, silver chains burning through their skin, keeping them restrained.

"Ah, shit!" Gabriel cried out from the agony. "What the fuck?!"

Adrian panted, biting his bottom lip to keep from screaming out. The silver chains burned his skin, embedding into his regenerating flesh. Sergio was going through the same thing, as was Miranda. Darian opened his eyes along with John and Christopher. They looked at their surroundings and saw their friends being tortured by their silver binding. Not one of them knew where they were. Both Darian and Christopher noticed they were free from bindings, and that concerned them a great deal.

"Welcome to my home, I hope that you're enjoying the comforts I've provided," Marcus greeted, smiling wickedly.

"Well, the dècor could stand to be a little more cheerful," Sergio retorted as he looked around at the dull, gray, bloodstained stone walls. He squirmed against the chains, trying to alleviate his pain. He was careful not to pull on them, further embedding them in his skin that healed around the chains only to be burned away again. The sensation was excruciating, but he fought hard not to cry out.

Marcus stepped forward. "That hurts my feelings … I decorated this room myself with the blood of others just like yourselves." He leaned his head backward, inhaling deeply. "Ahhh," he exhaled. "You know, most vampires can't stand the smell of old, stale blood … but not me, I love it. Not as much as the smell of fresh blood, but I do enjoy it."

"What are you going to do to us?" Christopher asked. He swallowed hard, trying to hide his mounting fear. The hunger inside of him churned, causing him to wince.

Marcus squatted beside the younger vampire, reaching out toward him. Darian, who had been sitting beside Christopher, moved to attack the older vampire, thinking he'd catch him off guard. Marcus struck out, hitting Darian across his jaw, knocking him across the room, his body forcefully smacking the stone wall.

The ancient vampire returned his attentions back to Christopher. "Now, where were we? That's right… you wanted to know what I've planned for you."

"Leave him alone, Marcus. We both know it's me you want," Darian growled, hoping to keep him away from Christopher.

Marcus snarled at Darian, baring two sets of fangs. It was the mark of the ancient vampires. The more powerful the vampire, the more fangs they have. It was to establish their dominance over the younger ones. Four fanged teeth at the top instead of two, could easily tell the vampire's age and level of power. It is said that the most ancient of their kind, the Original Founts had four pairs of fangs, two sets at the top, two at the bottom.

"Leave him out of this!" Darian said once again, standing his ground.

Marcus rose, advancing behind Darian, wrapping his hand around the younger vampire's throat. He tossed Darian against the wall, breaking two of his ribs. Before Darian could hit the floor, Marcus was on him again, kicking him repeatedly, breaking four more ribs and cracking his sternum. Darian cried out against his own will as one of his ribs puncture his lung. He spat blood onto the floor as he struggled to get to his knees; his body aching from the abuse he'd taken.

Sergio tried to break free of his chains, biting his lip against the pain. He rattled the chains fiercely, growling as he struggled.

Raven stormed over to him, backhanding him, breaking the tiny bones in his nose. "Be still!" she demanded.

Blood poured from Sergio's injured nose, dripping onto his chest, staining his bare skin. "Fuck you, bitch!" he managed to spit out before she punched him again, nearly knocking him unconscious. The room dimmed, tilted then straightened as he regained his senses.

"Now who's the bitch?" she taunted with an evil smile.

"You are," Sergio said feebly, his mouth turned up in a sneer.

"You haven't seen the bitch in me yet, but you will. I promise you," Raven threatened before turning her attention back to her Master.

Marcus picked Darian up by his long, silky, jet-black hair, bringing the vampire to eye level. "Your torture will be your inability to protect your coven. I find that having coven Masters watch as I decimate what was once theirs has been highly effective and enjoyable. However, I don't want you trying to make any more feeble attempts to stop me, so allow me a little taste." Without another second of hesitation, Marcus plunged all four fangs deeply into Darian's jugular.

Darian gasped and froze as if bitten by a poisonous snake. Both Christopher and John cried his name in vain. They hated seeing their Master so viciously mistreated. Darian gazed over Marcus' shoulder at Christopher struggling to break free of Alicia's hold. The young vampire's face was twisted in both rage and sorrow as he watched his Master endure the torture. Marcus pulled him closer as he drained him. Darian raised his hands, attempting to push the stronger vampire away, but he couldn't. He tried to fight against the intense pleasure he was feeling, but he couldn't. His blood flowed into Marcus and at the same time, a powerful orgasm was building within him.

"No," Darian whispered through labored pants. It was all he could say to express his true feelings. The orgasm exploded, causing his body to dance erratically in Marcus' arms. He thought the vampire would release him once his orgasm faded, but he didn't. He continued to drain him, only now, it was more painful. Marcus' pull grew more forceful. Darian could feel every drop of blood being sucked out of him, leaving him retched agony … the kind of pain he had never, ever felt before. Marcus finally released him, letting him fall hard onto the stone floor. Darian lay there immobile, severely weakened by extreme the loss of blood. His entire body throbbed with his intense thirst. Every ounce of him screamed out for blood; demanded it!

Marcus stood over him. "The sensation you're feeling now … it's new to you, isn't it? My, my, you have been spoiled … pampered. I bet you have inflicted this kind of pain on many vampires, haven't you? Yes, yes … do you feel your insides twisting into tangled and mangled knots as if someone is wringing them out as one would do a wet cloth?" He taunted Darian, smiling widely at the vampire's helplessness. "Does it feel like a thousand searing hot jagged blades stabbing you all at once?" The ancient vampire laughed boisterously.

Darian was still, unable to move or talk. Every muscle in his body ached from thirst. Every cell of his flesh burned with unrelenting hunger. The pain was agonizing and unforgiving.

"He's pitiful," Raven said, laughing as well.

"Tell that to your two freaks he killed back in Chicago, bitch!" John said. He had never felt such anger before. He wanted to rip them apart, he wanted to feel their skin shred underneath his nails... his fangs. He had never known such hate.

"Oh, feeling bad for your Maker? Save some of that sympathy for yourself, boy. Your time is coming up really soon," Raven shot back.

"Besides, he didn't kill Kiren. You all give him more credit than he deserves," Alicia said.

John laughed. "Darian had fucked him up real good. Kiren was dead before Adan put him out of his misery."

"Before this night comes to a close, I'm going to give you a lesson in real power," Marcus told John as he walked toward Christopher, who was still struggling in Alicia's grip. "Now… back to you." He looked at Alicia, "release him."

"As you wish," Alicia said, releasing the young vampire and stepping back. She knew what her Master was going to do and wanted to see every second of it!

Christopher tried to punch Marcus, but was unsuccessful. The stronger vampire held his balled up fist in his left hand. He squeezed, shattering the bones. Christopher screamed as his uninjured hand instinctively tried to pry Marcus' away.

Marcus laughed and released him, turning toward Raven. "Lift him up," he said, pointing to Darian. "I want him to see what I'm going to do next."

Raven nodded and approached Darian, propping him on his knees. She took hold of his chin, forcing him to watch what was going to happen.

Marcus tossed Alicia a knowing look and she smiled, stepping forward, she began to remove Christopher's clothes.

"No!" Christopher yelled as he tried to protest with one good hand. Alicia wasn't the least bit deterred by his efforts. She removed all of his clothes, leaving him naked on the cold stone floor.

Marcus pushed Christopher back, pinning him down. He smiled as the young vampire struggled under him, vainly. "If you relax, and play nice, I'll make it very pleasurable. However, if you fight me, I can make it very painful."

"You think I give a fuck?! I hope you fucking die, motherfucker!" Christopher yelled in a rage.

"I'm sure your body will give me much pleasure, Christopher. However, I seriously doubt I will die from it." Marcus laughed. "As a matter of fact, you give me an idea. Maybe I will fuck your mother when I'm done fucking you."

"I might even turn his little brother, Brandon," Raven threatened.

"Go, bring him here, you can turn him in front of his big brother," Marcus said.

"NO! Please, don't!" Christopher pleaded.

"Wait," Marcus said. "Does this mean you're going to play nice?"

Christopher hesitated before he answered. He looked at the

three vampires, knowing they weren't bluffing.

"Maybe he's just trying to stall us," Alicia said, doing her part to torture the younger vampire.

"No! Please, just don't hurt my family. Yes, I'll play nice," Christopher said, giving in. "Please, promise me you won't."

"I have no interest in attacking your family … now that you've decided to have a little fun with me. They're safe, I promised," Marcus said.

Christopher nodded.

"Open your legs," Marcus ordered him.

Christopher knew what was going to happen to him. He swallowed hard, fighting the tears that wanted to pour from his eyes. Reluctantly, he opened his legs.

"Wider."

He did as he was told. He didn't want to look down, didn't want to see what was going to happen. Marcus dipped his hand in a container of gel-based cream Alicia handed to him. He smeared the contents on himself, slicking his shaft. He slid his hands up and down his shaft, moaning in pleasure as he did so. Finally, he leaned over Christopher, guiding himself inside. Christopher gasped, his hands gripping Marcus' forearms. He closed his eyes tightly, not wanting to see the vampire above him.

"Ah, ah, ah, open your eyes, now." Marcus demanded.

Slowly, Christopher opened his eyes. He inhaled sharply as Marcus pushed deeper into him. The pain was beginning to subside as Marcus worked up a skillful rhythm, stroking him with smooth precision. Against all of his willpower, he began to feel the greatest sexual pleasure he'd ever experienced. He body ignited with fire as the ancient vampire stroked him. Both men moaned in ecstasy, one because he enjoyed what he was feeling, what he was doing and the other because he couldn't help but enjoy it.

Darian was forced to watch Christopher's assault. He could do nothing to stop it. Adrian, Sergio and Gabriel cursed the vampires for what they were doing. John turned away, not wanting to witness what was happening. Marcus looked up at them, smiled wider than leaned down, kissing Christopher, who tried to turn his head.

Marcus chuckled as he pushed deeper, causing the young

vampire to cry out in pleasure. With his mouth opened to him, Marcus plunged his tongue inside, attempting to force a passionate kiss from his captive, though he was unsuccessful. To make Christopher kiss him in return, he pulled away, biting his own tongue. Leaning downward, he forced his tongue into Christopher's mouth again and at the first taste of the ancient vampire's blood, the younger vampire sucked harder, pulling his tongue deeper into his mouth. Christopher became oblivious to what was happening around him, all he knew was the world of pleasure he was now submerged in. The precious, ancient blood that entered his mouth in droplets maddened him; he wanted more. His arms encircled Marcus, holding the vampire closer to him. His right hand pressed the back of the ancient vampire's head as his legs tightened around his waist. The blood combined with the pleasure his entire body was feeling electrified him. A powerful orgasm grew inside of him, erupting over him like a volcano. He cried out against Marcus' mouth, his body twisting and jerking underneath Marcus as the vampire continued to feed their combined pleasure, experiencing his own release. The moment seemed to last forever, their bodies sealed in the rapture. Then, all of a sudden it was over. His body was slick with various fluids as he lay on the cold stones. Marcus was rising from the floor, looking down at him. When Christopher became aware of his surroundings, he wanted to cover himself, he wanted to turn away, but he didn't. He looked at Marcus, not wanting the vampire to know how much he'd actually hurt him … humiliated him.

"Now you know what it's like to have sex with a man," Marcus said, referring to Christopher's curiosity concerning the matter.

Christopher looked up at him. "Let's hope the real thing is better," he retorted. He was so angry, ashamed and mortified. Still, he didn't want them to know just how much they affected him.

"Cute. Consider this act of kindness a favor as well."

"Just remember your promise," Christopher reminded him. He said nothing else after that.

Marcus snorted, before returning his attention toward Darian, walking over to him. He grabbed a handful of Darian's jet-black mane, jerking his head upward. Leaning down, he kissed Darian, letting him taste the remnants of the blood he'd given to Christopher.

Instinctively, Darian sucked the blood from Marcus' tongue; the tiny drops sending his thirst into a frenzy.

Marcus pulled back, laughing. "I have something else you could suck. How would you like a taste of how sweet it was to be inside of him?" He leaned forward, his penis in his hand as he aimed it toward Darian's parted mouth.

"You sick son-of-a-bitch!" John yelled as he turned his head again, not wanting to see Darian assaulted as well.

"Don't worry, you'll get your turn," Marcus said, with a hearty laugh. He grabbed Darian's jaw, pressing on it, opening his mouth wider. He was mere centimeters away when he paused. He let the Master vampire go, tilting his head upward, eyes closed.

"Master, what's wrong?" Raven asked.

"I sense other supernaturals here, shifters." He smiled. "It seems like your friends finally came for you."

"How did they know how to find us?" Raven asked, shocked.

"Quiet, I'm trying to read their minds." He stood still for several minutes then he opened his eyes. "They have another with them."

"An ancient one?" Alicia asked.

"Yes." Marcus frowned. "He must have been shielding their auras, because they're close now. He's protecting their thoughts, I can't read their minds. This vampire had to let his shield down in order to penetrate mine. I wonder who this vampire is?" He looked down at Darian. "Perhaps your Maker?"

Adrian laughed. "Whooo! Kysen's going to kick your fucking ass!"

Marcus smirked. "I seriously doubt that." He turned to Alicia. "Tie him up. … " He pointed toward Christopher. " … And follow me." He left the room with Raven behind him. Alicia began chaining Christopher to the wall with chains far too heavy and thick for him to break free from.

Adrian continued taunting her. "Your bitch-ass Master is going to die and so are you, 'cause if I know one thing, Kysen won't like that you messed with Darian."

"Shut up!" Alicia said, advancing on Adrian and striking him hard across the face, knocking him unconscious. She looked at Gabriel, Miranda and Sergio, giving them her most menacing glare before turning and leaving to help her Master prepare.

***

Kysen sped through the streets, groaning because he was forced to take the standard mode of transportation. He would have much rather preferred to fly, he would have gotten there faster. In the back seat of the car, Xavier fed quickly from Elise, nearly sending her into an ecstatic frenzy. He himself had enjoyed feeding from Adan giving the young shifter the most amazing orgasm he'd ever experienced. When it was over, and their eyes locked, he was pleased to see the expression on Adan's face was one of admiration and lust. In the back seat, Elise moaned loudly as Xavier finished feeding, pulling away, licking his lips. He adjusted himself in the seat.

"Thank you, Elise," he said.

"You're welcome." Elise brushed her hair from her eyes as she forced herself to calm down from the pleasure his bite induced. She smiled to herself, thinking about Sergio's reaction to that, how jealous he would be … she thought it was cute. She really missed him.

Xavier looked at Kysen. "How close are we?"

"Not nearly close enough as far as I'm concerned. This mode of transportation is pointless and slow," Kysen groaned. He pulled the car over, climbing out. "Xavier drive!" Mentally he gave him the address and directions.

"You're going alone?" Xavier asked as he climbed over the front seat into the cushion of their stolen Anaconda Pavilion.

"He knows I'm coming, I can't explain now." Kysen took to the sky without another word.

"Shit!" Xavier cursed under his breath as he shifted the automobile into gear.

"Try not to attract the police," Elise said, watching the buildings passing by in a blur as Xavier sped through the narrow winding streets.

"If I do, I'll send them away," he said, concentrating on the road, trying to get to Darian as fast as he could.

Adan leaned forward. "If he's already engaged in a fight when we arrive, what's our plan?"

"If the last remaining members of his coven are involved, we do what we can to kill them, or at least, distract them long enough for Kysen to kill their Master," Elise said.

"Hopefully once he's done with him, he can handle them."

"We're the diversionary tactic?" Adan asked.

Xander nodded sadly. "Unfortunately, they are far too powerful for our presence to have much of a physical effect against them."

"All right, 'diversionary tactic' we are then. I can live with that." Adan turned toward Xavier. The vampire seemed almost in a trance as he steered the car effortlessly through traffic. He looked out of the window and notice the cars were parting for them, he knew then that Xavier was manipulating the minds of the drivers, getting them out of their way. He thought that was very cool.

*** 

Kysen stood in front of the main entrance having just imploded the door with the force of his thoughts, sending thick wooden splinters into the castle. He stepped inside, needing no invitation.

Marcus entered the parlor, confronting him. "How rude. You know you could have knocked, I've been expecting you," he said, looking at the splintered remains of his heavy oak door.

"I'm not in the mood for false pleasantries. You have someone who belongs to me, and I've come to take him back," Kysen said. He eyed the female known as Raven moving along the side of the wall, closer to him. "Don't toy with me little girl; you'd be wise to stay where you are."

Raven hissed at him, baring her fangs. A low growl bubbled up from her throat as her nails turned into long claws.

Kysen scoffed, but kept his eyes on Marcus.

"You must be referring to Darian. I can see why you turned him; he's *magnificent*. I must say I'm very upset with you. I was just getting ready to slide myself through those luscious lips of his when you interrupted me." Marcus took another step closer.

"I have neither the time nor the inclination to stand here and trade remarks with you. I want him and I intend to go through your mutilated corpse to attain who I came here to get."

Without another second wasted, Kysen made his move, traveling faster than Marcus had expected, appearing behind him. Sensing Kysen was near, Marcus moved, but not before the other vampire had a chance to cut a thin wound across his bared neck. Marcus flew upward, landing softly on the ceiling. He looked down at Kysen who was looking up at him. Marcus smelled blood before he knew it was his. He dabbed his neck, felt the wetness there and pulled his hand away. He stared, shocked, seeing his own blood on his fingers. He looked back at Kysen, unable to hide his amazement.

"You're faster than I expected. There are ways to deal with that." Marcus growled low, baring his fangs at Kysen, who only stood there, his facial expression blank.

Raven advanced on Kysen at the same time Marcus did, expecting to complete a duel attack. Kysen vanished, teleporting across the room. Marcus stopped himself before he collided with Raven. Alicia saw when Kysen rematerialized, so she lunged toward him. As Kysen felt her presence, he punched her, knocking her through one of the beautiful handcrafted floor length windows, shattering the glass. She landed hard on the moss-covered ground, skidding across the pavement.

"Ah, too bad it's not high noon," Kysen quipped.

"Enough of these games!" Marcus growled, his frustration mounting.

"Now you've developed a distaste for games? I thought you were the ultimate gamer, as they say these days. Why, look at where your amusement has led us," Kysen said, making a sweeping motion around the castle.

Raven began to change, taking her strongest form. Alicia regrouped from the attack and came storming back into the house. Seeing Raven change, prompted her to do the same. Kysen looked at both females, not liking the fact that they were taking their strongest form. He could sense that he was stronger than Marcus, however, now he knew he would be taking a huge risk fighting all three at the same time. He smiled to himself, thinking about what his other companions said. *So they were right after all. ... He needed them.*

"What are you smiling for? Do you think you can win this?"

Marcus asked, snarling.

"I've never been unsure of anything in my life, and I don't plan to start doubting myself now. If you think you can take me, the three of you, then please do so," Kysen stood his ground, hoping he could stall them long enough for the others to arrive to provide him with the distraction he was going to need to eliminate Marcus.

The two women charged forward first, attacking from both sides. Kysen slashed his nails across Alicia's throat, catching her by surprise. Blood gushed from the wound, splattering Kysen's cream cashmere shirt. Raven tried to grab him from behind, but he moved, managing to avoid her hands, but inadvertently ending up in Marcus' who was using the opportunity to get a hold of him. Raven slashed at Kysen, but he kicked her hard in her midsection, causing her to double over. His other hand gripped Marcus' arms, stopping the vampire from breaking his neck. He could hear the seams of Marcus' clothing coming apart and knew the other vampire was transforming, which might give him the advantage. Not in four thousand years had Kysen been forced to take that form. Like most vampires, he thought the form ghastly, void of beauty, purely demonic. However, now it was necessary that he change, it would be the dividing factor between life and death. Kysen forced his change, ripping out of his clothes in the process. His skin became darker, almost black and leathery in appearance. Both of their hands grew wider, fingers elongating, as did their limbs. Muscles grew harder, more prominent under the skin. Both vampires stood together, taller, stronger and more hideous than they were only seconds ago.

Marcus growled loudly as Kysen began prying his hands from around his neck. Both vampires looked up, surprised by the car that came plowing through the opposite set of floor length windows, sending glass and woodwork in all directions. Xavier steered the car toward Raven, who was healing Alicia. She dodged it easily, landing softly near the fireplace. Xavier slammed on the breaks as Elise, Xander and Adan climbed out. All three were already in their strongest form. Alicia charged forward, grabbing Adan by his mane, claws coming down to rip his head from his body. Xander stopped her, biting deeply into her flesh, which he loathed doing due to the highly addictive aspect of vampire blood, but he had no time to hesitate.

Alicia hissed, jerking her arm away, slinging Xander across the room. Xavier took his strongest form as both he and Elise went for Raven. Marcus didn't have time to worry about the other members of his coven as he fought with Kysen. The other vampire was stronger than he had anticipated and he was beginning to feel the tiniest inking of fear creeping into his mind. Never had he fought with one so powerful! Kysen flipped Marcus over, clawing at his chest, attempting to rip the vampire's heart from its cavity. More hissing, snarls and growls between the two men as they battled to the death. As Marcus twisted from Kysen's grip, he flew upward, taking Kysen with him, slamming him hard against the ceiling. Plaster cracked and sprinkled to the ground. Marcus continued flying, dragging Kysen across the ceiling, colliding into the glass and chrome chandelier sending it smashing to the floor, glass shattering every which way.

In midair, Kysen flipped, pressing his feet to the ceiling he jumped off, slamming Marcus into the floor. The power of his force sent both men through the stones, into the basement level, their bodies crashing with a resounding thud as dust and debris clouded around them.

Adan tried his best to take Alicia out, but he was no match for her. She pressed him against the wall, her hand locked around his throat, choking him. Xander was unconscious, his body laying half in and half out of the Anaconda Pavilion's now shattered windshield where Raven had tossed him.

Alicia changed back into her human form and began laughing. "You're pathetic! I could kill you with one hand and I will. Why did you even bother coming?"

Xavier saw what was happening to Adan, but he was unable to help. Raven held Elise up with one hand, while she pinned him to the floor with her foot. Raven decided to change back into her human form as well, believing the two she held captive were not a threat to her.

"You came for your man, didn't you?" She asked Elise. "I'll say this… he talks a lot of shit. But just so you know, later on tonight, once we're done with you, I'm going to make sure he puts better use to that tongue of his."

Elise kept calm in spite of the anger she was feeling. She needed to slow her circulation down to gain the advantage. She pretended to lose consciousness from the strangulation, letting her limbs fall limp. When she heard Raven laugh and felt her grip loosen a bit, she lashed out, clawing out one of Raven's flame-red eyes. Raven screamed and tossed her away, sending Elise crashing into the car, knocking it onto its side. Elise changed back into her human form. She peeked over the car, seeing Raven staggering back, her hand clutching the now bleeding and empty socket.

Elise stepped around the car. "I guess you're looking for this," she said, holding up the bloody eyeball, the nerve endings dangling from its end. She dropped the eyeball on the floor, squashing it with her foot. "Well, you can stop looking now."

Raven screamed in rage, she charged for Elise, but Xavier intercepted from behind, wrapping his arms around her waist, slowing her down, but not tackling her. Elise took that opportunity to try to get the upper hand. She ran forward, but was stopped by Alicia, the vampire's hand punching through her back, shattering her spine, the vampire's fist coming out through her stomach. Elise gasped and coughed. Blood poured out from her mouth as she stared down at the hand protruding from her torso. Alicia pulled her hand free, then tossed Elise to the side. Xander came to in time to see what had happened to Elise. He went to her aid, licking and soaking the wound with his saliva as fast as he could. He wanted to find Miranda as another born shifter's blood of her own species would help her heal faster. However, he didn't want to leave her in such a critical state. Alicia saw Xander leaning over Elise, and began walking toward him. Adan called out to her. She turned.

"Yeah, you bitch!" Adan yelled across the room at Alicia. "I wasn't finished with you."

She advanced on him as he darted around the room, trying unsuccessfully to widen the gap between them. Alicia grabbed him by his hair, pulling locks from their very roots. Pain shot across Adan's scalp, but he refused to expose the vital areas he was protecting.

Raven pried Xavier's hands from her body then whipped around in front of him. "You've been more than a pest! I'm going to enjoy killing you in front of your lover!" She punched Xavier several times, faster than he had time to react to. Within seconds, he was knocked unconscious. She threw his body to the side. Then went to see if Marcus needed her help. "Alicia, take care of them but don't kill them. That's for later. I'm going to Marcus!"

"Don't worry about me, just go!" Alicia responded, before returning her attentions back to Adan. "The only reason I'd let you live is to see if Marcus still wants you."

"I was his original target, don't you think that still means something?"

"We'll see," she said. "If nothing else, I'll enjoy ripping your insides out inch by inch." She punched Adan, knocking him dizzy. Before she could punch him again, Xander came up from behind, biting her shoulder. She hissed and clawed his face, ripping open his cheek. Xander's bite was unrelenting and Alicia had to release Adan to pry the shifter off her shoulder.

Much like Adan, Xander was protecting his vital areas, making sure Alicia couldn't slice his throat even as her nails raked across his biceps and back, shredding his flesh, ripping chunks of skin away. Xavier came to as did Adan, and the two men converged on the vampire, hoping to keep her from killing Xander. They hoped their combined attack would at least buy them time.

Raven made it to the level below, which was in shambles. Glass, plaster, bits of stone, shattered furniture and wood splinters were strewn about. She could hear the two vampires fighting in the next room and she ran in just in time to see Kysen slamming Marcus into a huge mirror. Jagged pieces of mirrored glass stabbed the vampire in his shoulder. Raven ran top speed toward Kysen, hoping to keep him from Marcus long enough for her Master to regroup. Kysen sensed her coming. He had long since grown agitated with her interference and was now better prepared to deal with her. As she drew nearer, he waited, for the right moment, never taking his eyes from Marcus, who was pulling large shards of glass from his wounded shoulder. When Raven was close enough for his attack, he lashed out. His claws ripped her throat open, splattering blood over them both. With a backward slash, he severed the remaining flesh ending with a clean decapitation. Marcus screamed in a cloud of rage as he rushed forward. Kysen twisted around, catching the vampire from behind. Without wasting another second now that the opportunity was present, he buried his fangs deeply into Marcus' jugular, piercing his flesh. He drained the vampire quickly, feasting greedily, which healed his own wounds he'd acquired during their battle. Once Kysen had taken as much blood as he could hold, he changed back into his human form and leaned forward, toward Marcus' ear.

"Who's pathetic now?" he asked. He slid his claws under Marcus' chin then digging deeply, he punctured the flesh. With a quick jerk, he ripped the vampire's head from his body, killing him instantly.

"Nooo!" Alicia cried out, sensing her Master's life instantly drain away. She turned, leaving Adan, in hopes that she could flee the room. Kysen intercepted her path, blocking her. His hand reached up, catching her by her throat.

"Where do you think you're going in such a hurry?" Kysen said. He growled at her, pulling rank, flashing three sets of fangs. Two at the top, one set at the bottom.

"Kill me, I don't care!" Alicia managed to say through feeble gasps.

"Just what I had in mind." Kysen punched through her torso, impaling her on his forearm. In his hand, he held her heart, the bloody arteries still attached, dangling from their ventricles. Blood gushed up from Alicia's mouth spilling forth, splashing his shoulder and chest. Her eyes bulged forward, shocked by her own death. Kysen pulled his hand free, dropping her body at the same time. He looked at her heart as he held it in his hands, then he turned toward Adan.

"Hungry?" he asked, smiling.

"She was your kill, not mine. Besides, I want no part of them," Adan said, turning down the proffered meal. "Were you badly injured?"

"Not critically, but yes. I'm completely healed now, so no need to worry about me," Kysen said, tossing the heart to the floor. "My main concern is getting to Darian, he needs me now." He knew the location of where the others were. Adan followed him to a huge solid sterling silver door.

"Jesus!" Adan gasped, looking at the door.

"I assure you, he had nothing to do with the construction of this door, carpenter, though he was," Kysen joked as he turned the knob, breaking the lock. Before he opened the door, he turned toward Adan. "Let me go in alone."

Adan stepped back, nodding.

Kysen entered the room, looking around. He saw Christopher naked and chained, fluids he knew all too well were dried on his flesh. He turned to the sound of his voice being called out.

"Kysen, Darian's hurt and for that matter, so are we, please get us down," Sergio said, trying not to pass out from the intense pain the silver chains caused.

Mentally, Kysen broke the locks on the chains, freeing the supernaturals. The four shifters fell to the ground, weak, exhausted, and still suffering the effects of the silver as their flesh begin to heal. Sergio was the first to rise, followed by Miranda.

"Thank you, Kysen," Sergio said.

"Your woman's life is in danger, she may already be dead."

"What?!" Sergio looked at him. "Where is she?"

Kysen told him how to get to her then watched as he and Miranda sped from the room.

As Christopher was assisted by Adrian, he could feel sharp pains shoot through his stomach, causing him to double over. "God, I don't think I've ever been this hungry before," he whined.

Kysen looked at the two men. "He really needs to feed, he's young. Your father is upstairs; he's all right, although, badly injured as well," he told Adrian.

"Thanks," Adrian said as he walked past him, with Christopher. Gabriel followed the two men, nodding at Kysen as he passed by him.

John looked at Kysen. "Do you need my help?"

Kysen shook his head. "I'd like to be alone with Darian now."

John nodded and left the room. He had never seen Darian in that state. He, like the others, hated it. He respected his Master even more than before for what he had endured. He didn't think it was possible for him to love Darian more than he had, but he did. As he made his way up the staircase toward the others, he gave thanks that he was still alive.

Kysen watched John ascend the staircase then he closed the door. He looked down at Darian's incapacitated form. "My, my, my, what a fine mess you've gotten yourself into, my love." He walked toward him, taking a seat on the cold stone floor beside him. He lay down, taking Darian into his arms. His eyebrows creased as he witnessed a violent hunger pang rack Darian's body, causing him to whimper softly. The whites of Darian's eyes showed beneath his half-closed lids.

"Feed." Kysen opened a vein in his wrist, pressing the bloody wound to his immortal child's slightly parted mouth. Another violent spasm raced through Darian's body, causing his back to arch as the first drop of blood hit his tongue.

"That's it, Darian. Drink," Kysen urged.

Darian's pull was feeble at first, in spite of his raging hunger. The more blood he was able to bring into his body, the stronger his pull became. His limbs grew in strength and he took hold of Kysen's wrist. At that point, Kysen pulled his wrist free, breaking Darian's grip.

"More!" Darian growled, fangs bared.

"It's coming, my child."

Kysen offered Darian his neck and without a second's hesitation, Darian plunged forward, biting viciously into the pulsating vein protruding under his Master's dark chocolate skin. Darian crushed Kysen under him as he fed ravenously, drawing the blood into him with a forcefulness that was painful to Kysen. There was no pleasure, no rapture. It was need, pure and simple, Darian's need. Kysen only held his child as he fed, until the urgency of Darian feeding began to slow, becoming less painful. Kysen panted, feeling weaker the longer he was drained. A wave of nausea rippled through him and he swallowed hard, fighting it back, knowing it was an effect of the massive loss of blood and the speed in which it was drained. Finally, it was over. Both men released moans the moment they separated, Darian rolling onto his back beside his Master.

He lay still, catching his breath. "Thank you, Kysen," he said, once he was finally able to speak again.

Kysen looked over at him. "You're welcome."

"I wish I could have seen you killing him."

"Ah, but you did, through my blood."

"I mean with my own eyes."

Kysen smiled knowingly. "Well, one must take what one can get." He sat up, struggling a bit due to his own weakness then looked over his shoulder at Darian. He didn't like the expression on his face; it was a look of humiliation, uncertainty and a hint of defeat. "Darian, are you going to be all right?"

He turned toward Kysen. "I honestly don't know."

"Darian, you'll get through this. You're still here when he is not."

Darian sat up, facing him. "I couldn't protect them, Kysen. Not only that, I was … ." His voice trailed off and he turned away.

"Your pride is hurt, my child … nothing more. This happens, Darian. There have been vampires within your own coven over the years, who've come through this exact type of situation. There is always going to be a vampire stronger than you are … always. Some of them will wish you ill; they'll want to possess you, hurt you; this happens. It's one of the many predicaments I've tried to prepare you for."

"There was no way you could've prepared me for what happened."

"No, this is true. You were no match for him, and perhaps, I did fail in that sense. I should have taught you humility. If I had, you'd be handling this much better than you are now."

Darian's head shot up and he looked at Kysen, confused. "You're criticizing me for feeling the way I am? You have no idea what I'm going through right now, Kysen."

"You're angry, dejected, you feel humiliated because you were completely and effortlessly overpowered. For all of the impressive strength, ingenuity and self-confidence you possess, you were made to look absolutely useless, weak … pathetic?" Kysen leaned forward, toward him. "Does that sound about right?"

Darian winced, each word piercing a hole in his shield.

"Darian, I know you better than you think I do. Maybe you've forgotten that, but I haven't. You were always on top of the world, on top of your game … the best. Moreover, you still are. What happened here means nothing in the grand scheme of things. Wallowing here in self-pity will be your downfall, not what Marcus did to you."

Darian reflected on Kysen's wise words, he nodded.

Kysen chuckled. "Ahhh, the job of a parent is never done. You always keep teaching, your child will always need to learn more of life's lessons, even after sixteen hundred and fifty-three years, is it?"

Darian nodded. "Kysen, you mentioned that this sort of thing happens to all vampir-"

Kysen held up his hand, silencing Darian. "I know where you're going with that question. Don't."

"Kysen, has it ever happened to you?" Darian asked, ignoring his Maker's orders.

"Stubborn as always, I see. Nothing's changed," Kysen said, with a sigh. "If it will make you feel better about your own circumstances, then fine. I was about two thousand years old, living on my own with my own coven. It was what Irikara wanted for me. According to her, I'd been far too attached after eighteen hundred years together. I thought we would be together forever. …" He paused, reflecting on his own emotion at the present time as well as in the past concerning his love and worship of his Maker, Irikara.

"You love her very much, don't you?" Darian asked, watching him.

Kysen nodded. "Yes, as much as she loves me; as much as I love you. But, I digress. As I've said, I was on my own, I had six vampires living with me, four of whom I turned, the other two were those who pledged allegiance to me when I killed their Master and took over her territory. I had complete control over that territory for two hundred years, my reputation; much like your own had spread across the continents, reaching the ears of a vampire who was almost as strong as Irikara."

"I can't imagine the extent of her power. All I know is what flows through you and that's telling enough."

Kysen nodded. "Drinking from her has been one of my greatest pleasures and privileges. Now, back to the tale… This vampire, he came for me and I was powerless against him. He massacred my entire coven in front of me, and then took me for himself. You can imagine all of the things he did to me. I don't think I have to go into the specifics."

Darian shook his head. "I can imagine. Kysen, I would have never known."

"No, you wouldn't have. Irikara received news of what had happened to me. She came for me, challenging the vampire who had taken me, killing him. Much like you, I was ashamed, bewildered ... didn't know how I was going to regroup from what had happened. You must understand, Irikara is a Goddess and she chose to grant me the gift of her powers. And in one instant, another had shown me just how useless my powers were against him."

"What did she say?"

"Exactly what I'm telling you. Get over it. Darian, I chose you for a reason, this self-pity you're exhibiting now is not befitting a warrior such as yourself. When you left me eight hundred years ago, you did what I couldn't do with Irikara. You wanted to experience life on your own. You wanted to take this world into your hands, and make it your own. Whatever fears you experienced at that time didn't hinder you and your reputation grew over the years. Look at you, my love. You're Master of one of the most powerful cities in the entire world. Chicago has been your territory for over a hundred years; you have a coven that would die for you if you so wished it. You have friends who love you and would fight and die for you if need be. You have nothing to be ashamed of." He took hold of Darian's chin, lifting his face upward. Leaning forward, he kissed him passionately. Moments later, he broke the kiss. "My child... stand tall on your pedestal again, and show no shame or uncertainty. You are a powerful Master vampire, direct descendant of the Goddess, Irikara; the Original Fount of our line and my immortal love, my son ... my *Chosen One*. There is no greater honor."

Darian could feel his pride swell from within. He smiled. "Kysen, has anyone ever told you that you could have a future career in motivational speaking?" he asked, feeling more like himself again. The shame he was feeling was starting to fade away.

"No."

"Thank you."

Kysen smiled slightly. "Do try not to get yourself into this kind of trouble again."

"I wasn't trying to get myself into trouble at all. However, I'll keep that in mind."

"Oh, by the way, you may want to send someone back for your airplane. Marcus transported you all here in it."

Darian sighed. "The thought of him and his on my airplane," he shook his head. "I'll retrieve it later. Let's go, I want to check on Elise."

"She was injured badly, she's probably dead," Kysen said nonchalantly as he rose from the floor. Reaching down, he helped Darian to his feet.

"I still want to see for myself," Darian said, adjusting the tattered remains of his clothes in an attempt to make himself look presentable. The two men left the room, heading into the living room where Sergio was leaning over Elise, licking her wound, sealing it. Elise was alive but unconscious. Her strength was gradually returning, but she was still very weak.

Xavier walked briskly toward Darian, taking his Master and lover into his arms, kissing him. Kysen watched to two lovers reunite for a few seconds, then he returned his attentions to the shifters in the room.

Sergio was lifting Elise in his arms. "We should get going," he said, walking through the hole that used to be a wall of beautiful imported French glass windows.

"Is she going to be all right?" Darian asked, once he and Xavier broke their kiss.

"Yes, she just needs to rest so that she can heal completely. I've done all I can for her right now, the rest will have to heal on its own." Sergio looked down at his woman. Her eyes were closed, brows furrowed as she endured another spasm of pain. Her wound was healing slowly, in spite of Sergio and Miranda's help.

"We can take Marcus' limo back to the jet," Adan said. He looked down at his own wound, which was healing, but still very tender to the touch, sore. He wished he had his Matron there, if he had, he'd be completely healed.

Xavier wrapped his arm around Darian's waist and the two exited the mansion following the others through the large opening.

Kysen paused beside the limousine, looking around the property, admiring the landscaping. "Pity to leave such a beautiful territory, having just successful won it," he said, with a hint of regret.

Darian looked at him. "Thinking about staying?"

"No. I'm perfectly happy where I am. It's just … well, old habits die hard, as they say. I'm used to claiming territories I gain through victories, that's all."

"You'd be challenged for it constantly," Darian said, reflecting on how popular the territory was.

"Rome, it's old, rich in history and culture, of course others will want it and I have no interest in defending my territory every other day. Let's go." Kysen climbed into the limousine, mentally igniting the engine. Darian entered behind him.

"I'll drive," Adrian said, finally relieved to be free and reunited with his father. He pulled the long car out of the driveway steering it onto the road. His father sat beside him in the passenger seat, looking over one of his numerous wounds, which was still bleeding slightly. "Are you going to be okay, Dad?"

Xander nodded, but kept his eyes on the wound in his stomach. "I'm bleeding internally still, but it's healing. Mostly from the inside out, it's just taking a little bit longer than I'd like."

"I'm just glad all of this shit is behind us," Adrian said, navigating his way through traffic.

"I concur." Xander looked at his son. The bloody and burned marks that were on his wrist were practically healed in spots. Overall, his skin looked a little puffy and red where the silver chains once bound his wrists, torso and ankles captive. "I'm glad to see that you're healing well."

Adrian glanced down at his wrists. "Yeah, me too. For a minute, I thought those silver chains were going to burn their way through my bones. I had to really be careful to make sure I didn't add extra pressure."

"You have impressed me. Although, I wasn't expecting less from you, my son."

Adrian smiled. "I just did what I thought you would do in that situation."

"That's not true. All who you are isn't based on what you think I would have done. You were brave because that's the kind of man you've become. You've shown great strength and courage during this trying time and I couldn't be more proud of you, Adrian."

"Thanks, Dad." Adrian was honored by his father's words. His father was a man he held in extremely high regard.

"You're welcome." Xander settled more comfortably into his seat, wincing a little as he did. "Yes, my son, you'll make a wonderful Alpha one day."

Adrian glanced at his dad, his smile growing wider. "I'm in no hurry for that title."

"No, you're not quite ready yet, but soon, and when you are, you'll be perfect." Xander applied more pressure to his wound, grimacing slightly.

"Are you going to be all right?" Christopher asked him over the seat.

Xander looked over the headrest. "Sure, I'll be fine. How are you?"

Christopher looked down. "I'm starving, the pain is driving me insane, but other than that, I ... I'll be okay." He frowned as he turned back around in his seat. The memory of his sexual assault flashed in his mind. He shook his head as if he could erase the vision. Xander looked at him, but didn't say a word. He could smell what had happened to the younger vampire and felt it was in bad taste to initiate conversation about the incident.

Adrian drove to the jet and they all boarded and were airborne within minutes. Miranda lay next to Elise, giving her warmth as Sergio laid Elise's head gently down on his lap. He watched her sleep, hoping it was peaceful. Adan sat down in a chair, tossing one leg over the armrest. He eyed both Darian and Kysen from across the plane, wondering what words were shared between them when they were alone in the room. He knew that it was none of his business, but he couldn't help his own curiosity. Not to mention, Darian appeared to be unruffled by what had happened, and he wondered if it was because of something Kysen said to him. Xavier watched the two vampires as well, wondering the same thing as Adan.

"Darian, are you all right?" Xavier asked, coming closer, sitting beside him.

"Yes, Xavier. I'll be fine. The worst is behind us," Darian assured him. He looked at Christopher, who was sitting alone and very quiet. "I'm more concerned for him than myself at this time." He nodded his head in Christopher's direction.

Xavier looked at the younger vampire. "You should talk to him."

"I know, but now is not the time," Darian said, not wanting to discuss the matter in front of others.

Xavier nodded, understanding Darian's reasoning. "He needs to feed."

"Don't we all," Kysen commented, still feeling weak from feeding Darian.

"I'm all right," Darian said, giving Kysen a knowing look.

"Can you spare a few pints, then?" Kysen retorted.

"No." Darian smirked, enjoying their moment of closeness.

Adan had been watching and listening to the three vampires converse. He looked at Christopher, seeing him shake from his unrelenting hunger pangs. He rose from his chair, walking over to the young man.

"Christopher?" Adan asked, looking down at him.

Christopher looked up. "Yeah?"

"Here, you should feed." He offered him his wrist.

Christopher reached out desperately taking the wrist in both hands. "Are you sure?" he asked, softly, apprehensively as if he was afraid Adan would change his mind.

Adan nodded. "Go on, it's okay."

Christopher didn't need much convincing. His fangs extended and he plunged them deeply, sharply into Adan's blue vein, causing the shifter to gasp and jerk. Darian, Kysen and Xavier watched the two men. Kysen ran his finger over his bottom lip as he observed Adan undergoing the effects of the vampire's bite. A slight smile crept over his face. Darian turned from them, toward Kysen, noticing his *interest* in Adan. He remained silent, keeping his opinion to himself until he was ready to address his thoughts. Xavier also noticed the attraction both men seemed to share for one another, but he also said nothing. Adan moaned aloud as his climax rippled through him, buckling his legs. Kysen was across the plane in a fraction of a second, catching him before he fell. Adan leaned against him, panting as his orgasm faded. Christopher pulled away, sated.

He looked up at Adan, seeing Kysen standing behind him. "I didn't take too much, did I?" he asked, hoping he hadn't hurt the shifter.

Adan shook his head. "No, I'll be fine. I just need to regain my strength. Are you better now?"

Christopher nodded. "Thanks, I really appreciated that."

"My pleasure," Adan said. He looked up, over his shoulder at Kysen. "Thanks for catching me, you can let me go now."

"I'm a little parched myself," Kysen said, imploringly.

Adan chortled. "You're unbelievable, you do know that, don't you?"

"I take it you won't donate?"

"How perceptive of you."

Kysen laughed, caught off guard again by Adan's forthright approach. "How can you deny me after I've saved your Pride?" He smiled seductively as he waited for Adan's response.

Adan looked at Kysen, watching as his full, perfectly shaped lips parted in that alluring grin. He was beginning to desire the vampire more than he had anticipated and wasn't sure how he felt about that. "If you really need to feed, I'll let you, but you just don't look that desperate."

Kysen inched closer. "Who says I'm desperate? It's true, having been guzzled down by my young one over there … ," he gestured toward Darian. " … I *am* in need." He slid his hand underneath Adan's chin, gently lifting his face upward. "May I?"

Adan's heart began to race. He remembered how wonderful it felt the first time he had fed Kysen. He remembered how he had wanted it to go on forever. He nodded, before even realizing he was granting the vampire permission. Kysen winked, leaning forward, his lips parted revealing just one set of his razor-sharp fangs. He bit deeply, sealing his lips around the wound as he began to suck the delicious blood from Adan's veins. The two men stood together, held still by the glorious rapture of the vampire's bite. It was quite evident to the others who were watching them that there was more to their union than the simple act of feeding. They could all sense the attraction the two men shared for each other, and that attraction seemed to grow stronger as Kysen fed from Adan, causing the younger man to share the experience of indescribable pleasure and the powerful orgasm it created that rippled through both of their bodies. Finally, the two parted. Adan's legs collapsed, but Kysen held him up, keeping him from falling. He laid Adan on the sofa. Standing back, he watched as Adan silently drifted into a blissful unconsciousness.

"That was most satisfying," Kysen declared as he settled back into his chair.

"I'm sure," Darian commented, giving Kysen a knowing look.

Kysen rolled his eyes.

"I wanted to thank you again, for helping us, Kysen," Xavier said.

"You're welcomed." Kysen cocked his head sideways as he watched Xavier.

"Is there something wrong?" Xavier asked, curious as to why he was being observed.

"You've never been happier in your life than you are now, have you?"

"What do you mean?"

"Darian, Natasha, your children, your position within the coven … It's everything you've ever wanted, isn't it?"

"It is."

"Then you're a simple man to please."

"Is that an insult or compliment?" Xavier asked, not sure whether to be affronted or flattered.

"I could tell you to take the comment any way you please, but I'll go on and eliminate your confusion. It was a compliment. Darian doesn't need complicated, troublesome people in his life. He just doesn't have the patience for such," Kysen said, chuckling.

Xavier chuckled. "Thank you." He refrained from making the smart-aleck commit about "complicated and troublesome people", in reference to Darian leaving the ancient vampire eight hundred years ago.

"That was a wise decision," Kysen stated, having read Xavier's mind.

Xavier looked up sharply; confused at first then he quickly realized that the ancient vampire had mentally read his wisecrack comment. "I want more than anything to return to my life once again," he said.

"Things aren't going to be the same for some of us," Xander said. "Warren and Matthew will have to face the scrutiny of the S.U.I.T., having avoided them for the past few days. I'm sure they suspect that they're supernaturals by now."

"I hear it's a huge controversy across the country and in Europe as well. According to some, many people have expressed resentment toward supernaturals masquerading as humans in order to remain in the S.U.I.T., and on the police Force while others have expressed relief and rejoiced in the newfound information," Kysen said.

"Have you read the minds of the people in your territory?" Christopher asked. He had been impressed and amazed by Kysen from the moment the older vampire freed them. He had heard stories of Darian's Maker; of his character, his beauty, and his powerful aura and to meet the legend face-to-face was one of his greatest experiences.

Kysen turned toward the young vampire as he shook his head. "No, I gathered this information simply by turning on my television. Apparently, supernaturals all across the country have either been arrested or put on the fugitive list for evading arrest. What started out as an internal investigation within the S.U.I.T. has extend into an internal investigation throughout every faction of law enforcement. I suppose many supernaturals have fled back to their communities for protection."

"What?!" Christopher asked, incredulously. "We didn't hear about any of that on the news earlier."

Kysen shrugged. "Before you came to my home, I had been watching television. It was mentioned on the news then. And I heard more while I was on the plane. Amazing how quickly matters can get out of hand, isn't it?"

"They can't just arrest them, can they? I mean, they're cops too, they didn't do anything wrong!" Christopher said, outraged by what he had heard.

"Young one, being what they are has always been wrong in the eyes of the human world. The fact that they lied in order to infiltrate the government's various law factions, especially the S.U.I.T., which supersedes all others, is unforgivable enough to justify whatever punishment these humans deem worthy for such an offense," Kysen said, crossing one leg over the other.

"They weren't infiltrating!" Christopher was upset, angered by the overall response toward people he now considered friends and family.

"How do you know? Perhaps there are some who really wanted to help, like Warren and Matthew. There could also be others who wanted the inside scoop, as they say." Kysen interlocked his fingers, resting them on his stomach.

"I've known Warren and Matt for a long time, and as jealous as I was of their success, I knew them to be great cops. We have to do something," Gabriel said. He was also angry knowing what was happening across the country and the world.

"What can you do? You've already been kicked to the curb by the S.U.I.T.?" Adrian asked.

"I'm not going to sit on my ass while they pull the bullshit they're pulling," Gabriel said. "You guys have political contacts, right? People who are in the highest form of government? I mean, hell, if vampires can fucking hypnotize anyone you want to … you can do something." He looked at Darian, then back at Kysen.

"Why would I do that?" Kysen asked, one eyebrow rising.

"Why would you stand back and let them do this to other supernaturals?" Christopher asked, apprehensively, not sure if he was ready to hear the vampire's response or if he'd like it.

"Because I don't care. I've lived a long time and I've seen many rebellions break out. This one is no different. What will happen will happen, with or without supernatural interference. It's best to let things be and see where it all goes. You may be pleasantly surprised with the results once the dust settles," Kysen answered.

"Or maybe, I'll be completely aghast at what's happened, wishing I had done something to prevent it," Gabriel said. "I don't understand you guys. You're old enough, powerful enough to stop a lot of shit that's happening to people, but you won't, why?"

"Because we shouldn't try to control the world. When you start to think the minds and hearts of men are yours to own, you began to take away others right to free will. With this whole ordeal we've endured, you've gotten your first taste of a supernatural being who wanted to do just that. Tell me, was that experience just?" Darian asked everyone in general.

"Hell no, of course it wasn't!" Gabriel said.

"It is what happens when you start to believe that your power should govern all," Darian continued. "I do only what I must, and no more than that. I've seen over sixteen hundred years of human evolution, empires rise and fall and be reborn into something new … sometimes better, sometimes worse, but it's part of history. Everything that has happened has in some way had an effect on you, made you the man you are. The same can be said for me. You'll never learn if you don't experience both the good and the bad." Darian hoped to shed insight on why older, more powerful supernaturals tend to not interfere.

"Is that your reasons, too?" Gabriel asked Kysen.

"For the most part, yes. I understand Darian's reasoning and he's right. For me, however, I find this debacle somewhat entertaining." Kysen smiled.

"Besides, asking me and others like myself to step in and make all of the horrible things go away for you would be like us turning every human into a supernatural or giving them our blood simply because an outbreak of the Black Plague is consuming life. That epidemic was also something that had to happen in order for the world to remain balanced. Still, humans built a resistance and grew stronger over time in spite of losing over half of the world's population. Moreover, our kind had nothing to do with it. Truth is, with life comes death. It's what's natural for humans," Darian said.

"It's also human nature to destroy yourselves," Kysen added.

"Aside from that, when has the fight for freedom and equality ever been easy?" Xander said. "Let what will happen, happen. We'll know what to do once we see where it's all going."

Gabriel looked at the three wise men, reflecting on what they said. He turned toward Darian. "What's so wrong about giving your blood to science so that a cure could have been made?" he asked.

"During that time, it wouldn't have been a smart thing to do. I can just imagine the witch-hunts. Hell, even now, we're still not accepted, and they know what we could offer them. Face it, Gabriel, humans don't want our fucking help. Just ask those poor shifters who are on the run now. Or better yet, take a look in the mirror and ask yourself if you feel appreciated or wanted," Adrian said.

Gabriel opened his mouth to protest, but closed it, thinking about his own situation. How he felt betrayed by his government and other S.U.I.T. officers. He looked away, remaining silent.

"So, you're not going to do anything?" Christopher presented the question again to anyone who would answer.

"I'm going to be there for Warren, I won't allow him to go to jail, nor will I allow them to kill him. Whatever happens at that point, I don't know. I'll let Warren deal with this situation as he sees fit and step in only if or when the situation gets out of his control," Xander said, answering his question.

"I see, I guess this would be a part of the co-existence," Christopher said, slouching slightly in his seat.

"The good and the bad, yes. We have to look to the Council to take control of this until it looks like we must intervene," Xavier said.

"Enough of this chatter. We should all get some sleep, besides, the sun will be rising soon where we're headed," Kysen said.

"I see you're taking your time going back to Montana," Xander said.

"I am. Piloting this aircraft isn't an easy feat. It's draining. Besides, the urgency is past us. I'd much rather be relaxing at this point," Kysen answered.

"That's fine with me, I'm tired as hell anyway," Adrian said, stretching out completely on the sofa. He looked at Adan, who was sleeping on the sofa then at Miranda, Sergio and Elise who were cuddled together on the other sofa, sound asleep. He scoffed. "Just like some cats. I'm glad she's going to be okay." His eyes settled on Elise.

Xavier chuckled. "I remember when you first met her, I thought she was going to kick your ass. Not that you wouldn't have had it coming. You were out of line."

"When?" Adrian looked at him, eyebrows furled.

"In Moscow, a few years ago. You came in as if you were the *big deal*, cocky as ever. You laughed at her and I remember the words you two exchanged."

"Oh, yeah … that's right. I had every right to be cocky; I'm the shit. But I did step out of line and I knew it. Nagesa told my Dad about what had happened and he scolded me, too, for disrespecting her." Adrian smiled to himself, thinking back.

"Why would you be cocky?" Gabriel asked, breaking his own silence.

"Because they were in some pretty deep shit in Moscow and needed help. I'm an enforcer within my Pack and my father sent only Nagesa and myself to assist them. I knew he trusted me to get the job done and that's what I was going to do. Besides, I'm just cocky by nature." Adrian winked at him.

"Enforcer? What's that?" Gabriel asked.

"Well, that depends on your community. Most Prides don't have such appointed positions … hell, some Packs don't either. My Dad was in the military and needless to say, he's very structured," Adrian said.

"You didn't answer his question," Xavier teased.

"I was getting to the point," Adrian said.

"Eventually, I hope," Xavier retorted.

"Eventually." Adrian smiled widely at him. He turned toward Gabriel. "We enforcers are charged with tracking down rogue shifters who have entered my Dad's territory uninvited. We also seek out newly turned shifters whom our Alpha believes need help and a place to learn what they are and how to survive. We're also highly trained in tactical and physical defense."

"Oh, I guess enforcers are a good thing to have around," Gabriel agreed.

"I'm still hearing mindless chatter," Kysen interrupted, clearly annoyed.

"I don't think it's mindless," Christopher said. He had been enjoying the conversations, learning new things.

"I do," Kysen retorted, His head rested on the back of the cushion, his eyes were closed as he tried to rest.

"Should you be resting anyway? I mean, who's going to fly the plane if you're asleep?" Christopher asked, getting instantly nervous after he remembered how Kysen was piloting the plane.

Kysen opened one eye. "Afraid I'm going to crash the airplane?"

"Hell yes!"

Kysen laughed. "I'm not. Don't worry."

"What about fuel?"

"Would you believe me if I told you we ran completely out of fuel an hour ago?"

"What the fuck!" Christopher began to panic.

"I don't need fuel to keep this plane afloat. Don't worry," Kysen repeated. "It was just easier for me to do so when the aircraft had fuel."

"Christopher, it's going to be fine. Kysen is very powerful and you don't have anything to worry about," Darian said.

Christopher glanced at Kysen; he nodded as he slowly settled uneasily into his chair.

Darian looked toward the other end of the plane, seeing his gold sarcophagus in the corner. "I see you've kept my old resting place."

Kysen glanced at the sarcophagus, then back at him. "Yes."

"I've been meaning to ask you this, but is that made out of real solid gold and jewels?" Christopher asked, looking at the sarcophagus.

"Yes," Kysen answered. "Real solid gold and authentic and rare jewels, it's priceless. But not nearly as precious or beautiful to me as the vampire who used to rest inside." He looked at Darian.

Darian returned Kysen's gaze, smiling at his Maker and Master.

Christopher snickered. "I guess if you ever go broke you could sell it."

Kysen turned toward him, giving him the "look". The one that told Christopher he'd better not say another word as he was beginning to annoy the older vampire immensely.

Christopher turned away from Kysen's gaze. He was beginning to understand why John, Devin and Justin said they felt uneasy around the ancient vampire. "I guess I'll go to sleep now." He lay down on the floor in front of the sofa Adrian was laying on.

Xavier laughed softly to himself at both vampires. He settled more comfortably into the cushions beside Darian, laying his head on his lover's shoulder. Kysen watched the two men bonding once again, both happy to be reunited. He laid his head back against the cushion, closing his eyes once again. Within the hour, they were all resting, their bodies finally getting the relaxation it needed. Hours passed on the flight back. The sun was shining brightly when they finally landed on Kysen's private airstrip. Gently, he lowered Darian's resting body into the gold and jeweled encrusted sarcophagus. He gazed down lovingly at his child for a few minutes, remembering days of the past when this would be their morning routine. He smiled to himself before opening the second coffin, placing Xavier inside. For the third coffin, he placed John and Christopher inside. He stepped closer to Elise. Since she was fully healed, he tapped her on the shoulder. Her eyes fluttered open and she looked around.

"Are we home?" she asked in her soft French accent.

Kysen nodded. "Well, my home, but American soil, nonetheless."

Elise sat up, shaking Sergio awake along with Miranda. The three began to rise to their feet, stretching. Sergio woke Xander up then Adrian, Adan and Gabriel.

"We're home," he said.

"Shit, it's about time. I can't wait to see everyone else," Adrian said as he swiftly climbed to his feet. He made his way toward the coffin containing John and Christopher, hoisting it up onto his shoulder.

Sergio walked toward Darian's gold encrusted sarcophagus, stooping down to pick it up.

"I'll be handling that one," Kysen said, halting the shifter.

"Oh, I see. I'll guess I'll get the one that doesn't contain your *precious* one," Sergio teased.

"Please do," Kysen replied with a hint of agitation. He would be ecstatic once his uninvited house guests returned to their own territory, leaving him to his peace and quiet. He lifted Darian's sarcophagus effortlessly, carrying it as if it weighed nothing at all. They loaded the SUVs and headed for Kysen's mansion. Once they arrived, Kysen placed Darian's sarcophagus gently on the floor in the den. He watched the others as they hugged and kissed each other, looking over one another, making sure they were all right. Sebastian was extremely relieved and happy to see that his father was alive and unharmed. Elise had fully recovered from her injuries and was hugging Madeleine, thanking her for taking care of her little ones. Tatiana and Xander shared a long, passionate kiss, before she grabbed her son, covering him with kisses on his forehead and cheeks, hugging him tightly. Barry patted Gabriel on his back, coming out of a hearty hug, happy to see his best friend and partner back in one piece. Natasha peeked inside the two coffins containing her lovers and smiled. She would have to wait until nightfall to reunite with them properly.

Kysen gave them the time he felt was enough for their reunion before he interrupted. "I suppose you'll be departing at sundown?" he asked, looking to Elise, then Xander.

"You're really in a hurry to get rid of us, aren't you?" Adan asked.

Kysen looked in his direction. "You can say that. I do miss my solitude. Already, as I look around my mansion, I see a pair of shoes in the corner that weren't there before."

"Oh! I'm sorry, those are mine," Devin said, rushing over to the discarded shoes, hurriedly slipping them on.

Kysen continued to complain. "The incessant and annoying sounds of tiny children wailing have completely drowned out the tranquil trickling of my water fountain over there," he pointed to the beautifully hand-carved granite cascading water fountain mounted in the wall beside his throne-like chair.

"Okay, we get it. As soon as Darian and the others rise, we'll be out of your hair," Sergio said. He was as anxious to leave the mansion as Kysen was to have them gone. He didn't like feeling unwanted.

"Until sundown, then." Kysen turned, leaving the den to his "guests".

They watched him leave. No one said a word for several moments.

"I don't know about ya'll but I'm ready to get the hell out of here. Dude is *seriously* uptight," Sebastian said once he figured

Kysen was out of an earshot range.

"You know he can still hear you," Warren said.

"Oh," Sebastian's mouth was a perfect "O". "I didn't think about that."

"A lot of the ancient ones are that way. Most are completely jaded and often don't like being disturbed," Elise stated.

Adrian nodded in Adan's direction. "What's up with you two?"

Adan frowned. "What do you mean?"

"The thing that's going on between you and Kysen. You seem like the only one he can tolerate-correction, wants to tolerate. Well, you and Darian, that is," Adrian replied.

"Nothing. He's arrogant, obnoxious and far too finicky for my taste," Adan said, reflecting on the personality traits Kysen had that he didn't like. Although, he was greatly attracted to all the ones he refused to mention. Such as Kysen's exotic, breathtaking beauty, his strength, knowledge, charm and wit, just to name a few.

Adrian smirked, knowing there was something more to it, even if Adan didn't want to admit it. He decided to drop the topic. "Oookay," he said, turning away, finding a seat to relax in.

"So, we're here for a few more hours. We should get the planes ready for our flight home," Tatiana said. She used her cell phone, making the call. Elise did the same.

They waited for the sun to set. When the sun disappeared behind the horizon, Kysen returned to the den just as the gold and jeweled encrusted sarcophagus lid opened. Darian climbed out, stretching once he was on his feet again. He greeted the others then looked to his Master.

"Hello Kysen," he smiled at him.

"Good evening, Darian," Kysen replied.

"I have something I want to speak with you about," Darian said, walking toward Kysen, taking him by the hand, leading him out of the den. The others were curious, but no one dared to interrupt the two men.

Inside the privacy of Kysen's soundproof bedroom, Darian sat his Master down on the edge of the bed.

"Remember how wonderful it was the last time we were in this room together?" Kysen asked, hoping to seduce his young lover once again. He leaned back, giving Darian a perfect view of his muscular frame and the impressive bulge of his groin.

Darian's eyes devoured his Master's physique. For a moment, he wanted to mount that glorious body and devour him in a more physical and pleasurable way. He pushed his lust back and focused on the reason he wanted to be alone with Kysen. "That's not what I wanted to discuss with you … but I do remember." He flashed him his signature charming smile before continuing. "It's about you."

Kysen's interest was piqued. He sat up straight, one eyebrow arched. "Me?"

"You're lonely, I know this. You may be all powerful, but that doesn't protect you from the loneliness. You said it yourself the last time we were in this room together."

"Darian, as they say in this instant gratification era where people are completely void of tolerance or patience or both, 'what are you getting at'?"

"And they call me long-winded," Darian mumbled.

"I heard that."

"I'm sure you did. Listen, I want you to be happy."

"Then come back to me."

"You know I can't do that … I won't," Darian corrected himself. "At least not now."

"I get the sickening and distinct feeling you're trying to play matchmaker." Kysen lay back against the silken covered mattress, gazing down at his eternal child.

"And if I am, it's not as if there's nothing there. I watched Adan and you together. Your attraction for each other is quite evident even if you want to ignore it."

"I'm not ignoring it." Kysen cracked a smile without meaning to.

"Good. I mean it's been a while since you've been with someone. I think Adan would be good for you and you'd be foolish not to pursue him."

"I've thought about it. To have him with me on a more long term basis, but then I thought about his Pride. They would come trailing behind him and that was a less pleasing notion."

"It's not like your land isn't big enough, or home for that

matter."

"Not the point."

"Who did you take as your companion when I left?"

"One of my former children came back to me for a time, but there's been no one new."

"Who?"

"Julius."

"Julius!" Darian rolled his eyes. "He such a … as they say, 'twat'."

Kysen chuckled. "He said the same thing about you. Well, not in those exact words, that is. He helped me get through a tough time when you left me."

Darian lowered his gaze, feeling a bit guilty for the pain he had caused his old lover and Maker. "Again, I'm sorry that I made you go through that, but I did what I felt was best for me, Kysen."

"You don't have to explain, Darian. I understand. I understood then."

"Master, how many years do you plan to spend in solitude? How long is too long?" Darian asked, getting back to the original topic.

"You're really this concerned about my state of being?" Kysen was touched, although he wouldn't outright admit it.

"I love you, of course I am. You've taught me how to find peace and happiness. After eight-hundred years, don't you think it's time you've done the same?"

"I don't know … he's brash, outspoken, very young, and extremely cocky. Come to think of it, he does remind me of someone," Kysen said, smiling knowingly at Darian before his expression grew more serious. "He's not immortal. He's not a vampire. My time with him would end eventually."

"Even if he was, there may still come a time when you may want to part."

"Think you that I want to go through that pain again?"

"Your fear of that pain is what keeps you depressed, Kysen."

"Is this my old pupil teaching me a new lesson?" Kysen asked, one eyebrow rose. He was surprised and impressed by Darian's insight.

Darian smiled. "Well, someone has to. Don't let what happened between you and I or you and Irikara stop you from moving on. This really isn't a new lesson, but only a paraphrasing of what you told me last night."

Kysen was silent, thinking about what he had said. "You really think we're compatible?"

"I think you both have something to offer each other … yes, I do."

"We had a rather ill beginning."

"You exerted your power over him?"

"At that time, he was pretty to look at, but he'd aggravated me immensely."

Darian chuckled. "For as long as I've known him, he's been outspoken. Besides, I have an inkling your outburst may have turned him on, once he was done fuming over it."

"He likes powerful men. I did get that from him when he shared his blood with me, twice."

"You took advantage."

"Of course I did. I want him."

"So what's stopping you from pursuing him? Besides, I've learned something new during this whole fiasco."

"And that is?"

"If you give Adan your blood, there's no telling how long he'll live. You may or may not want to spend eternity together, but whatever time you do share, don't you think it's worth it?"

"Did anyone ever tell you that you have a secure future in motivational speaking?"

Darian chuckled. "No."

"I'll make this move. Once you and your brood vacate my home, I will see if he wants to join me."

Darian smiled pleasantly. "I'm glad to hear that."

"Remember what I told you. You're still powerful and the Master of your own territory. Don't let this incident make you weak." Kysen sat up on the bed.

"I won't. What you said to me meant a lot; thank you."

Kysen nodded. "Now, if you please, take your friends and those wailing children home with you."

"All right, Kysen, we're leaving." Darian turned heading for the door, when Kysen reached out, grabbing his arm. "Yes?"

"You, however, are always welcome," Kysen said. Then he leaned forward, kissing Darian passionately. The two men shared their moment, and then Darian broke the kiss.

"Thank you," Darian replied. He opened the door and they left the bedroom. The two men made their way back downstairs toward the den, which was now empty. The others had decided to leave the mansion and were now waiting for Darian to join them in the driveway.

"Hmmm … do you think I was a gracious host?" Kysen joked.

"What do you think? Your guests didn't even want you to see them out," Darian said with a chuckle.

Kysen rolled his eyes. "Refugees, is more like it. Not 'guests'. I'll walk you to the door." He led Darian toward the front door, opening it. Darian thanked him once again, before climbing into the same SUV where Xavier and Natasha were waiting. Kysen walked toward the SUV where Adan was sitting in the front passenger seat, he leaned in.

"May I speak with you privately?" Kysen asked.

"All right," Adan said, he climbed out of the truck to speak with Kysen away from nosy eyes and ears. The two went back inside the mansion leaving the others to speculate.

"You and your Pride are welcomed to stay if you like," Kysen said, once inside.

Adan's expression froze, shocked at Kysen's suggestion. "Are you serious?"

Kysen nodded. "Yes, I rarely joke, especially not about anything this important. I don't know the situation your own territory is in, or even if you still have it. But as you can see, there's enough space here for us if you choose to stay."

Adan looked at the ancient vampire. "Why did you suggest that I move in here with you?"

"Because I want you and I know that you want me."

"Are you always this … forthright?"

"Even eternal life is too short for regrets. I don't waste time when I see something … or someone I want," Kysen said. "You didn't give me an answer." He reached up, lightly stroking the smooth curve of Adan's jaw line.

Adan appeared to be thinking, he looked up at Kysen. "It gets really cold here."

"Intemperate climates really don't affect shifters. Besides, there are plenty of animals you can hunt over my vast land."

"My other home was warm and comfy."

"As you can feel, so is this one. There are no other supernaturals in this area and you'll never have to worry about fighting for your territory again."

"I don't know... you seem as if you don't like to share what's yours."

"I am very generous to those whom I share my life with."

"I'll have you know, I like to top as well."

"That's perfectly fine with me. Sometimes I enjoy being taken. Is this conversation going to continue on this way, us negotiating the terms of our relationship?"

Adan laughed. "I've been wanting to do this for a while now," he said. Reaching up, he grabbed the back of Kysen's head, bringing his face to his own, kissing the vampire hungrily. Their tongues caressed as their hands explored each other's bodies. Kysen pressed Adan's back against the door, his hands beginning to unbutton Adan's shirt. Before he could remove it, the doorbell rang, interrupting the two men. Kysen looked up, breaking his kiss.

"I suppose they're ready to leave," he said, looking down at Adan.

"I suppose." Adan buttoned his shirt, making himself look presentable. He gave Kysen another long, yearning look, biting his bottom lip as his eyes traveled up the ancient vampire's powerful and beautiful body. Regretfully, he turned, opening the door to see Danielle standing before him.

Danielle looked at both men, her nostrils flared slightly and she rolled her eyes, knowing what had just transpired between them. She looked at Adan. "Are you ready to go?" she asked, sarcastically.

Adan nodded. "Yes." He stepped over the threshold. Turning, he addressed Kysen. "I'll be seeing you later."

"Until then," Kysen replied. He watched the two shifters climb into the waiting SUVs then drive off down his winding driveway. He closed the door, relishing the peaceful quietness. Sitting down in his throne-like chair in his den, he looked around. The house was in order, his noisy guests were polite and didn't litter. He thought about Darian and his situation, knowing his fledgling would survive intact. He was strong enough to bounce back from his ordeal. He then thought about Adan and the relationship that was now becoming a possibility to him. He wanted Adan, he really wanted him! The fire inside of the young shifter, his passion, his personality was electrifying to Kysen. He excited him, much in the way Darian had done so many centuries ago.

Stretching out his long legs, he began to fantasize about the life he could share with Adan. All of a sudden, he began to frown. He thought about Adan's Pride. They would have to live in his mansion along with him and there would be children in the future. Whiny children. For so many years, he had lived a life of solitude, almost forgetting what it was like to live with others. Would he be able to tolerate the constant noise, the inner squabbling that so many shifting communities endured? Would he want to kick them all out by the end of a week's time? He chuckled.

"I guess only time will tell," he mumbled to himself as he reclined in his chair, relaxing his mind and body as he drifted off to sleep.

# CHAPTER TWENTY—TWO

On the plane back to Chicago, Natasha sat down next to Darian, sitting between him and Xavier. She took his hand into her own. "Are you going to be all right?" she asked, concerned. Her eyes studied him, watching for the slightest indication that there might be a problem. She saw none.

Darian nodded. "I'm going to start charging money to answer that question." He was beginning to get annoyed by how many people kept asking him if he was going to be "*all right*". He took it in stride, because he knew they were only asking because they cared. "Yes. I'll be fine. What happened is now over, we can move on. We should move on."

Natasha studied him for a few seconds more before nodding. "Okay. I know I'll be happy to be back in our own city, comfy in our own home."

Darian gave her a slight smile. He placed his hand over her stomach, resting his fingers where he knew their unborn baby lay curled safely. "How are you and the baby feeling?"

"We're both fine, happy our Daddies are doing well. To be perfectly honest, I'm more worried about Warren and Matthew, and what's going to happen with them."

Darian frowned, his perfectly arched eyebrows creasing slightly.

Xavier nodded. "This situation is going to get worse before it will get better," he said. "The best we can offer is support."

"I know. Besides, I'm sure Xander and Richard won't let any harm come to them," Natasha said.

"That's true, they won't, but that's not to say harm won't come to others," Darian stated, bringing up another issue. "Humans make it very difficult to handle things in a sensible matter."

"I don't know if I agree with that notion. People have fought for equality in a non-violent manner and have made wonderful progress," Natasha stated.

"And yet, there was still violence. It's almost a certainty that it's human nature to reject change. People become accustomed to their way of life and when they are forced to transcend into something unknown, they react badly. Mark my words, there will be chaos." Darian settled back against the cushion of his seat, allowing his two lovers and all aboard to reflect on what he said.

Warren had been listening to every word spoken, especially those concerning his future. He hadn't really wanted to think about what was to come; yet, he couldn't stop thinking about it. He looked down at his right hand, noticing that he had bitten two of his nails down to the quick. He frowned, biting his nails was a horrible habit, and one he had broken himself of when he was twelve. Doing so now, meant he was more nervous than he realized.

Adrian sat down beside him. "What's on your mind?"

"Just listening to Darian's forecast of gloom and doom," Warren replied, resting his hands on his lap.

"The shit's going to hit the fan, there's no denying that, but I have your back, you know that. Who knows, things might work out. You said you've got some people on your side in the S.U.I.T., right?"

"Marshall Galen and Captain Lawrence are the only people who know for a fact what we are. They may be on our side, although I'm not willing to take the chance in putting all my faith in them. It's us against the government, and the odds are shitty as hell."

"When you go back, they are going to want to test you and if you take the test, they are going to try to either fire you or arrest you. What are you going to do?" Devin asked, looking at Matthew then to Warren.

"I honestly have no idea. I won't know what I'm going to do until I'm in that predicament. Trying to come up with a scenario now just isn't working," Warren said.

"I think we should bypass the outing of the test results and simply confess to who and what we are," Matthew said, causing a few of them to raise eyebrows.

"Come again?" Gabriel said. "Matthew, do you honestly think

that's the best decision?"

"Do I think it's the best idea? I can't say. But it *is* an idea, one that will give us a sense of freedom from having to always be worried of exposing ourselves."

"Yeah, it'll give you a sense of freedom for about five seconds before they arrest you, thus taking your real freedom away," Sergio said, snorting.

"Sergio, I can deal without your sarcasm right now," Matthew said, startling some who were a bit surprised to see the young shifter get agitated. He was normally so very calm, levelheaded.

"Sarcasm aside, you go in there and confess, you better believe you'll get arrested. That's how the law works," Sergio said, without the cynicism.

"I still think Matthew's right. You should take the honorable high road and just come clean, state your case and hold your heads up high," Barry said, adding his opinion. "The court may be lenient if you do."

"Matthew is right. There's no way we can return to work like nothing's happened, especially considering our absence," Warren said, finally agreeing with what was turning out to be the best and only plan.

"Tomorrow morning, then?" Matthew asked.

Warren nodded. "Yeah, the sooner, the better. I hate this feeling. I hate the anticipation, the not knowing what's going to happen."

"I know what you mean. So, it's decided." Matthew gave Warren a sad smile. He too, was worried about their fate.

"Well, whatever the case, we're not going to let you two go to jail and we for damn sure won't let them kill you," Ignacio said.

"Is this where the violent part comes in at?" Natasha asked.

"I hate to say so, but yeah. Matthew is one of us. I'm fucking someone up if they think they're going to kill him just because he lied about what he is. He did that so he could help them. These people are some assholes as far as I'm concerned for even taking this shit this far!" Ignacio replied, frowning. His anger was palpable, and not one could disagree with his sentiments.

"I don't blame you. I remember when the S.U.I.T. arrested Darian. We had to haul ass to Russia, crack the case and sprint back to Chicago before all hell broke loose. Darian was going to break out of there one way or another," John said, remembering the urgency of that time, and all that had depended on their involvement.

Darian chuckled. "It's true. You all did a fine job, saved many lives."

"Just so we understand what's to come. Tomorrow, both you and Matthew will turn yourselves in; confess to being shifters and then what?" Xander asked, trying to get a broader understanding of what was to be expected.

"They'll probably arrest us, since we've committed perjury. It's a crime, punishable by law. If you're a government employee, jail is mandatory," Warren said.

Adrian snorted. "Bullshit, it's a crime if you're a shape-shifter and a government employee. For what you've been doing, if you were a human, the worst you'd get is fired, maybe a fine, but that's it. This is a dick swinging competition to see who's got the biggest one. And what really pisses me off is, you shouldn't even be getting arrested at all."

"That may be true, but we knew the law when we took the oath. Let's take the first step and then we can all see where to go from there, how about that?" Matthew asked, looking around the plane at the others.

"I still say we should bug you so we can monitor your conversation. Just in case we need to bust through some windows, crack some skulls," Justin said.

"That's not a bad idea," Warren said, pointing to Justin. "We should bug our conversation that might be helpful."

"Consider it done," said Michael, a member of Xander's Pack. "I've been meaning to ask you two this, but do you want me to find you a lawyer?"

"No need for that. I have a lawyer that I'm sure would love to take your case," Darian offered.

"Is this lawyer the same one who was about to rip the S.U.I.T. a new asshole when you were arrested?" Natasha asked.

Darian chuckled. "Yes. I only put my money behind the best. He's one of the top defense lawyers in the country."

"He looked like a shark in that courtroom before we showed up.

I almost didn't think you were going to need us," Natasha said chuckling.

"I'll always need you," Darian said. He lifted her hand, kissing it softly.

Natasha blushed. "All worked out for the best."

"He's got to be the best. He did rip the S.U.I.T. a new asshole in Darian's lawsuit."

"That's convincing," Matthew said, nodding.

"Well, if this guy's as good as you say, then yeah, I'd really appreciate his help," Warren said.

"Consider it done," Darian said.

"All I know is, I'm glad Marcus and his crazy fucking coven are dead!" Christopher said.

"Oh, hell yeah!" Devin added. "I don't ever want to go through anything like that ever again."

"You?!" Gabriel said. "You had it easy compared to me."

"What is this? A 'Who Got Fucked-Up The Worst' competition?" Sergio asked. "People died! Friends… Family… Good people. We should be honoring their memory, not debating on who suffered the most, because in reality, there's no competition." He looked at the younger shifters. He knew he'd gotten through to them by the now somber and shame-filled expressions on their faces. He then looked down at Elise, who was still resting from her ordeal, but at least she was alive and healed.

"I'm sorry, Sergio," Devin said, apologizing. "I didn't mean it that way."

Sergio gave him a slight nod. "I know you and I know you didn't mean to disregard those who've died."

"I didn't either. You're right. I'm sorry," Gabriel said, apologetically.

Sergio nodded, accepting his apology.

"As much as I would like to not have to ask you this, I must. Darian, would you happen to have any spare coffins we could borrow to take our members home in?" Xander asked.

"Actually, I only have a few. Not nearly enough for what you ask. But whatever I do have available, it's yours," Darian said. Silently, he wondered why so many assumed he had an abundance of spare coffins lying about, but he dared not voice his thoughts as the mood would have made such a statement extremely inappropriate.

"Thank you," Xander said. "We'll make sure we return your property to you." He paused with a sigh. "This isn't going to be easy."

Darian nodded in agreement. He too, was saddened to lose one of his loyal human servants and a member of his coven. Annabelle had been one of his for almost seventy years. To lose her with such a violent ending was disheartening. Still, he knew his pain could not compare to that of Miko's, who had shared more than companionship with Annabelle. He looked at Miko noticing her silence, he could see the anger she felt at her loss behind the caramel color of her eyes. He thought for a second of going to her, giving her words of peace, but what could he possibly say to take away her pain? There were no words to console the inconsolable. In the end, he decided to allow her time to deal with her loss, but leaving himself open to her if she wanted to come to him.

***

The airplane landed in Chicago an hour later. As they were driving back toward Darian's mansion, many were silent, not really wanting to face the carnage that awaited them. They didn't want to see their loved ones scattered about, lifeless, their bodies torn to shreds, bloodied and dismembered. The memory of all they had experienced grew clearer, more defined in Christopher's mind as they got closer to the mansion. Frantically, he called for Xavier to pull the SUV over. Bursting from the vehicle, he leaned over the railing of the overpass, vomiting a thin stream of blood into the water below.

"Should one of us go out there, and see if he needs any help?" Natasha asked.

Darian watched his young coven member from the passenger seat. He could imagine exactly which images were now burned into the young man's mind to cause him to become so sickened. "He's been exposed to a great deal in a short time. He's never seen death so up close, let alone, experience a true fight for survival. And there are other aspects that he must now come to terms with."

"He's just a bit rattled right now. He's going to need time to come to grips with it," Xavier said.

"Here he comes," John said as Christopher slid into the seat beside him, closing the door behind himself.

"All right, we can go," Christopher said, clearing his throat.

"Are you going to be okay?" Gary asked.

"Yeah, I think so. It's just … I wish I could stop thinking about it, but I can't." He shook his head, turning to face the window, not wanting to look at the others.

"This doesn't make you weak, Christopher. You went through a great deal in the past forty-eight hours and you've survived. Try not to dwell on the pain, it will eat at you if you do," Xavier said before putting the SUV into drive and pulling off.

Christopher sat in silence for several minutes, and then he spoke. "How?"

"Come again?" Xavier asked.

"How do I put everything behind me? How do you?" Christopher asked, innocently.

"You keep on surviving, living the life you have to live. There's no magic answer I can give you, Christopher," Xavier said, steering the car into the long winding driveway.

"Our lives are just as riddled with pain and suffering as those of humans. What matters most is how we deal with that pain. You can't let what happened to you take you over. You'll either end up insane or dead," Darian said, adding his own words of wisdom.

Christopher reflected on what the two older vampires said. He couldn't deny the wisdom in their words, and it gave him a sort of peace he hadn't expected to feel. Their words helped clear his mind, gave him a sense of direction on what he expected his life to be. He still had to find a way to deal with what happened to him, however, he knew he would. "Thanks," he said.

Xavier smiled before parking the SUV in front of the mansion. Sergio, Adrian and Richard pulled the other SUVs up behind Xavier's. All of them climbed out of the trucks and looked at the mansion, not really wanting to go in, but knew they had no choice. Darian entered first, looking around; the mansion smelled of rotten blood. It reeked of death, a scent he didn't enjoy at all. His nostrils crinkled as he moved further into the parlor. Xavier stepped up from behind, walking further into the room. One by one, each of them came into the mansion, making their way to the living room where most of the carnage took place. Once there, they looked around, tears flowed freely from several of them as they mourned.

"Jesus Christ!" Daniel said as he gazed at Darian's human servant, Troy's mutilated corpse. The body had been ripped to shreds; both his right arm and left foot were missing.

"I think I'm going to be sick again," Christopher said, struggling to keep down the bloody bile that threatened to erupt forth.

"If you're going to puke, please do that shit outside. The last thing I want to see is regurgitated blood spewing from your mouth. Once was enough," Sergio said, stepping past Christopher who managed to choke back a gag.

Christopher swallowed hard. "Sorry, it's just, I can't help it. I'm not used to this like you are."

Sergio turned sharply, looking at him. "You think I'm used to this?"

"Well," Christopher shrugged. "You seem to be handling it better than I am."

Sergio turned around, looking at the rotting corpse of his Pride member. Rachel's body lay sprawled on the blood soaked carpet. Her eyes held no sign of the spirited life she once exuded. His heart sank as his memories of her played over and over in his mind. He turned slightly, looking at Christopher from over his shoulder. "You never get used to this shit, no matter how many wars you survive. You never get used to losing people who meant something in your life."

Miko knelt beside Annabelle, tears flowing down her cheeks as she stroked her lover's hair gently. She leaned down low, her lips lightly brushing Annabelle's ear. "I'm so sorry I couldn't protect you," she whispered in Japanese.

Xander stood over the gruesome remains of Phillip's body. He thought about his now deceased member. Philip had been with him for thirty years. He'd once challenged Xander for control of the Pack and lost. Xander had allowed him to stay because he was young at the time. He gave the shifter allowances for his youth. After he'd been given the second chance, and not killed, he proved his gratitude with loyalty to Xander and the Pack. He hadn't bothered to challenge the Alpha anymore. Xander had seen Philip killed, had seen the very moment when Marcus ripped the shifter's heart from his chest with one powerful blow. It was at that point he saw Xavier ushering the others out of harm's way: Natasha and their children, along with Gary, Madeleine and David. He, himself had decided to distract Marcus' coven, doing his best to make sure his members and all of their friends were safe. He only wished he could have saved the others as well.

Adan's expression was full of sorrow as he gazed at the remains of his fallen Pride members. His Matron, Danielle was kneeling beside Patricia's corpse, tears streaming down her cheeks.

"We should cremate our dead," Adan suggested as he surveyed the damage and loss of life.

"I think that is a good idea. We can scatter their ashes in the wind over the lake. Patty, Stephanie and Lori would have wanted that," Danielle agreed.

"I actually like that idea. Allowing their remains to fly free as opposed to rotting away in the ground," Elise said, agreeing with Adan.

"I have no objections," Xander said. "We need to inform their families of their demise. Those are telephone calls I'd rather I didn't have to make."

"I'll contact Philip's sister, she needs to know," Tatiana said. Xander nodded solemnly.

One by one, they wrapped the bodies of their fallen brethren in sheets Darian provided. They had decided not to take Darian's only coffins, especially since there weren't enough for all of their dead.

Darian gazed as the bodies wrapped in white cloth linens. It reminded him very much of his time … the death shrouds one would wrap their dead in. Before he would send Annabelle's body into the flames, he would send her to her God in a ceremony worthy of a warrior.

Sergio loaded Rachel's body gently into the back of the SUV as the other remaining members of his Pride climbed inside the truck.

Elise climbed into the passenger's seat. After Sergio climbed in
behind the wheel, he gazed at her lovingly. He had thought he'd lost
her, and for a second, he didn't know how he could go on. Miranda
had helped save her life, had she not given Elise her blood at that
exact moment, he would have had to face a life without her. He
shook his head of the memory. Turning the key, he kicked started the
engine.

"Let's go home," he said, pulling away.

Xander pulled off in his truck after Sergio, ready to return
home, as were all of their members who trailed behind them in other
SUVs.

Richard put his arm around Matthew's shoulder. "Everything
will be fine. For tonight, try and get some rest."

"I'll try," Matthew said as he climbed into their Anaconda XL40
SUV. Much like Darian, Richard also enjoyed owning luxury
automobiles that were insanely pricey. They drove off, toward their
mansion in the northwest suburbs. They were quiet on the way home,
reflecting on all that had transpired and what was still to come.

***

Miko gently placed Annabelle's body into her coffin. Her gaze
lingered for a few more minutes before she closed the lid. Darian and
Natasha watched in silence from the doorway; neither wanting to
disturb her. Natasha couldn't image the pain Miko was feeling. The
loss of a soul mate, not to mention one you've shared your life with
for decades. She looked down, seeing Darian's hand at his side. She
slid her own hand into his. Darian squeezed her hand reassuringly,
turning toward her, wrapping his other arm around her shoulders,
bringing her closer. He kissed her lightly on her forehead. No words
were necessary to express what they felt for each other. After a few
moments had passed, Miko rose from the floor and left the room,
walking past both Darian and Natasha, giving them a sad smile.
Natasha thought about saying something to her, but decided against
it. What could she say? Should she ask her if she was going to be
okay? Would that be the polite thing to do? She opened her mouth to
do what she thought was the polite thing, but Darian stopped her,

shaking his head. Natasha nodded.

"The sun is rising, we need to rest," Darian said, leading Natasha to their bedroom.

"Darian, I don't think I can sleep here tonight. There's too much blood, pain ... I ... I ..." Natasha struggled to find the right words to express herself, but was unable.

"Shhhhh," Darian placed his finger over her lips. "It's all right. I understand. I'll instruct Billy to take you to the hotel, stay in our suite."

Natasha nodded. "I'll see you this evening?"

"Yes, I'll come by the hotel to visit you. However, I suggest you stay clear of the mansion until it is presentable. So make sure you take with you plenty of clothing and other provisions."

"I can do that."

"Good." Darian leaned forward, kissing her softly. "I must go now."

"Until tomorrow," Natasha said. Darian nodded then turned, walking away. She watched him make his way into their bedroom. Not wanting to spend another moment in the mansion as it was, she went into the nursery, scooping up their son. Packing all of her necessary items, she informed Billy of her plans.

"I can't blame you for not wanting to stay here. Just let me get my overnight bag," Billy said, and he did just that. Slinging the bag over his broad shoulder, he stepped up to Natasha. "Are you all ready to go?"

"Yes," she said, buttoning up her jacket, as the temperature had dropped a bit. She gathered her son and the three left the mansion, driving downtown, toward *Xavier Hotel*. Natasha had no problems getting the key to Darian's master penthouse suite. Billy raided the fridge, snacking on whatever was restocked. He looked at Natasha as she entered the room.

"How's the little guy doing?" Billy asked.

"Sleeping like a ... well, a baby," Natasha answered. She sat down in one of the luscious comfy chairs that adorned the room, making herself comfortable. "He's been so upset these past few days, and who could blame him; the screaming, the fear, the running. I never wanted my child to experience anything like that. Hell, I never wanted to experience anything like that."

Billy nodded. "Yeah, war is something a child should never see. Still, Darian and Xavier sheltered you both pretty well, all things considered. It's been rough, and I didn't think I was going to survive."

"I never really knew the extent of Darian's warning until now," Natasha said, staring forward in deep thought.

Billy's brows crinkled, his lips pursed. "I'm not following you?" he confessed, confused.

Natasha shook herself mentally, bringing her back to the present. "Before I became pregnant with Matthew, Darian once told me that their lives were dangerous. For some reason, I didn't think about a psychotic ancient vampire wanting to attack us as part of that danger."

"Having second thoughts about sharing your life with them?" Billy asked, wondering if Natasha was going to seek a more peaceful existence.

"It's not always like this. For practically two years, we've had a peaceful life and I'm very confident we'll have more years of peace. Honestly, Billy, I can't imagine my life without all of you in it. Does that make me an irresponsible mother? Am I being selfish?" she asked, greatly confused about her own feelings.

"I don't know if I'm the right person who you should be asking all of these questions."

"But you have an opinion? That's all I'm asking."

Billy took a deep breath, releasing it slowly.

"That's not a good sign," Natasha said, noting his apprehension.

"That's not it. I mean … Well, it's like this, when I took over the head security detail at the mansion, I knew the dangers I was getting myself into. The last guy was murdered by the mob of all people, so I knew Darian's life wasn't ordinary."

Natasha chuckled slightly. "Tell me about it."

"It takes fortitude to live this life. I never know when some glory-seeking vamp slayer is going to try a take out the Master vamp of Chicago, so I'm always on my P's and Q's. And if that's not enough, shit like this happens. The money I make is sweet as hell, and I'm able to send my son to college without struggling. So, to me it's worth it, because I'm ensuring a future for my child. But you, your situation's different. You've fallen in love, started a family and found your place here. Really, that's what everybody looks for, a place to call home. The mansion is your home. Darian and Xavier are your, I guess, men … lovers, I don't know, domestic partners, babies daddies? Shit, I don't know what cutesy terms you call them," Billy chuckled.

Natasha smiled. "It's cool, I get it. I'd like to be able to call them my husbands, but that would just be crazy."

"Not to mention illegal. But we're getting off subject here. You've been through enough shit with them to know what you were getting yourself into. You knew the risk and I'm guessing the rewards outweighed the risks. I mean, you're happy aren't you? The little guy up there seems very happy. You have two doting men, who love fatherhood and life with you. I don't think you're being selfish in wanting that to last." Billy took a swig of his soda.

"You don't think I'm putting my children in unnecessary danger?" Natasha asked softly.

"Would leaving Darian and Xavier guarantee they'd never be in danger again? See, the way I look at it, your children were in the same predicament Elise's kids were in, not to mention Tatiana's and Madeleine's. You sure you don't want to talk to them about this?"

Natasha smiled. "No, I think I have my answer."

"You do?" Billy looked at her, eyebrows raised.

"Yeah, I do. Thanks Billy," Natasha hugged him then rose from the sofa, heading into the bedroom. Deep down, she knew her answer was to stay with her lovers. All she needed was confirmation that it was the right decision. Elise's life is no less dangerous than her own, yet she lives it every day with the people she loves, regardless of what dangers may arise. She climbed under the sheets, content about her future and the future of her children.

# CHAPTER TWENTY-THREE

Warren woke up the next day, his heart heavy with the weight of his decision. His head throbbed with pain caused by the stress he was under. When he sat down at the breakfast table, Tatiana placed a plate loaded with delicious smelling foods in front of him.

He looked down at his hearty meal, inhaling deeply. "Shit, I hope this ain't my last meal as a free man," he semi-joked.

"I say if you're going to jail, let your last meal be the motherfucker who put you there," Justin said, shoving a forkful of cheesy eggs into his mouth.

Warren smiled. "It's a thought."

"Enough talk about jail, eat up," Tatiana instructed. She then placed a bowl of cereal on the high-chair tray in front of her daughter. "Eat all of it, too. No playing with your food."

"Mommy, can I have juice?" Nyah asked in her sweet childlike voice.

"You sure can," Tatiana answered. She poured her daughter a glass of orange juice and set it on the table beside her bowl of cereal. Satisfied, the toddler began to eat her breakfast.

Warren devoured his meal in a matter of minutes. Xander entered the dining room, dressed in a pair of black slacks and a red ribbed v-neck pullover. He sat at the head of the table as his wife handed him his plate.

"Sleeping late, Xander, you're normally the first to eat?" Justin commented.

"My mind and body needed the rest," Xander replied, scooping eggs onto his fork. He looked at Warren from across the table. "Are you prepared to face your commanding officer this morning?"

"Not really, no. I just know I want this all to be over. Matt and I are going to go in together," Warren answered.

Xander nodded. "Will Darian's lawyer be accompanying you?"

"No, not until they try to discipline us; that's when he'll get involved. I don't know what the punishment will be, if there is one." Warren sat back in his seat.

"They'll be one, all right. It's the only way humans can put themselves over us," Adrian said.

"Can we not make this a 'them verses us' argument?" Warren frowned as his Pack brother.

"You know what, Warren? You can live with your head in the clouds if you want to, but the truth is the truth. It's always going to be about us and them!" Adrian shot back.

"Are you calling me idealistic?" Warren asked sarcastically.

"More like unrealistic. Look, I know for a fact that there are some amazing humans out there who don't hold what we are against us. However, there's an outrageous amount of those who do. They vote in congress to keep our children separate from theirs. They create laws which govern the populace unfairly. They try and silence those who fight for equality. And every time one of us does something stupid like this Marcus guy, they use that against the entire supernatural population. You put your life on the line for them every damn day, how dare they call you into question with this ridiculous fucking witch hunt!" Adrian's anger ignited the room, and everyone could feel what he felt.

"I actually agree with my son in this debate, Warren," Xander said, breaking his silence.

"I don't do what I do to please them, Xander," Warren said in his defense.

"I know why you joined the S.U.I.T., but that still doesn't take away from the fact of what's happening now. Every supernatural had their own reasons for enlisting in the CIA, FBI, S.U.I.T. or any other Force, just like every human did, but only we are being persecuted. This was something that I feared would happen to you, but I allowed you to join anyway. Mark my words Warren, if this matter is not settled amicably … fairly, it will get worse. How much worse, I do not know," Xander said.

"Will you take action if the outcome isn't what you deem fair?"

Tatiana asked her husband.

"I will. As will Richard and most likely every supernatural leader whose members are caught in this scandal." Xander finished his meal, handing his plate to his wife who put it in the dishwasher.

Warren listened to Xander, reflecting on what he'd said. He knew what it meant, the threat behind his words. "I should get going. I'm supposed to be meeting Matt there." He rose from his seat, leaving the room.

Adrian watched him leave then he looked at his father. "I heard on the news, they killed one of their officers who resisted arrest."

"My God!" Tatiana gasped, shocked and horrified.

"I know. I read it in my morning paper." Xander said, sipping his coffee.

"That's totally fucked up. Here this guy is, keeping their asses safe, and they shoot him. I guess Law number two was in effect there. They reserve the right to kill any of us who try to flee. I'm having a hard time liking humans right now … except for the ones I consider family," Justin said.

"As far as I'm concerned, this matter has gotten well out of control at an alarming rate. It's mind-blowing, actually how horribly this situation is being handled," Xander said.

"I'm worried for Warren and Matt," Adrian said.

"Me too," Justin added.

"I won't let any harm come to either of them," Xander said, then he rose from his seat, leaving the room. He opened the door to his study quickly enough to catch the telephone before the voicemail picked up the call. It was Richard.

"Xander, it's pure chaos out there concerning this government matter," Richard said gravely.

"I'm aware of just how terrible things are. This morning I learned a hyena was killed because he resisted arrest. Shot down by his fellow officers, it's unforgivable," Xander stated.

"I actually called you to ask about the cremation of your member. My Pack and I would like to attend the ceremony."

"We're holding off on the ceremony until Warren is with us. I know he'd want to say his final farewell to Phillip. The cremation however, is to take place tonight, his sister wants to be present."

"Understandable. I was going to mention we should have the farewell ceremony when our members were present. It's good that we're on the same page," Richard commented. "All right, I know you're busy. I'll leave you to your own matters." He ended the call.

Xander replaced the handset back onto the base. Reclining back into his leather chair, he thought about what course of action he'd take if matters worsened for his young wolf. He prayed he wouldn't have to interfere.

***

Richard starred at the telephone for a few seconds, contemplating the conversation he'd just had. Ignacio stepped into the room, taking a seat across from him.

"I'm worried for Matt," Ignacio said.

"The worst I'll allow them to do to him is fire him," Richard said.

"Yeah, but what if they arrest him?"

"I'm sure they will. It seems to be their raison d'Ítre at this point," Ryan said as she entered the room.

"I still think one of us should go down there just in case some shit kicks off," Ignacio said.

"Well, they're wearing the wires, that should keep us abreast of their situation," Ryan said.

"Actually, I convinced Matthew not to wear the wire last night," Richard said.

"You did? Why? Now we won't be able to listen in on them," Ryan asked, confused.

"They would be searched upon being arrested. The listening devices would be discovered on their person and might shine negative light on them. They need to look defenseless and most importantly, harmless to the humans at this point," Richard answered.

"I see what you mean. What about Warren, is he still going to wear one?" Ignacio asked.

Richard shook his head. "No. Matthew spoke with him on the matter and he agreed."

"Too bad, I thought it was a great idea," Ryan said. "But you're right, baby." She kissed Richard's forehead.

"I really hope shit doesn't kick off now," Ignacio said.

Richard looked at the both of them. He knew Matthew would not try to resist arrest. Matthew would not give them any reason to take aggressive action, but still, he didn't trust the government and the latest events were making his thread of trust even thinner.

"I think what you said before is a good idea, Ignacio. You should go down there, just to keep an eye out," Richard suggested. "I want to know what's going on there, the mood, the gossip, keep me posted on everything."

"Should I tell them that Marcus is dead?" Ignacio asked.

"No. They'll have questions you can't answer. See if you can get in contact with this Marshall Galen. He has assured both Warren and Matthew that he is on their side. I want to know exactly how much influence he has, not to mention the extent of his support."

"Will do. What if things don't get under control soon? What if they try to do something to them?"

"As I've said, I'm not going to let any harm come to either of them and I'll do whatever it is in my power to ensure that they return to us."

"*That's* what I want to hear!" Ignacio grinned as he rose from his chair, leaving for the precinct.

Ryan looked at Richard. "You think it's going to get worse, don't you."

Richard nodded. "I know it will."

\*\*\*

Elise rolled over, her body still slightly stiff from her ordeal but fully functioning. With her hand shielding her eyes from the brightness of the sun shining through her bedroom window, she looked around the room, realizing that she was now safe and sound in her own home. She was so exhausted; she didn't even remember arriving home. Climbing out of the bed, she stretched all of her muscles, relaxing her body. Looking down, she noticed that she was dressed in one of her pink pajamas with the ostrich feather cuffs and trim.

"Sergio," she said to herself, smiling, knowing it was her lover who had dressed her. The first thing she wanted to do was check on her Pride. Quickly, the snatched up her pink bathrobe, slipping it on as she exited her room. The house was relatively quiet; all of the noise she could hear seemed to be coming from one room. She made her way to the den, where everyone was sitting, discussing their fallen members as well as the issue with the government.

"Hey Elise," several members of her Pride greeted her when she walked in, some of them rising to embrace their Queen. Sergio was the last, kissing her passionately.

"I don't know what I would have done without you," he said, running his hands lovingly over her shoulders and arms.

Elise reached up, caressing his cheek. "My darling, my brave king, I love you." She kissed him once again then Sergio assisted her to her chair.

"Elise, I've already contacted Rachel's family in your absence," Madeleine said. "I figured you could be spared having to do so, considering all that you've been through."

Elise smiled sadly. "Thank you, Madeleine. I do appreciate your doing so. How did they take to the news?"

"As expected. However, her family was please to know that we killed the ones responsible for not only Rachel's death, but for the death of all those innocent humans," Madeleine replied.

"It's been a great loss for many," Elise said. Her lips were tight as she struggled to fight back her tears for her deceased Pride member. Her memories of Rachel flooded her mind. She had known her for ten years. The two first met when Rachel was attending college for her teaching degree, but since she was a young shifter in a territory without a Pride to belong to, she was an orphan. Rachel had been so humble when she came to Elise to ask for a pardon. During that time, Elise's late husband had controlled the Pride and had forced Rachel to join if she didn't want to be killed. That was the day she became family to Elise. Rachel had been her friend; her family and her heart ached at the thought of never hearing her laughter again, or seeing her beautiful smile. Her very life, her future ripped away from her in a mindless act of violence. For Elise, there was no greater crime.

"Elise?" Sergio called to her, bringing her out of her thoughts. "Where did you go just now?"

Elise blinked, clearing her mind. "I … I was thinking about the first time I'd met Rachel, of what we've lost in losing her."

The others in the room were somber; they had all shared her thoughts at least one time since accepting Rachel's demise.

"Elise, when should we have the cremation ceremony?" Madeleine asked.

"We want to make sure everyone who wants to attend the ceremony can attend." Elise looked at Sergio. "Where is she now?"

"Her body is in the garden shed. We were going to take her to the crematorium this morning, but wanted to wait for you," Sergio said.

"I think we should wait until this crap with Warren and Matthew is over. This whole police business has got everyone in a frenzy," Daniel said.

"Humans are going the hell crazy, is what it is," Miranda stated.

"What else has happened?" Elise asked, remembering what she had learned.

Daniel nodded. "It's escalated in a very bad way."

"Meaning?" Elise asked, eyebrows creased.

"Meaning, it isn't just the S.U.I.T. under fire now, but all of law enforcement. What's worse is, they've already killed one S.U.I.T. officer they found out was a shifter when he tried to resist arrest," Devin said.

"My God! Have they gone insane?" Elise asked. Her face was a perfect mask of disgust, outrage and fear for what was to come.

"Yeah, they've fucking lost it," Sergio said. "News is spreading fast about them killing that cop. It's just a matter of time to see what reaction the supernatural community is going to have about it."

"The Council is going to have to step in and get things under control," Carmen said.

"Shit, that's if they can," Devin commented.

"How are Warren and Matthew?" Elise asked.

"We don't know. The two decided to turn themselves in, state their case and are going to see where that gets them," Sergio said.

"It's going to get them arrested, just like the others. I don't think they should do it," Devin said.

"They might not have a choice. They have people who support them, they're taking a chance, it might help them more than hurt their case," Madeleine said.

"All we can do for them is pray that it all works out," Elise said.

"That's all we can do for now. If things don't work out, *then* what do we do?" Devin asked.

"What we must," Elise answered.

The others nodded. Now that Elise was awake, they all dressed quickly and left for the crematorium. It was their first step in giving their friend a proper good-bye.

***

Leaving the members of his Pride to assist Darian's human servants in cleaning up the mansion, Adan had taken his deceased members to the crematorium Darian had suggested. He had paid the director a hefty amount, as was suggested for his services and silence. He left there with the ashes of three members of his Pride. He would contact the other leaders to see if they would be interested in having a combined ceremony in which all would say a final good-bye to their members. With his Matron sitting beside him, they drove the SUV toward Darian's mansion,

Danielle turned toward him. "What do we do now?"

Adan exhaled. "We see our friends through this difficult time."

"After that, then do we go home?"

"I don't know. I doubt if our land is even our land anymore. Besides, having been challenged by Marcus and being unsuccessful, we're going to be targeted for that land a lot."

"Marcus wasn't challenging us for our land. He wanted us to hunt."

"As you know, that doesn't really matter in our world. A challenge is a challenge, and all any other supernatural will see is our failure to defend ourselves," Adan said.

Danielle took a deep breath. She turned toward the window, looking out at the buildings going by in a blur. "Adan, what are you thinking?"

"That maybe it's time for a change." He tossed her a glance.

She turned back toward him. "What are you saying? That you want to stay here in Chicago? This place, though absolutely exquisite, is simply overrun with vampires and shifters. It's intolerable."

Adan chuckled. "Not Chicago. Not Illinois."

She studied him for a few moments before responding. "Perhaps you've found something you desire in Montana?"

"Perhaps."

"That man is insufferable."

Adan chuckled again. "He is."

"Then why?"

"Because I'm powerfully attracted to him ... I want him as he wants me."

"And this reason alone is why we should abandon what's ours?"

"You're treading a thin line. I'm the King of this Pride. All decisions I make are final," Adan warned.

"Forgive me. It's just ... we've been through so much. Is relocating us to a new land so that you can pursue your desires the best decision?"

"The pursuit of my desires is not the only reason why I am contemplating the move. I've grown bored of our current location. Not too mention, the very fact that I and I alone am constantly challenged for that territory and the challengers increase in power and strength every time."

"But you are powerful as well."

"Danielle-"

"-But you are."

"Don't be so naïve. You know they'll also know that I had help in defeating Marcus. They'll know that I couldn't protect my members on my own. It's only a matter of time before the attacks come again."

Danielle placed her hand gently on his arm. "Adan, we don't blame you for what's happened."

Adan patted her hand, silently thanking her for her words. "That means a lot to me."

Danielle smiled sweetly. "Adan, may I be frank?"

"Go on."

"Do you fear any other challengers?"

"Fear? No. To feel fear, I would have to fear death. I don't. However, I am weary of fighting. In the short time that I've been King of the Pride, I've been challenged thirteen times. When Rashad was King, he had ruled for nearly two hundred years and had only been challenged four times."

"And yet, you are still King, you were victorious all of those times-"

"Don't you understand, Danielle? I'm tired of fighting. Because I am a young King compared to other lion Kings, I am a constant target," Adan said. "And I am always concerned about what will happen to all of you if I should fall to defeat in battle. Will the lion that killed me take care of you, or will he imprison you?"

Danielle was silent as she thought about what he said. She never considered what it meant to him to have faced so many challengers on his own. He was only one hundred and sixty-six years old, yet he managed to become King of a Pride and had defended it successfully for forty years. But she had to admit it to herself, finally. Thirteen *Challenges for Authority* was excessive. She knew what it meant. It meant others found him weak, too young to rule a lion Pride. Although she was sure they had found their underestimation of him unfortunate in the end, it didn't take away from Adan's own suffering, his stress, his many sacrifices or his pain.

She nodded. "I understand."

"You do?"

"I do now. Adan, are you sure about this decision to go to Montana? What if he changes his mind?"

"There's always that, but I don't think he'll tire of us so quickly."

"He's ancient. The older ones are always fickle."

"Is my company that undesirable?" Adan asked, raising one eyebrow.

Danielle scoffed. "Of course not! It's just, what if he doesn't want us, but only you?"

"He knows he can't be with me, if he can't be with us."

"You then, you won't grow tired of us?" she asked softly, apprehensively.

Adan looked at her. "Is that what this is about? You think I want to abandon you as I am abandoning our land. You think I'm abandoning my position?"

"It is my fear, yes."

"Oh, Danielle, I would *never* do that. The decision I'm making isn't an entirely selfish one. It's true, I do desire him, but his land is vast. Instead of us owning a city, we'll have free and complete reign as the only shifter community in all of Montana. A land that is plentiful of hunting grounds. A land so luscious and beautiful! Do we not deserve this?"

"Well, when you put it that way." Danielle smiled sweetly.

"I thought you'd be open to that point of view," Adan chuckled, and then he grew more serious. "Not to mention, it will be a land free of challenges."

"Well, I'm still surprised Kysen is willing to share that land, when the man didn't even want to share his home." Danielle rolled her eyes.

"You don't like him, do you?" Adan asked, smiling.

"He's an asshole."

Adan laughed outright. "I saw a side of him that was sweet and gentle … loving. Give him a chance."

"I guess I don't have a choice. I'll give him a chance," Danielle said, not sure how the others were going to feel about this new arrangement.

"Still, I feel bad leaving them with all that's going on, knowing that a part of it is my fault," Adan said, thinking about Darian and the others.

"I don't believe that. It was bound to happen at some point. The government is growing ever more suspicious of its people every day. It was only a matter of time."

"Yes, but this particular exposure was brought about by my bringing Marcus to their doorstep."

"How long are you going to beat yourself up about that?"

"I don't know. Until I feel as if I've done something about it."

"What can you do?"

"I know I'll do whatever it is in my power to help them."

"Even if that means-"

"Yes, even if it means that."

Danielle nodded, willing to stand by his decision. The two drove on toward Darian's mansion. Once it was cleaned and in respectable order and the funeral ceremony was over, he would leave. There was no place for him in Chicago and he was looking forward to his life with Kysen and all the promise the possibility held.

***

As Warren was driving to the precinct, his cell started ringing. "Hello?" he greeted upon answering.

"Hey, Warren, it's me, Brian."

"How are things going for you?"

"Not good. Colin's been fired, not to mention, he's holding a grudge against me."

"Why? It's not like *you* fucking bit him!"

"Because I never told him what I was."

"Shit, he didn't make it easy for you to tell him. His hate for our kind didn't instill confidence, I'm sure," Warren said, greatly annoyed.

"No, it didn't. He said I should have trusted in our friendship enough to tell him. I think he'll get over it, but I wouldn't hold my breath, he was pretty fucking pissed."

"What about you?"

"My Captain's put out an APB on me. You know, it's pretty fucked up. They don't even know Marcus and his coven are dead, but this is there damn priority, getting rid of the only people who can help." Brian's anger was intense, matching Warren's.

"My Pack's pissed and for the first time I can't disagree with any of their sentiments. I tried, but my heart's not in it. Not when I see what's going on."

"What about you and Matt?"

"We're turning ourselves in."

"Are you insane?!"

"It was our best choice. We can't hide, if we do, we're already going to be labeled shifters, so there goes our jobs. Besides, it'll make us fugitives if we continue to avoid the inevitable. We don't want that."

"The radical human groups are demanding we all be shot dead, you have congress giving permission to our co-workers to kill us on the spot if we show any signs of resistance, it's really ugly, are you sure you don't want to wait until the smoke clears?"

"And then what?"

"You could … ."

"Exactly. Brian, I love being a cop. I love being able to help people and save lives. I want to work this out, and the only way I can do this is to show that I'm not a threat."

"Good luck, man," Brian said. He understood Warren feelings, he had them himself, but he didn't trust in the human government to be fair to him in how they would handle his case. His Alpha demanded that he steer clear, and he would obey his order.

"You to, take care of yourself."

"You sound like we're not going to ever talk or see each other again."

"We are, I'm just saying 'good-bye' in a nice way."

"I prefer 'see you later'."

"Okay, then. See you later."

"Sure thing."

Both men ended their call as Warren pulled into the parking lot at the S.U.I.T. precinct. He climbed out just as Matthew pulled into the spot next to him.

"Hey babe," Matthew said, kissing Warren passionately. He stepped back, looking into his lover's beautiful gray eyes. Reaching up, he brushed a lock of Warren's black hair from his forehead. "Are you ready to do this thing?"

"As ready as I'll ever be."

"Let's go, then."

Both men stood outside of the main entrance, looking in. Taking deep breaths, mentally preparing themselves for whatever was to come. Warren wrapped his fingers around the handle, opening the door and the two men entered.

To Be Continued.

Oh yeah! … I ended this on a cliffhanger, baby!

Love ya!
D.N.

## ABOUT THE AUTHOR

D. N. Simmons lives in Chicago IL., with a rambunctious German Shepherd that's too big for his own good and mischievous kitten that she affectionately calls "Itty-bitty". Her hobbies include rollerblading, shooting pool, bowling, reading, watching television and going to the movies. She has been nominated at Love Romances and More, winning honorable mention for best paranormal book of 2006. She has won "Author of the Month" at Warrior of Words. She was voted "New Voice of Today" at Romance Reviews and "Rising Star" at Love Romance and More.

To learn more, and have the opportunity to speak with the author personally, please visit the official website and forum at www.dnsimmons.com . D.N. is always interesting in meeting new and wonderful people.